Fran O'Brien is a Company Di[...]
Just Curtains Limited with her sister, [...] ....., in 1978.

Steeped in a literary and theatrical tradition, her granduncle, Professor Liam O'Briain, one of the founders of An Taibhdhearc Theatre in Galway, and also a writer, has been an influence on her life. She spent many years on the amateur drama circuit, and enjoys theatre at home and abroad.

To switch off from the daily grind, Fran writes in the early mornings, evenings, weekends, on holidays, boats, trains and planes, whenever she gets an opportunity.

THE MARRIED WOMAN

FRAN O'BRIEN

To Ann —
Best wishes
love — Fran

McGUINNESS BOOKS

THE MARRIED WOMAN

Published by
McGuinness Books
19 Terenure Road East,
Dublin 6.

ISBN 0-9549521-0-3

Typeset in Sabon by Martone Press

Printed and bound in Great Britain by
Cox & Wyman Ltd, Reading, Berkshire.

Cover design based on an original painting by
Trudi Doyle.
www.trudidoyle.com

For Arthur
who is the love of my life

Acknowledgments

Thank you to all my friends in The Wednesday Group.

Special thanks to my editor, Muriel Bolger.

Thanks to artist Trudi Doyle for allowing
the use of her paintings on the cover.

Thanks to Anne Dunphy for all her help.

Thanks to my sister Mary, and friend Tricia,
who listened so patiently to the lives of these
imaginary characters on a daily basis.

Fran.

Chapter One

A light drizzle was falling from an ominous grey sky when Kate left the house just after six. There was a lot of work to be done before she could fly out to Spain tomorrow and she was anxious to get into the office long before the traffic built up. But almost immediately the gods let her down when the engine of her Toyota Corolla coughed once and died, not a spark out of the battery. Dermot, her darling husband, still snored his head off in bed, and their sons, Shane and Conor, wouldn't appreciate being woken up at this hour, so she opened up the bonnet aware that she would have to go to the trouble of trying the jump leads, or phoning for a taxi. Either way, she would be delayed, so she decided to make an attempt to start it herself. Kate hated to be without wheels.

She hurried back into the house, her hair was getting wet, and her white jacket had a large damp patch from where she had leaned against the side of the car. She took it off and in the utility-room she pulled on an anorak, rubber gloves, and went outside to the shed where she searched among boxes of tools, garden implements, tins of paint, and God knows what else, until finally she found the jump leads hanging on a hook right in front of her eyes. Within minutes she had Dermot's Mercedes purring beside her car, and she was nervously trying to decide if the red lead went with the plus sign or the black, or was it the other way around? Red...black...positive...negative...her heart thumped as she wondered whether the cars would explode if she got it wrong, and how she would explain to Dermot that his precious CL 600 was no more.

'What are you doing to my car?' There was a sudden shout from above, and she looked up sharply to see Dermot leaning out of the bedroom window with a furious expression on his face.

'Mine wouldn't start.' She took a deep breath and carefully positioned the red with the positive, and the black with the negative, determined to do this herself before he arrived down. She turned the key in the ignition, and was delighted when the engine roared and held.

'Why didn't you use one of the jeeps?' He stood over her, tall and broad-shouldered. His hands on his hips, wearing just pyjamas and dressing-gown, his generous bulk flopping over the belt.

'What difference does it make?'

'It makes all the difference. God knows what you might have done to mine, it's brand new, and isn't to be touched by anyone else.'

'Dermot, stop worrying.' She began to remove the leads, confident now that she knew what she was doing. 'Will you go inside, you're getting wet, and would you mind putting away the leads, please, I have to get going.' She held them out to him, smiling.

'I will not, put them back yourself.' He turned off the engine of the Mercedes, locked it, and pocketed the key.

'You were lucky I didn't ask you to do it for me.'

'I was lucky something woke me. God knows what you'd have done if I hadn't got down here in time.' He marched back into the house.

She stared after him, exasperated.

In the downstairs loo, she tried to put some shape on her damp newly-styled short hair, loving the white blonde hilights. And the fact that she could simply run her fingers through it and she looked well. As she slipped into her jacket, she couldn't help admire herself. The thrill of the transformation was fantastic. For years she had tried to lose weight but had no success. Now in a matter of months and with huge self-sacrifice and struggle she had lost two stone. Most of the loose skin had tightened up from the exercise routine which she did religiously every day. Her face looked thinner too, and her blue eyes larger, and she thought she looked even younger than her thirty-nine years.

But on her way into the office, she couldn't get that little bust-up with Dermot out of her mind, although it was just one of many of those loud-voiced sessions which exploded out of nowhere. The last few weeks she had tried hard to keep things at home on an even keel until the holidays, but it was difficult, and like walking on eggshells around Dermot. His mood was so volatile, it was impossible to predict whether he would be full of the joys, or down in the depths at any time of the day or night. Even last year, twice they had booked to go out to their house in Torrevieja, and twice he had cancelled the day before they were due to leave. First it had been contracts which had to be closed on some new property he had purchased, and not very keen to go alone, she had abandoned their plans, and gone back to work. Later in the year it was a trip to Prague to check out property there which apparently was an opportunity that couldn't be missed, and once more she had to unpack the suitcases.

The thought of it happening again tomorrow filled her with a sense of dread. She had tried to pinpoint when things had started to change between Dermot and herself, and lately had to face the truth and admit that it was almost as far back as the time she had gone to work for Carol and Mags five years ago, and the death of his mother, always inextricably linked in her mind.

It had been strange. She had enjoyed that first day in the office so much, and had come home full of excitement looking forward to giving Dermot all the news. But his face when he came in the door did not encourage her to launch into a vivid description, so she said nothing and quietly served up the dinner.

'My mother died,' he said as he opened up the newspaper after she had cleared away the dishes and they were alone. It was a blunt emotionless announcement like a television news report.

'I'm so sorry, love.' She put her arm around him, but he shrugged her off, and turned a page. 'What happened?' She went through the motions as if it was a normal situation, which it

3

wasn't. Dermot had not seen his mother since that day he had told her they were going to get married. Kate had not seen her since the time she took the boys over. They were aged four and two and she felt strongly that their grandmother should meet them, and hoped that she would soften when she saw the little innocent faces. But the woman who opened the door might have been a stranger. Her cold eyes flicked over them for a few seconds and without a word she closed the door again.

'She was found by a neighbour, and had been lying there for a few days. I suppose it must have been a heart-attack or something like that,' he muttered as he threw down the paper on the table in a crumpled heap, and went out of the kitchen into his study. She followed him, and watched the door close, the firm click warning her off.

In Lee O'Donnell Design it was hectic as she followed up on which fabrics were in stock or on order. Checked the status of curtains and blinds. Chased quotations, dealt with clients' queries, and made sure that all the work-in-progress was as far advanced as she could manage at this point in time.

During lunch when the phones had died down, she rang Uncle Bill. 'How are you?' She tucked the phone under her ear as she re-read the report she had just written on the computer.

'Who's that?' he asked through a loose chesty cough.

'Kate.'

'Faith?'

'It's me, Kate.' She raised her voice.

'Don't know any Faith,' he said abruptly, and then all she could hear was the tone.

It was difficult to talk to her uncle on the phone, in spite of the hearing aid he still got things mixed up. At eighty-three, he was sprightly, but lately had begun to show his age, a little forgetful and obsessive about certain things; his money which she had invested for him was a particular bugbear.

'How much have I?' he would ask in a tetchy suspicious manner. She gave him the approximate value.

4

'Where is the book?'

She tried to explain that there wasn't a book with that type of account.

'Get my money for me now. I want it.'

She argued that he couldn't keep that amount of money in the house, and if anyone found out, it might be stolen.

'If anyone breaks in here I'll deal with them, I have my walking stick.'

And she told him that he would lose his interest.

'I don't want any interest.'

Usually she gave in and promised to withdraw everything the following week, hoping he would have forgotten their conversation by the next time she talked to him. Although on one occasion, she did exactly as he instructed and presented him with a cheque made out in his name, the original amount invested increased by a small percentage. 'That much extra? Sounds good, put it back there again wherever it was,' he ordered.

She rang him again before she left the office, glad that he knew who it was this time, although she was entertained to a long-winded description of the strange woman who had phoned earlier.

'Her name was Faith, first I didn't know who she was but then I remembered I knew a girl of that name when I was young. Do you think it could have been her? I never thought I'd meet her again...'

'No, I don't think so; it was probably a wrong number.' She tried to push him off the subject. 'I wouldn't worry about it. Are you taking that bottle I gave you, the medicine for your cough?'

'What?'

'The bottle?' she repeated, looking at the first drawings of the window treatments which she intended using for Castle Dracula, their nickname for the pub in Cork which was to be renovated in an extreme Gothic style.

'Coddle? I haven't had that in years.'

'No, cough bottle.'

'Bring some when you come over with my mince pie. Faith might call around for supper. You are coming tonight, aren't you?'

5

'Yes, but I mightn't have time to make coddle, I'm going away tomorrow.'

'I don't want you to borrow it, just make it yourself. Surely you know how?'

'I'll see what I can do.' Kate groaned. But then decided it wasn't the end of the world. She had to go to the supermarket anyway, and she could throw a few potatoes, sausages and bacon into a pot for him and let it sizzle there while she did the packing.

She cleared her desk and left the office, and as she sat into the car her phone rang.

'Kate?' Her name was shouted in a nervous shriek.

'Yes Irene?' she sighed, Irene, the one person who could be relied upon to stir things up.

'I'm in a bind,' she wailed in her most melodramatic fashion.

'I'm very busy,' Kate said, 'you know we're heading off tomorrow.'

'My car is in the garage and I'm at the beauty salon and I can't get a taxi. Could you come and pick me up?'

'I'm running late myself and I don't know when I'll be leaving here,' she lied. 'Why don't you give it a bit more time?' She really didn't feel like going out of her way for Irene. There was just too much to be done tonight.

'It's rush-hour and I'll have to wait at least forty-five minutes, the taxi people tell me.'

Kate could visualize the beautifully-turned out woman at the other end of the phone, her stepmother, forty-two and looking like twenty-two. She ground her teeth.

'What about the bus?' she tentatively suggested, but knew deep down that it wasn't a runner, so she pulled out into the traffic and turned the car in the direction of town.

'Are you serious? Have you any idea what I've just gone through to get ready for tonight? I've a really important dinner engagement. Can you imagine me trying to squash on to a bus with a crowd of God knows who with their screaming kids? Kate, you've got to bail me out. The limousine is coming at seven-thirty.'

'All right, I'll get over as quick as I can.'

Kate wondered why she always gave in to her stepmother. But her father had asked her to look after Irene before he died and she really didn't have to ask the question. It had been a shock to the whole family when barely two years after Kate's mother had passed away, he had married Irene on a Caribbean Island. He was in love, he declared, and happier than he had ever been before.

Her brother Pat felt the marriage besmirched the memory of Mam, but then he was in Boston and didn't have to confront it every day. Kate eventually came to the conclusion that there wasn't much to be said to a man who had been given a new lease of life, even if her stepmother was only a couple of years older than herself.

So she just had to grin and bear it. The family home in Shankill was sold, and a modern apartment purchased. His beloved Rover was traded in for a racy open-topped hair-flying sports car. Even his wardrobe was updated, all the old suits thrown out for fashionable gear, and what grey hair he had left was tinted. Irene turned her father into a trendy, and he loved every minute of it.

It was almost one o'clock in the morning when Kate finished the packing, and took a quick look around for anything else they might need, but nothing caught her eye and she decided it was time for bed. She had to be up early in the morning again.

Dermot slumped in front of the television, and she leaned over and kissed him slowly. She had been looking forward so much to getting away she wanted to be on good terms when they flew out, and had forced all the aggro of this morning out of her head. She turned off the television, stretched out her hand and took his. 'Come to bed, love.'

'I'm knackered,' he muttered, and pushed himself to his feet.

She walked close behind him as he climbed the stairs her hands almost touching places she should know so well, but somehow didn't, and all the more excited because of that. In the bedroom, he dragged his clothes off and pulled on dark blue pyjamas, creased from where they were folded flat under the pillow, all with a tight energy in his movements, a rushing, as if he had to be in bed first. Like when we were young, she thought suddenly, as she slipped on her nightdress and climbed into bed beside him, hugging close, finger tips playing him, down his chest, across his stomach, and further.

'Dermot, it's going to be great to get away from it all. Are you looking forward to sunshine and blue skies, I know I am.' She breathed in his body aroma. That sharp sweaty underarm smell mingled with deodorant that could get her going, deep breaths of it, like glue or nail-polish remover. Dermot used to laugh at her, and promise to bottle it so that she could take it everywhere she went and they would never be parted.

But tonight there was no response from him, and he didn't notice what she was doing. He made no attempt to push down the narrow straps of the nightdress and reach to touch her, or try to get beyond the soft folds and twirl and curl in search of the woman who waited just a breath away.

'Dermot?' She moved her fingers, but after a few seconds, she was still too, knowing there was no point in trying any longer. He was soft, small, and asleep.

The following morning it was a rush as Kate tried to get the house in as good an order as possible before she had to leave for work.

'Dermot love, will you make sure you're back here by eleven at the latest? That will give you time to shower and change. The taxi is booked for eleven forty-five,' she said as she gave the fridge a quick clean.

'Yea,' Dermot grunted from behind yesterday's newspaper.

'Mum, is my football gear washed?' Conor, her eldest son asked.

'I haven't done it in the last few days.' She closed the fridge door.

'Why? I've a match this evening,' he complained angrily.

'Conor!' Dermot barked.

'Where did you leave it?'

'Maybe it's still in my bag,' he muttered and wandered up to his room, reappearing a few minutes later with the mucky gear.

'Why didn't you give it to me?' she asked.

'Forgot.'

'I'll throw it in the wash now but it won't be ready for a couple of hours.'

'That means I'll have to come home to pick it up,' he groaned.

'Sit down and have your breakfast. What do you want to eat?'

'Flakes.'

She poured them out for him, tossed a handful of chopped fresh fruit on top and put the bowl in front of him. Then quickly, she threw the clothes in the washing machine, put in the powder tablet, and switched it on.

'Mum, any chance you could get them in to me?' he asked.

'You know we're going away today.'

'Couldn't you do it on the way to the airport, they'll be dry by the time you come back here, and you could divert, it won't take you long.'

'No way.' Dermot pushed himself to his feet and shrugged into his jacket.

'Come home at lunchtime, I'll have them dried for you before I go,' Kate suggested. She knew there would be no time for stopping on the way to the airport, it was always a last-minute rush.

'If you can't do that you can play in your birthday suit.' Dermot swept past.

Conor grimaced.

*

'A dozen of those red ones there, please.' Dermot pointed to the vase full of dark velvet buds. Always had to be roses, it was all Irene would accept, and she demanded them on a regular basis, pouting "you don't love me, Dermo, you don't love me anymore" if too long went by and he forgot or just didn't bother.

As he drove over to the apartment, he ran the electric shaver over his chin, five o'clock shadow, or worse still, nine-thirty in the morning shadow, was something which would not be tolerated. He had worn his good suit, and a crisp white shirt, Irene had little patience for a crease or a curling edge.

'Darling.' She met him at the hall door, after keeping him waiting outside for at least five minutes. Nervously he had moved from one foot to the other and glanced up and down the corridor, dreading the moment when one of the other doors would open and curious eyes would stare and demand reasons why he was loitering there. 'Sorry, my love, I was just making myself respectable.'

She wore a white satin dressing-gown, a clinging, revealing thing that suggested she had nothing else on underneath. Every blonde shoulder-length hair was in place, her just-sprayed perfume wafted sensually towards him, and he wanted her immediately, now, there in the hall, reluctant to wait even a few minutes.

'You look gorgeous.' He whipped out the roses from behind his back dramatically.

'Roses for me? You're a pet. And this isn't even my birthday.' She smiled, and then kissed him, full lips open, so inviting. 'Come on in, I've just made coffee.' She led the way down the hall of the luxurious penthouse suite.

'I haven't got that much time. I've to go back to the office and deal with a few things, and be home by eleven.' He followed her, already undoing his tie.

'I wish you weren't going away, I'll miss you terribly. I think you're very mean not to let me go with you, I can still book a flight at this stage, please, please?'

'Rene, you know that's crazy. Do you want Kate to find out about us?'

'Kate isn't the suspicious type.' She helped him off with his jacket.

'Don't wreck my head, Rene, I couldn't cope with the two of you over there. Anyway, there's so much going on at the moment

10

I can see myself coming back after a week. Kate doesn't understand what it's like to run a business as big as mine, she can float off whenever she wants from her piddly little job.'

'I'll be delighted to see you back.' She picked up the coffee pot.

'Don't bother with the coffee.' He kissed her passionately and then he pressed her down on to the couch and pulled aside the dressing-gown to reveal her slim, taut, tanned all over body.

'Let's go into bed, it's more comfortable, my back's at me.' She moved under him.

He stifled an irritable response with a kiss. He was ready for it now. The walk into the bedroom could ruin all that. His momentum would be interrupted and he might collapse like a sail without wind. 'No, love, let's stay, I like it here.'

'But my back, Dermo, it's hurting.' She put a red-tipped foot on to the floor.

He groaned and she giggled.

'It's more fun on the couch.'

'Fun, are you mad, and a six-foot waterbed waiting for us?'

'I don't want a bed, I just want you.'

'This schoolboy stuff doesn't turn me on,' she said in a flat bored voice.

'You'll love it like this, wait and see, if I go into bed I might fall asleep and then where would I be?'

'You'd be with me,' she laughed.

'And what about all the work I still have to do this morning?'

'Forget it.'

'Wish I could,' he said. And wished he could forget all about going out to Spain too. Three whole weeks of lounging by the pool with Kate, swimming and sunbathing, boring repetitive stuff that would drive him to distraction.

'Let me go out with you, I can still arrange it. Go on, Dermo, say yes.'

'I told you no,' he said emphatically.

'Just for a few days?' she begged.

11

'You need to have your head examined.' He pressed her down on the couch again.

'My back, Dermo, my back,' she squealed.

*

It was late when he arrived into the office and began to work through the files he would need to take with him. He had told his secretary to hold all the calls, but she put her head around the door a few minutes later.

'Yea?' He didn't bother to look up.

'One of the Chinese tenants from Mountjoy Square is on the line, it's urgent.'

'Put him on,' he sighed.

It was Ling, and he sounded worried.

'Mr. Mason, we have problem, some men have broken down the door and they won't leave, please come over.'

'What men?'

'Quickly, please.' The phone was cut off.

'What is that all about?' he muttered to himself and rushed out to his car. When he approached the apartments, he phoned Ling again. 'What's happening now?'

'We are on the landing, they won't let us in.' His voice quivered.

'What do they want?'

'To live here, but we don't want them.'

'How many?'

'Four.'

'There isn't room for one more, let alone four. What sort of guys are these?'

'Very dangerous. They have knives and other weapons, very dangerous yes Mr. Mason.'

Dermot sucked in his breath. He certainly didn't want to get involved with these people, whoever they were, so he decided to phone the police and let them handle it. He rang Ling again and told him that. Then he parked down the road from the

12

apartments, not even daring to go inside on his own.

But the police didn't arrive, and he waited impatiently as the minutes ticked past, eating up the time.

'Come on, will you, come on,' he muttered to himself, tapping his fingers nervously on the steering wheel. 'Where are the police?' He craned his neck and peered out the window. 'Never around when you want them.' It was a quarter to eleven now, and then ten to, and five to, and he turned off his phone, aware that Kate would probably call any minute wondering where he was. He knew he was going to be late and she would do her nut, he might even miss the flight. At that thought a self-satisfied grin slowly spread across his face and he relaxed back in the seat.

Chapter Two

Kate checked and re-checked, until finally she was almost pushed out of the office by Carol and Mags, and told to go. She wasn't indispensable, and did she think they weren't able to manage to run the company in her absence? She loved working in Lee O'Donnell Design and never felt like an employee as such, Carol and Mags were her best friends and insisted that everyone work together as a team. Now they steered her into the lift, and she reminded them that someone should follow up on a quote she had sent to a client the other day, and that there was a good chance of getting the job.

'Yea, yea, now have a great time, we don't want to see you for three weeks. I'll look after Uncle Bill, so you can forget about everything.' Carol handed the briefcase to her.

'Thanks a million. Wait a minute, did I ask you to contact Irish Rollashades re the delivery of the blinds for the college tomorrow, and put through that order for the poles to Cramptons?'

'Yes you did, bye,' they chorused as the door slid closed. But when she reached reception she had to talk to Carol again. 'Will you phone Prestigious? I requested some samples and as soon as they arrive send them out to the client immediately, that's urgent, and there are orders due in from Venice and DWS as well, and Fontington and...'

'Yea, yea, yea! Now I'm putting the phone down, goodbye.'

'See you,' Kate laughed, and hurried to the car park. It was always the same whenever she went anywhere, her mind would take a week to wind down out of work mode.

At home, she showered and changed, and then carried the suitcases downstairs, and left them at the front door. She glanced at her watch and looked out of the window praying Dermot's car would swing in at any moment, but the gates remained closed, and that sense of dread which had lurked in the pit of her stomach during the last twenty-four hours suddenly began to build up into something much more disturbing.

'Dermot, I'll kill you if you do this to me again,' she said out loud, and thought how hard she had tried since "that incident" to be the person she imagined he wanted her to be. Suddenly her mind swept her back to New Year's Eve, and the events rolled again.

It had been their turn to entertain the family, Dermot's sister Mary one year, Kate and Dermot the next, and it was a great night according to everyone as they drifted home at some ungodly hour. No-one made any comment or even the slightest allusion to the confrontation which occurred somewhere around three o'clock, most of the people left at that point laughing at Dermot's discomfiture. It all began when someone mentioned New Year resolutions, and took off from there.

'I'm going off the fags.'

'Cut back on the drink.'

'Joining a gym.'

'Try not to get any points on my licence.'

'Going to spend more time with my beloved.'

But it was the subject of losing weight which occupied the minds of most of the women there.

'I stick rigidly to my diet, and I work out in the gym every day, and that's why I look like this.' Irene ran her hands down her slim taut body. 'Am I not an advertisement for the perfect figure, as good as any young girl?' She swung around, and there was a general murmur of approval, a few whistles from the men, and a whoop or two.

'If you walk regularly, avoid the fatty foods and the junk, then you'll never put on any excess weight,' Mary advised.

'But you don't look like Irene, so you must be doing something wrong,' Des chortled. 'When the clothes come off, it flops out in all its middle-aged glory. Any chance of another drink?' He waved his empty glass in the air.

'Rat!' Mary retorted.

'Have to say Irene does look pretty good.' Dermot led Des into the dining-room and they refilled, grinning at each other.

'Like to get underneath all that glam, see what the real thing looks like,' Des murmured.

'I can tell you it's all there, like you wouldn't believe, as good as any young one.' Dermot slurped his whiskey.

'You know all about it? Has she put you to bed lately, like she's your Mammy?' Des warbled, his voice slurred.

'I could tell you a thing or two,' Dermot said with a sly grin as they sauntered unsteadily back to the couch and flopped down.

'I'm really going to try hard this time. Last year it was a pound down one week, a pound up the next, and I lost nothing at all in the end,' Kate was saying.

'That's the trouble, Kate, it always goes back on, doesn't it?' Dermot sniggered. 'You've always been fat, and you'll never be anything else but fat no matter what you do.'

Kate stared at Dermot as he sat there grinning, and a sudden rage exploded inside. She raised the almost full glass of G & T and flung it over him. There was an ominous silence for a few seconds.

He jumped up furiously amid an explosion of laughter from the crowd. 'What did you do that for? I'm soaked, and this is my good suit, are you mad or what?' he snarled as he pulled out a handkerchief from his pocket and dried his face.

'Dermot, you deserved every bit of that, it was a desperate thing to say to Kate. You fellows don't give a damn how you look with your big fat paunches flopping over your trousers as if you were nine months pregnant, which you wouldn't have a clue about anyway, being such wimps, the pair of you. If the roles were reversed the world population would be extinct.' Mary was furious.

16

'Surprised you could say so much without taking a breath,' Des remarked with a sarcastic smirk.

Irene and the other women there began to jeer. 'Good for you, Kate. He got what was coming to him. Kettle calling the pot black. Don't mind him.' They took her side, and she had to laugh as well, but inside she was already crying, his words had cut deep.

She awoke on New Year's Day feeling very rough, with a general seediness which made her want to turn over and go to sleep again until tomorrow. About twelve o'clock, she forced herself up, and left Dermot humped under the duvet. It was a beautiful crisp day of blue skies and sunshine. She pulled on a heavy fleece, and sat outside under the pergola, breathing in draughts of the cold air into her lungs. She tried to dispel her upset about last night, and the realization that Dermot was right. She was...too heavy, and she had to do something about it. But now she had to get to grips with what must be done today. Irene and Aunt Betty were coming for dinner. Uncle Bill was staying over, and the place needed a major scrub-up after last night.

Dermot surfaced an hour or two later, and came into the kitchen where she was making a pavlova.

'You certainly lost your cool last night, you made me look a right eejit.'

'It was good enough for you.'

'I had one too many.'

'You shouldn't have spoken to me like that.' It spurted out in spite of her good intentions not to get into a row about it. 'I swear, if you ever do that again, I'm out of here,' she threatened.

'It was just drink talk, everyone was at it. You were ridiculous.'

'I hate it when you make insulting remarks to me in front of other people.'

'Anyway, it was the truth, you can't get away from that.'

'That's not the point,' she snapped.

'It is the point, not that you've got very many, you're an all rounder.'

'There you go again, sarcastic bastard, how dare you!' she shouted, but had no satisfaction as he turned away from her and went into the television-room where Shane was stretched out on the couch, and Uncle Bill watched some war film.

'Up you.' He dug Shane with his knee.

'Hey Dad, what did you do that for?'

'I want to sit there, I'm not feeling well.'

'I was here first.'

'Up, or I'll brain you.' Dermot dug him again.

'OK, keep your cool, man.' He slid off and stood up.

'And where's the remote?'

'Here, although it's Uncle Bill's call now.' Shane handed it to him, and went into the kitchen. 'Think I'll go around to Kev, Mum, see you later.'

'Dinner's at seven.'

She opened the oven door, put in the joint of beef, and checked the time. Then she took out the vacuum-cleaner and began to clear up, so tired now it was a huge effort. Most of the dishes she had put into the washer earlier, but there were still dirty ashtrays, and glasses in hidden corners, on the floor, the window-sills...the most unexpected places. Doggedly she worked on, and wondered if she carried out her threat of leaving, would she bear the guilt of abandonment on her head for the rest of her life? She imagined walking out now and leaving notes around the place. Get your own dinner. Clean up the house. Take Uncle Bill home. Make sure he has enough food. Do his washing and ironing and all your own too. She flopped into an armchair, and let go the nozzle which fell on the floor with a loud thump, and wished herself a Happy New Year.

Now Kate pressed in the code and the gates slowly opened. She stood looking out through the window praying that Dermot's car would appear, but after a moment, realizing that there were still things she had to do, she hurried into the kitchen. To double-

18

check that there was enough food for Conor and Shane, who were men now at twenty-one and nineteen and should have been able to look after themselves. But as ever, Kate had done her motherly thing and made sure that the quantity of pizzas, burgers, beer, and other junk in the fridge and freezer was enough to keep them going for the three weeks that Dermot and herself would be away.

In a rush now, she scribbled a note on the yellow pad to remind the lads to water the flowers. The weather could be quite warm in May and all her plants might be withered by the time she came back if they didn't get enough moisture. Another note on how to operate the new dishwasher, a reminder to put on the alarm when they went out, and lock all windows and doors. She stood with pen in hand and tried to think of anything else she needed to do, suddenly remembering to take Conor's gear out of the dryer.

She caught sight of the clock on the wall, the minutes creeping closer to the time they were due to leave, and walked down the hall again. As she looked out the window, real anger uncurled itself in her stomach. Her pulse began to race, and she could feel that old familiar band of tension across her forehead which always made itself felt when things seemed to be going wrong. She punched in the digits of Dermot's number, and walked up and down impatiently, the phone pressed to her ear so hard it zinged. But all she could hear was the answering service so she left a rather irate message. She tried the office but his secretary told her he had gone out, and that he'd be back soon. Where was he? There was no time for going back to the office at this stage.

The bell rang, and praying it was him, she opened the door, but it was the taxi which waited outside. A diminutive woman climbed out and walked smiling towards her, and Kate lifted the two suitcases on to the step with a chill in her heart.

She tried his number again without success, but suddenly her mobile rang.

'Where are you?' she shouted.

'I'm over at one of the apartments.'

Her anger overflowed. 'What are you doing there?'

'I'm sorry, Kate, but something's come up, a problem with one of the tenants.'

'Can't it wait?' she demanded.

'No, the police are involved, I'm waiting for them now.'

'The taxi is outside the door, you can't do this to me, not again.'

'I'm sorry, we'll re-schedule.' He seemed only very slightly regretful.

'But everything's arranged, the car, everything, and I won't be able to take time off again this summer.'

'Why not?'

'Because other people have booked their holidays.'

'What if you were sick or something, they would have to do without you then, wouldn't they? Look, defer it for a week or so and we'll head off as soon as I've got this sorted. I have to go over to close the contracts anyway.'

'We're supposed to be going on a holiday, not closing contracts,' she snapped, furious at his inference that her job didn't count.

'There's nothing I can do, must go, I'm in a rush.'

'And so am I.' She cut herself off, something she wouldn't normally do no matter how angry. Then she took the tickets and passports out of her bag, separated his and threw them on the hall table. Lastly, she rapped on the converted garage door, her youngest son's music studio, and living quarters, but there was no response, the dull thump of rock music from inside drowning out any sound she could make. Frustrated, she rang his mobile which he answered as soon as it began to vibrate.

'Shane, I'm on my way now, open the door please.'

He was her baby, and even though he was six feet tall, without a screed of hair on his head, wore studs in his nostril, his lip, and his ear, and apparently had a couple of tattoos in intimate places which she hadn't seen for a long time, she still loved him to bits. He appeared in the doorway, a plectrum poised between his thumb and forefinger over the strings of the guitar.

'How is your throat?'

'It's fine today, don't worry. Any chance you'd make us some sandwiches before you go? Kev and Jake are inside, we're getting a bit hungry.'

'Shane, the taxi is at the door, there's plenty of food in the fridge, you'll just have to rustle up something for yourself.'

'What will I make?'

'The place is bursting with food, will you please start behaving like someone your age, you're hopeless.'

'Yea, yea, cool it Mum, cool it.'

'I'm off then, look after yourself.' She hugged him, and he hugged her, always the more affectionate of her two sons.

'Have a great time, Mum.'

'I've left plenty of cooked meals in the freezer and all you have to do is defrost, so there's no need to be hungry, and you might learn how a kitchen works.'

She walked towards the taxi, still concerned about Shane's throat. She worried most about her youngest son, always seeing the curly dark-haired boy in him in spite of his bald pate. Conor was harder, more independent, like Dermot.

'I'll have to take back that dark-blue case, we're not waiting for him.'

The taxi woman opened the boot and lifted it out. Kate grabbed hold of it, marched half-way up the drive and dumped it in the middle of the garden.

As she slid into the back seat of the comfortable car, she closed her eyes, and tried to calm the racing of her heart. He'll give me a stroke one of these days, she thought, if I let him. He doesn't give a damn.

Something was wrong, terribly wrong, and she knew that she hadn't wanted to see it before now. Even the fact that she looked better than she had in years never registered with Dermot. And she had been longing to get away with him to Torrevieja, just the two of them alone. Her imagination taking her to that warm lazy place where they would make love after they had wandered back

21

from the beach, lips tasting of salt, skin tingling from too much sun. And showering together, leisurely soaping, kissing, and touching, unable to stay away from each other even for a few minutes. Later, they would sip an aperitif at the edge of the pool, and share a romantic dinner on a balcony overlooking the whispering moonlit sea. But that scenario was looking distinctly improbable now.

'Catch up with you later?' The woman's eyes met hers in the mirror.

'Doubt that, he doesn't want to go, that's the bottom line,' Kate spat it out vehemently.

'Men!' she laughed sympathetically.

'Can't prise him away from his business, no matter what I do, even if I offered him sex on a plate, morning, noon, and night, it wouldn't attract him. Mind you, it wasn't always like that, but nowadays I think he just sees me as his housekeeper.'

'Mine is a football fan. He heads off most weekends to Man United matches in England, and then there's the European Cup, and the World Cup, and the this Cup and the that Cup.'

'Wash, cook and clean.' Kate wasn't really listening to what the other woman had to say. 'He doesn't want to know what I think any more, or what I do when we're apart, doesn't want to know full stop.' Her angry feelings came out in a sudden rush, and she was surprised at herself telling a complete stranger.

'I took this job cosying for a friend, and it gives me something to do so I'm not tearing my hair out waiting for him to come back. You should be looking at alternatives, don't let him control your life.'

'He doesn't really, I do my own thing,' Kate replied, but the woman's words kept repeating in her head for the rest of the journey, particularly the control word. Control. She should stand up to him more often, she knew that, but she always gave in for the sake of peace and avoided confrontation, and if she admitted the truth she was probably afraid of it. Except today, for the first time she hadn't let him away with it. She uncurled her body out of the slumped position, sat up and straightened her shoulders as they pulled up outside Departures. She stared at the people getting out of cars and taxis, loading baggage on trolleys, kissing and hugging, and felt a sudden loneliness, but she knew there was no turning back now.

At the check-in desk, she asked automatically for an exit seat, thinking of how Dermot liked to stretch his legs, but then decided there was no need to think of him at all.

'I'll have to up-grade you,' the girl said.

'Thank you.' First time that's ever happened, she thought, and smiled with satisfaction. On her way now, she was going to try and make the best of it, and went through into the shopping area where she treated herself to some expensive perfume, moisturising-lotion, foundation, nail-polish, lipstick, and charged it to their joint credit card with pleasure.

On board, she had a wide comfortable window seat. The day was still dull and grey, ideal weather for escaping to sunnier climes, and she tried to drum up enthusiasm, visualising sparkling blue sea, golden beaches, and the pleasure of opening their house in Torrevieja for the first time in over a year. As people came through the door of the plane, she glanced up in hope, still expecting to see Dermot arrive, but soon all the seats were occupied by strangers. A large oily-haired man overflowed in the seat beside her, his head buried in a newspaper. Even though the seat was extra wide, it didn't seem to be big enough for him, and his elbows almost touched hers, so close it was uncomfortable.

Finally the doors were locked and the seat belt sign switched on, and she knew it was too late. He wasn't coming. She swore under her breath, those choice words she hardly ever uttered, but even in her head they gave satisfaction.

The hostess went through the usual safety precautions and she wondered if she would ever know which cord to tie or pull if she was falling into nothing? Or would she pass out before ever reaching land or sea, all the oxygen sucked from her lungs, and her clothes torn off? Always wear clean knickers, her mother used to say, you never know what might happen. A lot of use in a crash, she thought, her crumpled body would be naked, starkers, for all to see. She forced that unpleasant thought to the back of her mind, as the plane began its forward thrust down the runway until it achieved lift-off, and then slowly cut through the diaphanous swirl of grey cloud into bright sunshine and blue sky. The nervous flutter of her heart abated, and she felt better when the smiling hostess offered her something to drink. The G & T was sharp and cool, and it slipped down a treat, but when wine was served with the meal she resisted, and reminded herself that she had to drive to Torrevieja from the airport. The in-flight magazine passed the time for a while, and after that she tried to sleep, but it was impossible. She just sat there thinking about Dermot, until eventually, to her relief, the plane slowly began its descent into Alicante. She slipped on her shoes again, and tightened the seat belt as she heard the landing gear grind into position. The hostess gabbled something in English and Spanish, but she couldn't understand either, and just waited breath-held until the wheels hit the runway with an uneven series of shuddering bumps, sighing with relief when it finally came to a halt.

In Arrivals, the bags came out onto the carousel quickly, and she went over to the car hire desk to arrange collection of the Mégane Coupe. It was brand-new shining silver and gave her a sudden unexpected moment of pleasure to have the car to herself. Dermot always drove, this was his domain.

'We're on the opposite side of the road, it's dangerous, and you've no experience,' he had said the last time.

'When I was at that trade-show in Paris with the girls we shared the driving and had no problem,' she responded.

'It's different here, the Spanish drivers are crazy.'

'And another time in Rome, where they are complete maniacs,' she said mildly, just wanting to get the point across, but not really caring.

Now she sat into the comfortable air-conditioned car, drove out to the motorway and headed for Torrevieja, definitely the one in control this time.

Chapter Three

To Dermot's relief, the police took the men away for questioning. Then he arranged for a new door to be supplied and had to wait around until his maintenance-man arrived. In the meantime he talked to the terrified tenants and tried to persuade them not to rush back to China because of a few heavies, but there was no changing their minds. Eventually he did a deal with them on the deposit, very annoyed that he would have to go to the trouble of re-letting.

In spite of his intention to get home early, it was after seven when he opened the gates with the remote, and jerked the car to a scrunching halt on the gravel driveway, glad to see Kate's car parked there. Then he reached for his briefcase, and a bunch of flowers which he had just bought at the garage. It was a long time since he had given her any, and he hoped the gesture would put her in good mood after what happened this morning. He walked towards the front door, but stopped suddenly, his forehead creased in puzzlement as he noticed his suitcase in the middle of the garden.

'Kate, what's my case doing outside?' he yelled, dumping the flowers on a chair, 'my stuff is going to be all damp.' He carried in the case, banged the front door, and stomped into the kitchen. It was like a bomb-site, with dirty mugs, plates, half-eaten pizza, and empty beer cans everywhere.

He went down the hall to the garage and could hear a dull unmusical sound as he stood at the door, knocking hard at first, then pounding, until eventually it was opened and Shane's head appeared out through the small gap. 'Where's your mother?'

'I 'dunno.' He peered suspiciously at his father. 'Thought you were supposed to be away?'

'Obviously, I'm not,' he growled.

'Shane, come on,' one of the others called him back inside, and he began to close the door.

'You didn't see her at all today?' Dermot demanded.

'I saw her this morning before she went. Must go, Dad, we're in the middle of something.'

Wondering where Kate was, Dermot marched into the television-room and plonked into an armchair. He clicked the remote, stared at some news programme for a few seconds, then switched from one channel to another. He had come home anxious to patch things up with her. He could probably manage to get away in a few days, or a week or two, but where was she now?

He turned off the television, stared frustrated into space for a moment and only then thought of phoning her. But he was even more annoyed when he discovered the mobile was powered off.

He hated it when Kate was absent. Something in him needed to know where she was at any given moment. And nowadays he didn't always know, and hadn't for years. He shouldn't have let her go back to work; if she wasn't so involved with her little job, she would have more time for him and the lads, he had plenty of money for them all to live quite comfortably. He could never forget that day when she went out at eight o'clock to drop the boys off at school, and didn't return until after four, and in between those hours it was as if she had disappeared into the ether.

'That's fantastic, she's gone on her own, wow!' Irene threw her arms around Dermot. 'Just as well I didn't arrange to go.'

'I'm hoping she hasn't. But it was something about the case, standing there in the middle of the garden. Such a weird thing to do. And my passport and ticket were thrown on the hall table. She never did anything like that before, wouldn't have thought she had the guts,' he grumbled.

'If she's gone, then we can be together every night, I can't believe it, let's celebrate.' She poured two glasses of whiskey.

'It's all very well for you, but I have to deal with Shane and Conor and the domestic stuff as well. The kitchen is a mess already and its only been one day. Shane and his friends are a shower of lazy...the lot of them. She'd better be home by the time I get back, I'm not cleaning up, that's her job.'

'Do you want me to come over, I'll look after you.'

'You can barely look after yourself, Irene.' He swallowed the whiskey.

'You'd be surprised at what I can do if I want to.' She sat beside him, her skirt flipping back to reveal long suntanned legs.

'And have the lads put two-and-two together, and get four.' He raised his eyebrows in horror.

'Am I not part of the family? What could be more natural? Mother-in-law comes over to help while the wife's away.' She ran her fingers through his hair.

'You're a most unlikely mum-in-law.' He leaned his head back on the soft cushions of the black leather suite.

'I was married to Kate's father for ten years, and he really loved me.' She kicked off her shoes.

'You were able to wind him around your little finger, and he gave you everything you wanted.'

'That's what bugged the family most, the money, well, all of them except Kate, it didn't seem to bother her very much.'

'Money isn't really important to Kate, not like someone else I know.' He slid his hand slowly along her body, thinking how fantastic she always looked, this evening dressed in black, with carefully understated gold jewellery.

'Stay the night,' she suggested softly.

'And how would you have me explain to Conor why I'm coming in when he's going to work?'

'They won't get up until lunchtime if Kate's not there to call them.'

'Probably not, still I don't want to make waves.' Sometimes Conor looked at him in a curious appraising way as if he knew what was going on all the time.

'Take the risk,' she whispered, opening the buttons on his shirt.

'Irene, before we...any chance of something to eat?' Dermot suddenly became aware of the emptiness in his stomach. 'I'm starving.'

'For me?'

'For sustenance.'

'I'll make you a sandwich later.'

'I can't do anything when I'm hungry Irene, you know that, can you cook me up something a bit better than a sandwich?'

'Ham or cheese, that's it, nothing else in the fridge, you know I'm not the domesticated type, I'm not your Mommy.'

'For God's sake, Irene, is that all?' He was irritated.

'Fancy a bowl of cereal, nuts and fruit? That would fill you up, and it won't take long to eat.'

He made a face. Suddenly his phone rang.

'Leave it, leave it, you'll only get involved.' She pushed him against the cushions and leaned on him.

'Must take it, I'm waiting for a call from Manuel.' He reached past her for the phone which was on the coffee-table.

'Flipping Manuel,' she muttered, her face unattractive with discontent.

'Get off me, Irene.' He tried to extricate himself from her legs which were entangled around his.

'I won't let you,' she said in a little-girl voice.

'Irene, stop.' He shoved her away, and grabbed the phone. 'Manuel? Manuel?' He listened for a few seconds. 'Irene, I've missed that call, and it was important.'

She resettled her clothes, disgruntled.

'It's always important,' she sighed deeply with an air of tragedy.

'Irene, it won't take a minute, you make the sandwich and a cup of coffee, then we can...' He tried Manuel's number but couldn't get through.

'I don't feel like making anything now. Think I'm Kate, do

28

you? I was looking forward to an uninterrupted evening together and now this.' She lit a cigarette and lay back on the couch, a sulky dissatisfied expression twisting her beautiful features.

'Come on, just a bite to eat and then I'll be ready for anything,' he coaxed. But she stared across the room, and wouldn't meet his eyes.

'OK then, don't bother.' He picked up his car keys and jacket, and marched out of the apartment, trying to button up his shirt and form a knot in his lemon tie as he hurried along the corridor, hoping he wouldn't bump into anyone. In the lift, he shrugged into his navy-striped jacket, and closed one button to cover his ample stomach, automatically taking a deep breath to reduce his rotund shape. He exhaled as the heavy door slid back silently, and his eyes met those of a young woman who waited for him to step out. He felt self-conscious, and brushed past her, thinking that he should do a bit of training. If he enrolled at the gym again, and lost a few pounds, he could pull someone like that. He wasn't bad looking, he thought. His hair was still black, not a grey hair in sight, and he looked pretty good with the new shorter cut. He had plenty of money to give her a good time, and that was all any of them wanted these days. Over the last few years he had extended his modest building business into property speculation on a grand scale, particularly in Spain. The lucrative property deal he had contracted with Manuel and his colleagues was mind-boggling. A development of hotels, shopping centres, golf clubs, commercial, residential; the biggest investment in which he had ever become involved. He had mortgaged everything to raise the millions of euro needed, and the profits he expected to make would change their lives radically.

But Kate was all part of that. The thought of her going off to Spain alone was just too much for him. How would he manage without her? He couldn't imagine what it would be like to wake up in the morning and not hear her calling them to get up, or come home in the evening to a cold empty kitchen. A very uncomfortable feeling swept over him. A sensation of loss which made his stomach clench; his heart began to race rapidly.

Chapter Four

Kate pressed her foot on the accelerator-pedal and filtered into the traffic on the motorway, enjoying the handling of this car, the response of the controls sharp and unused. She opened the window and could feel the soft warmth of the breeze on her face, breathing in the aromatic scent carried in the heavy air, reminding her that she was far away from the cloudy damp day at home. An hour later, she drove up the driveway to their house, which was positioned on a height overlooking the beach. It was built in typical Spanish style, with white-painted balustrades, and windows covered with black wrought-iron grilles. The gardens were colourful with bougainvillaea, and the sparkling water in the swimming-pool was so inviting she wanted to jump in immediately.

But first she wandered through the cool spacious marble-floored rooms getting to know the house again. She opened the heavy wooden shutters and windows to let in the air and then she attended to the utilities, gas, electricity and water. Later, she sat at the edge of the pool, and watched the sun go down. It was quiet and very secluded, protected by trees and shrubs, the chorus of crickets the only sound. Then an idea occurred to her. She switched on the lights in the pool, took off her clothes, and dived in. Loving the freedom of nakedness, she laughed, imagining Dermot's shock-horror if he knew what she was doing. Skinny-dipping just wasn't something a woman her age should do. What if someone arrived, and you were caught? she could hear him ask. Maybe Eddie from next door, maybe the fellow who looked after the place, the postman, the pizza-boy, or any

30

Tom, Dick, or Harry? She raised two fingers in the air to his invisible presence, turned a back-flip, then treaded water and stared down at herself. As she moved, the ripples distorted her shape, and she thought that she looked even thinner than she was. Her body all liquid now, glimmering white through the water. She smiled, thinking that she would have to get the blonde hilights in that little patch as well. But what was the point? Dermot probably wouldn't even notice, he didn't go there very often these days.

More and more she found her mind drifting back through the years to when they were young and in love and couldn't spend enough time together. Since she was twelve she had been mad about the dark-haired boy who went to the school down the road, and who everybody fancied; the one she had finally landed. They had to be very careful. Her parents didn't approve of her having a boyfriend at all, and expected her to do well in her exams and go on to college. But Kate wasn't interested in doing that, all she wanted was to be with Dermot. Their own secret hiding-place in the thick green undergrowth behind where they lived provided that chance, and there experimental teenage kisses led on to a much heavier scene, until they crossed all boundaries.

It was the summer of '83, and that day the sunshine glinted through the mesh of greenery around them. He had his back up against a tree and she lay on an old rug on the ground with her head on his lap, nibbling a blade of grass.

'I've already started to save to get married,' he confided to her.

'So have I,' she admitted shyly.

'Although it's going to be hard, you know I have to hand up a fair chunk of my wages at home, and I try to give the others some pocket-money as well.'

'I wonder when we'll have enough?' She turned her head to smile up at him.

'Never, if my mother has her way.'

'She doesn't want you to leave home?'

'She wants my wages.' He had a sullen look on his face.

'But she has a job.'

'There's talk of the factory closing down.' He ran his fingers through her long fair hair, and she turned to kiss him, and the import of his words went straight out of her head until the day she told him that she was pregnant.

There was war. Her parents were furious, disappointed, hurt, and succeeded in making her feel very guilty and ashamed. But after a few tense frosty days they put all that aside, and began making plans for the wedding.

Mrs. Mason's attitude was very different.

'She said I was letting the family down, and that she always depended on me to help her keep going since Dad died.' Dermot was upset. 'If I leave, they'll be living on the breadline, and Brendan and Owen won't be able to finish school because they will have to get jobs. She went on and on, and then she hit me across the face.'

'My love.' She put her arms around him.

'It was when she called you a...that I saw red and walked out. I'm never going back there.'

'You can come and stay with us, I'm sure if I explained to Mam and Dad...'

'I'm going over to Uncle Paddy, he has room in his flat for me.'

'It won't be for long, we have to get married soon.' She was excited.

'Yea, and then we won't have to come down here any more, we'll have a place of our own.' He kissed her.

But that little place in the greenery was long gone under a concrete-jungle and with it the innocence and wonder of young love.

Over this last year, she had probably tried too hard. Often she found herself making the most foolish of remarks to try and open up a conversation, and endless suggestions to do things together.

'Fancy going to a show one night this week, Dermot, we haven't been out in ages?' she had asked, but the shake of his head as he watched the television was dismissive.

32

'How about meeting me after work for a drink?' was another offer which met with a vague inaudible mutter.

'Let's go out to dinner on Saturday night, put on the glad-rags and hit the town?'

'I have to see clients, inspect a site, meet the accountant, the solicitor, a councillor, a man-with-a-dog,' he would say, or more often than not, it was the vague work-late excuse. Like a snake sloughed his skin, the new Dermot seemed to be totally bored with everything around him except his business.

Or maybe it was her? Had she wandered off down a narrow country lane where there were no signposts to tell her which way to go? Like a blind person, she reached forward to hold on to the familiar. Ridiculous things that suddenly meant so much. The salad-bowl he had bought her in Portugal, all bright yellows, reds and blues, a reminder of happy holidays. And that little soft teddy he had surprised her with one Valentine's Day. And so much more.

Worst of all was the length of time since they had made love. Real love. The very quick version that was Dermot these days had obviously made little impression on her. A hurried coupling one night in the dark, the result of a few drinks, when Dermot climaxed within minutes, and her delicately-achieved orgasm was a non-event. She had almost forgotten what that felt like, and longed to rekindle the love they once had known which filtered into everything, and made life worth living.

She found excuses. It's always too late, he's tired, growing older, I can't expect him to have the same drive. But it became something she could not ignore, and now she began to wonder where he was at night, nearly always out until twelve or one, and last Tuesday, it was almost four in the morning. When she lay in the bed unable to sleep, stiff and cold, as her ears strained for the sound of his car coming up the road and crunching to a halt on the gravelled drive, the click of his key in the door. Her mood changed from anger that he couldn't take the trouble to phone to explain what had happened, to worry that maybe he was involved in an accident. Or perhaps he was over with his sister Mary, having a drink and chatting, without a thought for her. She had tried his number but couldn't get through, and finally got up at three, unable to bear the sleeplessness and inaction any longer. She pulled on her dressing-gown, made a cup of tea and stood in the hall staring out through the window, willing him to come home, her treacherous mind taking her to all sorts of uncomfortable places.

What was she to him now? A housekeeper? Caring for the three men in her life, cook, cleaner, washer-up, who hovered in the background with her hand held out permanently with the necessary. Paraded in front of friends and clients like the specimen of the perfect wife.

'People are impressed by solid marriages, good homes, well behaved kids. They want to do business with dependable people. I know, I want to do business with people like that, and I've invited the directors of that new firm of architects over on Saturday night, pull out all the stops, they're important contacts,' Dermot had announced after dinner.

'How many altogether?' Her mind switched into cooking mode immediately.

'Eight, including the wives.'

'Would you like rack-of-lamb this time, or maybe roast-beef, or how about Italian?' But Dermot never had much interest in the food, the wines were his forte.

I hate doing pasta for a big crowd, so no to that, she thought. Could do salmon stuffed with prawns and crabmeat, that went down a treat the last time, and have a couple of steaks for anyone who doesn't eat fish. And maybe a mixture of vegetables, aubergines, courgettes, for the vegetarians, and potatoes done in the oven with garlic and cheese. She began to scribble down a shopping-list.

But that was then and now she had changed into a wild thing, spitting fury, when he came in at three fifty-six exactly.

34

'Where have you been until this hour, I was worried about you, I thought I'd have the police at the door any minute telling me you had an accident, why didn't you phone?' she demanded.

He stared at her for a few seconds, pushed past, and stomped up the stairs. She ran after him, wanting a confrontation, a question-and-answer session which would satisfy all those nagging doubts which had escalated out of all proportion during the last few hours. But he went into the bathroom and she climbed back into bed, lying rigid with anger mixed with relief, wanting to pummel him and make him understand her concern. But as he flopped down beside her suddenly the anger faded and she put her arm around him and cuddled.

'I'm sorry for losing the rag, love, but I was really worried...' She ran her fingers down his body, and then leaned across and kissed him.

'Go to sleep, Kate,' he murmured, the smell of whiskey strong.

'I can't, I'm too upset, give us a kiss.' She hugged closer to him.

'I'm wrecked, I haven't the energy.'

She moved back on to her own side, as memories of past times tumbled into her mind and she realized how much she missed the tease of his hand caressing her as she stood at the cooker preparing dinner, the sensual whisper in her ear which promised an early night, the touch of his lips when he come home during the day and they did it all hurried and giggling on the couch, praying the boys wouldn't come back from school unexpectedly.

It seemed to Kate that she didn't know her Dermot any more. She felt their once close relationship had subtly changed into a bare nodding acquaintance with each other. So much so, she deliberately took a good look at herself, honest enough to think that perhaps she had a responsibility as well. Maybe she hadn't tried hard enough to lose weight? Maybe her clothes were frumpish? Maybe she needed a new hairstyle? Maybe she needed a complete make-over?

After her swim, she dried herself off, and stood in front of the full-length mirror in the bedroom. She did look so much better, and to her disappointment, Dermot hadn't really noticed, and he wouldn't be here to see how well she looked in her new clothes. Her hopes for a reconciliation were ground into nothing. But she still had a sense of satisfaction when she showered and changed into one of her lacy camisoles and a skimpy thong, a pair of white shorts and a blue T-shirt, and liked the person she saw in the mirror.

After that, she walked down to the nearby shop to pick up some food, looking forward to a meal of tasty meats, cheese, olives, crusty bread, some red wine, and was just setting it out on the table beside the pool when her phone rang. She hesitated for a few seconds, almost sorry that she had switched it on again, quite sure that it was Dermot and really not keen to talk to him, but it was too hard to ignore and there was always the possibility that he was on his way.

'Kate, what are you doing there?' he demanded abruptly.

'What do you think?' She was suddenly freshly annoyed with him.

'Listen, you can't leave me here with everything, once I've got this problem sorted I can get away, why don't you come back tomorrow, then we'll go out together again?'

'Are you mad?' she asked.

'It's your place to be here, I can't be doing all this stuff, and it looks odd, I don't want people to be wondering what's going on.'

'My place? What do you mean exactly?' She stared out at the water in the pool, the moonlight reflected on the surface.

'To be at home looking after things, I haven't time for cooking and cleaning,' he blustered.

'Go and stay in a hotel then.'

'I'll check the flights and get back to you,' he said, and cut off.

She sat there waiting, and tried to compose herself. Whatever he said or threatened, she wasn't going to give in.

The phone rang again.

'I've arranged it, jot this down,' Dermot said.

'I'm not going back, it's ridiculous.' She was quietly determined.

'The flight is at 11.10 out of Alicante to Madrid, can you make that?'

'You're not listening to me. I said no. I'm on my holidays,' she enunciated carefully.

'Kate, you do what I tell you!' he roared down the phone.

'See you Dermot.' She clicked off deliberately, and sat thinking. All the little things which had happened in the past few years coalesced into one big thing. She suddenly realised that he thought she was his slave.

Curiously, the following day, she did exactly what a slave would do, and began to clean, although this time it was her own decision. When she had finished the house, she tackled the garden. The maintenance-man came around every week, but there was still a lot to be done there too. She was busy, so very angrily busy, and she had kept her phone switched off, only ringing Uncle Bill to check that he was all right, and texting the lads, always a little anxious about her boys, never quite able to see them as grown men.

By Friday, she decided it was holiday-time, and she planned her day, dividing it into segments. Swim, sunbathe front. Swim, sunbathe back. Swim. Sandwich. Drink. She went down to the beach late in the day after most of the families and the footballers had gone, and when all she could hear was the soft ssshhh of the waves on the sand, the endless over-and-over of water hissing, and surging. She lay with her eyes closed in the still-warm sunshine, and put out her hand in a tentative searching movement, as if she might touch Dermot and find that he was there all the time. She imagined she might press her lips against his, and that his response would be immediate, needing and wanting her. But that was how it was twenty-odd years ago. She sat up and stared along the gleaming curl of the surf at the edge of the aquamarine sea, watching the local fishermen set up their rods at the far end of the beach, shadowed now as the sun moved slowly down behind the land. There was a dull pain in her heart, of knowing and understanding something which had been just around the corner of consciousness for God knows how long.

Chapter Five

'You'll have to keep this place clean, it's like a pigsty,' Dermot shouted at Shane who was carrying a tray of something towards the garage. 'Your mother's not coming back.'

The tall gangly figure stopped and the shaven head turned around. 'What?'

'You'll have to pull your weight, or I'll cut the slush fund.'

'What did you say about Mum?'

'She's staying out in Spain for her own little holiday, doesn't care what happens to us here.'

'Thought you meant gone altogether.'

'She'll be back in her own time, when it suits her.'

'Probably needs a break from us.' Shane continued on down the hall.

'Did you hear what I said?' Dermot followed him.

'Yea Dad, yea.' He disappeared into the garage and closed the door.

'I expect this place to be spotless when I come back later,' Dermot yelled, and wandered into the kitchen, muttering to himself. Kids! We've spoiled them rotten; these days they don't even listen to you, that's what you get when you give them too much. And how could Kate go off like that, and refuse to come back, forcing me to look after everything? Dermot's pathetic efforts amounted to boiling the kettle for a cup of coffee in the morning, after he had fallen in and out of the same unmade bed. In the bathroom, he kicked the dirty towels into a corner for one of the lads to pick up. A small percentage of the clothes made the wash-basket, others missed and sank their smelly selves in a pile around it.

But he hadn't always been like that. When he was young, there was a time when he had to give his two brothers and sister their breakfast in the morning, check they were properly dressed, and get them to school. And in the afternoon, he would collect them from a neighbour's house, make sure they had something to eat, and did their homework. He hadn't really minded that. What he hated most of all was the empty house, his mother never home from work until after six. Those first few seconds were always the worst as he heard the slight creak of the opened door and walked down the hall, the sound of his footsteps loud on the shining lino, the rooms full of echo. Those were the moments which came back to haunt him in nightmares.

After the death of Dermot's father, Kathleen Mason ran her household like an army-camp, and exercised such discipline on her children that they almost stood to attention whenever she spoke, except Mary, her only daughter, who seemed to lead a charmed life in her mother's eyes. But Dermot, the eldest, was always the one expected to achieve the highest standard in everything he did. He tried to reach her expectations, but didn't always succeed and he received no congratulations for obtaining ninety-five per cent.

'If you can achieve those marks then you should be able to make the hundred.'

But it was impossible to satisfy her however hard he worked. All his life, he longed for her to hug him, tell him he had done well and that she loved him. But none of her boys knew the touch of her lips or a soft hand, and her attitude to Kate, and decision not to attend their wedding hurt him so deeply they had never reconciled.

In his office, he rang Manuel. 'I've got those contracts signed for that development, twenty-nine apartments sold, mostly 2-beds, yea, I'll send you an email, yea, si.' Dermot had picked up a few basic words of Spanish to get through most situations, but his pronunciation left a lot to be desired, and he was liable to get quite mixed up at times. 'I'll be out with you next week, say

Tuesday, si, si, ciao, adios.' He put down the phone, and with a small key he opened a drawer and pulled out a stack of legal documents.

'Number three,' he murmured to himself as he leafed through them, and extracted it. 'The new Lotto millionaires, lucky beggars, the ideal candidates.' He pulled another out and laughed, remembering the hard sell to the sisters who wanted to invest some of the money amassed on the disposal of their large house.

It was a scheme that Manuel had devised, a lucrative plan which gave Dermot a neat little backhander. The con was perpetrated on a select group of clients who thought they owned one-hundred-per-cent of their properties in Spain but through the clever notaries used by Manuel, actually only owned twenty-per-cent, the balance held by his company. It was like a time-share, the people chosen always first-time buyers with too much money.

Chapter Six

Suddenly Kate's world repositioned itself, and round pegs settled into round holes and fitted perfectly. From this distance she was able to look at her life and see that it fell far short of the ideal. But although she tried not to, she couldn't prevent herself wondering how things were at home. In the past when she had been on holiday with Dermot, Dublin had simply faded out of her mind completely, but this time was different. She was still very angry with him and couldn't make up her mind whether she wanted to see him arrive, or not. Mixed up with all of that was a dread that Irene would turn up since she had mentioned she would love to join them, and worry about Uncle Bill. That evening when Bill hadn't known Shane, and seemed to think her father was still alive continued to nag at her.

'The television won't come on, I can't get Coronation Street.' Uncle Bill waved the remote-control, but the screen remained stubbornly blank. 'Hurry up, nothing's happening, I'll miss the beginning.' He peered at his wristwatch. 'Kate, it's gone half seven.'

'OK, just a tick.' Kate turned the fillet-steaks on the pan, added a little olive oil, and garlic, and went inside to turn on the television. There was a ring on the doorbell. Quickly she returned to the cooker and moved the steaks around the pan again before she went to answer it, wondering if Dermot had forgotten his key, or Conor. She smiled as she opened the door, but was slightly taken aback to find Irene standing outside. Togged out in a smart navy-and-white suit, no doubt designer, with matching shoes, bag, and probably matching underwear, too, Kate thought.

'You're looking stunning, are you going somewhere?' Kate smiled.

'I'm visiting you.' She put a delicately-shod foot on the step.

'Well, you'd better come in, we're entertaining in the kitchen tonight.'

'I've already eaten, thanks, I'll just have a glass of something.' She sat down at the table, crossed one slim leg over the other, and took a packet of cigarettes out of her bag. 'Where's Dermot?'

'He hasn't come home yet, if he doesn't arrive soon, his steak will be frazzled, glass of wine?' Kate took a bottle of Chateau Bechereau, one of Dermot's favourites, from the sideboard and opened it.

'Thanks, you don't mind if I smoke?'

'No.' She would have preferred if people didn't smoke in the house but with Dermot's cigars, Conor and Shane's cigarettes, it seemed a bit much to ask visitors to refrain from polluting the air as well.

'How are you?' Kate checked the vegetables in the oven.

'Fine thanks, fine.' She positioned a cigarette in her holder, lit it with her gold lighter and took a deep pull.

'Uncle Bill's here.'

'He's such a pain.' Irene grimaced, a flash of indented lines in the golden hue of her carefully-made-up face, a sudden ugliness which previewed how she might look twenty years on. Irene had no time for him at all, and never had, even when Kate's father had been alive. In her opinion, he had been the odd weirdo elder brother who lived in a hovel in Rathmines, and she wouldn't have him put a foot across the threshold of their pristine apartment.

'He likes to come over.'

'Rather you than me, I don't know how you stick him, sure you can't exchange two sensible words with the man, all gobbledygook.'

Kate went into the television-room and brought him in, and then phoned Shane to tell him the dinner was ready.

'Hi, Irene, how's it going? Bill, you're looking sharp.' Shane patted him on the shoulder as he sat down.

'Who's he?' Bill asked Kate.

'For God's sake, that's Shane,' Irene said.

Bill stared suspiciously at him.

'Why is he sitting at the table with us, Kate?'

'Me big chief grandnephew.' Shane pounded his chest, grinning.

'Don't know you.'

'It's Shane,' Irene sighed.

'You're a right bitch!' He turned to her, a sudden malice in his faded blue eyes. 'You took my brother to the cleaners.'

There was silence around the table for a few seconds. Kate's heart began to thump at the mention of her father.

'You're a vindictive crabby old man who never learned to keep his mouth shut,' Irene hissed.

'You'll be thrown out one of these days, he won't put up with you.'

'What do you know about anything, living like a pig in your ramshackle house? I made that man, gave him back his life.' She pressed the tip of the cigarette into the ashtray until it was extinguished, and then lit another with quick jerky movements.

'Where is he anyway, he's late.' Bill looked towards the door.

No-one said anything. Even Irene was quiet this time.

'Uncle Bill, Dad won't be coming, he's...' Kate began.

'Why not? He's always here at this time.'

'Don't you remember, he's not with us any more,' she said softly.

'What do you mean?' He stared at her.

'He died a few years ago...' There were tears in Kate's eyes.

'Why didn't someone tell me?'

'You were at the funeral, Bill, what's wrong with you?' Irene snapped.

'That's typical, you didn't even tell me my brother had died.'

43

'You're going senile, old man,' Irene retorted.

'She didn't mean that, Uncle Bill.'

'Heap big Indian chief love steak,' Shane said in a deep voice.

'There's a bloody-odd crowd here this evening, Kate, why did you invite them?'

'It's only Shane, Uncle Bill, he's just joking.' She forced a smile. 'Well, Irene, how's life treating you these days?' Kate asked, anxious to change the direction of the conversation.

'As ever.' Irene stubbed out her second cigarette in the ash tray, with white tipped nails. She had hardly smoked any of it. 'I'll have another drop of that wine, it's good.' She helped herself from the bottle, although Kate could have cheerfully poured it over her beautifully-arranged hair.

'Time for Coronation Street.' Bill looked at his watch, clattered his knife and fork down on the plate, and drank the last of his milk.

'It's over,' Irene smirked.

'I must find out what happened.' He began to push himself out of the chair.

'I'll bring in your apple-tart and tea.'

'It's over by now, Bill,' Irene said loudly.

'I tape it and he watches it again.' Kate rose to help him.

'OK Mum, leave him to me.' Shane took his arm, but he shook him off.

'You can't force me into your tepee, I know all about you with your bows and arrows whooping around the campfire and taking scalps, they must have done you already.' He stared balefully at Shane.

'Me Arapaho.' Shane drew himself up. 'Heap big Indian.'

'Shane, leave it,' she said. It was the first time she had seen Bill react in that way to someone he should have known so well. The sudden venom he directed at Irene was strange, and forgetting that her Dad had died was worst of all and a very disturbing development.

Kate phoned Bill from Spain every day, and she received various responses. Sometimes he was angry that she hadn't been around to see him, and couldn't seem to grasp that she was away. Other times he didn't know who she was at all, then again he could be very pleasant and normal.

At the weekend, Chris and Eddie arrived. They lived next-door and Kate knew that their invitations for drinks, lunch, dinner, or whatever else, were going to be difficult to refuse. This evening was Eddie's sixtieth birthday party, and as she had agreed to help Chris with the food, there was no way out. It was still warm when she arrived back from the beach, and she poured herself a gin, added tonic, and two cubes of ice. In the garden she sat under the shade of the umbrella and stared into the greenness, at the smooth of the lawn, the flowering shrubs with their soft round lines, the tall trees in the distance. It was beautiful, but she wondered what had been the point of buying this house. Dermot had been so full of enthusiasm at the time, and talked about coming out regularly, perhaps even at weekends, and closer to retirement they could live part of the year out here. But that was a lot of hot-air, exaggerated as usual. She never had a comfortable feeling about the house, Dermot was so unpredictable she could imagine him selling it tomorrow, taking no account of whatever way she might feel about it.

Regardless, she would have preferred to sit here alone for the evening rather than go next-door, but she had promised, so eventually she forced herself to take a shower and get ready. The first thing to her hand in the wardrobe was the white linen dress and she decided to wear that, clipped on her gold earrings, and ran a comb through her hair. The deepening-suntan made it look brighter, she noticed vaguely as she outlined her lips with a soft peachy colour.

Chris looked flustered in a pink frilly apron over a glamourous little blue silk number, and her bright blonde hair had that gleaming just been at the hairdresser look. She rushed towards Kate the moment she saw her, kissy and huggy and up to ninety. 'Lovely to see you, thanks for coming over early, but Jack's arrived, and he's great in the kitchen so we're reasonably well organised.'

His dark-brown eyes and shy smile flashed into Kate's mind, and she remembered meeting the artist some months before, the man Mags had fancied.

It was his first solo exhibition at the Nestor Gallery in Dublin and that evening Kate had managed to fit into the black leather trousers for the first time, having lost about a stone since the New Year when she had made that decision to do something about her image.

'I'll fit into those some day, I'm determined,' she had informed Carol and Mags when she bought them, and they had smiled and nodded agreement, of course you will, but hadn't really believed her. So many banana diets, cabbage-soup diets, calorie-counting, cutting out foods to which she was supposedly allergic, and even pill-popping on one occasion, had been tried, but all to no avail, until this year. Now who would have egg on their faces as she swanned out this evening looking, dare she say it, almost slim? She ran a comb through her hair, and re-did her make-up. A little more eye shadow, pale blue edged with white, blusher, lipstick, and a spray of perfume. Then she slipped on her black full-length coat, the one she had kept in its own special case until today. All done, she twirled in front of the mirror and laughed, feeling like a kid all dressed up in her Sunday best.

Mags appeared in the doorway, followed by Carol.

'What do you think, girls?' Kate twirled again.

'Wow, you finally managed to squeeze into them.'

'The coat looks really cool.' Mags repaired her make-up, and spiked up her short red hair.

Kate looked at the three of them in the mirror, all so different to each other, Mags vibrant, Carol sultry, and herself? She thought she was looking pretty good tonight as well.

'Remember all those arguments about total extravagance when you bought it and the threat of murder if either one of us ever opened our mouths to Dermot?' Carol reminded her of that day with relish.

'First time I'd ever kept anything from him, but he'd have thrown a fit about the cost of it, so it's been kept in mothballs until now. This is the launch of the new trendy me, gone are the sensible middle-aged clothes, belly-tops here I come,' Kate laughed.

Vincent, the owner of The Nestor Gallery, met them almost as soon as they arrived. The flamboyant, rather camp character, dressed in his burgundy damask jacket and casually but no doubt deliberately arranged cream silk cravat, was all over them, kissing on both cheeks, darlings this, dear hearts that.

'White or red wine?' He clicked his fingers. A waiter carrying a tray of glasses appeared at their side and they helped themselves. 'You'll have to be quick if you want to buy, they're selling at an amazing rate. Jack is very well known in the States and Europe, and does most of his work in Spain. Have a good look, and then I'll introduce you to him afterwards, now I must get around everyone, see you anon, dears.' He worked the crowd, shaking hands, kissing, hugging, the complete social animal.

They wandered around looking at the paintings, meeting an occasional person they knew through work, and others they would see regularly at these gatherings. Then an excited voice called Kate's name and she looked around. Chris hugged her with enthusiasm and Eddie kissed her. 'You haven't been out to Torrevieja in ages.'

'Twice we cancelled because Dermot was too busy, but I'm hoping to persuade him to take a break in May.'

'We're going back next week, I can't stand the dampness of Dublin at this time of the year.' Chris shivered theatrically.

'And I'm looking forward to a few rounds of golf,' added Eddie.

'That's all he thinks about.' Chris raised her eyebrows upwards.

'I wish I could get out to Spain more often, but with work and everything it just doesn't seem to happen. Do you particularly like this artist?' Kate asked.

'You could say that...he's my brother. We had to come to support him, the rest of the family don't appreciate what he does.'

'He's the radical.' Eddie finished his glass of red wine, and looked around for the waiter.

'I think his work is wonderful, we're going to buy,' Kate said.

'You are?' Chris looked at her with surprise. 'You must be doing very well, I have to wait until he's throwing something out.'

'For a client.'

'We're hoping it's going to be a big success, he's a nervous wreck, come on over and I'll introduce you.'

'Could we do that later? I'd better join the girls and make the final selection before they're all gone,' Kate excused herself, and made her way through the crowd until she found the others standing in front of a large canvas.

'What do you think, Kate?'

'Can our budget stretch?'

'Just about.' Carol glanced down at the list.

'Right, which ones do you like?'

'Once more around and then it's decision time.'

They chose four of the large paintings which were dramatic compositions of the Spanish people and landscape. Bright sunshine cast deep-blue shadows across the mountains, inter-cut with the faces of Spain, dark and brooding, layered one over another in an impressionistic style. Kate took a note of the numbers and gave them to Vincent.

'I presume there will be the usual discount,' she asked.

'Of course.'

'And we need an extra five-per-cent this time, can you do it?' Her voice was low, but adamant, she was always the one to get the best deal.

'Well, I don't know.' He looked at his list, and bit his lip.

'Go on, we're good customers, and we're buying four this time.' She had been determined to do better, he made enough on it.

'OK, I capitulate.' He had a rueful smile on his face as he made a note. 'Now come and meet Jack.'

She grinned at the others and followed him, looking forward to finding out what made this Jack Linley paint pictures like these. She imagined him bald, dressed in wrinkled shirt and jeans, or long-haired and paint-splashed, but he was neither, being tall, lean, with dark tight-cut hair and intense brown eyes.

Carol and Mags gushed, particularly Mags. Kate could see that she fancied him, always able to tell with Mags, the youngest of the three of them and the only one who had never been married, or had a long-term partner. The one who felt she had missed out big time, although she was still only twenty-eight.

Kate stood a little on the outside of the circle, and listened to the banter between them. Love your work. Where have you exhibited? Do you spend much time in Spain?

The girls plied him with questions, but Kate didn't contribute much to the conversation; she just noticed things.

How he listened intently to whoever was speaking, hesitating before he replied; how his dark eyes became more alive when he spoke about his work. How the corner of his black shirt-collar was curled slightly under the leather jacket, and she had a sudden urge to reach out and straighten it, like she would with Shane or Conor.

Vincent reappeared, followed by a man who was then introduced, and Jack's attention transferred to him with an apologetic grin towards the girls. Vincent's attitude was one of polite dismissal as he concentrated his energies on this prospective client, with a you've-had-your-few-minutes-with-the-maestro wave of his hand.

They said goodbye, and moved away.

'He's a bit of all-right,' whispered Mags.

'I knew you'd fancy him, knew straight off,' Kate teased.

'He's late-thirties or early forties. Probably married with six kids. And far too old for you,' Carol said.

'I could ask Chris about his marital status,' Kate offered.

'Don't bother, the ones I like are always tied up in knots.'

'Come on girls, I'm starving.' Carol led the way towards the door.

'Yea, need comforting. That Jack has me all...upset!' Mags grinned.

Kate glanced around for Vincent, but as she searched for him over the heads of the crowd, it was dark eyes she met, a smile, and a nod, which she returned, suddenly understanding exactly what Mags meant.

Kate followed Chris through the house and out to the patio. Eddie, a big rugby player type gone to seed, raised his glass of whiskey.

'Welcome, Kate, welcome.' He planted a sloppy kiss on her lips, and she could see that he had started drinking early. Chris and Eddie were the leading-lights of the social scene in Torrevieja, and had been living here for a number of years, having taken early retirement when they sold their pub business in Galway.

'Happy sixtieth.' She handed him a silver-wrapped parcel and a bottle of wine. She had forgotten about a present, and in a panic, had given him a Neil Diamond CD she had brought out for Dermot.

He thanked her profusely, picked up a glass and started to pour. 'Plenty of gin and not too much tonic, that's the way you like it, I seem to remember.' His broad smile revealed sparkling white-capped teeth below a brown moustache, which contrasted oddly with the grey monkish fringe of hair which befrilled his shining bald pate.

'No thanks, I'll just have something soft for now otherwise I won't be able to do anything at all.'

'Go on, just have a small one to start you off?'

'OK, but it's plenty of tonic Eddie, plenty.'

'Cheers to the birthday boy.' They raised their glasses and drank a toast. He dimpled shyly, chubby features glowing.

'Now what can I do?' Kate asked.

'Follow me.' Chris toddled on extremely narrow high heels

into the kitchen, where her brother Jack worked at the counter, chopping peppers or something in that amazingly fast professional way Kate could never manage.

'Our helper from next door has arrived.' She put an arm around him and kissed his shoulder, just as far as her five-feet-nothing allowed her to reach.

'Hi, Kate, good to see you again.'

'Right, what's next?' Chris fluttered her hands in an agitated fashion.

'Let's see...Chris, you put out those dishes of olives and cheeses. And Kate, could you slice that salami please?' He handed her a knife.

'Right sir.' Chris saluted, lifted two large platters and walked unsteadily towards the dining-room.

'Maybe I should have asked you to do that, hope she makes it. But doing the salami would be much more dangerous, we could have fingers and God knows what else to flavour it.' His smile was warm.

Kate giggled and did what she was asked, and unexpectedly it seemed like tonight might be fun. On her second G & T maybe she was a little high already, and while she had only met Jack once before, she was suddenly stirred with unfamiliar long ago feelings of schoolgirl excitement.

When everything was prepared, they sat by the pool. Chit-chat and humour flew between them. Eddie was one of those people who had a great memory for the most hilarious stories and as the laughter grew louder and the jokes funnier, Kate relaxed, and began to really enjoy herself.

People arrived, and she was glad of the opportunity to serve the food, and keep busy rather than stand around with a glass in her hand. Jack was doing the bar, and they didn't come into contact, although she was very much aware of him as she did her cocktail-party thing later, meeting some people she knew vaguely, and others who were complete strangers. When the celebratory cutting of the birthday cake and all that fuss, congratulations and back-slapping had ended, she decided it was time to say goodnight and leave. She skirted the patio where a few couples had begun to dance, and saw Jack ahead of her.

'Going already?'

She nodded. 'It's getting late.'

'Will you have a dance with me before you go?' He held out his hand.

She hesitated, unexpectedly shy, the excuses which hovered on the tip of her tongue froze, and she was in his arms before she could say any more.

'We move well together,' he murmured.

'I haven't danced in years, except at weddings.'

'I've usually got two left feet.'

He looked down at her, and Kate's normal sensible thoughts scattered as her senses took over.

Kate was up early the following morning. She hadn't slept much at all, her mind possessed by Jack's eyes and his smile. She had twisted and turned in the bed as she tried to shut-down and put his unbidden presence out of her head, but he wouldn't go. She knew nothing at all about this man only that he was an artist whose work she admired and he was Chris's brother. During the evening they had hardly talked, there was no mention of Dermot and her sons or his wife and family, it had all been so immediate. Although she found out that he lived some of the time here, the weird throaty pronunciation of the place he mentioned was completely foreign to her and she couldn't even remember it.

Now she made a quick decision to head off and see a little more of Spain. Although when they walked back to her house last night or early this morning, he had said he would see her today and she had smiled in agreement. But after these last few hours, she knew that it wasn't a sensible decision to make. Whatever way she felt about Dermot, she was a married woman with a family and that was her life.

When the Tourist Office opened, she came away with maps and brochures which she browsed through over coffee at a nearby café. Then she remembered that there used to be a copy of The Rough Guide at the house but she never really had the opportunity to use it, Dermot refusing to spend even one day sightseeing.

'You go yourself,' he had said on more than one occasion.

And when she did plan a trip to a town a few miles away, he put the squeeze on.

'Are you sure you'll be all right? A woman alone in these parts? Never know who might hassle you, steal your money or credit cards. It's a hell of a risk wandering off, I'd be worried about you.'

'Why don't you come with me?'

'You know it's not my thing, and I have to meet Manuel, and I'm expecting phone calls from Dublin, my business doesn't stop when I'm out here you know, Kate.'

He took the good out of it, and she didn't bother after that. Now she realised how malleable she had been in his hands, like a dull uninteresting piece of putty.

She decided to head inland to Murcia by bus, preferring to travel with the people instead of alone in the car. And anxious to get going, she packed quickly, suddenly full of dread that Chris or Eddie would come in or, God forbid, Jack. She was running scared, afraid of herself, afraid of him, and those strange unfamiliar feelings which had sprung out of nowhere. In the event that Dermot might arrive while she was away she scribbled a brief note to him, and propped it against a small flower vase on the window-sill. Lastly she crept up the driveway next door, and put another addressed to Chris in through the letter-box. She had to say she was going away. She wouldn't have put it past them to phone the police and report her missing if they found she wasn't there.

*

Jack was up even earlier, and he had sat reading on the terrace reluctant to disturb Chris and Eddie by moving about the house. But the essay on modern art which he found fascinating yesterday, now seemed dry and uninteresting and he was unable to concentrate, his mind a few hundred yards away in another house where a woman lay sleeping in her bedroom. As the morning grew brighter and hotter he had to resist the impulse to go next-door and knock, to make contact with her again and see if last night had even been real.

Chris surfaced eventually around lunch-time and came into the kitchen, groaned and flopped on to a chair. She was wrapped in a multi-coloured satin dressing-gown, with her hair scraped up untidily in a bunch. The bags under her eyes were ridged from lack of sleep like wind-blown sand.

'Coffee's perking.' He poured a cup and put it on the table in front of her. 'Hard night?'

'You might say that, God I feel rough.'

'Eddie still in the wad?'

'Yea, lazy lump.' She yawned, unclipped her hair, and sipped the hot liquid with obvious pleasure.

'There's a letter, I found it in the hall.' He picked up a white envelope and handed it to her.

'You read it, my eyes can't focus.'

He opened it, pulled out a card, and his pulse began to race as he read the contents aloud. He could hear Kate's voice as if she was standing just beside him, and was disappointed that he wouldn't see her, unusually so.

'That was good of her, she's always so thoughtful.' Chris lit a cigarette and pulled deeply. 'It's a pity, I was going to ask her over this evening for a barbecue, although maybe that mightn't be such a good idea, you seemed to get along very well with her. One minute she was going home and the next thing I see is the two of you wrapped around each other. Just as well Dermot didn't suddenly turn up!'

'I think that's a slight exaggeration. She's very nice, I like her. There was something...I can't really explain,' he said vaguely, always able to talk to Chris, the only one who knew everything.

'You need someone in your life, I've told you that more than once, but Kate isn't for you. It's been a long time since Paula, and

I haven't heard any other names being bandied about, what have you been doing with yourself?'

Since Paula? Since he had been a happily married man, with a wife, a home, a dog, and almost a family?

'I'm going to London at the weekend,' Paula had announced over breakfast that Monday morning.

'Maybe we could take in a show, I'll see what's on,' Jack said.

'I'm going...'

'On a shopping spree?'

'No...not exactly.' She poured a little milk into her coffee.

'I thought we promised each other never to have secrets,' he asked with a grin.

'I was going to tell you.'

'You don't have to, you're entitled to your privacy, Paula, I was only joking.' He spread marmalade on his toast.

'And I'm sure you'll agree with me that this is the best way of dealing with...this situation,' she said.

He jerked up his head and stared at her. 'What situation?'

'I'm pregnant.'

'But I thought you...we...weren't going to have a baby just yet?' he stuttered, taken aback.

'Obviously something went wrong.'

'But that's wonderful news!' He rushed around to her side of the table and put his arms around her. 'I can't believe it, when is the baby due?'

'Sit down, Jack.' She lowered her head.

'I can't, I'm too excited. My love, I am so happy, were you worried that I wouldn't want this, is that it?' He kissed her.

'No, I knew you would, it's myself I have to contend with.'

'What do you mean?'

'The timing isn't right. I can't have a baby now, not where I am in my career.'

'But we can employ a nanny, and I'll do as much as I can in the evenings and at weekends, we can work it out between us.'

'No, I don't want this.'

'But you have no choice, there's a little person growing inside you now.'

'I'm going to have an abortion.'

There was a sudden coldness in the atmosphere.

'You can't do that, Paula.' He stiffened.

'I've made my decision, it's arranged.' She rose from the table.

'Please don't do it, Paula, please.' He moved towards her, cupped her face in his hands and forced her to look at him. 'I love you, and I love our child as well, there's no separating the two of you in my mind.'

She turned away from him, and went upstairs to the bathroom.

He followed her. 'Paula, please reconsider, let's talk. I don't have to go to work, I've got all day.' He stood in the doorway and watched as she brushed her teeth, and then applied lipstick, and sprayed perfume. Her behaviour was so normal, it accentuated the horror within him.

'I have to get into Court.' She brushed past him, hurried downstairs again, grabbed her briefcase and left.

'Please Paula, don't go, there has to be some way around it, you musn't do this dreadful thing.' He rushed after her and stood watching as the car disappeared out of sight.

He didn't go to work that day, his mind twisting and turning as he tried to think of ways in which he could persuade her to change her mind, and by the time she came home that night, he had a plan which he put to her.

'Why don't I give up my job? I might do some painting, maybe even sell a few. Then I'll be able to look after the baby and you can continue with your career, go as far as you want, all you've dreamed about, I don't mind. In fact, I think it's a great idea.'

He left that suggestion with her, hoping that she would come around to seeing it his way, and struggled through the week. He even went into a church one morning and sat at the back. It had been a long time since he had been there, and he didn't know how to pray any more. But that day he opened up his soul to the unseen God, the entity he still believed in, and asked for the life of his child to be given to him, and not sacrificed to convenience.

He had said nothing else to Paula until she came home late on Thursday evening, but then it erupted again. He felt it was his last chance and pulled every possible stroke, but she had a glazed look in her eyes as if she wasn't really there with him and made little response to his reasoned arguments. His bursts of anger. Or even his emotional entreaties, in tears finally as he ran out of words and sat down heavily on the couch, his head in his hands. She left him there and went to bed and he followed much later but lay awake stiff and tense as the hours crawled by, it was the longest night in his life.

When she came back on Monday, he tried to be sympathetic and caring, but the love they had felt for each other seemed to have disappeared. Within weeks he had moved out.

He dragged himself back to the present, feeling stupid, almost childish, for having told Chris how he felt.

'She's a married woman, Jack.' Her tone was soft.

'I knew that, I know that,' he said. But somehow when he met Kate all of that information had flown out of his head and with it, the adult reserve which should have made him behave like a grown-up.

'There's no point in starting something, it will only lead to problems further down the line,' she advised, playing the big sister mammy role.

'You're right,' he said with a wry laugh. Deciding that it was just physical attraction probably, her touch, her smile, the scent of her hair. Add to that a few glasses of wine, the music, the moon and the stars. With that recipe the imagination could work overtime and create a fantasy to fool the most sensible middle-aged man into thinking he was twenty-one again.

*

It was a novelty to travel alone. Kate had to wait around for the bus to Murcia, and she sat in the station watching the people, fascinated to see them arrive and depart, the ordinary Spaniards going about their lives. She was the only tourist in the bus, among housewives with full shopping bags, noisy children, young people with ear phones listening to their own private concert, and a couple of army recruits going back to base, or home on leave. She wondered about them all as the bus travelled down the motorway, glimpsing towns in the distance with romantic names, Elche, Orihuela, villages tucked into the folds of the land, ruined castles which still stood guard on distant hillsides, mysterious needing to be explored places.

In Murcia she stepped down from the bus, gripped her bag and slowly walked out into the hot afternoon, the city drowsy and quiet in siesta.

First she followed the river, a pleasant cool walk under the trees. Then she turned into the old city, wandering through the narrow streets until she spotted a sign for a hostale above a taverna. It was quiet, with only a few oldtimers sitting inside, and she could feel their eyes on her as she walked in.

'Do you have a room, por favor?' she asked the man behind the bar hesitantly, wishing now that she knew a few basic words of Spanish. The man nodded and shouted for a Maria in an irritated why do I have to be bothered with this tone. Probably the husband, Kate thought, or the father, or the brother, another bully, they're everywhere. After a moment, a woman appeared, hurriedly pulled off her floral apron, and beckoned Kate to follow her up the cool white-tiled stairway. On the first landing she opened a door into a pleasant twin-bedded room which was simply furnished in traditional style. She showed Kate around proudly, even the loo-seat in the spotless bathroom was lifted up for inspection.

'Gracias.' Kate nodded, smiled, and the deal was done. When the woman had gone, she opened the long wooden shutters and stood on the little balcony looking down into the narrow street below which was suddenly much busier now. Murcia had woken up for her again.

Chapter Seven

'Dad?' Conor lounged in the doorway.

'What?' Dermot packed his clothes into the new suitcase on the bed, then at the last minute decided to include a pair of shorts, and some T-shirts, thinking he might stay on with Kate for a few days, maybe, if he felt like it.

'Can you give us a few euro?'

'No.' He rang Kate's number again, anxious to let her know when he was arriving, she would have to meet him at the airport with the car. He banged the phone down with a noisy crash.

'What gives?' Conor asked.

'I can't get your mother, she's gone AWOL.' He threw in underwear, socks and his toilet bag, and then looked up at his tall son, who was broad-shouldered, muscular, and fit as the proverbial fiddle, the way he used to be. 'How come you've no money, didn't you just get paid, every fortnight isn't it?' Irritation began to balloon inside him.

'I owed a few people.' Conor's good-looking features were unconcerned, and he stood there with a so what shrug of the shoulders attitude.

'You should learn to manage your money, what if I'd gone out to Spain last week?'

'I'd have to get it from someone else, I suppose, but it could be difficult.'

'I'll bet.' Dermot knelt down and searched at the bottom of the wardrobe for his good black shoes. He could never find anything when Kate wasn't here.

'I'll pay you back.' It was his usual promise which never materialised.

'When?'

'The end of the month,' Conor said. Then he grinned in the exact same way that Dermot looked when he got things his own way.

'For God's sake, what about all of the money you owe me already?' Dermot threw shoes out on to the floor in an ever-widening circle.

'You're not waiting for it, are you?'

'Maybe I am,' he growled from the depths of the wardrobe, his voice muffled.

'For a few hundred euro?'

'That's not the point.' Dermot stood up and stared at the array of shoes around him. In shades of brown, black, and navy, it looked like every shoe he had ever owned was there, even his dress shoes which he hadn't worn in years. Dermot never liked to throw anything out, he was a hoarder, a never-know-it-might-come-in-handy sort of person.

He picked up the phone and tried the number again. Maybe Kate could tell him where she had put his shoes. If he couldn't find them he would have to buy another pair tomorrow and there just wasn't the time, where are you, Kate, where are you? But the same man rattled off his announcement that the phone was powered off and to try later.

'Just a couple of hundred, Dad, please, help me straighten myself out, then I can start afresh next month.' Conor kept at him.

'A likely story.' Dermot marched out of the bedroom and went downstairs into the study.

'We've ordered a Chinese take-away, want some?' Conor strolled after him.

'You know I don't eat rice and stuff, and will you tell your brother to tone down that racket, it's driving me bonkers, I went to the expense of sound-proofing that place and I can still hear it.' He waved towards the garage door.

'They'll be breaking up shortly.'

'I'll be breaking up if they don't shut it.'

'Look, are you going to lend us some money?' Conor never gave in, persistence was his middle name.

Dermot pulled a roll of notes out of his pocket, licked his thumb and peeled off a few from the top.

'One hundred is all you're getting, you'll have to make do with that.' He pushed it into Conor's hand.

'We need cash for the take-away, the lads are inside with Shane.'

'I don't know why you eat that junk, your mother left the freezer full of food.'

'Don't feel like it,' Conor grunted, squashing the money into his back pocket.

'What would you do if I wasn't here?' Dermot demanded.

'You are, so it's hypothetical.'

The doorbell rang.

'That's the delivery guy.'

'What if...' Dermot's voice raised a few decibels, but then he suddenly spotted his shoes in a corner under a chair and the shout was tempered with satisfaction as he bent down to pick them up.

'Dad?'

'Ah for God's sake, here.' He pulled the money out of his pocket again and handed Conor thirty euro.

'I hope that's enough, they've increased their prices.' Conor looked at the money doubtfully.

With a deep sigh, Dermot gave him another twenty.

'Thanks Dad.' He loafed down the hall.

Chapter Eight

Kate wandered around the dusky interior of the cathedral, dwarfed by vast pillars which soared upwards. She stopped at each chapel to look at the gilded statues. Dressed in ornate clothing, and lit by banks of long white flickering candles, their painted faces stared tragically at her, and she was suddenly reminded of her childhood. Taken by her mother when they lived in Milltown to the large churches in Rathmines, High Street, John's Lane, and many others, a small girl who stared up at the carved images of Jesus, His Mother, and the Saints. They attended all the ceremonies, Mass, Sodality, The Miraculous Medal, Easter Vigils, Novenas, and she remembered with greatest clarity the visits to the seven churches, one after another until her little legs were exhausted, although now she couldn't even remember the reason for that particular ritual.

She would have loved to share all this with Dermot, but knew he wouldn't have lasted more than a few minutes before having to get out to have a drink, or make a phone call or invent some other excuse to escape. This morning she had talked to Carol and told her how she was getting on. Well, not quite everything. Not the intimate details of her unexpected response to a man she barely knew, which was for herself alone to deal with. Then she checked-in with Uncle Bill, an unusually satisfactory conversation as he asked how she was enjoying herself in Spain, and to bring him back a souvenir. She made no contact with Dermot, but sent a text about having a great time to both Conor and Shane. She wondered would it mean anything to them? Both grown up now, long past needing anything from her other than the basics of food, washing, ironing, stuff anyone could do. An unexpected feeling of uselessness swelled inside. The person deep within, the real Kate Mason, wasn't needed any more.

She turned her phone off again, unable to bear Dermot's annoyance that she was doing her own thing without his say so. And she had already decided to travel further, having picked up a leaflet at the Tourist Office about a festival in a place called Mojacar which began on Thursday, and thought perhaps if she made it that far she might spend some time there.

Exploring Murcia, she stopped to look through elaborate wrought-iron gates which led into flower-filled courtyards whenever she felt like it. She sat down when she needed to rest, and wandered in and out of shops as the mood took her. No what do you want to do that for? No come on, hurry up, I'm not going to hang around here all day. Dermot's usual song and dance act.

The following day she took another step out into the unknown. She travelled through arid land broken by lines of Cypress trees, and haciendas with tiled roofs golden in the sunshine. She came towards a town. She read the signs and tried to get her tongue around the pronunciation. Mediterraneo. Was that the name of a place or a road or the sea or what? Minofret, a factory which she thought might manufacture freezers? Repsol sold petrol, and to her surprise she spotted a cash-and-carry, the English words startling in the midst of this Spanish landscape.

Lorca was an ancient frontier town, and although she didn't know if there was any connection with the Spanish playwright, she loved the place instantly. From the dusty baroque architecture to the Roman column which marked the distance between Lorca and Cartagena on the Via Herraclea, the road which had been built by the Romans through Spain from the Pyrenees to Cadiz. She was fascinated and snapped all the time, to keep a record of how things looked and felt, the heat pressing down into the streets relentlessly, the brightness on one side, the cool blue shadows on the other, the quick rise and fall of Spanish voices, the aromas, particularly that strong musky aftershave or soap that the men used. It made her glance at them, admiring their smooth dark skin, giggling to herself as she appreciated the sight of a neat bum, and how the clothes they wore, though simple, were always clean and neat. No scruffy trainers, or sign of poverty, people begging, living rough, but that didn't mean it wasn't there, she reminded herself.

She spent a second night and a third, enjoying the impulsivity of her decisions, stay if you like, move on if you've had enough. Then the bus took her into the land of greenhouses. There those fat red tomatoes and other vegetables grew under miles and miles of sun-glinted stretched netting or plastic sheeting. And as she travelled further away from Torrevieja, at last Dublin began to drift out of her immediate consciousness and she was drawn into the everyday life of Spain.

In Torrecilla a group of children climbed on, full of chat and laughter. In Cuevas del Almanzola she was amazed to see that some people still lived in houses built into caves cut from the soft stone of the hill, and quite comfortably too it seemed, with their satellite dishes pointing up to the sky.

The names of places stayed in her head for a few seconds and were forgotten almost immediately. St. Maria de Nieva, Huercal Orca, Tanorio, Vero. So tantalising she wanted to shout stop and get off but the bus whirled her away from the plain through a tunnel bored into the mountainside. An old church was the last thing to be seen before the brightness was turned off like someone had flicked a switch. Dim yellow lights lit the concrete walls which shot past, and she was suddenly reminded of the death of Princess Diana. An unpleasant feeling of trepidation spread through her until she was out again into sunshine which dazzled. The bus travelled towards the coast, where waves crashed on wild empty beaches for a stretch before civilisation sanitised nature with the growth of holiday apartments, hotels, bars, and restaurants, rows of sun-beds, bright blue and yellow umbrellas with edges fluttering in the breeze. The whole tourist bit.

*

Dermot flew into Alicante at about ten o'clock, annoyed that he had been unable to contact Kate, and deeply resenting the fact that he had to take a taxi to Torrevieja. When he arrived he spotted the car in the driveway, but the house was in darkness, so he let himself in with a loud 'It's me, I'm here' and went upstairs to the bedroom where he flicked on the light. But the bed was neatly made, and very much unoccupied. He was dismayed. It was after eleven now, and late for a woman to be out on her own in a strange place; for a wife without her husband too late altogether. Maybe she had gone into Chris and Eddie. Yea, that was probably it, he convinced himself, and after a shower and change he went in next-door but found no-one there either. Disgruntled, he went down to a bar and had a few drinks. One of the things he hated with a vengeance was to be left in the dark about anything which he was when he returned to find the house still empty.

He threw himself into bed, asleep within a couple of minutes. Nothing would keep Dermot awake. But the morning didn't start well when he couldn't find the keys of the car either. He hated to start the day like this, he needed to be clear-headed and on top of things, that was vital. So as he dressed, he tried to think more logically.

Kate wouldn't be bothered playing around, she was far too conservative. He was the only man in her life, the first man who had made love to her. He possessed Kate, she was his, and he had done the right thing by her when she had become pregnant in spite of the way his mother treated him. He concluded then that she had probably gone off to do some sightseeing, she was always trying to persuade him to take her somewhere or other, and that explanation satisfied him.

At nine, he met Manuel to finalise the contracts with his clients. He liked doing business with the slim, dark, good-looking Spaniard, who danced flamenco in his spare time. But his habit of clicking his fingers and tapping his heels even in the office drove Dermot spare. Little ponce! For all that, he was a smooth clever operator, and had a good thing going with a small group of well-placed people. Dermot considered himself very lucky that he had been invited into that circle when he had first purchased property in Spain.

'Numero tres y numero doce.' Manuel passed the documents across the desk.

Dermot jotted down a few figures on a pad.

Manuel smiled, his even teeth whiter than white against his tanned skin.

'I'm pretty confident neither the Browns or the Needham sisters will realise what they are signing. They're innocents abroad, and all they want is their nice new house on the Costa. And they want it now. It should be a breeze.' Dermot leaned back in the comfortable leather chair. He always felt he was rubbing shoulders with the high-rollers when he was here, and loved the luxury of the offices and the huge colourful modern paintings on the walls. He didn't know what they were about, but had asked Manuel about them on one occasion as they walked along the corridor, trying hard to sound knowledgeable.

'I'm not familiar with that artist, he's Spanish I presume?'

'No, Irish.'

Dermot was at sea now, he wasn't into the world of art, that was Kate's department. 'Oh yes, what's his name?' he stuttered, wishing he hadn't opened his mouth.

'Jack Linley. He is well known in Espana. I make a good investment, these are worth a lot of money now.'

'Oh yes of course, Jack Linley, Jack.' His self-conscious laugh had a ho ho Santa Claus ring about it. 'Don't know where my brain is today, si si I know him, of course.'

'You should buy with the profits you will make, then you have much money when you sell in a few years time.' Manuel stopped in front of a large painting. 'But they are hard to get. This one here I buy in New York, if I can I find one for you.'

Dermot had thought about it at the time but didn't have the cash, and every time he passed them he was reminded of his plan to become an art collector, to go to exhibitions and mingle with the rich and the famous, and perhaps even to commission artists to paint whatever he wanted.

'When these contracts are closed and the deeds they are issued, we will be able to raise the money to start work on that new parcel of land south of Torrevieja. See here the plans, what do you think?' Manuel spread the drawings out on the desk. 'It is a large resort with a marina, theme parks, residential, and commercial, even bigger than Calpe.'

'I'd say we're talking a few hundred million there?' Dermot was excited.

'It is hard to say exactly at this point.'

'How soon will the contracts close on the development at Calpe?' Dermot asked, trying not to appear too anxious. His financial position was extremely tight but this was something he kept hidden from Manuel, as far as he was concerned Dermot was a millionaire many times over in Ireland.

The phone rang, and Manuel picked it up. 'Si?' He stood up, straightening the fall of his dark well-cut jacket. 'Your people have arrived.'

'Right, I'll wheel them in.' It all went according to plan. Over the next few days the contracts would be closed and monies paid on the houses and apartments, and his share of the profits lodged into his account. He didn't have to do another thing, it was so easy. And within a few weeks, the next phase would be completed, and the whole procedure repeated.

On the way out at lunchtime he stopped to talk to Manuel's personal assistant, Carmen. He looked down at the slim dark-haired beauty, her full cleavage barely held in place by the clinging white top she wore, and took a deep breath. The rush of excitement which swept over him almost made him put his arms around her there and then, but he managed to resist and in a low whisper suggested they meet later. Manuel only ever invited him to the club where he pranced about on his high-heels, and waved his hands in the air in company with the other members of the dance troupe whose haughty eyes flashed and feet pounded the floor in shuddering flamenco rhythm. Dermot was able to get out of it this evening, smoothly using Kate as an excuse.

It was the ideal relationship. To have a woman waiting for him whenever he flew over to Spain for a couple of days. Who listened enthralled as he talked about life in Ireland and expounded his ideas about politics and business, although how much of it she understood was questionable. Still he enjoyed her child-like adoration. The way she pronounced his name, Derrrrmot, made him shiver inside. Most of all he loved the different foreign taste of her.

But first he had to go through the preliminaries of the evening. Dinner and champagne in a candle-lit restaurant on the edge of town before he could take her back to the large apartment. There all formality disappeared, and Carmen ran the water in the huge sunken marble bath, turned on the Jacuzzi, and they lay in the blue-tinted water and played with each other.

'Derrrmot, I think I will come to visit you in Ireland soon, I do not like to wait until you come to Spain, it is too long for me,' Carmen whispered later as she massaged him with a smelly lotion.

'Mmmmmm keep doing that,' he moaned.

'I want to look after you. Manuel is not warm like you and he doesn't love me the way you do.' Her hands worked. 'He has given me all that I have, my apartment and my car, my clothes, my jewellery, but I am bored, querida, it is you I desire now.'

'He's obviously very generous.'

'Yes but when one falls out of love it means nothing any more. When I come to be with you in Dublin you can arrange for me to live in one of your apartments and buy me a nice car.'

He didn't respond to that last little speech, and he pulled her down on top of him and shut her up with his lips.

'Slowly Derrrrmot, slowly,' she murmured, but he wasn't able to wait and did his usual thing in a rush, selfishly.

The following morning, still wife-less, Dermot wondered about going next door, maybe Eddie and Chris would know where Kate had gone. To have to admit that he had no idea, that was his worst nightmare. He was returning to Dublin tonight and he wanted her with him. He had no intention of hanging around now to suit her. But in the end he didn't have to ask any awkward questions, as Eddie knocked on the door. Full of hail fellow well met, they went through the usual pleasantries and inevitably Kate's name came up and he found out that she had indeed gone away for a few days. Where and with whom remained a mystery.

He tried to control his anger so he forced a smile on his face.

'She's doing her historical bit, she loves poking around old castles and that sort of thing.' *Bitch, why hasn't she got her phone on?*

'There are some very interesting places around here,' Eddie said.

'I'm sure there are.' Dermot nodded. *Very interesting piles of old stones.*

'You should join her, take off for a few days yourself.'

'I have to go back, no rest for the wicked, someone has to make the money.' He just about managed to joke.

*

The white houses of Mojacar clung to the side of the mountain overhanging the blue Mediterranean. The town was very old with narrow streets curling this way and that, long flights of steps from one level to another, bars, restaurants and shops tucked into the most unlikely places. During the day Kate spent the time on the beach opposite the hotel. In the evening she took a taxi up to the town to join in the celebrations of the festival of Mouros y Cristianos, the place thronged with people, many of whom were dressed in traditional costume. The women wore colourful frilled flamenco dresses, their dark hair done up in combs and mantillas. The men were handsome in short jackets and tilted black hats, some of them on horseback, the livery shining and betassled. Many of the children had similar outfits, and she even saw a poodle in frills. He was ridiculous, and she pitied the poor thing.

69

She enjoyed wandering on her own. Away from the excited crowds, she explored the back streets, and quiet courtyards, whose only occupants were thin undernourished cats who stared at her with suspicion. She climbed up to the top of the town and sat in the shadowy church, a quiet island. But she didn't pray. She just listened to the creaks, clicks and sighs of the old building, and in the distance, the sound of birds twittering, the bark of a dog, the crying of a very young baby. After a while she was drawn back to the square where she found herself a good vantage point and waited for something to happen.

It grew dark and people packed around her, at times too close for comfort. The eyes of the men stripped her, bold and inviting. The women's sideways glances made her conscious of her difference, the oddness of her presence there, the few tourists around lost among the hundreds of local people. It was the last night of the festival, and the excitement became more intense as the sound of a drum-roll was heard in the distance, a loud dumm-dumm in marching time, a threatening funereal sound which heralded the arrival of the Moors and Christians.

The Christians were dressed as crusaders with a large red cross on white costumes, the first group from Almeria according to the banner they carried. Fearsomely, they marched to the rhythm of the drummers in rows of six, their arms linked together as they stepped to the left and right in their high leather boots, while the leader of the group brandished his sword at the crowd.

The Moors wore even brighter costumes, satins and velvets, gold and silver sequinned, and the tall dark bearded men flashed scimitars. In the square, the groups challenged each other, and mock-battles were staged encouraged by the shouts and screams of the people.

As one group disappeared out of sight, and before the next had arrived, Kate thought she heard someone call her name, but she didn't even look around, convinced it was her imagination. Then she heard it again, and deliberately stared ahead, deciding it was probably something in Spanish that just happened to sound the same. But the possibility that by some fluke Dermot might have followed her down here made its unwelcome way into her mind, and suddenly her freedom seemed about to be curtailed. Like a runaway she would be dragged back to become again Mrs. Kate Mason, housewife and chattel, and she swore to herself that she wasn't returning until it suited her. Suddenly a young woman beside her tipped her on the shoulder and pointed back. Reluctantly she was forced to look in that direction, surprised to see Jack Linley waving at her. He beckoned, but she shook her head. It seemed almost impossible to get through the crowd, and anyway, she didn't know whether she wanted to or not. She dithered nervously for a few seconds, but logic intervened and persuaded that she couldn't avoid him now. So she began to move back, stepping on toes and bumping into people in the crush, until her hand was caught in a strong warm grip and she was beside him.

Chapter Nine

Dermot surveyed the scene in the kitchen. Beer-cans, bottles, and glasses stood on the counter tops, take-away boxes were thrown on the tiled floor, scattered cold chips mingled with stubbed-out cigarette butts and other weird unrecognisable bits of stuff, and was that the remains of someone's curry and rice adhering stickily to the white roller blind?

'Conor, Shane!' He stood in the hall and shouted, but it was a waste of energy, there was no sound, both still out for the count after an obviously late night. While he had agreed they could have a few friends around, he hadn't expected the house to be in this state. He picked up an empty gin-bottle from the floor and then put it back deciding that he wasn't going to start clearing up.

In his study he sat in front of the computer, and tapped into his files which contained detailed lists of houses and apartments, tenants, rents, expenses, valuations, bank loans, kept under code names and numbers to which no-one else had any access. This was his other set of books, the one the tax man and the accountant didn't see, but he was careful enough, didn't cream too much off the top, just a little here and there, easy enough when a high proportion of his rental income was in cash.

Conor appeared a while later and began to clean up.

'Bit of a mess,' Dermot said.

'Had a few people around last night.' He yawned.

'Looks like it was more than a few.'

Empties were thrown into black bags, with loud crashes of tin and glass.

'Conor, can you get me a towel, please?' A pretty face with tousled blonde hair came around the door.

'Yea, sure.' He stopped what he was doing and walked quickly over to the girl who stood on one bare foot, the other curled around her ankle, her body only partly-covered by his blue shirt. He hustled her back upstairs, and a moment later clumped into the kitchen again, his black baggies dragging on the floor over his trainers, the laces hanging loose, and continued to clean up. He put all the takeaway boxes in another black bag, and the delph into the dishwasher, and made a dismal effort to do something with the mess on the blind.

Dermot sat at the table sipping a mug of coffee and watched.

'Don't know what your mother's going to say about that blind.'

'I've something to tell you, Dad.' Conor sat opposite.

'You're going to buy a new one?'

'Yea, maybe.'

Dermot sighed and drained the mug.

'As I was saying...'

'What?'

Conor ate a chocolate biscuit and pushed the open packet towards him.

'I'm going to move in with Nicola.'

'Darling, you're all broody tonight, what gives?' Irene put a finger under Dermot's chin and stared into his eyes, which were a tired blue, the skin shadowed underneath.

'Nothing,' he snapped, swallowed the drain of liquid left in the glass and held it out to her.

'Another? Please don't have any more, I've a lovely bottle of wine open and I want you to enjoy it over dinner.' She toddled back into the kitchen, the high-heeled sandals clip-clopping on the wooden floor, her bottom waggling from side to side in the white skirt. But tonight it did nothing for him, his mood foul.

'I need a drink,' he barked impatiently, in that belligerent way of his.

'I don't want you to fall asleep at the table.' She forked a small fillet steak on to a plate for herself and a large sirloin for Dermot which was rather black and crusty around the edges. On to his plate, she spooned some yellow corn, a portion of chips, and put it in front of him. 'Now doesn't that look tasty, I think I've really excelled myself this time.'

He pushed himself to his feet, and went over to the drinks cabinet, where he quickly poured himself another whiskey, and came back to the table again. 'Looks good, thanks love.'

'Eat up, you've probably had nothing all day.' She poured a little of the mature claret into a crystal glass and held it out to him.

'Want me to taste?' He sipped it.

'Yes, I need your opinion.'

'Seems OK.'

'OK? It should be much more than that, it cost me an arm and a leg.'

'That year was excellent.' He cut into his sirloin and took a mouthful.

'Don't eat so fast, it's bad for your digestion,' she reminded.

'Don't turn into another Kate,' he said as he speared the chips with his fork and stuffed a few at a time into his mouth. He enjoyed Irene, and liked the way she was so disorganized and scatty. But in a very short time she had re-invented herself. She insisted on cooking his meals for him, and invariably it was steak, or a chop done under the grill, anything else came out of a packet and was cooked in the micro-wave, even though she seemed to spend hours shopping and poring over cookery books. And the latest, she wanted to do his washing and ironing, and had even attempted to sew a button on to his shirt the other night.

'There's no need, I don't care about this shirt, I'll throw it out first. Come here to me.'

'I'm just going to get a needle and thread.' She made a move to stand up.

'Where would you find such a thing?'

'I bought some the other day.'

'Irene, forget about such mundane stuff, there's no need for you to waste your time like that. I don't want you with your apron on I want you with nothing on.' He pulled her down again and kissed her.

She giggled.

'Kate will be back soon, so you won't have to be slaving in the kitchen any longer, and we can get back to normal.'

'But I don't mind.'

'Well, I do, I'm not going to turn you into a housewife, so dull and boring, you're none of those things.'

'OK, anything for you.' She blew him a kiss. 'Anything.'

'I do this every year and you say no, but I never give up.' His sister Mary had phoned earlier today, and it hadn't helped his mood.

'What are you talking about?'

'It's mother's anniversary, and we're having a Mass on Tuesday at ten o'clock. Why don't you come? The first time is always the hardest, after that it won't be so difficult, and, you never know, it might be good for you.'

'No, I can't, I've meetings all morning.' Something clutched at his heart and twisted.

'That's a pity, there will only be myself and Des...we could have done with the company.'

'How on earth do you expect me to go to the Mass when I didn't even go to the funeral? It would be hypocritical to say the least.'

'Will you mention it to Kate, she sometimes comes with us?'

'I can't, she's not here.'

'Where is she?'

'Spain.'

'What's she doing there? Is it business?'

'Having a good time, no doubt.'

'Oh.'

He felt strung out. Kate had not been in contact at all and it was driving him spare. He had clients to entertain, but was afraid to make any appointments because he wasn't sure whether she would return on the original flight. And if she didn't come back, what would he do then?

Chapter Ten

'I was shouting for ages, I thought you would never look around.' Jack drew her out of the crowd, and through a door which he closed behind them, shutting off the sounds from the square. In the narrow marble hallway, he kissed her lightly on the cheek, put his arm casually around her shoulders and ushered her along. 'What are you doing here? I can't believe I'm looking at you, just turning up outside like that, it's incredible, come on up.' He led the way into a courtyard, in the centre of which was a white marble fountain, with sparkling water spraying out of the mouth of a blue dolphin balanced on his tail, the crystal clear sound bouncing musically off the cool white walls.

'I didn't realize this was where you lived, the name you mentioned didn't sound a bit like the way I pronounce Mojacar.'

'Replace the J with an H, cough out the C, and drop the R, Mojacar.'

'I really need to learn some Spanish, my version of it sounds terrible, no wonder no-one understands me.' She followed him across the courtyard to a winding-stair. 'You have a beautiful place here.' She looked around her at the colourful flowers which were planted in earthenware pots, and trailed from baskets hung around the walls.

'Paqui is the one with the green fingers, she rents the ground floor, and I'm upstairs in the roof apartment with plenty of light and space.' They took the stairs to the balconied upper level which overlooked the courtyard, and she followed him through an open door into a large room.

'You'll have to excuse the mess, but this is where I work and it tends to build up. Sit down on the couch there while I get us some wine.' He stood smiling at her for a few seconds and then disappeared.

The scene was a kaleidoscope of reds, yellows, greens, and blues, up here even brighter than the courtyard below. Great vibrant sweeps of paint were applied thickly on canvases which were stacked against the walls, propped on window-sills, on the bench, chairs and easels, amid a clutter of large tubs of paint, smaller tubes, brushes, palettes, the smell of oil paint and turpentine strong. She was reminded of Francis Bacon's studio which she had visited at the Hugh Lane Gallery at home, and she felt rather than saw the vibrancy of the work here, an expression of one man's thoughts and feelings.

'There is so much movement and life in the paintings, so different to when they are framed and hung in a gallery,' she said when he returned holding a bottle and two glasses. She was quite taken aback by the drama of the bright colours, her eyes drawn in to try and understand the essential message contained in the landscapes. His other work which they had purchased for a client didn't have the same energy as these paintings, and she wondered if perhaps she was seeing them differently now.

'I don't know how many will ever be finished.' He handed her a glass. 'I remember you like red...' She nodded and sipped the wine which had a musky earthy flavour. 'Let's take a look at the goings-on from the terrace.' He led the way outside. 'You were standing below me there, your blonde hair stood out among all the Spaniards, I wasn't even sure that it was you, and just went down in the hope.' He turned to watch what was happening below. 'The Moors and Christians festival is always very enjoyable, the people in Mojacar really know how to celebrate, any excuse at all and they're off again.'

Now Kate saw another side to the man. This was the real Jack in his own environment, speaking enthusiastically about his life here, gesticulating with paint-stained hands. She looked at him as he leaned over the edge of the balcony, dressed in blue jeans and shirt, but he caught her glance, his brown eyes so intent on hers she almost felt embarrassed, and directed her attention once again to what was happening below.

They stayed there until the finale, and shared another glass of wine as the night sky was lit up by the fireworks display. After he had excused himself to shower and change, they went out to one of his favourite restaurants, a little place tucked into a shadowy patio with blue lamps twinkling on the tables. They sat in a corner, and had another glass of wine while he ordered the food. She let him choose for her. She wanted to be surprised, and was surprised, to find herself sitting here with him.

'Your work is wonderful, so vibrant, I love it,' she said.

'I've a lot more to do.'

'I used to paint.'

'You're welcome to use my stuff if you feel creative.'

'Years ago I went to classes, but didn't get past a jug and some fruit arranged on a carefully-creased tablecloth. I lost interest after a while, obviously wasn't cut out to be an artist.'

'We all started there. I'm an accountant by profession, a career in art was something I didn't even dream about when I was young.'

'And you gave that up?'

'Circumstances of the time. I was at a loose end...my marriage had broken up, so I decided to take my chances over here. I worked in restaurants and bars for a crust until I held my first exhibition in Almeria, and then I got lucky, I suppose.'

'I'm sorry...about your marriage.'

'It was a long time ago.'

'Have you children?'

'No,' he said abruptly, and there was a sudden silence between them.

She sensed a reticence from him that barred any further mention of the subject.

The food arrived, and they shared all the dishes, which consisted of various types of fish, the best custard she had ever tasted, and delicious coffee. They talked about everything. She mentioned Dermot, Conor and Shane as a matter of fact, and discovered that his family came from Inchicore. He loved his art above anything else, and when he got the chance, he liked to read, particularly biographies and thrillers, enjoyed sailing, and played the guitar. He didn't say that there was anyone in his life at all other than his family and friends, and she certainly wasn't going to ask.

'Better get you back to your place.' He glanced at his watch, a plain gold piece on a worn brown leather strap. Her eyes followed his, noticing the tiny dark hairs which grew on his forearm. 'It's almost three.'

Her heart did something with a pang of disappointment.

He drove out of the town and down the winding road to the beach, and pulled up outside the hotel, the only sound that of the crashing surf a few yards away.

'Thanks, it was a lovely night,' she murmured as they walked up the steps.

'Likewise. What's on the schedule for tomorrow?'

'Probably be on the beach, I suppose.'

'We could drive somewhere quieter,' he suggested.

Her pulse raced, and she didn't know what to say for a few seconds. 'What about your work?' She tried to be practical, reluctant to let him know how this sudden possibility of seeing him again affected her.

'I can take time off, I'm my own boss.'

She hesitated, not knowing what to say.

'I don't want to push you...why don't you think about it and I'll give you a call in the morning. Do you have the number of the hotel?'

Immediately she decided that he was being polite probably, and felt he had to ask because she was on her own. But she pulled the card from her bag anyway and he noted down the number.

'Sleep well.' He kissed her on the cheek, and she stepped in shyly. She felt like such an idiot, a mature woman behaving like someone on a first date.

'Buenos noches.'

She closed the heavy wooden door between them and he was gone.

As soon as she arrived in her room, she took a quick glance through the window, surprised to see his jeep still parked in front of the hotel. Where was he? She stared out over the beach, but it was dark, and she assumed he must have gone for a walk, but was slightly disappointed that he hadn't asked her to join him.

The phone shrilled. Kate opened her eyes and reached to pick it up, knowing instantly who it would be.

'Have you just woken up?'

'This minute.' She lay back on the pillow.

'It's a lovely morning.'

She glanced towards the shutter and could see slivers of bright sunshine slide around it.

'Have you decided what you're going to do today?' he asked. Straight to the point, no beating around the bush, she liked that about him.

'I haven't had a chance.' She crossed her knees and stretched one leg up in the air, golden brown like the rest of her body, white skin only visible where her bikini had covered. She giggled.

'You sound in good form this morning.'

'I am.'

'Why don't I call down to you, maybe we could have breakfast together?'

'Yes, why not,' she agreed, quite unable to say she was definitely going to do something else that didn't include him, and tell him that she was a married woman and under no circumstances should she give in to whatever this was. She was still drying her hair and nowhere near ready when there was a knock on the door. She had taken too long in the shower, soaped and creamed, and painted her toe-nails racy red. Then she had the difficult task of trying to decide what to wear, so much choice in her meagre wardrobe.

'Just a minute.' She pulled on a white linen top.

'Kate, I'll wait for you on the terrace, I've ordered coffee, rolls, and tortilla, so don't be long.'

She rushed then, and got down in five minutes. He stood up

81

when she arrived at the table, and gave her his usual perfunctory kiss on the cheek before pulling out a chair for her. She sat down and thought how well he looked in navy T-shirt and shorts, as fresh as if he had a good eight hours sleep. This morning they didn't talk very much, and to her surprise she felt much more relaxed even than last night as she sipped her coffee, and bit into the tasty omelette.

'Well, have you decided what you're going to do?' he asked, when the dishes had been cleared away by the waiter.

'I'm not sure,' she murmured. Imagining how he would react if she came out straight and told him that she was too scared to spend even another few minutes with him. And that she had a husband at home who would...would what...if he knew what she was doing now?

Jack leaned forward across the table and stared directly at her, his face serious. 'Just say no, if that's the way you feel. I'm going to be devastated, heart-broken, but I'll try to deal with the rejection. If I can't manage to live with it, then maybe I'll hang myself, or jump off the balcony, there are any number of choices available to me.' His eyes were full of laughter.

'Stop messing!'

'Right, it's make your mind up time.' He stood up.

'OK, you're on, where are we going?' She knew that there was no decision really.

'I was thinking...the beach is always going to be there, have you ever been to Granada?'

'No, but I'd love to go.'

'It's a couple of hours drive on the motorway.'

They walked up the stairs to her room, and she opened the door and stepped inside.

'I'll wait for you,' he said.

In the bathroom, she freshened up, and then came out and began to comb her hair in front of the big mirror in the bedroom.

He called from the landing. 'Kate, in the event that we don't get back tonight, why don't you throw a few clothes in a bag?'

She stopped what she was doing suddenly, and in her

reflection could see surprise send her eyebrows up and blue eyes widen. She wondered had he planned this already, his gear already packed in the jeep, full sure of her?

'I'm sorry, that sounds...don't take me up wrong.'

She could hear uncertainty in his voice.

'It's a good suggestion.' She reminded herself that she was a grown-up now.

'I have no ulterior motives, Kate, believe me.'

'Let's do that, we could get delayed.'

'I'll have to go home to collect my stuff, I'll be back in about twenty minutes.'

She heard the sound of his footsteps on the marble staircase diminish into the distance. Quickly she pushed almost all the clothes she had brought with her into the bag. I'm well able for him if he turns out to be the type who tries to take advantage, she thought, I'm a bit long in the tooth to be seduced.

In Granada, that magnificent ancient Moorish city, he took her to the Alhambra, the palace fortress of the Nasrid Sultans, rulers of the last Moorish kingdom in Spain. There they spent hours wandering in the splendour of the Royal Palace with its magnificent patios, fountains, and pools, and the harem where the women who belonged to the sultan once lived in seclusion.

'Sixteen princes were murdered here, because their chief Hamet had fallen in love with the Sultan's favourite Zoraya,' Jack told her the story as they stood looking up at the wonderful ceiling in the Hall of the Abencerrajes.

He drew her attention to the rust stains on the fountain below. 'That's supposed to be the blood.'

'Gruesome!'

'And over here is the Hall of the Two Sisters, the principal room used by Zoraya.'

'It's wonderful,' Kate murmured softly, the atmosphere of the place so evocative of the past she could say very little. They continued on then to the Queen's Tower, and he showed her where they burned perfumes under the floor to waft up through

83

a marble slab in the corner. And to the Royal Baths, decorated with rich tile mosaics. The central area for reclining and the balconies from where musicians and singers entertained, and who according to legend were always blind to ensure that the royal women couldn't be seen by strangers.

Kate was enthralled, feeling she hadn't seen half of it by the time they were forced to leave when the place closed in the evening.

'Fancy spending the night there with all those ghosts?' Jack asked.

'No thanks.' She shivered, and he put his arm around her, a warm friendly hug which didn't remotely fit into the seduction category. After that little intro, she waited for him to suggest they stay over, expected it almost, but he said nothing.

Dinner that night was in another small intimate restaurant, he seemed to know exactly the sort of place she liked.

'It was a great day,' she said, when they had finished.

'For me too.' He picked up the bottle of wine which was still more than half-full. 'You'd better drink the rest of this, I have to drive.'

'No thanks,' she protested, determined to be more careful tonight, and at least stay relatively sober.

He put down the bottle again.

'It sort of cuts the evening off, having to get back,' she said slowly.

He didn't make any response.

'Let's stay the night, what a waste to go back so soon. This is a fantastic place, it would be a sin to rush through it.'

He looked at her, and his brown eyes showed surprise. 'I had decided that perhaps it wasn't the most kosher thing to suggest. I regretted my impulse this morning.'

'I'd love to go back to the Alhambra again tomorrow, but will we get somewhere to stay at this hour?'

'I know a place not far from here. It's a small hotel but there should be availability at this time of the year. Do you mind waiting while I check it out?' He stood up, quite obviously chuffed, kissed her on the cheek, and then he was gone through the door into the darkness.

She felt her face grow warm, amazed that he seemed so delighted at her suggestion to stay over. She sat there and sipped her wine, unable to stop smiling. It was ridiculous. She was caught in some sort of fascination with this man, who enjoyed her company so much he wasn't interested in talking to anyone else. Not like Dermot, who almost always insisted on friends or acquaintances joining them no matter where they were, quite unable to sustain a conversation with her alone. She stared around the packed restaurant and noticed a couple at another table, both staring into the distance beyond each other. Without doubt, a Dermot and Kate on holiday. The man lifted a glass of beer to his lips, the woman sipped a coffee. Their blank eyes snapped open and shut, like they were camera lenses, each frame to join the next to create something complete in their memory. Recollection convinces them that they had really enjoyed Granada, the empty spaces filled up, unaware that they ever existed.

And she was with a man who had no interest at all in what was going on in the middle distance, or even in the near distance, he was right here in her face.

He reappeared after about half-an-hour, and another coffee later, and settled the slight worry which had begun to build up in Kate's mind about not coming back, the crazy things you think of when you don't know someone very well.

'We're all set, two rooms booked.' He was out of breath.

'Here, have some.' She poured wine into his glass. 'You can enjoy it now.' They clinked glasses.

'To...' he said.

'A good time,' she finished the sentence.

They sipped their wine and stared at each other silently for a few seconds and then Kate burst out laughing.

'What's so funny?' he asked with a grin.

She giggled again, but couldn't put her finger on why, it was as if she had remembered the punch line of a joke long after it had been told. She twirled the stem of the glass in an effort to focus on something which would stop this uncontrollable burst of mirth, when suddenly his hand covered hers, soft-skinned, and she was reminded of the night they had danced at Eddie's birthday party. She looked into his eyes, and wondered was he thinking about that night too, but then gently she moved back. The movement was territorial, don't try to take a part of me, I draw the line. She didn't know where that was, but knew she had to put out a marker and let him know that she wasn't easy, he couldn't start something and expect her to follow.

He came with her to the door of her room.

'There's much more, you know,' he said, his head slightly down, eyes concentrating on the ground, hands pushed into his pockets.

She didn't answer.

'To see, I mean.' He looked at her then. 'I'd like to show it to you.'

The next day was spent in the Generalife, the summer palace of the sultans. They wandered through enclosed gardens and walkways, cooled by the shadow of tall trees, and fountains sparkling in the sunshine. Most beautiful was the Patio de los Cipreses, dark and secretive, surrounded by sculpted Junipers where the Sultana Zoraya was suspected of meeting her lover Hamet.

Kate felt quite relaxed now. At night safe and secure in her own room, protected from temptation, managing to sustain the myth of platonic friendship with Jack. They were behaving with perfect propriety, and she decided that it was like knowing someone at work, a person you like but wouldn't dream of thinking about them in any other way. She was still angry with Dermot, and decided that as it seemed he couldn't be bothered to spend time with her, then why shouldn't she enjoy the company of someone who did?

They didn't talk about going back at all now, it was taken for granted that they were going to spend this time together. Out of

Granada they travelled up into the Sierra Nevada, Jack driving his jeep along narrow dirt roads barely wide enough for one vehicle, Kate praying they wouldn't meet another coming from the opposite direction. She was a very bad passenger but he seemed to tolerate it reasonably well. Occasionally they stopped and walked along the edges of sheer grey rock cliffs, steep gorges falling away sharply to dry tree-filled river beds at the bottom, a head-swimming drop. They sat and breathed in the sharp air, cooler up here away from the coast, and watched the goats, amazingly nimble on their little hooves.

Another day, they tackled the tough climb to a monastery cut high out of the peak. There they visited the ancient church, the cloister, the vegetable gardens, and under the shade of a large tree in the courtyard, they were offered small cups of dark coffee and dry biscuits made by the monks themselves, all three of whom seemed to be well into their eighties.

Then they headed down to the coast and he took her to a quiet beach which they had almost to themselves. She was quite modest in her bikini, and didn't dare to go topless, although a couple at the far end of the beach were quite obviously nude. It made her even more conscious of herself, glad that she had gone through the excruciating experience of a leg and bikini wax before she came away. She remembered that it had all been for Dermot's benefit, but now that excitement and preparation for a holiday which never happened seemed very far away.

'Lunch,' Jack announced, and went up to the jeep for the cooler box. He had organised everything early that morning, and she hadn't been asked to do a thing. He poured two glasses of ice-cold sparkling wine, and raised his. 'To us.'

'To us,' she had the courage to say it now.

There were cold meats, salads, fresh bread, followed by luscious glistening dark red cherries, and they sat under the shade of the overhanging trees and munched. The white sandy beach glimmered in the heat, too hot for the feet without sandals. The sea was a bright blue, the surf crashing at its edge like a picture postcard.

'You're spoiling me.'

'Why not? Everyone needs to be spoiled occasionally.'

'Yes, why not, I deserve it.'

They raced into the sea and dived into the cool water, under the waves and up again, searching for each other and swimming close. Occasionally they touched, hands in contact momentarily as they gambolled, but she spun away from him, afraid of where it might lead. They threw the towels down on the sand at the edge of the water and lay there to dry off.

'I love it here.' Kate turned her head towards him, but with the sun in her eyes she couldn't see him.

'Thanks for spending the time with me, I haven't enjoyed myself so much in years.'

His keen artist's eye watched her every move, the way she stood, walked and sat, and he could see her model for him. He loved how she laughed at the least thing, so light-hearted, and how she grew heated, emotional almost, when they discussed more serious subjects. They held similar views on all the big issues, only the smaller ones showing the differences between them.

He couldn't believe that he had her all to himself, no-one else to interrupt, or to pry, and the days passed, each better than the one before. In the mountains, or at the beach, they wound their way back to Mojacar, enjoying each other. But it became more and more difficult for him to hide the way he felt about her. He hadn't analysed it, but knew that it was something momentous for him. She kept herself slightly reserved, he had no idea how she felt. And why should she feel anything more than friendship? She was a married woman, with a husband and family at home, who was just passing the time with him, and he respected that. He would have to deal with his own feelings when she had left him.

Chapter Eleven

'When is Kate due back?' Irene asked sleepily.

'She's supposed to be coming back on Tuesday, but who knows?' Dermot curled around her.

'I hate the thought of it.' She nibbled his ear.

'In some ways I do too, in others, I can't wait to get her back, I miss her around the house.'

'You could have me instead, didn't I make a nice dinner for you the other night?'

'Yea, you did, fair dues, and I needed it I can tell you.'

'Maybe Kate should stay away?'

'I don't think there's much chance of that, thanks be to God.' He closed his eyes.

'What if she never came back? Imagine what life would be like then?'

She ran her fingers across his chest and tickled.

'I don't want to imagine,' he groaned.

'Maybe we should tell her, come out in the open.'

'Tell her what?' He opened his eyes again, raised himself up on his elbow and stared at her.

'About us, that we love each other.'

'Are you mad?'

'Of course I'm not, I love you, and you love me, so what could be more natural than for us to be together? Once everyone is over the shock, they'll accept us. Go on. Say yes, please, please?'

But that wasn't part of Dermot's plan. He would be driven spare by her demands, forced to do everything her way. And the expense of it. Her clothes were all designer labels, only the best would do there. Her jewellery had to be 18 or 24 carat, the word "imitation" didn't exist in Irene's vocabulary.

'I think it would be wonderful. Trying to grab a few hours here and there is so frustrating. Leave Kate, and move in here with me, we could have such a great life.'

'How would you explain to your posh friends that you're living with your step son-in-law?'

'I've heard worse. Anyway I don't care about them, it's you I want.'

'We'd be like two alley cats living together, scratching each other's eyes out.'

'That's not funny,' she pouted.

'Don't take it to heart, I was only joking. It's late, I'd better be off.'

'It's only just after twelve.' She leaned across him.

'Rene, I have to be up early in the morning, I've a busy day tomorrow.'

'When will I see you?' She clung to him.

'Soon, there's a lot going on at the moment. I'll phone you.'

'Tomorrow?'

'Don't know. Now let me out of this bed, Rene, you're a terrible tease.'

'I won't let you go until you say yes.' She tightened her grip.

He played the dummy. 'Yes what?'

'You and me, my love, you and me. We're an item, we're partners, you know that, all we have to do is make the decision to be together.'

'That will have to keep for another day, Rene, this is not the time. Let's leave it until the Spanish project is completed, then we'll know where we stand.'

'Maybe we could go away and live somewhere exotic. Oh Dermo, I can't wait.'

'Neither can I, Rene, neither can I.'

Chapter Twelve

'Let's celebrate...being together. I know a really nice place, there will be just the two of us there,' Jack suggested.

She nodded, a catch in her throat as a wave of loneliness came over her, a sudden I'll miss you feeling. The end had come far too fast after the headiness of the last week, of his wanting to spend time with her to the exclusion of everything else in his life, put on hold because she was there. And his extraordinary generosity, refusing to let her pay for anything, the hotel bills the only expense she managed to settle herself.

In one way, that last day which they spent near Mojacar wasn't much different to those other days at the beach. The same sun shone overhead, the sea broke on the sand, the gentle breeze cooled. In another, it was altogether different. Now she watched him constantly, and tried to imprint his very essence on her memory. She laughed louder than usual, she ran down to the sea faster, dived deeper, and swam further. Everything was more extreme.

After lunch, he produced champagne out of the cooler-box, cool bubbly which heightened her awareness of even the smallest thing.

'This is crazy, we'll be out for the count in no time, snoring away the afternoon,' she giggled.

'I'll dump you in the sea if you fall asleep, wasting the last of our time...I'll twang a few chords, that should keep you awake.' He took up the guitar.

'I love the sound you make, it's beautiful.' She sipped the cool drink.

'It's a piece by Juan Martin.' His fingers rippled over the strings, and she was lulled into a state of dreaminess, her eyes closed.

Later they played with the sand like two children, and Jack took a stick and drew her name in huge letters, and she did the same.

'To us, for posterity!' he shouted.

'How long will it last?'

'Until the wind blows and other feet walk over.'

In her head she noted the hours, hoping that when she thought it was about four, it was really only three. She wanted the day to last long after their names had disappeared in the sand, but knew it wasn't going to happen. She would probably never see Jack again. For him it was just a brief holiday friendship, time out of his busy schedule. For her it had begun the same way, and should have stayed like that, but now she didn't want to let go. She felt frustrated, unable to say what was in her mind. She longed to ask him how he felt about her, and regretted that line she had drawn between them on the first night.

'Kate?'

She turned her head. He smiled and his fingers traced the shape of her face. There was a silence, an intense holding of breath as he moved closer to her and lit a flame which coursed between them. They lay skin to skin, and she could feel his heart thudding in time with hers, a symphony, a wild Beethoven Fifth cacophony. Their lips reached, and came together. His arms enfolded her body and drew her into him. She didn't think that this was wrong. She didn't think at all.

They stayed on the beach until late, and absorbed the beauty and wonder of the final minutes of the evening as the huge orange sun sank into a dark blue sea. They went back to the little restaurant of that first night, and he ordered the identical dishes and wine. They ate slowly, their eyes on each other. It was strange, like they were caught totally alone in some mystical dream place. Afterwards they walked to his house, and sat out on the terrace which was in shadow except for the light of the full moon, shining silver. He poured more wine, and they drank a little, but then he moved closer and put his arm around her. There was no decision taken, it was a continuum of that moment this afternoon when as of one mind they had turned to each other and submitted.

His fingers threaded a diffident course through her hair, and he closed his eyes for a few seconds and took a deep breath. All of his sensible decisions were swept away in this wave of aching desire. He wanted to keep her with him for always, and he cupped her face in his hand and kissed her. Then he stood up, and drew her with him into the bedroom, where very slowly he undressed her.

She didn't move, just let him unfold her, and she felt herself quiver with anticipation as he quickly stripped off his own clothes, and his arms curled around her again. Her brain was no longer operating logically, her body was in charge, every nerve-ending demanding satisfaction. They lay on the bed, skin damp from the heat of the night, and moved in tandem. He did all those things she had imagined. He kissed her eyes, her lips, her breasts, probed into her belly-button, and then, shuddering, moved beyond.

Anxious to give her the utmost pleasure he took his time, wanting it to last for ever, and when the moment was just right, he looked down into her eyes, into their blueness, and let her guide him inside that soft warm moist place that was Kate.

He awoke early and slipped out of the bed quietly, anxious not to disturb her. He showered and afterwards stood watching her as she lay there, the white sheet thrown off, her hand curled under her cheek. He picked up a pad and charcoal, and began to sketch. There was an aura about her body created by the shafts of sunlight which sifted through the shutters, and he made individual drawings of her face, her arm, hand, foot, every part of her, each one a delicate loving perception of this person who now meant so much to him.

Suddenly she opened her eyes and looked around her.

'Kate?' Smiling, he moved across the room the instant he saw her move.

'No!' she snapped, and climbed out of the bed.

He was puzzled, and taken aback by her vehemence. 'What's wrong?'

'Give me my clothes!'

He handed them to her and she quickly put them on.

'Don't know where your pants went, I think they were flung up in the air at some point,' he smiled.

She searched under the pillow, and began to drag the sheet off the bed.

'Calm down, we'll find them, come out on to the terrace and I'll make us some breakfast.' He moved closer, his hand touching hers.

'I can't wait for that, I have to go.' She shrugged him off.

'Kate, my love, why are you so upset?'

She slipped on her mules, and rushed out of the bedroom, grabbing her handbag from the table as she went.

'Kate, don't go.'

She clattered down the stairs, and ran across the courtyard to the front door. Jack called her from above but he had to go back inside and pull on some clothes before he could follow her. Taking the steps two at a time he hurtled down, but by the time he was through the door she had disappeared.

Kate hurried along the narrow street, almost falling more than once over the uneven ground, praying that the wind wouldn't suddenly squall, and whirl up her dress exposing her nakedness to everyone. All she wanted to do now was to take a taxi back to the hotel, pack her stuff and leave. When she awoke earlier, she had got such a shock to find herself in a strange bed, and remembering what had happened the night before, she found that the magic had paled and, like Cinderella, everything had disappeared at midnight. In her case it was eleven in the morning when the fantasy had exploded.

In her room she hurriedly showered and changed, and threw her clothes into a pile on the bed. She was just pushing the lot into the bag when there was a knock on the door. She stopped what she was doing and straightened up, knowing that it had to be Jack. She listened to him knock again and call her name, but ignored him. After a few minutes he went away.

She rang reception, to be told by the girl that there was a bus to Alicante at one, and booked a taxi to take her to the stop. Then slowly she opened the door and went down the stairs, praying that Jack would have already left. But as she walked into the reception area, her heart did a somersault when she saw him coming towards her.

'I'm sorry.' She was embarrassed.

'Have a cup of coffee with me?' His eyes pleaded.

'I must pay the bill.' She turned towards the reception desk.

'I'll order.'

It took a few minutes to settle the account and after that she had nowhere else to go but outside. She sat opposite him at the very same table under the big blue-and-white striped umbrella where they had had breakfast that first morning together.

'I'll take you back to Torrevieja, if that's what you want,' he said.

'I'm catching the bus.' She looked everywhere but in his eyes. Her heart thudded uncomfortably, like it had done yesterday when the day began to run away with her.

'I'm sorry about last night, if I thought you didn't want to, I wouldn't have dreamed of...it's not something I feel proud of now.'

'I drank too much wine.'

'I took advantage.' He sipped his coffee.

'It doesn't matter.'

'Doesn't matter?' He curled the paper-napkin into a ball in his fist.

She stood up, her cup of coffee untouched. 'I must go.'

'Come with me?'

'No, I'd rather not, it would be better if I...' She bent for her bag and he reached for it at the same time. Running out of energy, she let him pick it up, and they stood in silence outside the hotel until the taxi drew up.

'Let me drive you back, please?'

She didn't reply, and stepped into the taxi.

He was aware that he was losing her, and had known that this would happen. But that was before yesterday, and now he wanted to drag her out of the taxi, to explain that he hadn't meant to hurt her. Above all, he longed to tell her that he loved her.

'Bye Jack.' The door clumped shut.

He stood and watched the taxi drive away. Then he ran to the jeep, followed the car to the bus-stop, and walked quickly to where she stood in the queue.

She didn't look at him and moved along with the other people until she climbed up the steps, paid for her ticket, and found a seat. It was only after the last of the passengers had got on, and the bus finally pulled away from the stop, that she glanced back to see him stand alone, his figure blurred through her tears.

This time she didn't notice anything on the journey, the world outside the bus spun by in a vague stream of colour which meant nothing. There was no anticipation of discovery or excitement any longer, only a feeling of depression. She tried to understand why she had let herself lose control so readily, and decided that such a strong sexual attraction to a strange man had to be a reaction to Dermot's indifference. But he wasn't a strange man, a voice in her head argued...you know him now...you like him...you love him. She closed her eyes and tried to shut out the memories of the night before, and the awful thought that she had left her knickers somewhere in his bedroom.

Back at the house in Torrevieja, she noticed the dried-up granules clustered at the bottom of the coffee mugs, the unmade bed, the towels thrown around the bathroom, the stains of spilled water on the floor tiles, all signs that Dermot had been there. Anxious to keep occupied, she immediately threw herself into a cleaning spree, almost glad there was something to do, but the anxiety refused to die down and although she scrubbed and polished vehemently, she felt no better and thought she would never manage to put in the hours until it was time to go to the airport tomorrow evening. She longed to get home, to sit down in her own kitchen, and sleep in her own bed, but she baulked at that image as she thought of Dermot and suddenly wondered had he met someone else? And if she knew that for certain, would it make her feel any different, her own actions justified, tit for tat?

But there was another chore, and that was to go next door and see Chris and Eddie. She dreaded the thought of Jack's name coming up in conversation, or that he might even walk in while she was there. She cringed as she imagined being described as an easy lay, and accused herself of being all of that and worse. She couldn't see the black jeep parked outside, and felt slightly more relieved when she went in to find that they seemed genuinely pleased to see her.

'Dermot was here for a couple of days, but you had disappeared so quickly, we couldn't tell him very much,' Eddie said.

'It was a pity he didn't have the time to join you.' Chris was sympathetic.

'He's not interested in sight-seeing.'

'And you were on your own? I'd hate that.' Chris began to prepare a salad, and was standing in the exact same position at the counter where Jack had stood on that first night.

Kate looked away.

'You have to be so careful who you meet these days, I would have warned you against going off alone, G & T?' Eddie poured drinks.

'No thanks, I'm on the dry now. But I must go, there's so much to do before I fly home tomorrow.'

'This is your last night, you can't spend it on your own.' Chris put the large bowl of salad on the table. 'Dinner is just about ready.'

'One drink.' Eddie proffered a glass. 'With plenty of tonic.'

She gave in, and was drawn into the conversation in spite of herself, to hear them talk about Jack, so much a part of their family, the much-loved younger brother.

'You two seemed to get on very well.'

'Yes, he's nice.'

'But a right loner, all wrapped up in that painting stuff.' Eddie puffed on a cigar.

'He has an exhibition arranged for later this year in Dublin, so he's working like mad at the moment.' Chris took a roast chicken out of the oven.

Kate smiled.

'It's a totally erratic kind of life.' Eddie topped up his drink. 'No room for family, or friends. He never keeps in touch with anyone, doesn't bring his mobile with him, and there's no phone at the house in Mojacar either. Of course, we could ring Paqui and ask her to give him a message, but it must be life or death, nothing less.'

'I wish he'd meet someone and settle down.' Chris began to serve.

Eddie chortled. 'Sure no normal woman would put up with him. If he had kids he'd see them so seldom he would probably paint them by mistake. And any time we've been down at that place of his, I felt like a bull in a china shop, afraid to move in case I touched one of his precious pictures. What a way to live,' he sighed.

'He's an artist, they're not like the rest of us mortals.' Chris poured white wine into glasses.

Kate swallowed the cool refreshing drink. On top of the G & T, it seemed to soften the rawness of the ropes around her heart which had tightened since she had left Mojacar. Suddenly she wanted to know more about him, so she drew them out, and Chris was quite happy to chat, remembering the days when they were young together.

'Always scribbling and painting when he was small, he would have liked to study art when he left school but it was only when he split with Paula that he took it up seriously.'

'Paula?'

'She was a hell of a girl, brains to burn and gorgeous as well, I could never understand what went on there.' Eddie re-lit his cigar and wafted aromatic blue smoke.

'Things happened. He didn't want people to know.' Chris pursed her lips.

'He could have told us, we're family. I always thought she met someone else, or he did.'

'No, it wasn't anything like that.'

'I remember asking him at the time could I help, you know, friendship and all that, but he practically took the head off me. He was like a bull terrier.'

'He's a very private person, Eddie, you could never understand that.' She stood up and began to remove their plates.

'Hey, I'm not finished.' He grabbed his, and began to mop up what was left of the sauce with a piece of bread.

Suddenly the atmosphere changed, and there was a slight coolness between them. A can never understand your family resentment from Eddie, a we're not going to tell you secrecy from Chris. But after an uncomfortable pause, the conversation reverted back to the normal everyday.

Kate was disappointed. She would have loved to hear more about him, so that when she put him away with the photos and gifts he had given her, he would be a person with a background and a family, not a brief one-night stand whose face she would never recognize again.

Chapter Thirteen

Dermot tried to scrub some of the grime off the sink with a lump of steel-wool, but he wasn't having much success. Eventually, he threw it there and marched down the hall to the garage where Shane was practicing. It took some thumping on the door, and a phone call, before he put his head out.

'Your mother's due back in a few hours, and the place is in a mess, get out here and clean it up.'

'Dad, we're in the middle of something new, I'll do it later.'

'Well, make sure you do.'

He nodded, and retreated inside.

But as the door closed, Dermot knew Shane hadn't got the slightest intention of doing anything, and he realised that he would have to do it himself. Surprisingly, he was very nervous today. Since Kate had gone away, he hadn't heard a word from her, she seemed to have dropped off the planet, and he really didn't know whether she was coming home or not. He finished the sink, swirled the water, and wiggled his fingers in the plug-hole to help the last of the waste to flow away. Then he filled the dishwasher with the rest of the dirty plates, mugs and bowls, and switched it on.

Worst of all was her absence from Torrevieja, and while he had tried to convince himself that she had just gone sightseeing as Eddie had said, he still wasn't too sure about that, and wondered if she was getting her own back because she had found out about Irene or Carmen. He stood in the middle of the kitchen, hands on his hips, and tried to decide what to do next. Should he clear up the mess on the table, or start with the floor, which looked as if someone had spilled beer or something on it? He bent underneath and picked up a coffee jar, a bottle of ketchup with the curl of hardened red sauce congealed on the top, and an empty milk carton which smelled.

So things weren't like they used to be, and he wasn't so interested in sex any more. Irene and Carmen provided what he needed there. Marriages become dull over time, he decided, when people reach middle-age it's more of a friendship. He still loved Kate, well sort of, but thought he should make more of an effort, just in case she decided to take herself off altogether.

Kate didn't expect Dermot to be at the airport, and was more than surprised when she saw his figure detach itself from the crowd at Arrivals and walk smiling towards her.

As she felt his lips brush her cheek, she smiled too, an automatic response to a devoted husband meeting his darling wife. He took the trolley from her, and began to wheel it.

'How was your flight?'

'Good...thanks.'

'On time for a change.'

She followed him outside, and he paid the parking charge and located his car. She felt strange, as if Dermot was someone she had not met in a long time.

'How are the lads?'

'Grand, except that Conor has gone and shacked up with some new bird.'

'What?' She stared at him in astonishment.

'He's madly in love, and moved in with her.'

'Who is she?'

'Don't ask me, all I know is that her name is Nicola, and she works in his office.'

'What is she like?'

'I only caught a glimpse of her one morning with long skinny legs sticking out from underneath his shirt,' he guffawed.

That was a surprise, but not so much as Dermot's attitude, which was unusually friendly and good humoured, like she used to know him.

'Well, did you enjoy yourself?'

That question at last.

'Yes I did, actually.'

'Where did you go?'

'I travelled down south and visited a few interesting places.'

'Suppose you were with a tour?'

She stiffened. 'No, I went on my own.'

'I was worried, you know, when I arrived and found an empty house.'

She could hear the irritation in his voice, and for a few seconds she wondered what to say. Was this going to be a slide-back into the normality of Dermot's sharp responses, sarcasm, and even bullying, or was that too strong a description of him? No, it was just right, he could be a bully at times. Her decision was made dispassionately, as if she was looking down on the scene from the objectivity of a great distance, like people describe when they have had a near-death experience.

'I wrote a card and left it on the window-sill, didn't you see it?'

'No, I didn't.' He turned into the drive.

'I'm sorry if you were worried.' She stepped out of the car, and walked into the house.

'I don't know why you couldn't have phoned me. You managed to talk to the lads more than once.'

'I didn't have anything to say to you after our last conversation.'

'Oh that...well...'

She went into the kitchen.

'The house is in a bit of a mess, I tried to clean it up but...and you'll probably need to get a new blind.'

'Don't worry.' She began to unpack the shopping bags. A bottle of whiskey for Dermot, perfume for Irene, cigars for Uncle Bill, and cigarettes for Conor and Shane. She could see the state of the place, but didn't really care.

'Good, Black Bush, thanks.'

She busied herself making coffee.

He helped himself to some biscuits she had brought. 'These are nice, haven't a biscuit left in the house.'

'I'll do a shop tomorrow evening.'

'There's plenty of frozen stuff still there, Shane ate Chinese mostly, he couldn't be bothered defrosting. I ate out.'

They made desultory conversation for a while, and then went up to bed. She decided to leave the unpacking until tomorrow, reluctant to have Dermot looking over her shoulder. There was something of a truce between them, a stand off, and she wanted it to last as long as possible. It was like walking on a tightrope, every move carefully considered. He switched off the bedside lamp, and to her surprise turned to her, his hands searching in the darkness.

'Kate.' He pulled her to him.

'I'm tired, Dermot.'

'Come on, you've been away so long, I've missed you.'

'Maybe tomorrow.'

'Why are you putting me off? That's not like you.'

'I told you I'm tired, the journey...'

'Never held you back before.'

She gave in eventually, afraid that he would become suspicious, and their love-making, if it could be called that, was all over after a quick fumble. No sensitive fingering which set off alarm bells of strange intrusions into secret places. Dermot was a smooth universal highway, boring, desensitized, and she went along it, hoping that her memories of Jack would be obliterated. But that didn't happen, it only emphasised the difference.

Chapter Fourteen

Jack dipped the paint-brush into the mixture of blue and yellow and applied the greeny result onto the canvas. He worked for a few minutes but then lowered his hand, dissatisfied, the dryness of boredom in his mouth. He put down the brush, and rubbed his hands with a rag to clean off the paint. Then he walked out to the terrace, flopped down in a chair, and thought about Kate. These last few days had been some of the least productive since he had come out here in February, although he was happy enough with the quantity of work he had done this year, and had intended to return to Dublin soon. Now he didn't want to go back at all, quite sure that he wouldn't be able to stop himself calling to her office, phoning, or emailing. And there the uncertainty butted in. Would she want to know him now, back home and settled into normal life again with her husband and sons? Was he someone who only existed in Spain; a holiday-romance person who she could slot into a photograph album and forget?

He made himself a sandwich, opened a can of beer, and sat watching the comings and goings in the square. It had become more crowded with tourists and he wondered about moving on to one of the smaller villages. He knew the area well, fascinated by the bleak red desert-like landscape depicted in many of his paintings; the time he had spent there with Kate now etched in his memory. The photographs had been enlarged and there were some particularly good ones of the two of them together, taken with the camera on automatic. But he regretted that he had not held himself back on their last night. If he hadn't pushed the situation over the edge maybe they would still be friends. But he asked himself if that would have been enough for him, and he knew the answer was no.

It was much better this way, a clean break. Anyway, he should have been more prepared, he reminded himself, but then he hadn't expected to feel like this. To be in love. It sounded almost stupid at his age. I am in love with Kate, a woman who was amazingly compatible; the chemistry between them so strong that when he touched her he was immediately swept up into some crazy place and all sensible thoughts deleted. He had smiled when he found the handful of white lace under the bed, and was sure she was feeling absolutely mortified about that. He put them away in the hope that he might return them to her one day.

He moved on the following week with his basic equipment, canvases, paints, and set up his easel in the mountains. He was a man dwarfed by the drama of his environment, trying to capture something of this country, and there was a frustration deep inside which made him work furiously to catch the moment before the light changed, keenly aware of the echoes of their days spent up here. The sigh of the wind through red-pink rock canyons and valleys, along the edges of cliffs, the tinkle of the bells which hung around the necks of the goats. All of this he put into the layers of paint, his most vibrant colours used to express the happiness which he had known with her. Until the light faded he worked on a number of different canvases. The delicacy of pale lemon-pink as the sun came up, the shocking red-yellow-greens of the hot midday, the deep-blue-lilac of evening shadows. He waited the following dawn for the exact same moment to continue. To brush thick wedges of glistening paint on to the canvas, to recreate a sweep of the mountainside, emphasise the shadow of a rock formation. To capture the gleam as it touched and brightened silver, and caught the shape of the wooden roof of a shepherd's hut, the strange twisted trunks of olive trees below, the iridescence of the distant horizon.

Now he fell asleep the moment he put his head on the pillow, a change from those first nights after she had left when his mind

105

was tortured with feelings of loss. He grew even more impassioned with a crazy longing to express his love for Kate, and headed out into the darkness obsessed with the need to get there to that place and commune with her memory.

Chapter Fifteen

Kate was forced back into the routine of normal life by the alarm clock ringing that first morning, and the radio news bringing her up to date.

The girls hugged her.

'You look fantastic, did you have a good time on your own? Tell us all,' Carol asked.

'Where did you go?' Mags sat on the corner of her desk, long brown legs swinging under a tiny strip of beige linen she called a skirt, her spiked hair dyed a red-blonde combination...a new look.

'Down south.'

'Where exactly?'

'Murcia, and other places in between.'

'I can't believe you went off on your own, travelling on buses with a small bag over your shoulder, it's just not you. Next year you'll be back-packing in India.'

'Maybe I will.'

'I don't think that sort of holiday would be Dermot's cup of tea,' Carol laughed.

'Well, who did you meet?' Mags pressed.

'No one in particular.'

'It's like pulling hens' teeth trying to get info out of your woman, isn't it Carol?'

'There's not much to tell.' Kate was defensive.

'And we didn't come down in the last shower.' Mags swung off the desk and stood in front of her. 'Will you for God's sake tell us what happened? We know something did, it's quite obvious from the look on your face.'

107

'Nothing happened.'

The girls looked at one another, eyebrows raised.

'Come on, enough about me. How's business?'

'I think the only way we're going to hear the details of this particular little vacation is to quiz her under the influence of a few drinks, you know how talkative she can be then.'

'How many orders did you get in my absence?'

'Top of the list is the restoration of that castle in County Meath. The brief demands that everything must be the genuine article so we've already been over to a factory in France who will reproduce the silk wall coverings from the sample we found behind the wood skirting, and we've got an antique dealer searching for the original pieces. It's a real challenge. The fabrics for the drapes will have to be especially woven so we need to work on the designs, like yesterday.' Mags took a breath at last.

Kate opened the diary.

'We've an appointment tomorrow to meet with the architect.'

'What time?'

'Ten.'

She entered the details. It was the only thing she had to do in the week so far, and she wondered about making no more appointments, leaving one blank page after another. She imagined what it would be like to do things spur of the moment as the whim took her, but it was just a momentary weakness, her brain always caught in a vague cloudy place when she returned from holiday.

'The bank want more of Jack Linley's paintings,' Carol mentioned.

'I tried to contact him but he must be away,' Mags added.

At the very sound of his name, Kate felt her heart begin to thump, and her face grow warm. This would be all it took for the girls to put two-and-two together, but Carol was looking at Mags and took no notice of Kate who sifted through the large sheaf of emails and letters on her desk.

'Our Mags still fancies Jack.'

'What about Nigel?' Kate asked, a tiny swirl of jealousy making itself felt.

'Fizzled!' she grimaced.

'You don't need people like that. We said he was too good to be true, there will be someone else on the mat in no time.' Carol stood up and adjusted the full-length grey skirt she wore.

'I hope.'

'Kate, you get yourself together, and we'll conference about eleven, I've a million and one things to do in the meantime. See you then.'

'And I've got a meeting at ten.' Mags followed her.

They left together, and Kate stared at the pile of correspondence. She had a crazy urge to throw it in the bin, and she made no attempt to lift the phone, or go down to the workroom. She sat there doing nothing, her mind full of Jack.

During the following weeks, she tried hard to put him out of her head, and behave in exactly the same way as usual, but there were still moments when another part of her insisted on going back. The hint of Spanish rhythm took her to a small dimly-lit bar they had found one evening, the crowd silently listening to the sound of guitars strumming. And there were so many Spanish students in Dublin this summer, at times she felt that she was back in Mojacar. Even the sight of a product on a supermarket shelf which had been made in Spain could suddenly remind her of the smallest incident. She had told no one about Jack. No-one knew about the loss of her monogamous virginity to a man she hardly knew, or the unexpected feelings which had swept her along. She put away the gifts he had given her, remembering exactly when and where, the small blue glass cat he had bought her in a village in the mountains, the wonderful multi-coloured shawl which he had insisted on buying from one of those old gypsy women outside the Alhambra, the gold chain in Mojacar. Last of all were the photographs, the ones she couldn't show anyone or even watch on the screen, unable to look in his eyes, to read things there, and fool herself into thinking that this man felt something special which would turn her, like magic, into a desirable woman.

Dermot had reverted back to his old ways, and sometimes as they lay in bed together, fuzzy-pyjamas-silky-nightdress clad people, she would stare at his back and fling accusations. You don't ask me how I am with something real and true in your eyes...you don't kiss me...you don't put your arms around me and hold me close...you don't want me.

Kate and Mags admired Carol's tall willowy eighteen-year-old daughter, all done up for her birthday celebration in black taffeta. Long blonde hair was piled on top of her head in a series of tiny plaits, narrow satin ribbons in tones of blue and black weaving through, the ends cascading on to her bare shoulders. She preened and giggled, delighted with their admiration.

'Wish I looked like that,' Kate said wistfully.

'So do I,' Mags added.

'I used to...when I was her age, do you want to see my photographs?' Carol flicked her straight shoulder-length dark hair and fluttered her long eyelashes. 'I'm not such a bad looker.'

'No thanks, we've seen them all.' Mags stared out the window as Amanda was ushered into the white stretch-limousine by her current boyfriend.

'Right, time for a drink. Sit down, take off your shoes and put your feet up.'

'And no nibbles, please, Carol. The weight has piled on again and I really have to make an effort, I shouldn't even be drinking,' Kate groaned. Feeling bigger than ever when she looked at her two friends...Mags was barely a size ten, and Carol could usually fit into a twelve or a fourteen depending on the design.

'You can't go off the jar, for God's sake.'

'I find it difficult to get into my new gear again, particularly the underwear.'

'Can you image Mrs. Sensible Kate going around in those little skimpy lace thongs, can you Mags?' Carol shrieked.

'Anything would be better than big pink knickers.'

'My Auntie Annie wore a pair of white ones under the pink ones just for good measure.' Kate sipped her drink, ice cubes bobbing among the slices of lemon, and decided to forget about diets for tonight. She would start on Monday again, and make a real effort, maybe even tomorrow, all the bread, potatoes, chips, and sweet things ditched.

'Passion killers. Although some men might be turned on by the challenge in getting through, all that elastic to be snapped, maybe we make it too easy for them?' Carol hitched up her blue skirt. 'Not much there to be pulled.'

'I don't think it makes much of a difference really.' Kate smiled.

'But you haven't any experience in the field, other than with dear Dermot,' Mags pointed out.

'I met a man in Spain and none of that seemed to matter to him, or the fact that I was overweight, not particularly beautiful or clever, or whether I wore knickers or thongs.'

The two stared at her, their eyes wide open.

'So we hear at last,' Mags whispered in a heavily accented French undertone, like Hercule Poirot in one of Agatha Christie's murder mysteries.

'I knew there was something, you couldn't fool us.'

'Reveal all.' Mags moved closer to her on the couch. 'Who is he?'

'A gorgeous flamenco dancer?' Carol twirled her fingers in the air.

'A dashing matador?' Mags jumped to her feet, and began to pound the floor.

'No, he's Irish.'

'Boring.'

'Don't mind her. Just tell us where and when, his name and everything else, particularly the technicolour bits, most importantly, those bits.'

'Top up?' Carol did that generously, adding the tonic out of the cooler, ice and lemon. 'What did we say about finding out

111

about everything when her nibs here is under the influence?'

'I'm not that far gone,' Kate protested.

'No, you're perfectly sober.' Mags nodded at Carol. 'Now, just start at the beginning.'

Which she did, and somehow getting it off her chest made her feel better.

'For God's sake, one night? You're worried about that?' Mags shrieked.

'It could have happened more than once if I had given in to my feelings earlier.'

'And you ran, like a kid caught by her mother kissing a fellow behind the bicycle shed, leaving your knickers behind?' they exploded with laughter.

'With lover boy after you, begging you to come back.' They fell around the place.

'It wasn't so funny at the time.' She tried not to laugh, but at this remove, it did seem absurd, and she joined in the hilarity which seemed to last and last, the tears pouring down their cheeks, snorting and snuffling until it finally faded away due to sheer exhaustion.

'Girls, it's not something fantastic, it's anything but. He's probably already moved on to someone else, you know what it's like over there, women ten a penny all out for a holiday fling.' Kate poured more gin into her drink.

'Like you.' Mags began to laugh again.

'I didn't plan for it to happen.'

'But you didn't say no either.'

'So it gave you a hell of a buzz. Your one night of romance made Dermot seem like something you dragged in out of the rain?'

'How'd you guess?'

'What's his name, you haven't told us that yet?'

She hesitated for a second as she tried to think of a name. 'David...'

'David what?'

'That's all I can tell you.'

112

'We don't know the guy, so what difference does it make?'

She shook her head, adamant.

'So by the laws of deduction, it's possible we do know him, and that's the reason why?' Mags banged on the coffee table with excitement. 'Right, Carol, let's start listing.'

They began with anyone they could think of with that name, each suggestion more preposterous than the one before.

'Yea, he's exactly my type, blowsy, bald, and ready for retirement, what do you think I am?' Kate giggled.

'Love is blind, isn't it?'

'Yea, but I'm not. Anyway, you haven't come near, you're cold as ice.'

'Maybe the reason yer woman is so secretive is that it wasn't a once-off after all and continues on. What about that scenario?'

'No way, girls, I'm a happily married woman, didn't you know?' Kate began to help herself from the bowl of nibbles, barely aware that she was doing it.

'We thought you were the ideal couple, I looked up to you, the pair with the best marriage in town.'

'No such thing.'

'That's not so funny then,' Carol said slowly.

Chapter Sixteen

Jack was so involved in what he was doing he didn't even notice how exhausted he became. He worked on more than one canvas at a time, giving them a chance to dry in the coolness of his room, but didn't bother to examine them with his usual critical eye for the faults which normally drove him to distraction, a painting often dumped if it didn't come up to standard.

One day in the late afternoon he took a break, and suddenly realising that he was hungry, he sat on a rock and ate a ham-roll, washing it down with water. He repositioned the battered yellow straw hat which he wore to protect him from the sun, the band tight around his perspiring forehead, and looked at the painting which stood on the easel, wondering if it was finished. It was something he never knew until in the middle of a brushstroke perhaps or a knife-cut, he would stop and feel instinctively that it was done. It was complete as far as he could take it, as far as it wanted to go itself. Like Kate and himself, a whirlwind which had its own length too, a natural phenomenon which had a beginning and an inevitable end. As he stared at the swirls and movement of colour he knew, quite unexpectedly, that he had come to an end, that he had given so much of himself there was no more to give for now.

While he had known women in the years since he had broken up with Paula, not one had been allowed to get close, so inevitably the relationships had failed, sometimes to his regret, sometimes not. There was a reticence in him, a vulnerability deep inside which had always made him stand back from commitment, until Kate.

As he loaded the jeep, he wasn't sure whether he was pleased or not with the results of his recent work, his "after Kate" paintings he had begun to call them. He was almost afraid to start picking faults, loving them in one way for what they represented, but still uncertain whether the galleries, which usually carried his work, would like this more extreme form. Still he had almost enough of his earlier work to mount an exhibition, the first one booked at the Nestor in December.

He had to go back to Mojacar soon anyway, Chris and Eddie were coming down that way for a week or two, and he had said he would be there. She was anxious to see his work, and always a good critic, he depended on her opinion, although Eddie wasn't really interested and he knew it. The evening he returned, he found them sitting in their favourite bar across the square, and he was almost beside them when Chris turned and looked, hesitating just for a second.

'What's with the beard and the long hair? My God, I almost didn't recognise you.' She hugged him.

'Haven't had time, probably look a sight.' He fingered the smooth black hair growth.

'You're the real thing now, scruffy clothes, wild hair, a right hippy,' Eddie laughed.

'It'll be shaved off pretty soon.'

'How did the work go this summer?' Chris asked.

'Good...I think.'

'Let's have a gander?'

'I haven't put them in the studio yet, give me a chance to have a beer, I'm thirsty.'

Eddie ordered, and Jack sat down. They chatted for a while, and then he drained his glass and stood up anxious to unload.

'I'll help you,' Chris offered.

'No, you stay here. Enjoy your drink, I'll give you a shout.'

'For God's sake, what's got into you?'

'Don't know what you'll think of these, they're different. I can't really describe...'

'Get on with you, I'll give you a hand. Be back later, Eddie.'

She followed him.

Jack opened the doors of the jeep. The paintings stood in a metal structure he had especially designed, and were held securely to prevent damage. He lifted one partially out, but there was no sound from Chris, no scream of elation, no hesitant well-eh of disappointment. He looked at her, somewhat puzzled at her lack of reaction.

'It's fantastic,' she whispered after a moment.

'You like it?'

'I love it.'

*

It was October when he finally returned to Dublin, unable to stay away any longer because of the exhibition in December. He still hadn't come to terms with Kate's rejection of him, and to accept that their brief relationship had been just a once-off. It was strange to walk and drive the streets again, to know that she did the same thing, and that only a quirk of fate prevented them from bumping into each other. But he was glad to be home, to see the family again, particularly his mother and father. It was good for him, he was too long away from all he knew. It had made him more introverted, and he had forgotten how enjoyable it was to be with that wide extended family who insisted on putting their spoke into everything he did. They had been really shocked when Paula and himself had divorced, the first and only one to which this had happened in the strict Catholic family. And as for giving up his well-paid permanent job and heading off to Spain to paint, that horrified them and they wondered had he lost it altogether.

But he had laughed at them and over the years had proven to them that it was the right decision. But they never realised what it meant to him, they had little appreciation of his work. Even a painting he had given his mother and father which used to hang in the sitting-room had disappeared after a while.

'What happened to the painting?' he had asked casually, and they had the grace to look at each other with a certain amount of discomfort.

'It was awkward.' His mother fidgeted with a hankie in her apron pocket.

'Don't worry, it doesn't matter.' He had tried not to be put out about it.

'Everyone who came in asked us what it was all about, but we couldn't tell them, so your mother was embarrassed and I put it under the stairs,' his father said abruptly, and left the room.

'I'll take it back, I presume nobody else wants it either?'

The painting was brought in. It was one of his earlier ones, an abstract work in the bright warm colours of the Spanish landscape.

'It's too big anyway for this room, we're dwarfed beside it.' His father shuffled awkwardly.

'Don't worry, I'll find a client for it.'

'I can't imagine anyone paying money for that.'

'People do.'

'More fools they,' he snorted and pulled a cigarette out of a packet and lit up.

'If they didn't, I'd have to find a job,' Jack said, keeping a smile on his face, reminding himself that they didn't understand and would never grasp what he was about. Their generation had never heard of anyone who painted for a living, and as for having someone in their family who called himself an artist, that was just too much.

Chris was the only one who was really interested, the others had a wouldn't-want-that-thing-on-my-wall-in-a-fit attitude.

'I'll be doing roast-beef on Sunday, I know you like that,' his mother had said yesterday, giving him no chance to refuse. It was assumed if he was home he would come over to Inchicore for Sunday lunch. 'And your Dad wants you to look at the lawnmower, it hasn't worked properly for ages. You know how good you are with things like that. And Lorraine will be here with the new baby, so don't be late.'

'There's a few other things to be done as well, nobody around here can do anything,' his father grunted.

On Sunday, the moment he arrived he gave himself an excuse to leave early, he had limited tolerance for new babies. 'I don't know how long I can stay, I'm very busy at the moment.'

'You need to get some good food into you. I don't think you're looking well, you've lost weight.'

'It's the heat, Mam, you lose fluid, that's all.'

'Fluid my eye, you just haven't been eating properly,' she admonished, always a mother. Sometimes, she treated him like he was still six years old and he found that extremely irritating, but when she put her arms around him, the annoyance drained away, and he asked himself why he should upset them, they mightn't be around for much longer.

'Now this will put a few pounds on you.' She took the joint out of the oven, and as she put it down on the counter, she saw one of her grandsons sneak up to the fridge and open it. 'Ian, get out of there!' The tea-towel, always slung over her shoulder when she was in the kitchen, was pulled off and flaked in his direction. He ducked and ran out the back door into the garden. 'Little brat, thinks he could pinch something without my knowing, doesn't know I've got eyes in the back of my head.' She stood in the doorway waving the towel at him. 'I'll put manners on you!'

'Leave him be, sure we were always up to something like that,' Jack laughed.

'You got whacked for much less, I can tell you.' She pushed a skewer into the meat.

'Jack, can you check the strimmer for me, it seems to have gone on the blink as well.' His father came in the back door. 'I don't want to be taking things out in the spring to find they're not working.'

'After dinner, Dad.'

'Just take a quick look.' Thomas Linley didn't listen, he just turned and led the way out to the shed, his prize-winning garden was his only interest. Jack followed and together they examined the machine.

'Could be a loose wire, I'll take it apart later,' he said.

'Dinner's up,' his mother shouted.

'Just when we're in the middle of something,' Thomas groaned.

'Come on, or we'll be in the dog house.'

They went inside to sit at the big table in the dining-room. Rose was there with her three, her eldest with the first great-grandchild who was just a few weeks old, and Tricia had dragged her two reluctant teenagers over to see Gran and Grandad.

'I don't want cabbage,' one of them moaned.

'I hate that meat,' another said.

'You'll eat what's on the table, your Mam ate everything that was put in front of her. If she didn't, she went hungry,' their grandmother snapped.

'Can we have chicken nuggets?'

'I want chips.'

'Shut-up for God's sake, you little beggars. I told you that you'd have to eat the dinner Gran made for you, she's gone to a lot of trouble.' Tricia was annoyed.

'No point stuffing it down their throats, but they'll eat the apple-pie and custard no doubt.'

The kids giggled among themselves.

'Who'd have kids?' Rose grimaced. 'It's all ahead of you, Lorraine.'

'Drive you around the twist. Aren't you a lucky man, Jack, you've got no hangers-on at all. You can do what you like when you like. I'd give anything for just a week of your life. Maybe we could swop, you look after my lot, and I'll swan about in Harrington Park, no-one but myself to worry about.'

He smiled but made no response. It was what he always did, but somehow her light-hearted inference to his single status cut sharply today. At last he had met the one woman with whom he wanted to share his life but he had been knocked back again, and he resented that. They ate quickly, as always, a throw-back to the days when all eight of them were growing up, and meals were divided into two sittings. There was never enough room at the small kitchen table for everyone to sit down together, and the dining-room was reserved for Sundays. They were a busy family. Thomas spent his working life as a bus-driver, while Mary looked after her children. To make extra money, she made clothes for her own and half of Inchicore as well, turned garments inside out, and altered old into nearly new. She knitted for them as well, and her Aran sweaters, which she supplied to a shop in town, were perfection. She did it for a few pennies, and never wasted a moment. That work ethic was still carried on by her own children, and in their opinion Jack was the only one who had opted out.

Chapter Seventeen

'The plasterwork is wonderful.' Kate stared upwards at the curving vines and heavy bunches of fruit which were interspaced with figurative groups.

'I'm delighted with the way this job is going, wonder will "Irish Interiors" do an article on it?' Carol grinned down at them from where she stood on the painter's ladder.

Kate tried to seem interested. A lethargy had infused her since she had come back from Spain, and she found it hard to drum up enthusiasm for anything these days.

'Trouble is, there are very few people who can afford places like this, and even the ones who possess them can't finance the upkeep.'

'Thanks be to God for the Bob Bensons of this world, and that someone decided to mention our name. Come down off that ladder, Carol.' Mags put a hand out to her.

'You shouldn't have worn your good boots, Carol, are you mad? Black suede and a full length skirt on a building-site,' Kate chided.

'I might have bumped into Bob, always need to be prepared.'

'He's in the States at the moment.'

'Well, you never know with people like him, anyway, don't worry, they'll brush up.'

In the reception rooms, which were almost complete, they admired the silk wall-covering, and the wonderful Bossi mantelpieces which had been expertly restored. They then inspected the upper floors, going through the check-list with the foreman, reasonably pleased with progress. Afterwards, they went down to the modern block which had been built underground at the back and which housed offices, swimming pool, gym, and recording studios.

'We need some paintings for this area, I'll have to try and make contact with Jack again, I hope he's home soon,' Mags said.

'Why don't you call around,' Carol suggested.

'Might do that.'

Kate said nothing. On the way home later, she went into Superquinn to do the shopping. It was her usual habit every couple of days, and now she stood in the aisle and stared at the boxes of Cornflakes, All Bran, and Muesli, but suddenly she didn't know which she wanted, if any. She wandered vaguely along the shelves, her hand moved towards a box of tea, a jar of coffee, a loaf of bread, but she chose nothing, and hesitantly gripped the smooth handle of the trolley again, like she was hanging on to a lifeline. Any other day, she didn't even have to think. Whatever she needed would have been already flung into the trolley by now, the whole shop done in a matter of minutes. But the rather slow-moving individual who pushed an almost-empty trolley around the supermarket this evening was a woman who didn't seem to know where she was.

Chapter Eighteen

Jack stared at his "after Kate" paintings. At this distance and passage of time he could look more critically at the outcome of those days spent in the mountains. He examined each one carefully, searching for sections that needed a touch of paint or a highlight, but couldn't find any. There was a completeness about them that amazed him. Normally when he came home he re-worked what he considered unfinished paintings for months, almost never satisfied, and even when they hung in the gallery, he still spotted things which he didn't like. These he could show Vincent.

'Dear boy, how was Espana?' Vincent floated in with his hands waving excitedly. He wore a long black leather coat, his hair was tied in a neat pony-tail, and a bright red and yellow striped wool scarf was wound a couple of times around his neck. They shared a glass of wine and discussed the market, who was exhibiting, who was collectable, and what prices were being fetched. Jack picked his brains, the man knew anything there was to be known about the world of art.

'Let me see what you've been working on?' he asked later, but Jack hesitated. His paintings were so much a part of himself that whenever he showed his new work he felt stark naked. This would be his second exhibition at the Nestor, but he felt as nervous as he had been that first time. He wanted to make his mark at home, but if Vincent didn't like them, then what after that? His reputation would be ruined by a mere whisper, or a word behind a hand, and although his paintings were snapped up in other countries, he knew there were no guarantees anywhere.

Vincent stared at the painting on the easel. Then he took up various positions and moved up close to examine the detail. 'Much more interesting than your other work, Jack, shows a new departure.' He smoothed his black moustache with long fingers in that flamboyant way of his, then slid one of those narrow cigarillos into a mother-of-pearl holder, and lit it with a gold lighter.

Jack put another painting on the easel, his heart thudding inside his chest.

'You've been working hard.' Vincent looked at it critically, and wandered around the studio examining the collection of work. 'Will you be ready by December?'

'Yes.'

Vincent pulled a small red book from his inside pocket, and then perched a pair of gold-rimmed half-glasses on the end of his nose. 'I have you booked in for the fifteenth, that still OK for you?'

It sounded about right. The paintings would need that length of time to be framed, and the following morning, Jack was up and at it very early, going through the large body of work, deciding which paintings he would include. He had to list, number, and give them suitable titles, the sort of admin he hated. If Chris were home she could have helped, but there was no-one else who would be bothered, and as he made an attempt to put some order on the studio, he found the sketches he had made of Kate as she lay sleeping in his bed. The love that he had felt for her whipped through him once more. Suddenly he was charged with the need to work on them. It would bring her close to him again. Someone he had loved for such a short time, and still loved in spite of his efforts to push it behind him and persuade himself that it was only a quick thrill, a physical new person attraction.

But that evening she was brought even closer when he listened to his messages and heard Mags ask him to phone to discuss some paintings they required for a client.

*

'I've a meeting with Jack Linley tomorrow morning at ten,' Mags announced.

Kate's heart began to thump, the typescript on the papers in front of her jumbled up as she searched for a business-like response, which wasn't really necessary as Carol dived in immediately.

'You finally made contact?'

'Yea, the answering machine was switched on yesterday so I left a message which he returned.' There was a very pleased cat-got-the-cream look on her face.

'I know what you're at. You can have him all to yourself. I've to meet with the antique dealer about the furniture so I can't make it.' Carol closed up her file.

'I must go out to Cremins Moiselle...' Kate stuttered, making up the excuse on the spur of the moment.

'Maybe I'll change the time, invite him to lunch, what do you think, girls?'

'Good opportunity, then you can find out what makes him tick and discover all his dirty linen and whether you're prepared to go there or not.'

The phone rang, and to Kate's relief the girls departed. For a few minutes she had to concentrate on the call, but when she had dealt with that matter, her mind took her back to Spain, to that night when the silver moon gleamed through the open door which led on to the terrace of his house in Mojacar, their bodies dark against the rumpled bed sheets, the fan slowly circling above them on the ceiling. She closed her eyes and could feel again the touch of his lips, the softness of his hands, and breathed deeply, overwhelmed suddenly by the aroma of paint which she could sense and would always associate with him.

For the rest of the day, the thought of Mags having lunch with Jack put her in a vile mood. She spent the time searching for reasons why she needed to take tomorrow off, terrified that she would bump into him coming or going. Just as she was leaving the office, her stepmother phoned.

'I can't make my mind up about a new couch I'm buying for the study, can you come around to the shop and give me your opinion?' Irene was keyed up as ever.

'Well, I'm quite busy this week, would Saturday suit?'

'Too late, I'm afraid it might be gone, I never trust them when they say it's held. Can't you make it sooner?'

'I'm not sure if I'll have any free time during the day, I'm not the boss you know, but...maybe I might be able to meet you tomorrow, perhaps around mid-day.'

'Great, we can grab a bite somewhere, I'll book a table.'

'I wouldn't have time for lunch, Irene, maybe a cup of coffee if we make our decision quickly,' she said it just for the sake of sounding agreeable but knew that when Irene was buying anything it took twice as long as expected, and lunch would have turned into dinner by the time she made up her mind.

That night Kate caught sight of herself in the mirror as she undressed, suddenly horrified at the amount of weight which had piled on again. Her hips and stomach seemed to have taken the brunt of it, her suntan had faded and she hated herself. She hadn't stood on the weighing-scales since her return from Spain and her mood was so low these days that she picked and nibbled on bars, or crisps, or anything that came her way, convinced that she would start the diet again tomorrow.

She opened the wardrobe, and had a look through all the really nice gear she had bought before she went away, the smart jeans, with their coordinated shirts and sweaters, and the linens. The hangers clinked with a hollow unused sound, and she wondered about giving some of the clothes to Carol, who managed to stay between a neat size twelve and fourteen. These days, it was back to the sensible business-suits, and a size sixteen. But this morning's choice was her favourite black dress with the zip pockets. It had a young trendy look. She put on her make-up carefully, creaming on the new foundation she had bought going to Spain and which had sat on the dressing table unused until now. On her way into work she had her hair done, and in spite of her initial reaction at the thought of seeing Jack, deep down she knew she would have given anything to meet him again.

But there was no opportunity, as she spent quite a while in Cremins Moiselle, and went directly from there to meet Irene in Arnotts.

'What do you think of this one?'

'Well, it should suit your colour scheme.'

'I like it, but then I wondered if I was being too conservative, and thought I should go for something dramatic like that one there with the oriental look.'

'But don't forget you have a silk carpet and it's similar.'

'They're both oriental.' Irene looked as well turned out as usual in a pale pink dress and coat. Today, in her seedy, low esteem mood, Kate was jealous of her stepmother's chic.

'But they may not coordinate, and might actually scream at each other,' Kate pointed out with a sigh. They would probably choose the first couch in the end, it was always the way, but she would have to jump through all the hoops arranged by Irene before any decision could be made.

'I think the blue flowers on the black background looks well. Is there blue in the rug at home?'

'There's more than one.'

'It could still work, couldn't it?'

'If you're going to buy this couch, throw out the rug,' Kate said flatly, losing patience. She glanced at her watch, it was almost two o'clock.

'But it cost so much.'

Kate wandered through the range of furniture, but she could see nothing else that would suit Irene's room.

'Maybe you'd better have a look in some of the other shops,' she suggested. Careful to avoid even mentioning the possibility of making it up especially for her. They had done it before, and it had taken weeks to get it right.

'But I wanted it for the weekend.' Her disappointed wail could be heard all over the shop.

'I don't know what to say.' Kate shrugged with exasperation.

'But you're the interior designer.'

'I told you what I think.'

Irene sulked, sitting down in an armchair with a childish pout.

'What's so important about the weekend, is the queen coming for tea?' Kate smiled.

'No, I just want it quickly, you know I hate waiting.'

'Leave it for now. You'll spend all that money and you won't be happy.' She glanced at her watch. 'I'll have to get back.'

'I thought we were going to have a bite of lunch, although it's a drink I need now. Let's go somewhere and quench our thirst.' She thrust a manicured hand towards Kate.

'I'm not a lady of leisure like you, Irene.' She hooshed her out of the soft-cushioned chair.

'Maybe I should go for my first choice after all, I was probably a bit over the top considering the other one. Let's have another look.'

'Irene, I haven't time. If you decide on that one, then I feel it's a good decision, must go...good luck.' She walked out of the shop, all the time thinking she was hearing anxious little steps behind her, but thankfully, she made it back to the office without sight or sound of Irene, and was just in the door when the phone rang.

'I bought it,' Irene squealed.

'Good, I'm delighted,' she said, not even bothering to find out which one.

'You must come around and have a look, they're delivering Friday. Promise you will? Promise?'

'Yes, yes, I'd love to see it.'

She sighed, and stared down into the street below, wondering would Jack be dropping Mags off after lunch, excitement building up inside her as she strained to get a better view.

'Kate.' Carol appeared armed with wallpaper books. 'Can we have a look through these, I need your opinion?'

She whirled back from the window, almost annoyed at the interruption.

'Right, let's have a look at what we're dealing with.' She opened up the lap-top.

'Is Mags back yet? I want to see her about something,' Kate asked.

'Not at all. Still out with Jack, the poor man doesn't have a chance with our Mags.'

*

Jack walked through the doors of Lee O'Donnell Design at about twelve-thirty with a sense of apprehension. Would he meet Mags only, or might Kate be there as well, and what was he going to do when he saw her, the first time since that morning in Mojacar? Asked to wait by the receptionist, he stood looking at the large photographs of interiors which took up most of the wall space, his hands nervously bunched into fists and dug deep into the pockets of his black cord trousers. Then his name was called and he turned to see Mags coming towards him, looking particularly glamourous in a cream outfit, with an extremely short skirt and high leather boots. He glanced beyond her, disappointed not to see Kate.

'I've booked that new Italian place in Ballsbridge. Hope you like it there, we were lucky to get a table.' She rushed him into the back seat of the waiting taxi chattering all the time. Inconsequential stuff to which he only had to nod or give a yes or a no to keep the conversation flowing until they arrived at the busy restaurant and were ushered to a table.

She looked at him over red-tipped fingers clasped beneath her chin. 'How's your work going?'

'Fine, thanks, I've another exhibition coming up in December.'

'Hope it goes as well as the last one.'

'So do I!'

They mulled over the menus for a few minutes and ordered, and then the conversation began again with business. She told him that the bank really loved his work, and wanted more, and this new client was in the market as well. Somewhere in the middle of all that, he asked after Carol and Kate.

'They're well, of course we're madly busy on all sorts of projects, and you must be the same preparing for the exhibition?'

'It's always a rush, I'm not long back from Spain.'

'Kate was there earlier this year, although, to be honest, I prefer the Caribbean.'

'Did she enjoy it?'

'Seemed to. She went off on her own apparently, made no bookings, just took whatever was available when she arrived. It was so out of character for our Kate, she's usually five star or more, loves her bit of luxury.'

He wondered about that. The Kate he knew had seemed quite happy with the simplest of things.

'Could we book some of your paintings in advance, do you think, so that we're not forced to join the crowd at the opening night?' Mags asked a little later.

'Of course. Why don't you come around to the studio and have a look, although they're only at the framing stage at the moment.'

'When would suit?'

'It really doesn't matter. What about some evening after work? Allow enough time to have a glass of wine, choosing paintings shouldn't be rushed.'

'I'll check my diary and give you a call.'

'And why don't you ask Carol and Kate as well? I presume you make decisions like that together,' he added quickly.

'I'll mention it to them.'

'Tell me about yourself, Mags, what gets you going apart from your business?' He was all fired up now at the thought of seeing Kate again.

'I enjoy life, Jack, a few jars, the theatre or cinema occasionally, a game of tennis, working out in the gym. And I love to travel of course.'

'What have you planned for this year?'

'I'm hoping to go to the Virgin Islands.' Mags pushed her prawns around the plate, but left most of the meal behind.

'It's beautiful there.'

'Have you been?'

'I did some sailing in the area a couple of years ago.'

'I would love to do that but I need someone to teach me.'

'When you're out there, there will be no shortage of people willing to take you out.'

'You think so?'

'I know so.'

They finished the meal with coffee, and then he glanced at his watch and murmured something about getting back to work.

'I suppose,' she said.

He asked a passing waiter for the bill.

'Hey, that's my call.'

'It's mine.' He finished the last of the cheese that was left on the plate.

'What do you mean? I invited you.' She tried to grab the bill which the waiter had placed beside him, but he got there first and picked it up.

'I'm getting it, so don't argue with me,' He laughed as he put it down again with his credit card beside it.

'This is business.' She refused to let it go.

'You're one of my clients, I should be taking you to lunch.'

She sighed dramatically. 'Thank you.'

Mags took a taxi back to the office, but he decided to walk, needing time to think about what he would say to Kate if he saw her again. Did the girls know that they had met in Spain, or was that a closely-guarded secret?

Chapter Nineteen

The evening they were going over to Jack's studio, Kate wore her black trouser suit, with the white silk top, and prayed she looked slimmer. She was furious with herself to have let the pounds go on again, and had immediately gone back on her diet when Mags mentioned that Jack had invited them around to view his work. But that was only a week ago, and didn't allow enough time to lose the stone which was needed to bring her back to where she was last May. Full of angst she toyed with the possibility of finding some excuse to opt out, but that was as far as she got. Her heart won.

'Hey, that's a nice outfit, what's up?' Carol asked.

'Didn't we arrange to go around to see Jack Linley's paintings?' Kate pointed to the entry in the diary.

'Oh yea, forgot, about six isn't it?' She looked over Kate's shoulder. 'Are they the plans for the house in Wexford?'

'I've decided to use John Wilman fabrics, and Montgomery as well, I hope the clients are going to like the look.'

'Who's driving?' Mags put her head around the door.

'Don't know. We won't all fit into your little knee-crusher,' Carol replied.

'Why don't you two go over together, and I'll go on my own.' Mags flung out her arms and moved in a slow circle to show off her purple leather suit. 'What do you think?'

'You might get a draught up yer bum, so better be careful.'

'This is what turns them on, girls, didn't you know?'

'You look great, it's new, isn't it?'

'Yea!'

'Wish someone had reminded me, you two look like you're going on the town.' Carol glanced down at her own beige trousers and loose-knitted cream sweater.

'I don't want him to be looking in your direction, I want his eyes on me all the time.'

Kate sat quietly beside Carol, hands twisted tight in her lap. They were in the thick of the evening traffic and she could feel her heart thumping as she watched the cars ahead inch forward bumper to bumper. It was dark now. Lights reflected on shining surfaces, as people dived out of offices and shops cutting across the road through the cars, ignoring the stabbing of angry horns. It took some time to get to Harrington Park. They drove slowly, checking the house numbers, and although Kate knew exactly where the house was situated, she went through the charade for Carol's benefit.

'Can you see Mags' car? She's probably already arrived.'

'There it is.'

Carol drove in and parked. Almost immediately the door opened, and Jack walked towards them.

'Hi there, that was a neat bit of driving, Carol, it's not easy to manoeuvre a car in here.'

'If I'd known I was being watched I would have probably crunched Mags' sports job in bits.' Carol climbed out.

In the passenger seat, Kate fumbled with her handbag, wanting to delay for as long as she could.

Jack moved around to her side of the car, and instantly she was back in Spain, in the velvet darkness, his body all around hers.

'Kate?' His smile was wide and glad as he put out his hand and helped her out of the car, the touch of his fingers so familiar.

'How are you?' she stuttered, and began to follow Carol. She felt like a light had been switched on inside her and that all of them could see the glow, a luminosity which couldn't be explained.

'Good,' he said, as she walked beside him into his home. It was a lovely restored Victorian house, the colour scheme neutral, with a cream leather suite in the sitting-room similar to her own, the old floorboards blending with the slatted wooden blinds on the windows, everything low-key to allow the large painting which hung on the wall to dominate.

'Who did the restoration?' Carol asked, as she plumped into an armchair.

'I bought the house restored, and unfortunately I didn't know you when I was getting some of the other bits and pieces done. Needless to say, I would have appreciated your advice.'

'If you want anything else, don't forget to give us a call.' Mags crossed her legs and revealed another few inches.

'Carol, white or red for you?' Jack asked.

'Red, thanks.'

He poured the wine and handed a glass to Carol, and one to Kate.

'That painting is wonderful,' Mags said.

'A commission.'

'I love it,' Kate added.

She sipped her wine, sitting very straight on the edge of the cushion on the couch, thinking that he hadn't asked her whether she liked white or red, and so he must have remembered. She smiled, foolishly pleased at that, and shocked by the excitement which had burst through her when he had taken her hand.

'How's business?' he asked and sat down at the other end of the couch, which was too close altogether for Kate.

'We're very busy.' She was first in. 'Up to the eyeballs. There are some very interesting jobs in the pipeline,' she babbled on, unable to stop herself, so nervous she could feel her knees shake.

'Good to hear that, there's a huge amount of property development happening in the country.' He sipped his wine.

'We do a lot of restoration work as well.' She looked at Carol and Mags. 'There's almost too much on at the moment.'

'I'm sorry but I'm a bit pressed for time. Do you think we could have a look at your paintings?' Carol glanced at her watch.

He led the way upstairs, and into the studio. For Kate it was like being in Spain again, the room filled with bright colour, sunshine, and blue skies, and so much heat she was suddenly silenced.

'These are fantastic,' Carol whispered with a sense of reverence in her voice.

Kate stared around her, swept up in the magic of knowing exactly where some of them had been painted, particularly the views of the mountains. She remembered one day when they had shared lunch and a little wine, and afterwards lay down on a rough patch of grass to stare at the arc of the blue sky. He told her how much he loved it here, away from the rat-race, people, and everything else in society. 'It's a mad mad world!' he had said, and she had laughed with him as if they were the only two people left in it.

'What's the idea behind these paintings? The people have so much character, are they real, or imaginary?' Mags turned to him.

'Very real, they're all people I've come across. But as regards what is behind them, that's more difficult to explain.' He looked over at Kate, but she didn't notice. 'It's the soul of the place, you can't capture that in words.'

'Which ones will we chose for this job?' Carol asked.

'They're all so good it's difficult to decide, Kate, what do you think?'

She didn't reply, her mind lost in the Sierra Nevada.

'Kate?'

'She wouldn't stop talking a minute ago, and now we can't get a word out of her.'

Jack moved, and stood beside her, and she turned her head to look at him. For a long second, probably that's all it was, she melted into the brown eyes which smiled at her, and knew without a doubt that the feelings which had drawn her to this man were still as strong and vibrant as ever.

'Your opinion is needed by your colleagues,' he said.

'I think these are even more dramatic than your previous work, particularly the ones with the late evening light, though the paler more delicate ones are good too...' Words tripped off her tongue, and she was terrified that if she didn't keep talking, she would blurt out, I love you, Jack Linley, I love you.

'We want three this time,' Mags said.

'I'm going to have to leave, so you can decide. Are you coming, Kate?' Carol asked.

'Oh yes...' Her reply was uncertain.

'Mags will make the final choice, Jack, I'm sorry.' Carol walked towards the door.

'It's a pity you have to go, Carol, I was hoping you'd stay for a bite to eat, but maybe Kate and Mags might?'

'I've been trying to persuade Kate to take up Yoga, and the course starts tonight,' Carol said pointedly.

'I'm sorry, Jack, suppose I'd better go as well.' Kate knew exactly what she was playing at.

'Don't forget to come to the opening of the exhibition. It's on the fifteenth of December, but no doubt Vincent will send you an invite.'

'I've nowhere special to go this evening, so I'll accept your offer, my gain, your loss, girls.' Mags was chuffed.

'Right, let's go.' Carol sped down the stairs.

Kate said a quick rushed goodbye, and followed her.

'I'll see you out.' He moved close behind, and she was very much aware of his proximity, already regretting the plan she had made with Carol a couple of weeks ago.

'Mags is over the moon by the look of her,' Carol said as they drove out through the gates.

'Yea,' Kate agreed.

'It's a great chance for her, and he must be unattached, can't see him inviting us for a meal if his wife is going to arrive home any minute.'

'I don't think he's married.'

'Fantastic! He's a nice guy, and Mags really likes him.'

'That's quite obvious,' Kate murmured.

The exercise routine they were put through by the extremely

supple young woman was tough even for a first night. Asanas, a series of postures which put Kate's body under some strain, symbolising the connection between the earth below and the heavens above. In the microcosm, the spine along which the energy centres of the body are aligned is the source of health. She liked that idea, and enjoyed the exercises, and although she wasn't so steady standing on one leg, she found Downward Dog, Triangle, and the sequence of movements, Surya Namaskar, Salute to the Sun, somewhat easier. The names went into her mind and out again, all mixed up by the time they reached the meditation. She was supposed to be concentrating her mind on a point of focus, the breath, to be attentive to the present moment, memories and imagination both distractions. But however hard she tried, she wasn't able to erase Jack, blank him out and send him back to where he belonged. His eyes and smile were her point of focus.

And what about Mags, who so longed for someone to share her life? I have everything, she reminded herself. Dermot isn't the ideal, but who has that? Maybe it's fate that Mags likes Jack. Maybe they were meant to be together.

At the end of the class, she listened to the teacher talking about Yoga, how it is the stilling of the restless fluctuations of the mind, and the search for silence, the beginning and end of all thought, hoping for nothing, desiring nothing. That particular aspect of it struck a discordant note, and her feelings all coalesced into a jumble of confusion, the complete opposite to what she was supposed to achieve. The memories of those days she spent with Jack had been resurrected and dusted down. She imagined herself lying on a beach beside him, or in the car listening to a CD of that guitar music which he loved, sitting opposite him at dinner, or kissing, or touching, or...she dragged her thoughts back with difficulty from where they had gone, and concentrated on the voice of the teacher. She wasn't going to be a very good candidate for this, her mind uncontrolled and transitory.

'You did very well.' Carol pushed the gear into her sports bag.

'You're fit enough.'

'I don't know if it's for me, everyone else seemed to know what they were doing, and I'll probably be stiff as a board tomorrow.'

'That'll ease out, I promise you, and you'll feel so much better, particularly if you get the hang of the meditation. I do ten minutes morning and evening and it helps me deal with an eighteen-year-old who thinks she's twenty-eight. You'll come again next week?'

'I probably will, I've booked in now anyway.'

'And try and make time to pick up the mat, blocks and a belt in one of the sports shops. Then you'll be able to practice at home.'

'Yea.'

'You don't sound all that enthusiastic.'

'I enjoyed it, but don't know if I can do it. I felt like a baby elephant to tell you the truth. I was the heaviest there and the only beginner as far as I could see.'

'That's silly, people come in all sorts and sizes, and as you're back on the diet the pounds are bound to come off again if you stick with it. And remember it's non-competitive, everyone has their own level.'

'Yea.'

Kate called in to see Uncle Bill most evenings, always anxious about him. He was so much more unsteady on his feet lately and showed his age, although he wouldn't admit it. He still insisted on going out every day for his walk, refusing to change his routine for anyone.

She kissed him, and they walked in together. 'How is the pain in your back?'

'I'll survive.'

'Did you eat that casserole I cooked for you?'

'Of course I did. Come in, I'm watching a film.' He led the way into the kitchen and pointed to the other armchair, the rambling-roses loose cover now beginning to show its age also. The dark moquette covering of the original upholstery was showing through, and she decided that she must try and do a job on it sometime. But she said nothing and sat down. It was difficult to drop in on Uncle Bill for a few minutes. It had to be at least an hour to watch whatever was on the television, and she couldn't open her mouth while the programme was on, not a word. But it suited her tonight, and she lay her head on the back of the comfortable chair and closed her eyes, feeling worn out. Meeting Jack this evening had sent her into shock. All she wanted to do was sleep and forget, wondering would she always be reminded when tall dark-haired men appeared, or black jeeps, or when she heard someone mention Spain? And would these unexpected feelings destabilize her life, her steady successful life at which she had worked so hard over the years, all her time and energy invested in her family? She was a happily married woman who had let herself be carried away by another man's attention just because her husband was too busy to spend time with her.

'How about a cup of tea?' Bill asked as soon as there was an ad break.

She pushed herself out of the chair slowly.

'Bring in the chocolate biscuits, there should be a few left.' He looked at his watch. 'The film will be on again soon, so hurry up.'

In the small back kitchen, Kate made tea for them both and took out the crumpled packet of chocolate biscuits. There were only about three or four left and they were mostly broken, so she searched for a fresh packet which she found eventually behind the row of tinned soup in the press. She carried in the tea and the biscuits on a small tray and handed him a mug.

'Where are the chocolate ones?' he asked.

'They're broken.'

'I told you to get them, they're the ones I want, not these pinky mushy things,' he rapped, his lips pursed and forehead creased, a Steptoe lookalike.

She returned with them and sat down again, watching him break the biscuits even smaller with his fingers and then pick the pieces out of the packet one by one. This was something new, the normally fastidious man had crumbs all over his grey cardigan. She thought it was strange and so out of character. She had a sudden vision of him doing all those unexpected things people with early Alzheimers do, and thought perhaps that it had already begun to happen. Kate looked at him there, intent on the television, and tried to put it out of her head, she couldn't bear to think about it.

Chapter Twenty

With his work for the exhibition finished and already delivered to the Nestor Gallery, Jack took out the sketches he had made of Kate. Since he had met her again they appeared to be so much more alive, her natural warmth and beauty superimposed on them. Her hand seemed to move, eyelids flickered in sleep, and skin blushed, not golden tanned, but softly fair, the real colour of Kate. He flicked through the different drawings, already seeing the sizes and shapes of the paintings. Some would be oblong, others oval, or round, to suit the shape of her body. Excited, he squirted paint on his palette and began.

He took a view from the side of the intricate bone structure that was her shoulder, the light catching the curve as if she was standing against pale yellow sunshine, with that ethereal quality of the dawn, the rest of her body sleeping in shadow. He was so glad she wasn't just skin and bone like Mags. There was a roundness to Kate, a soft tenderness which he loved, and a very special beauty that he knew was going to be difficult to capture on canvas.

On the evening of the opening of his exhibition, people filtered in slowly. They were a mixed bag as usual, and Vincent quickly singled out the people who were more likely to buy and introduced him. While some of them loved to discuss every detail of his work, others shied away, preferring to browse without feeling that they were being put under pressure. Jack would have preferred to have stayed out of the whole thing if he had a choice.

'Now, Mr. Linley, do tell me of your inspiration when you painted this particular work, the subliminal message, the erotic symbolism?'

This came from an elderly woman, her arm tucked in his.

And then the typical Dubliner, the tough guy.

'Jack, I don't know much about this art stuff, all that mad colour, the mixed up look, but I like them, can't understand what you're getting at, but I like them.'

And the flowery buxom woman with the loud jolly laugh who informed everyone within hearing distance that she had already purchased two of the larger works.

'You must come around to see our collection. We'll have to put some of the other paintings in storage to make room for yours, but I'm tired looking at them. I'll give you my number, be sure to call me.'

He played the role as was expected, it was part of the territory and had to be endured. There were a lot of well-known faces here from the entertainment world, radio, television, the literary establishment, and he had to include them also. But every now and then he glanced towards the door, and wondered whether Kate had arrived, but it was so packed with people it was impossible to tell. Then someone called his name, and he turned to find Chris and Eddie struggling through the crowd towards him. He was glad to see them, particularly as it seemed that no-one else in the family was going to bother even though he had invited them last Sunday when he was at home for lunch.

He brought his attention back to the present and forced himself to do the PR thing, laughing and joking, until suddenly Mags and Carol were there. Mags smiling, hand outstretched to hold his as he kissed her on the cheek, an automatic response, he had been doing it all evening.

'You've reserved our paintings?' Her eyes were bright and excited.

'Yes, don't worry.'

'How is the exhibition going?' Carol asked.

'There have been quite a few sold apparently, according to Vincent.'

'We're so glad we had a preview and could buy directly from you, we wouldn't have had our first choice here.'

142

'Have some wine, girls.' He waved to the waiter who pushed through the crowd with his tray, and they accepted a glass.

He glanced around, hoping that Kate would suddenly appear behind them, and finally, unable to hold himself back any longer, he asked if she was coming as well.

'Something came up, she asked us to give you her apologies,' Mags explained.

He was silent for a few seconds, his gut tight with disappointment, and couldn't think of anything to say, only then realising that he hadn't introduced the girls to Chris and Eddie. He did that and they talked for a while, until Vincent hustled him up to the top of the room and the Spanish Ambassador made the formal opening speech, which was followed by press photographs. There were a couple of shots taken with Mags, who happened to be standing beside him, posed and giggly, smiling "cheese" for the camera.

Kate had eaten alone. There was no-one at home this evening, and she sat at the table staring into space, her thoughts with Jack at the Nestor. Her excuse had been trumped-up, Dermot and his client nowhere near the house this evening. But she was restless, and wandered into the lounge carrying her mug of tea. The large room was perfectly appointed, dominated by her most precious possessions, the two landscapes for which she had scrimped and saved years before. She walked across the room and adjusted the fall of a cream silk curtain. Her footsteps seemed loud on the wooden floor, and she was suddenly struck by the extreme quiet, so unusual for this house, the vibration of Shane's music always there in the background. She went through into the dining-room, and sat at the gleaming mahogany table, putting the mug of tea on the smooth surface, uncaring whether it marked or not.

Suddenly she was irritated with the perfection all around her, something she had created, something which she was not. Maybe that was why she was so fussy. There was so little she could do with herself, she put all her energies into her home. She remembered their previous house with its ethnic décor, strong

143

colours and loud patterns which were probably out of fashion even then, and always full of kids, untidy and noisy. And she was relaxed and happy in the middle of it, a few stone heavier than she was even now. In those days Dermot loved to be at home. He played football with the boys, took them to matches and on fishing expeditions. All four of them spent long days at the beach, and had picnics to the country, they were a real family then.

Now she lived like a museum piece in her beautiful house, no boys running in looking for her to kiss a bruised knee, or dry tears, or hug, and promise that Mum would make it all right. And no Dermot shouting "I'm home" in the evening, grabbing her as she tried to get the dinner, and kissing her amid the screams and shouts of excitement as the boys fought for his attention.

Suddenly, she hurried upstairs, took a quick shower, changed her clothes, and within a short time she was driving into town. It was almost eight, but Jack should still be there, people always hung around at these things enjoying the last of the free drink. At least she hoped so, driving too fast, urging the red lights to turn green, and the green not to turn orange, like cats' eyes blinking at her. In the city she had to contend with the busy late night shopping crowds, and it was difficult to find parking. It was almost eight-thirty when she walked towards the gallery, anxiety in her step, her heart fluttering, the compulsion to get there quickly before he had left forcing her almost into a run. She turned the corner and could see the open door of the house across the road, and then, just at that moment, a group of people came out. Jack was to the forefront, Mags beside him, followed by Chris and Eddie. They climbed into the first taxi which was parked outside, Vincent and others she didn't know took the second. She stopped abruptly, numb with shock and disappointment, and then turned to hurry back the way she had come.

'I feel much closer to Jack after the other night,' Mags sighed.

'You'll be invited around for Sunday lunch next.' Carol sipped her glass of red wine.

'And wait until you see this, girls.' Mags pulled a photograph from her bag and held it out for their inspection. 'I knew the photographer there and he gave me a copy. It's a really nice shot, isn't it, just the two of us together?'

'He's quite attractive in a craggy sort of way. You make a lovely couple.'

'I'm praying he'll ask me out over Christmas, it's such a romantic time of the year. There will be dinners and parties, and afterwards back to my place, or his, and maybe even stay over.'

'You can engineer that, no better woman.'

Kate said nothing as she ate her dessert, luscious sinfully gorgeous bread-and-butter pudding, something she could never resist. The craving within her had taken over again, and these last few days she was bingeing like an alcoholic. Comfort eating it was called, and she understood all about that as her mood had swung downwards since the night of the exhibition, like the pendulum of a broken clock.

'And he drinks in the Old Stand. I've been in there countless times with the girls and I've never spotted him, so that will be the place from now on.'

'I somehow think this guy is going to find it very hard to escape you.' Carol finished off her chocolate cake. 'What do you reckon, Kate? Can you see them as an item this time next year?'

'Yea...' she agreed. But listening to Mags going on and on about Jack almost made her feel sick.

'If he does ask me out, I'll have to buy him a Christmas present. You know his sister very well, Kate, has he any interests apart from painting? I know he likes to sail, but I don't know if it's a regular thing with him these days so I think I'll steer clear of buying anything in that line.'

'I've no idea.' She denied any knowledge of him. Jealousy surged again. It spoiled everything these days and grew stronger and stronger inside her. So much so she couldn't even bear to see

Mags and be subjected to a further episode of what she had said, or he had said, and should she phone him, or call around, or invite him, and what do you think, Kate? It came into every conversation, even ruining their Christmas lunch.

'Another glass of wine, Mags?' Carol held the bottle over her glass.

'Why not, pour away.'

'And Kate, same again for you?'

'Go ahead, what are a few calories one way or the other at this stage?'

'Looks like the diet has gone out the window?' Carol filled her glass.

For Kate it was as un-Christmassy as it could be. Normally she threw herself into the season with great enthusiasm, but this year was different. She had had to force herself to ask Shane to buy a tree, and then dressed it, arranged the gold leafed garlands on the mantles, the holly wreath on the front door, and lastly had set up the little crib on the hall table. She had done it on her own, no-one else in the family particularly interested.

*

Jack lost track of time, bringing out the images from the depths of himself. It was a slow emergence, like trying to find someone in a dream and he remembered that morning as he sketched Kate lying in his bed, the charcoal flying across the page, building the shadows and undulations of the intrinsic softness that was Kate as she had slowly emerged from sleep.

It had all come back with a vengeance since he had met her again, and as he worked he felt he should be able to send messages to her as if they were telepathic, and wanted her to come to him through some deep inexplicable need that she had. The need that had shown itself on their last night in Mojacar.

*

The parcel was sent up from reception in the mid-afternoon, and sat on her desk with the other post while she dealt with various last-minute items which needed attention before Christmas. It was their busiest time. Most of the orders had to be completed for clients who wouldn't wait until the New Year, and every second mattered at this late stage.

At the end of the day, she picked it up only then noticing that it was marked "personal", and assumed from its square flattish shape that it was a diary, or chocolates. She unfolded the paper, amazed to see a painting of the courtyard in Jack's house in Spain. The white marble fountain was exquisite, with vibrant cherry red flowers cascading onto the old terracotta tiles. Sunshine sparkled through the spray of water, and caught the sheen on the back of the blue dolphin. It was beautiful. She touched the rough surface with her fingers to feel the ridges and sweeps of paint, and the image blurred suddenly as her eyes moistened with tears. Her immediate impulse was to phone Jack and thank him, but she knew she wouldn't be able to control herself and then he would know everything. But practicality told her that he had probably given each of them a painting, and all of the excitement evaporated.

That night she went to bed early, and in the privacy of the bathroom pulled the accompanying card out of the envelope again. It was in aid of the Home Again charity, and inside was the usual Christmas greeting, and he had written "To Kate" at the top and his own name at the bottom. His handwriting was large, with a strength about it that she could almost feel. But she was disappointed that there were no flowery love wishes, or see you in the New Year wishes, nothing else.

The company had sent him a card, posted in a batch by one of the girls in the office. A present at this stage, in response to his, would be far too obvious a return gesture.

She looked at the painting constantly, going over every moment of those days in Spain again, and then she took down the print which hung on the wall in the bedroom. It was a cheap and cheerful thing she had picked up because it matched the pale yellows and whites of the décor, and she replaced it with Jack's painting. She rang the following morning from the phone at reception, thinking that it would be the best place, with too many people passing by for her to speak softly, or be emotional. 'Thank you so much for the painting of the fountain. It's beautiful, an original Jack Linley, I'll have to start a collection now.' He seemed pleased, and they chatted for a couple of minutes about work and after that there wasn't a lot left to say. Just Happy Christmas, and have a great New Year, enjoy.

'Guess what, Jack Linley sent me a case of wine for Christmas, did he send the same to you two?' Carol asked excitedly.

Kate nodded, but kept her eyes on the papers she was leafing through.

'Yea, just a business gesture by the look of it.' Mags' eyes were green pools of tragedy. The corners of her mouth curved downwards with disappointment. 'And Gypsy Rose told me that we'd be together by Christmas, and that he was the man for me. She even described him, tall, dark, and creative, I was so sure it was Jack.'

'You'd believe anything that woman tells you, it's a load of rubbish.' Carol scribbled notes. 'Could be anyone, a farmer, a carpenter, a writer, there are tall dark creative men everywhere.'

'But I thought we'd spend Christmas together, late nights, and long mornings, breakfast in bed. I had it all planned, and I'd even bought some new sexy underwear.'

'There's still a couple of days to go.'

'I rang him and thanked him for the wine, but not a word out of him, not a squeak about wanting to see me over the holidays. He's going to be working, would you believe, except for Christmas day, when he has to put in an appearance at home.'

'Enough about your personal life, Mags, we're busy.'

Kate was glad of Carol's sharp interruption, she wanted to cut this conversation short as well and keep her mind on work. She shouldn't be thinking of how she knew him so intimately. She could have told Mags all about the shape of his shoulders, and the smoothness of his body. How her fingers had worked along the edges of his bones and then to the softer parts of him which were warm, like satin, and responded to her touch instantly. She remembered that night when they lay in his bed close together, their rhythm exactly right, slowly at first and building. Now she could feel tiny beads of moisture on her forehead, her pulse raced, and she wondered why he had sent her the painting.

'It's ruined Christmas for me,' Mags moaned.

Kate intervened, ready to scream "shut-up" by this stage. 'Carol, what's the progress on that Morgan job? When are the carpets going to be fitted? We can't finish the curtains until we have final measurements.'

Carol pushed a box of tissues across the desk, and Mags snuffled into a sheaf of them.

'Look, he's probably not the type to dive into the deep end of anything, you're jumping the gun as usual.'

'I can't help myself, I'm in love.'

What's being in love? Am I in love? Kate wondered. Surely that's only for teenagers, not for someone who's nearly forty, a middle-aged married woman. Following the plan which had been cast in a church when she was seventeen, the first half of her life, like an act in a play, was almost completed now. She thought about the early days, when Dermot told her constantly that he adored her and making love was great. Those happy baby powder puke days, the he took mine, he hit me days, the moody grunting not telling you anything days, the growing up into tall young men days. And now the success and having plenty of money days, when Dermot didn't tell her how he felt at all, and when making love had become a quick roll over. She was almost into the second half, and the love they had known had waned like a spent candle.

'You'll just have to play a cool waiting game if you want him,' Carol advised Mags.

Kate's thoughts ran riot. Was the painting full of hidden nuances? A secret code which was saying let's have another fling? Did he think she was easy because she was a married woman and unavailable, and he was a man who could pick and choose, eat the cherry off the cake, and leave the rest, the mundane, to the boring too-long married people. Or was there something more?

*

Jack worked day and night only finally surfacing to the realisation that there was an outside world when the doorbell kept ringing insistently. Unless he knew someone was coming, he didn't bother to answer it, but now he was forced to lift the intercom.

'Would you for God's sake get down here and open the door. I'm freezing,' Chris demanded.

'It's you playing a tune on the doorbell, is it?' he bantered.

'If you keep me waiting for one more second, Jack, I'll do for you.'

Reluctantly, he went down and opened the door, and as she stepped in she bent to pick up some letters from the floor which had been delivered.

'Your post.' She threw it on the hall table, and then hugged him.

'Hey, be careful, I don't want to get paint on your expensive gear.'

He stepped back, but she just laughed.

'I'd be valuable then. You could put my clothes into the exhibition, I might even make some money.' She went straight upstairs, and he followed, praying she wouldn't recognise Kate in the painting on the easel, and in the sketches scattered about.

'Have you had lunch? I could do a pasta,' he offered, anxious to divert her.

'No thanks, I'm meeting Eddie in town, I love Grafton Street on Christmas Eve, and I still have to pick up a few last-minute bits and pieces.'

'It's Christmas Eve already?'

'Yes, and I suppose you've got nothing done?' She wandered around the studio.

150

'Actually, I'm a bit better than usual.' For the family he had taken the easy way out and given vouchers. Gifts for friends and clients were wrapped and delivered by a wine merchant on his behalf. The only one he dealt with personally was the painting for Kate which he had taken around to her office. He had asked to see her, but was told she was at a meeting, and left no message.

His mother had called him last week and discussed the plan for Christmas Day. Chris had invited him to her place in the morning for drinks, and he had other friends who had to be seen as well, but while he had agreed to meet everyone, all the arrangements had flown out of his mind as he worked.

He would have given anything to be spending Christmas with Kate, wandering down Grafton Street together, listening to the Christmas Carols being sung by the Simon group and savouring the atmosphere, sauntering in and out of the shops, and buying her something really special.

'Fancy a glass of wine or something else?' he asked Chris.

'A cup of tea will do fine.'

'Come downstairs.' He waited for her to follow him.

'I'll be down in a minute, I want to see what you've been doing.'

He turned and took the stairs two at a time, anxious to make this the quickest tea he'd ever made, and get Chris out of the studio before she started asking questions. But he had only just put the water on to boil when there was a shout from above and he finished what he was doing at a more normal pace, put out two mugs, milk, sugar, biscuits, and went back upstairs.

She was standing in front of a painting of Kate in profile and holding up one of the sketches. 'This is really something else.'

He stood back and tried to see it through her eyes.

'It is supposed to be Kate, I presume, based on the sketches?'

'Just happens to look a bit like her, coincidence.'

'Come off it, do you think I'm stupid?'

They continued to look at the painting for a moment in silence.

'Let's go down,' he said.

In the kitchen, they sat at the table.

'So you didn't take big sister's advice after all?' She nibbled a chocolate biscuit.

'It was just one of those things.' He had a sudden very strong feeling of loss. A beginning and an end. That analogy reminding him of the death of his unborn child, something else over which he had had no control.

'Have you seen her since you came home?'

'Only in a business context.'

'It's just as well, I told you she's not for you. Anyway I thought it was Mags who was featuring in your life these days, the pair of you seemed to get on like a house on fire at the dinner on the night of the exhibition, and both of us thought she seemed ideal for you.'

'No, it isn't Mags,' he said abruptly.

After she had left, he flicked through the post. Bills, a bank statement, and a couple of Christmas cards which he opened. The first was from Vincent, and the other from one of his friends. He propped them on the mantle, and noticed the card he had received the other day from Lee O'Donnell Design. He opened it, and felt again that despondency which had swept through him when he read the rather impersonal greetings from all three of the girls. Kate's phone call in response to his gift of the painting had been polite and had given him no hope. He went back to work then, but he had lost his enthusiasm and sat staring at the painting, dissatisfied with it and life in general.

Later, there was another ring at the doorbell, and he went to the window and glanced out, not sure whether he was glad or not to see Mags outside. But the thought occurred to him that where Mags was, Kate could be, and it was enough to send him hurrying down.

'I'm heading into town to meet the girls for Christmas drinks, fancy joining us?' She looked attractive as ever in a black suede coat trimmed with fur.

'Yes, why not, I could do with a break. But I'll follow you in later. I presume Kate and Carol will be there?'

'No, they're all tied up with their domestic duties, not fancy free like me.'

He was disappointed, but he had committed himself now, and it didn't seem that he had anything better to do.

Chapter Twenty-One

Christmas Day was a performance. All the Masons and extended in-laws, including Uncle Bill and Irene, were invited over to Dermot's sister, Mary, and husband Des, to mingle with their friends and family. The house in Donnybrook was decorated like something out of winter wonderland without the snow, the trees in the large garden were festooned with sparkling lights, and inside the theme was red-gold, glimmering baubles and painted leaves on every possible surface. There were magnificent arrangements of red roses, lilies, and what seemed like hundreds of thick gold candles. Shane, Conor and Nicola, came over and Kate was pleased that her sons didn't have to be dragged to such an event as in other years. Everyone was dressed in new Christmas gear, with a lot of glitter. She was sorry she hadn't worn something more glamourous, her wine velvet jacket and full length cream skirt looked even less than ordinary.

'G & T for you, Kate.' Des poured the gin into a crystal glass, added tonic, ice, lemon, and handed it to her. 'And Dermot, I've a nice ten year old malt for you, how does that sound?'

Kate sipped the cool drink and helped herself to crisps which she dipped into a pinky garlic sauce. She wandered in search of Mary, anxious to offer her assistance if it was needed. The kitchen was shining steel grey and chrome, the counter tops clear of any food, or implements, or anything which looked out of place. So different when she was doing Christmas dinner. Every possible space occupied by something or other, people always congregating there while she tried to work around them.

'Hi Kate.' Mary rushed in, dressed in a dramatic bright red suit, her glass of vodka in one hand and a cigarette in the other. 'My husband has ordered the kitchen staff to bring him some more lemons,' she said heatedly.

'I'll get them,' Kate offered.

'No thanks, they're just here.' She removed the cover from a silver dish. 'But he can get them himself next time, who does he think I am, one of the hired help?'

'Anything else I can do?'

'You're not supposed to be doing anything today, have a few drinks and enjoy yourself.' She disappeared again.

Slowly Kate walked through the crowded house, smiling and nodding, but joining no-one. Eventually she went into the conservatory where she found Uncle Bill sitting with a few of the more elderly relatives. She sat on the broad arm of his chair, and dropped a kiss on his forehead. But he made a disagreeable face, and sipped his glass of Guinness. 'Happy Christmas again,' she said.

'What's happy about it, would you mind telling me? You can't hear yourself think with all these people.' His snap was typical Bill, even more cranky than usual out of his own environment.

'Most of them will be leaving later, and then it will be just ourselves,' she said, but he humphed in response.

She attempted conversation with the other people there but was met with mostly stolid silence, but then Aunt Betty piped up through pink smeared lips, and loose hairy double chins. 'Have you put on a few pounds, Kate? I thought you were slimmer the last time I saw you.'

'I'm going back on my diet in the New Year, Betty.'

'When I was young I hadn't a pick on me, thoroughbred stock, my Tommy used to say.'

'I had the winner of the Grand National, sixteen-to-one, did you know that?' someone else said as they began to wake up.

'I won fifty euro at the bingo.'

'I know a woman who was on the Lotto programme on the television. She lives down the road from us and won twenty-five thousand, a car, and a holiday.'

'I hate that programme. It's stupid.'

'Don't you send in your three stars?'

'I've sent in hundreds of them, but I was never pulled out of that plastic thing they have.'

'There were hundreds killed, thousands killed, in the Second World War,' Uncle Bill muttered.

'I was only a child then.'

'Pull the other one.'

They argued on, and she went back to Des for another drink. Her own state of mind was not helped by the level of their conversation, all shunted out of the way by Mary. She walked through the crowd again, watched heads nodding, mouths opening, closing, heard high-pitched chattering, shrieks, loud guffaws of laughter, then suddenly a familiar voice close by, and she was embraced by Irene. 'Where's Dermot?'

'Somewhere around.' Kate hadn't seen him since they arrived.

'This is fabulous isn't it? Mary really knows how to do it.' The gold-lame clad figure posed.

She's like an Oscar, thought Kate, and wanted to laugh. But wouldn't you like to look like an Oscar? she asked herself. Some chance, snowball in hell. Suddenly, she wanted to go home, flake out in front of the television, and watch old movies, Judy Garland, Fred Astaire and Ginger Rogers, this was all just too much of an effort.

'Oh there he is over there. Come on, he's probably wondering where we are.' The glimmering figure moved away from her and she followed automatically. Irene called his name, but he was deeply-engrossed with a skinny model type. She was probably early twenties, tanned from a couple of weeks in the sun, or maybe that false tan they were all using these days. Long dark hair framed her pretty face in a casual untidy fashion, her figure was encased in tight black, and she smiled up at him, listening intently to whatever he was saying. Kate watched. Her stomach tightened like a fist in its lumpy cellulite folds, and sent a swirl of heartburn up into her throat, sick-making.

'Dermot?' Irene moved closer to him.

156

He dragged his eyes away from the girl and stared at her. She kissed him and insisted on being introduced. Kate moved back a little, feeling uncomfortable, noticing the telltale frown between his eyes which always appeared when he was annoyed about something. Then she turned and headed for the downstairs-loo where she sat and knocked back the rest of the G & T in the glass. Something exploded inside her then, and she wanted to get a lipstick and scrawl all over the black marble walls, and across the mirrors which seemed to be everywhere. Even the ceiling reflected and gave no compliments. She had an urge to throw down the white embroidered towels on the pristine floor and stamp on them, run the water, and leave the place the way Dermot left the bathroom at home. I hate this house of mirrors, I want out now.

She thought of Jack. He never made her feel like an oversized hippo. It hadn't seemed to bother him, but of course she wasn't this weight when they met. She knew that she shouldn't be thinking about him at all, but still couldn't forget him, a man who wasn't much more than a stranger to her.

How can you love someone you don't know?

What is he like first thing in the morning when he wakes full of grouch, with a grizzly beard and red-rimmed eyes? And how would he react if it appeared you had done something to annoy him. What did you do with my after-shave? Who moved the telephone book? Where are my car keys? Would he go on and on like Dermot as a small thing escalated into a huge thing, the whole family involved until no-one knew what started it? And that's the way it is when you love someone you do know. There was a rattle at the door, and quickly she washed her hands, and exited the place with as much aplomb as she could muster. Now people were leaving and she was drawn into the smaller family circle, forced to make light conversation, on her third G & T.

Des was pontificating. 'They'll be voted out before the next election, the people won't put up with it.'

'Politics, who wants to talk about it?' Mary groaned.

'They're not the worst.' Dermot puffed on a large cigar.

157

'No? What about health, the hospitals, the cut-backs, while they line their own pockets, making the most of their stay in power?'

'They're a crowd of chancers.'

'All tarred with the one brush.'

She watched Shane, Conor and Nicola sitting across the room talking with the cousins. Drinking cans and putting in the hours because they were expected to by the parents, but bored stiff really.

Dermot gulped his whiskey, and stood on the balls of his feet, moving backwards and forwards with a self-satisfied smirk on his face, his generous belly overhanging the belt of his navy pin-stripe trousers. It was all about weight, she thought. As usual, imagining herself to be even heavier than she actually was. She undid the button of the jacket, and tried to find a comfortable position on the couch. She was on her fourth drink now, and that was probably a good proportion of the points allocation for the day already.

I'll think about that tomorrow, she decided.

Chapter Twenty-Two

Kate found it difficult to get herself motivated this year. There was a crippling dullness in the pit of her stomach which grew steadily stronger and as she sat at her desk on the first day back, more than once she stopped what she was doing, and stared into space, feeling so...trapped. It was the first time the word had entered her head, and it seemed to explain her mood exactly, which was like being lost in a maze of high thick green hedges, running frantically this way and that looking for the exit but each time ending up in a cul-de-sac. To get out of the claustrophobic atmosphere, she went into Carol's office. 'Will you go through these estimates with me, please?' She sank into the chair in front of her desk.

'And you can tell me what you think of my ideas for the pub job.' Carol pushed a drawing across the desk.

'I hate pub jobs.'

'You didn't always hate them, they were our bread-and-butter once upon a time.'

'I was almost relieved we didn't get that Cork job, Dracula's Castle.'

'I thought it would have been fun.'

'It's completely over the top, all that reproduction Gothic rubbish. Did you see the final thing?'

'I saw a photo in the paper. Anyway, this isn't much better, they want a medieval theme as well, but not so extreme.' She looked at her. 'Hey, what's going on with you? You're pale as death. Is something wrong?'

'No, I'm just a bit tired.'

'It's the New Year blues. Why don't you plan your holidays, book the flights to Spain? I always find even making the decision gives me a boost. I'm definitely going somewhere really exotic this year. I wouldn't have minded going with Mags to the Caribbean, but then we both can't be away at the same time.'

'I've gone off Spain.'

'Well, what about the Canaries, or one of those romantic places, Rome, or Prague?'

'There's very little chance of getting Dermot to take time off work.'

'Go on, persuade him, you should know how to do that at this stage,' Carol giggled.

'Happy New Year!' Mags appeared dramatically through the door, and hugged the two of them.

'And it seems to have been good for you, coffee?' Kate poured three cups from the percolator.

'It wasn't that exciting, but I caught up with a few friends, and enjoyed myself. Ate, drank and slept a lot, so now I'm raring to go.'

'With a new man in your life?' Carol asked.

'No, not exactly, but I had an interesting Christmas Eve with someone we all know.'

'Would it be our artist friend by any chance?' Carol glanced at Kate and laughed.

'Yea, I called around to Jack on my way into town, and asked him to join us, and we had a great night.'

'And did it work out the way you wanted?'

'No, unfortunately he headed off home early, but I enjoyed seeing him again.'

'And since?'

'Sadly no, but I've great hopes for the New Year.'

Carol was doing all the talking, and Kate had to force herself to seem enthusiastic for Mags' sake. If they were going to be an item then this was something she would have to accept, and not fall apart every time his name was mentioned. Suddenly, at that moment, she resolved to push herself out of the doldrums and make the most of what she had.

First, she decided to go on the cabbage-soup diet, and that very night made a big pot of it and began. It was hard at first to eat soup only, and fruit, but as she added a little more food each day it became easier, and she was delighted to discover that she had lost five pounds by the end of the week. It was a great start.

She tried to make things better with Dermot. A few days away together might give them a chance to talk. She wasn't looking for much more. It was probably up to her to make an effort, married to Dermot for better or worse, in sickness and in health, until death do us part. She asked herself if she believed in that and the answer was yes. This wild talk about leaving was meaningless emotional drivel, and her attraction to Jack Linley pure fantasy.

Over dinner, she broached the subject with him, suggesting that they take a trip somewhere altogether different.

'I've no time for holidays. I have to be in Alicante next week on business.'

'Could we have a few days off, do you think, combine the two?' she asked tentatively. Although she didn't want to go back there, she knew it was something she would have to face some time, particularly since they had their own house and would obviously holiday there for years to come.

'I'll be over and back as quick as I can. There will be no time for lazing around, I'm far too busy.'

'What about a weekend somewhere? I feel we've drifted apart and I want us to spend some time together, just the two of us,' she appealed to him, suddenly wanting it so much and willing to forget all that had gone before.

'What are you talking about? There's nothing wrong with us. We're as good as we ever were, you're imagining things.'

His gruff crusty response held no understanding of how she felt. Fixedly, she watched his hands move, and winced when the knife scraped the surface of the plate with a little squeak as he quickly cut and swallowed what was left of his dinner.

'Right, I have to make a few calls,' he said and left the room.

'I had that fellow around the other day,' Uncle Bill said.

'Who was that?' Kate asked.

'You know the man...'

'Oh yes.' She nodded as if she understood.

'I've taken her out of it, old bag.'

Now she knew, the solicitor.

It was nothing unusual, Uncle Bill had changed his will at least twenty times over the past few years. He liked doing that. His money which he had saved was left to various people, charities, the church, relatives, neighbours, they were all in the will at one time or other. Should someone be very nice to him, as many of the neighbours were, they spent a bit of time on it until they looked crooked at him or didn't do something he expected and the solicitor was called again and they were deleted. He never mentioned whether Kate was in the will or not, and she didn't want to know.

'Can we look at the bank stuff? A letter came the other day, but I couldn't understand it.' He sent her off to fetch the box in the sideboard where he kept all his statements and correspondence. Once again, she explained how the statement worked, but he shook his head, puzzled.

'Look, that's your pension going in every month.'

'Yes, yes.'

'And there are the direct-debits which pay the phone and the electricity.' She pointed to the column. 'And the cheques that you write sometimes.'

'I see, now I want you to take this to the bank for me.' He pushed a bundle of money across the table. 'And put that in the building society.' He handed her another, and she picked them up noting that each contained one hundred euro. She was about to warn him against keeping too much money in the house, but didn't bother, he never listened anyway. 'And could you sew a couple of buttons on to my jacket? And tell that Mrs. Murphy next door to keep her kids out of my front garden. They're always kicking their football in.' He paused for breath.

'Yes sure, I'll do that,' she said. But didn't add that she certainly wasn't going to pass his message on to Mrs. Murphy who was a most kind and generous person.

'What did I say then?' He looked at her quizzically a moment later. 'And what's all that money doing there?'

'It's yours.'

'What? Where did I get it?'

'I suppose you saved it out of your pension.'

'No, no, it's yours, it must have fallen out of your bag. Put it back in before you lose it.'

She did as he said, worn out a little with the signs of his increasing senility. She had discussed it more than once with Dermot who was no help at all.

'He'll have to go into a nursing home, and I hope he's got enough money because I'm not paying. The house will have to be sold to cover it, but then who knows how long he will live and whether the money will last. Better off if the old ticker gave up and he kicked the bucket tomorrow.'

'The problem is that he won't consider a nursing home, not for a minute,' Kate had said, always the thought in the back of her mind that she would look after him herself if it came to the worst, although how she was going to do that she didn't know.

'If he's lost his mind, then he won't know what's happening, will he?'

'But it's not constant. Sometimes he's fine, and then other times he can't remember what he has just said. I'm worried about him.' She was very concerned, and Bill seemed to be aware of what was going on in her mind as well, which was strange.

'You won't put me in one of those awful places, will you Kate?'

'Of course I won't, you'll be fine here, don't be worrying about it.'

'It's just that Tom down the road has gone to a nursing home, and so has Gladys, and there's not a word from either of them since, and they haven't bothered to visit, or write, I can't understand it at all.'

And that was today, one of his good days.

She stayed for the afternoon and did the usual cleaning, roasted a chicken, and baked a sponge cake. Bill was actually quite well able to look after himself, and was tidy in his habits, a throw-back to his naval career, but he still needed to be minded. She hated leaving him later and was sad to see his forlorn wave as she climbed into the car. In her mind, she could see him walking down the hall and into the kitchen to sit alone for the evening, no-one to talk to, or laugh with, or even ask a question, just an old man and his television.

Chapter Twenty-Three

In Alicante, Dermot was looking forward to seeing Carmen again. The first couple of evenings he had to be polite and have dinner with Manuel and the other directors and investors, ending up in the music club watching Manuel do his thing up on the stage. While he hated the dancing, he hated the singing even more, that wild keening from deep folk memories was probably great stuff if you were Spanish, but for Dermot it was a boring dirge that had to be endured. On the third night he managed to excuse himself on the pretext of visiting friends in Torrevieja and called around to see Carmen, who was her usual accommodating self.

'Derrrmot darrrling.' She embraced him in that wonderful way she had.

'Carrrmen,' he murmured, rolling his r's as he tried to pronounce her name correctly.

She looked stunning tonight, dressed in red, but as ever he had to curb his impatience and wait for the real Carmen to emerge when they returned to the apartment much later.

*

Manuel let himself in quietly, drawn there by a whispered comment about his woman which had made his blood curdle. Carmen had been seen leaving and returning with another man earlier that night.

'Who?' Manuel had rounded furiously on his informant.

'I don't know, Senor.'

'You'd better find out for me,' he demanded. No one messed with Manuel, no one poached his possessions. To think that some man had moved into his space was enough to make him want to challenge him to a duel.

Now he stood by the side of the bed, his eyes focussed on Carmen who was sleeping, her body only half-covered by a black satin sheet. He grabbed her arm and dragged her out on to the marble floor. Suddenly awoken, she screamed in fright.

'Manuel? What are you doing, Manuel?'

He lashed her face with the flat palm of his hand and she burst into tears. 'Manuel, please don't hit me, please.'

He did it once more, and then stood back and watched her pathetic efforts to clamber up from the floor on to the bed. 'Now, tell me the name of the man.'

'What man?'

'His name?' He hit her again.

'I don't know what you're talking about,' she whimpered.

'That's a lie, tell me or I'll kill you.'

'There's no-one else, Manuel, I love you, I love you.'

The argument went on and on, but she did not expose Dermot. He raged and threatened the most horrible of tortures, but still she said nothing. 'If you don't tell me the name of this pig then you can leave, I never want to see you again.' He crossed the room and swung back the wardrobe doors, mirrored and finished in brushed chrome, designed by one of the top interior people in Madrid. He began to pull her clothes out on the floor. Her casual gear in her favourite creams, beiges and soft blues were thrown in a heap, and after that her business suits, and her precious evening clothes, colourful glittering sequinned dresses, trousers, tops and swinging silk skirts, all by her favourite designers.

'Manuel, what are you doing? My clothes will be ruined,' she cried, crouched on the bed like a fearful rabbit.

But he said nothing, and continued until everything was yanked off the hangers. His attention then switched to her shoes, so many designs and colours with handbags to match, then her underwear and negligees of silk and lace. He emptied the drawers of each skimpy thong, then he opened the French doors and kicked the pile along the floor out on to the terrace.

'Manuel!'

Slowly, deliberately, he began to throw them over the edge of the balustrade. Carmen came to the door wrapped in a sheet, her dark eyes wide with horror. He was meticulous, even her collection of silk scarves did not escape, and were thrown down the two floors of the building in a soft floating rainbow of colour. In the lounge he drew back the drapes, pressed in a code on the keypad, and smoothly a panel in the wall slid back to reveal a safe. Then he emptied her magnificent collection of jewellery into a plastic bag which he found in the kitchen.

Carmen stood watching, a little child lost look on her face.

'Get out of here tonight, but I warn you, take nothing that doesn't belong to you.' He picked up her keys which lay on the hall table, the plastic bag, and a bottle of olive oil. Then he walked through the door, and closed it with a thump behind him.

'Manuel?' She followed him into the corridor, trying to keep herself covered with the sheet, but the doors of the lift slid silently closed as she reached it. She ran back inside to search in the wardrobe for something to wear, but the empty spaces yawned back at her and it was only then she remembered that in the wash-basket there should be a pair of jeans, a sweater, and the underwear she had worn last night which would have to do until she retrieved her clothes from below. But as she pulled on the jeans, something drew her back to the balcony. She looked over the edge to breathe in the acrid smell of smoke, and saw all of her clothes engulfed in flames below. It was only then she realized the significance of the olive oil.

She ran to the phone and dialled Dermot's number, but there was no reply. She left a message and then turned to look around her beautiful home. She fingered the exquisite ornaments, the pieces of art, remembering that she had thrown out almost all of her own possessions over time, placing no value on them. Now she realised how foolish it had been as she faced the prospect of walking out into the world empty-handed.

Dermot pressed in the digits of Carmen's number and waited as it rang out.

She burst into great choking sobs as soon as she heard his voice.

'What's wrong?' He was puzzled.

'It is Manuel. He came last night and it was terrible. He burned all my clothes, and he has taken my keys and now I have nada, nada.'

'Calm down Carmen, I can't make head nor tail of what you're saying.'

'I need you Dermot, I have nowhere to go now, can I come to you?'

'I'm leaving today, Carmen, I'm sorry.'

'But I have no apartment and I am afraid of Manuel, I do not know what he is going to do.' The tears began again.

'You're exaggerating, Carmen, you've just had a tiff, it will all blow over in a day or two.'

'He has found out about us. I do not know how, but I didn't tell him your name even when he kept hitting me.'

Dermot's stomach did a somersault, and dropped down with a horrible sense of being caught out. Initially, he hadn't realised that Manuel and Carmen were an item, and when she did mention it he had not taken it seriously, too comfortable with their little arrangement, confident that here in Spain people did it all the time and no-one took a blind bit of notice. But now, the thought of what Manuel would do if he found out caused his carefully constructed financial empire to shudder right at the very bottom.

'I leave at four.'

'Take me with you, Derrrmot, take me?'

'Are you mad, Carmen? I've a wife and family at home, didn't I tell you?'

'That does not matter to me,' she whimpered.

'What about your friends, why not go and stay with one of them?'

'I'm going with you, Derrrmot, I will book a ticket for the plane to Dublin.'

'Carmen, you can't, it's not possible, you have to think this through more carefully, I'll be back in a couple of weeks, we can talk then.'

But she had already put down the phone.

Dermot went to the airport late, and checked in at the last minute. He glanced furtively around but couldn't see Carmen, hoping that she had changed her mind about coming with him. He walked quickly to the departure gates, and as he passed the entrance to the shopping area, he dashed in, grabbed a couple of bottles of whiskey and made it to Gate 10 with the stragglers. He felt a bit more relaxed climbing up the steps of the plane. He had expected Carmen to be waiting for him, crying on his shoulder, but she wasn't there and he was very relieved when he found his seat, pleased to see that there were two young women sitting beside him.

'Been on holiday?' he asked.

'In Torrevieja.'

'I've a place down there.'

'We were staying with our aunt and uncle, in a villa.'

'Very nice.'

Then they were in the air and the business of the flight began.

'Girls, fancy a drink?'

They nodded and giggled, and both asked for a vodka.

He ordered whiskey for himself, and sat back. This would be a pleasant little interlude. Carmen had obviously thought better of coming back to Dublin with him. He decided to steer clear of her in future, he didn't want a confrontation with Manuel. So now he concentrated on the girls, Dermot could be so charming when he wanted.

The captain announced they were approaching Dublin.

'I know that bar, it's on a corner, maybe I'll see you in there some night.' They left the plane together, walked through Passport Control, and into the baggage hall. He took his opportunity then to offer them a lift home, but was disappointed to be told that someone was picking them up. There was a crowd around the carousel and he leaned forward to try and spot his suitcase, but for a change he wasn't in any hurry. Normally he was an irritable why-can't-Aer-Rianta-get-their-act-together person. He had even been known to make serious complaints to anyone who looked vaguely official, send emails, write letters, but he never got anywhere with his blustering angry approach, and always had to wait in the end with everyone else. But today he didn't care if there was a couple of hours delay. It would gave him his chance with the girls who were gorgeous, probably early twenties, he guessed. Both tall, slim, with that long blonde hair that he liked.

He felt someone touch him, and ignored it at first, assuming it was accidental, but he felt it again, and the hair on the back of his neck did something uncomfortable, as if there was a sudden draught of cold air.

'Derrrmot darrrling.'

'What are you doing here?' He stared at the dark-eyed woman who stood in front of him, holding a large statue in her arms.

'I was on the same flight, but I waited to surprise you, I am so happy to be here in Ireland,' she smiled at him.

'But you can't, can't...' Frantically he looked around at the girls who were chatting together. 'Look, I'll see you later.' He moved away a little. 'Outside, I have to talk with some people.'

'Oh there is my bag, look, the red one, lift it for me, please, Derrrmot darling, rapido.' She pushed him and he had to lean over and pull it off the carousel, and then quickly reach for his own which was sailing into the distance.

'Thank you, Derrrmot. It is all I have, these cheap store designs I bought this morning. I am so glad I had saved a little money, enough for the journey here too, Manuel cancelled my credit cards. But I look forward to doing some shopping in Dublin, you can take me to see the Irish designers. Will you carry

170

my Madonna for me, please?' She pushed the statue, with its red velvet dress and white mantilla, into his arms.

'I'm not carrying that thing.' Embarrassed, he thrust it back at her. 'What do you think I am? Get a trolley, woman.'

'But she is so precious, my grandmother gave her to me.' Her eyes filled with tears.

'Hi Dermot!' a voice said from somewhere to the side, and he looked around to see the man who managed the local service station grinning at him.

'Hi Dan,' he responded in a half-hearted way, furious to be seen with Carmen by anyone who knew him.

'Been away in the sun?' Dan asked.

'Business, business,' he said.

'Derrrmot darling.' Carmen put her hand out and softly touched his cheek. 'Will you lift my bag for me?'

'Get off, Carmen, will you, this is Ireland and you can't be doing that sort of stuff in public,' he muttered, and quickly moved through the crowd to where the girls had been, but they had disappeared. He stared around, annoyed, then strode quickly towards the exit hoping to catch up with them, followed by Carmen.

'There's nobody in Customs usually, I don't know how they ever catch people,' he said as he marched in, so preoccupied he didn't hear the Customs Officer, and was walking on ahead when the voice was raised and the "Sir" finally caught his attention. He turned back and was instructed to lift his case on to the counter, unable to believe that he had been chosen out of all the people going through.

First the man took out his shoes and placed them on the counter, then he picked up a dirty sock and wrinkled his nose. What does he expect to find there? Dermot fumed. Next he took out his toilet bag. The bottle of after-shave was shaken, the liquid sniffed. Dermot was very embarrassed when he noticed that the blade of the razor still had congealed shaving cream on it since this morning, and that the toothpaste dribbled thickly out of the uncapped tube. He was red-faced now with mortification as the man began to forage through his clothes, and checked the contents of his hand-luggage. Dermot was about to make a wisecrack about the whiskey but then decided to keep his mouth closed. Finally, all of his belongings were stuffed untidily back into the case, the lid pushed down with some difficulty.

'Thank you, Sir,' the man said politely and swung the front of the case around to Dermot.

'Thank you.' Dermot was very tempted to add the "Sir" in appreciation of this wonderful experience but held himself back from that bit of witticism. They might decide to search him for secreted drugs. That thought kept him quiet.

Outside, he mopped his brow with his handkerchief.

'What was he looking for?' Carmen was puzzled.

'Drugs, contraband, rashers and sausages, heads of cabbage, can't bring anything like that in any more.' He marched towards the car park.

'He didn't examine me,' she said.

'Lucky for you.'

She tried to keep up with him, the weight of the suitcase and the Madonna beginning to slow her down.

'I told you to get a trolley, but you wouldn't, typical woman, expecting me to carry the whole lot. Well, you can take a running jump for yourself.'

'I couldn't find one.'

'You look as if you're planning to stay on a permanent basis?' He deliberately began to walk even faster.

'I hope so.'

'Well, if I were you I'd turn around and go straight back. You'd never get used to the cold weather, or the strange food, it's much cheaper to live in Spain anyway.' He turned to the right, and marched along the line of parked cars in search of his Mercedes.

'But I thought you would be pleased to see me, Derrrmot?'

'You thought wrong, Carmen. I've a busy life here, there's no time for playing around.' He turned again, to the left this time, and marched up another row of cars. 'Where is it? I definitely parked it around here,' he growled, bad-tempered as he listened to the uneven clatter of Carmen's footsteps behind him.

'Derrrmot, I must rest, I am very tired.' Her voice was soft and limp.

At last, he found his car. He put the case in the boot, and waited for Carmen to arrive, wobbling on her high-heels.

'You are strange today, my Derrrmot.' She let the suitcase slide out of her hand on to the ground.

He drove her straight to the airport hotel, booked a room, and then they went up together.

'I am so tired, Derrrmot, let us go to bed, I have such a headache. Look what Manuel did to me, he is such a terrible brute.' She raised her hair to show him the purple marks on the side of her face.

'That looks awful, it must be very sore,' he said, trying to force some measure of sympathy into his voice.

'But I am feeling better now that I am here with you, my Derrrmot.' She reached out to him but he shrugged her off.

'I have to go home, Carmen, my wife will be waiting for me.' He stood there, hands in his pockets.

'But you will come back to me later?' Her dark eyes filled with tears.

'It's almost eleven o'clock at night, Carmen, I can't.' He moved towards the door.

'But I thought you love me, querido?'

'I am very fond of you Carmen, but I never suggested that you should come here. Dublin is a small place, no such thing as mistresses, or paying for apartments and cars the way Manuel did. I'm a respectable person, with a wife, a family, a successful businessman in the community. I'd know ten people in the bar downstairs, how do you think I'd explain you?'

'But I will be so good for you.' Her hands joined together as if she was about to pray. 'Maybe you could give me a job, I can speak four languages, it would be such an advantage to you. Then I can do everything for myself, I don't want you to have to pay. Manuel, he was different. Kiss me, Derrrmot, I need your arms around me again.' She leaned against him.

'Carmen, no, I told you, no.' He pushed her away, floundering for explanations.

'I can't believe you have changed so much.' She began to cry with long mournful sobs. 'Derrrmot, querido, Derrrmot.'

'Carmen, will you shut-up!' he shouted.

She stared at him, her mouth open, and the sobs became one long moan.

'You will have to pull yourself together.' He grew heated, took his handkerchief from his pocket and handed it to her. 'Stop snivelling. Go to bed, get some sleep and I'll book a flight for tomorrow. You'll have to go back, you can stay with your family or your friends.'

'But I am afraid of Manuel.'

'Go somewhere else for a while, Spain's a big place, and anyway he's bound to be wondering where you are, probably searching for you at this very moment.'

'To kill me.' Her moan began again, even more high-pitched.

'Don't be ridiculous. So what, you had a bit of a fling, that's nothing, you don't kill a person for it.'

'You don't know him like I do.' She wiped her eyes.

'I know him well enough, I'm in business with him. He's a normal guy, well, apart from his dancing.'

'He is not normal.'

'You're crazy. Stop this. I'll check on the flights, and call you later.'

'Oh Derrrmot, I am so frightened.'

'I'm sorry, I'm very sorry, but there's nothing I can do, it's the way it is,' he said abruptly. Without another word, he left the room. Then he hared down the corridor, taking the stairs in preference to waiting for the lift.

In the car, he opened up his lap-top, and booked her on a flight to Madrid the following morning, with a connection to Alicante later in the day. Then he rang her, it was easier to talk at a distance, but, to his surprise, she seemed to have changed in that short span of time. The pitiful crying had stopped, she sounded more in control.

'I'll come out to collect you about eight.' He tried to assuage his guilt.

'It is not necessary, I will take a taxi,' she snapped.

'But I'd like to see you off.'

'Don't worry, there is no need, goodnight, I must sleep now.' She put down the phone.

He couldn't believe it, she seemed to have taken it so well in the end.

Chapter Twenty-Four

'You should get out more, you're like a hermit,' Chris said.

'I am a hermit,' Jack laughed.

'No, seriously. I'll bet you haven't been outside this place since Christmas except for the odd Sunday at home.'

'I haven't had the time.' It was true, all caught up with Kate these days. He was happy with the series of paintings, eleven so far, and wasn't sure whether there was one more, feeling he had almost come to the end.

'Will you exhibit these?' She sipped a glass of white wine, ensconced in the Director's Chair at the window, elegant in her beige silk suit.

'I don't know.' He picked up his own glass. 'There aren't enough paintings for an exhibition, and anyway they have to be sold together.'

'All of them?'

'There's a link between them, they're parts of a whole person, you just couldn't separate them.' He wandered over to the one which stood on the bench. It was a painting of Kate's hand, and the colours he had used were more natural than his usual strong primary shades. Warm earthy golds, rusts and creams, the cooler blue-green of the sea, and the myriad of tones in between, all intermingled to produce something very different.

'I see what you mean. It makes it difficult for someone to afford them, although maybe a corporate buyer might invest.'

'I don't really care, I'd rather not sell them at all.' He wondered should he ask Kate her opinion of them, maybe she wouldn't want to be sold like a product on the supermarket shelf.

'Can you see them dominating the boardroom of some bank or big organisation, they wouldn't get any work done.'

'Won't have that affect on the average person.'

'They're so varied. What type of frames will you use?'

'Carve them out, it will take time but I'm looking forward to doing it.'

'Well, I have to make tracks. We're having a few people around next Saturday, why don't you come over?'

'Wait until I check my diary, I might be booked up.'

'Yea, I believe it.'

'OK, I will, but I won't stay long, just enough time to give you a hand with the food.'

She hugged him, and then left in her usual flurry.

When she had gone, he checked his messages.

First it was Tony, someone he hadn't seen since Christmas.

'We're having a bit of a party tonight. See you in the pub, we'll all be there.'

He wasn't very enamoured of the idea.

Then it was his agent in Spain wondering when they could arrange an exhibition.

And finally, his mother, whose call he returned immediately.

She attacked him straight away. 'I haven't heard from you all week, where have you been?'

'I've been working, Mam.'

'Working?' She sounded puzzled.

'Yea, working.' She was so funny in her own way.

'What at?'

'Are you going all dolly-dimples on me?'

'No, I'm not.'

'You know what I do.'

'For a minute I thought you were after getting a real job, you know, that you'd go to every day, and then you wouldn't be disappearing for months on end.'

'How are you and Dad?'

'We're all grand, but we'd be better if we could see you tomorrow. Most of the others are coming over, it will be a full house, one of the kid's birthdays.'

'Which one?'

'Andrea, Rose's young one.'

'I'll give her some money.'

'She'll be delighted with that, she's mad into the style. Now don't be late.'

She put down the phone abruptly.

That was it, tomorrow gone.

He wasn't interested in this party, but he hadn't seen his friends in ages, and about ten o'clock he decided to go in for an hour or so. He was warmly welcomed, and found himself unwinding over a cool pint of Guinness, glad now that he had made the effort. To his surprise, a little later, someone called his name, and he saw Mags, dressed tonight in a silvery outfit, pushing through the crowd towards him. She smiled and kissed him on the cheek. They chatted for a few minutes; then Tony drew her into the inner circle, no problem to Mags with her sparkling repartee. He bought a round and sipped another pint, trying to follow the gist of the conversation, which was uninteresting talk about sport. Then two friends of Mags arrived, and the noise grew louder, but out on the edge he switched off. Seeing Mags had reminded him of Kate. His mind took him away to another place, to those days of love, or in love, or whatever it was called, those days that wouldn't go away. He wondered was he going to have to exist in this strange half-light for the rest of his life? Unable to have a relationship with the woman he loved. Destined only to exist for his art which had seemed to be enough, the ultimate in joy or desperation such a short time ago.

After closing time, he found himself hustled back to Tony's apartment, no opportunity to make excuses as he was persuaded to give some of the crowd a lift. The place was packed with people; he wasn't even sure who half of them were, but he opened a can and stood there talking until Mags, pretty well tanked up at this stage, pulled him towards the centre of the room where a few people were gyrating to some rock music.

'Come on, shake a leg.'

'I've two left feet, all I can do is shuffle.'

'That will do me.'

'You can't shuffle to that music.'

'Hold on there, I'll put on something else but don't move until I come back.' She wagged her finger at him and disappeared in the direction of whoever was organizing the music.

'How about that, a slow number, that has to suit you.' She put her arms around him and they danced in the small space pushed around by other bodies. She was wearing a low-cut stretchy top and hugged so close to him, he thought he could have made a move here if he wanted to. But he wasn't really aware of her, not the way he should have been, instead his mind wandered with the music to a night in Torrevieja.

'You're somewhere else,' she said with a knowing smile.

'What do you mean?' He came back with a start.

'Your eyes were all misty. You were miles away, admit it.'

'I was listening to the music.'

'Don't go off there again, you're with me now and I want your undivided attention.'

'Here I am, mind and body, you have me.'

'You shouldn't have said that.' She hugged closer.

'You're crazy, you know that.'

'About you, baby.'

It was a late night, and Mags had had far too much to drink. He managed to persuade her to leave her car parked at Tony's and took her home himself.

'I don't want to go in, want to stay here with you.' She snuggled up to him.

'It's late, Mags.'

'I don't feel well.'

He went around to the passenger side to help her out.

'I think I'm going to pass out.'

'Don't worry, you'll be all right, which floor are you on?' He put his arm around her.

'Ground.'

'Can you manage it that far?'

She nodded, pulled the key from her handbag and handed it to him. He opened the door and she held on to him tightly as they followed the corridor.

'Stay with me for a few minutes, just to make sure I'm OK?' She headed immediately for the bedroom.

He helped her to sit on the bed. 'Do you want anything before I go, a drink perhaps?'

'No, I need to lie down.' She lay back on the pillows with a deep sigh. 'Jack, hold on until I'm sure I won't be sick.'

'If you close your eyes, you'll drift off and be fine in the morning.' He moved towards the end of the bed.

'Maybe I will have some water, the kitchen is the first door on the right.'

He fetched a glass. As he bent down towards her, she raised her head from the pillow and curled her arms around his neck, reaching with her lips to touch his mouth. But there was an immediate resistance in him. He drew away, kissing her lightly on the cheek.

'I'd better go, Mags.'

She reached her hand up to him, but he didn't take it.

'Goodnight.' He walked to the door.

'See you soon.'

'Look after yourself.'

There was just one more painting. It came out of that episode when he had turned away from Mags. He felt so foolish, like a boy. But he wasn't attracted to Mags, and although he could have satisfied himself, God knows he had been celibate for long enough, that didn't sit well with him.

As he worked his mind took him into the realm of fantasy. This was a full portrait of Kate as she lay in bed that morning relaxed in sleep. He laboured over this the longest, knowing that it was definitely the last in the series.

Then, unexpectedly, something exciting and different happened. A theatre company approached him and offered a contract to design the staging for their next production written specifically for the opening of the new state of the art theatre in the docklands area of Dublin. It was unusual, something he had never done before, but a thrilling prospect none the less. He responded immediately, and then met with the director to discuss it in-depth. The contemporary theme dealt with young people who lived on the edge of society, with all the dangers associated with alcohol abuse, drugs and prostitution, the whole gamut.

The timing was perfect. Kate's paintings were completed now and new work hadn't yet revealed itself. He was second choice, as the original designer had been taken ill, but that didn't bother him in the slightest. It was a great opportunity and the maudlin mood which had dogged him lately suddenly disappeared at the prospect of this new challenge.

Chapter Twenty-Five

'You're looking great, you must have lost at least a stone,' Carol admired.

'Almost, I can manage to pull up the zips now without holding my breath, and to give myself a treat I had a facial yesterday, the eyebrows waxed, a massage - the works.' Kate felt good.

'I'm so glad to see you in such good form. I was worried about you after Christmas.'

'You needn't have. I'm getting things together again...let's go on a shopping spree on Saturday.'

'No better woman.'

Beginning the day with breakfast in town they enjoyed themselves in the shops. Kate went mad. She bought some nice casual gear, delicious underwear, and make-up. But the best buy was a fabulous skirt and tunic in a rich aubergine shade.

'It looks wonderful on you.' Carol circled around her as she stood in front of the mirror.

'Is it a bit tight?' Kate asked doubtfully.

'Get that size, you'll fit into it comfortably in another week or two, and it will be an incentive to keep up the diet. You couldn't leave this gorgeous thing hanging in the wardrobe,' Carol persuaded, flicking through the rail of clothes in search of something for herself. 'And I can borrow it from you.'

So her credit card was produced again and they walked through Grafton Street laden down with bags and went for lunch, a carefully chosen meal, the days of splurging gone.

Carol raised her glass of wine. Kate was abstemious and drank water.

'To the new Kate.'

'To the new me, thanks for coming.'

'Everyone needs a make-over from time to time. I wonder what Dermot will say.'

'He won't even notice probably, and if he did, it would probably only be a complaint about the amount of money I've spent,' Kate said in a light offhand way, but hoped deep down that he might make some compliment. She needed that.

Chapter Twenty-Six

Irene stared at a photograph of Dermot and kissed it, tears blinding her eyes. 'Dermo, where are you, Dermo?' she mumbled incoherently as she pulled a tissue from her pocket. It had been weeks since she had seen him, other than when she visited Mount Asher Road and then he almost cut her dead, with barely a nod in her direction. Suddenly she decided that she had to see him. Quickly she repaired the damage to her make-up, changed into her newest outfit, a vibrant blue creation, and headed into town.

Dermot's secretary looked up at her with vague recollection when she asked to see him.

'Have you an appointment?'

'No, just tell him a friend has called to see him.'

'Whom shall I say?'

'Don't say, it's a surprise.'

The girl looked uncertain.

'Go on. He'll be delighted, I know he will, just tell him.'

The girl buzzed through.

Irene had never worried about Dermot's secretary. She was dull, uninteresting and plain, no threat whatever. After a moment, she told her to go in, and she made an entrance with a sweep, standing just inside the door in a dramatic pose.

He stared at her, surprised.

She moved gracefully across the room towards him, with an exaggerated swing as if she was a model on a catwalk.

'Sit down, Irene.' He indicated the chair in front of his desk.

'I'll perch here, I don't like to feel I'm being interviewed, not with you Dermo, definitely not that.' She placed her bottom on the corner of the mahogany desk and crossed her legs, the skirt riding up to reveal well-shaped knees clad in the lowest denier stockings she could find.

He swivelled his chair and fiddled with some papers.

'Have you missed me, darling?' She leaned forward so that he might catch the aroma of her perfume.

'It's been very busy, Irene.' He bundled up the papers together, smoothed their edges and put them down a couple of inches away from where they had been before.

'I haven't seen you in ages, Dermo, let's get together again. Life has been so dull without you.'

'I'd love to, Irene, but it's not possible. Kate began to get suspicious that I was up to something a while back, so I had to lie through my teeth. If she finds out about us I'm for the chop.'

'You do still love me then?'

'Of course I do.' He straightened his tie and buttoned his jacket in a protective don't-touch-me way.

'Look, why don't we come clean? Just tell Kate out straight. You were going to do it, you promised me.'

'It's not as easy as that. If I tell her now, we're facing divorce, and I'm not in a position to pay her off, not at the moment.'

'I can help there, I've plenty of money.'

'Thank you, Irene, but I'm an independent person. I have to be my own man. You know what I mean?'

'Dermo, you're deliberately finding reasons why we can't be together.'

'It's difficult, Irene.'

'You're breaking my heart.' She pulled out a tissue and dabbed her eyes. 'I can't live without you. Look at me, I'm skin and bone. Why don't you call around this evening on the way from work. You needn't stay long, Kate will never know,' she coaxed.

'No, Irene, I can't, I have an appointment.' He shook his head and opened the large diary.

'Tomorrow night?'

'Irene, I'm really busy at the moment.' He ran his fingers through his short hair in a distracted fashion.

'I thought you said you still loved me?'

'I do, but...'

'You're just trying to put me off.' It was the "but" that did it, and she was suddenly angry. He was saying one thing and he was doing another.

'I told you the reason.'

'You're playing some sort of a game with me.' She slid off the desk.

'No, I'm not.' He shook his head.

'You've got someone else, is that it?'

'No, I haven't,' he mumbled.

'You don't care about me.'

'It's very awkward.'

'So you dumped me to suit yourself, you bastard.' She burst out into loud husky sobs. It was a deliberate ploy, knowing he couldn't bear it.

'Irene, stop that crying. Let me get you a cup of coffee.' He stood up and as he moved she threw her arms around him.

'If you don't come back to me, I'll kill myself.'

'Don't be ridiculous, Irene.'

'I have plenty of sleeping pills, I just have to take a few and I'm gone from the world. If I never wake up again, it will be your fault,' she screamed at him.

'Sshh, sshh, for God's sake. Here, you'd better have a drink.' He pushed her down in a chair and took the bottle from the drawer, his hands shaking as he poured a good measure for each of them. 'Knock that back, Rene.'

'I can't live without you, Dermo.'

'We have to be unselfish and not make life difficult for Kate. She'd be desperately upset if she found out, so we can't see each other for a while. Maybe later on, who knows, things may change. Then we can get together again.' He put his arms around her.

'Oh Dermo.' She relaxed against him.

'You know I love you, so don't worry, it will all sort itself out

186

in the end.'

She left the office in slightly better form, determined that she wasn't going to let Dermot drift away from her. He was hers and she was going to keep him.

Dermot was anxious. He wouldn't put it past Irene to get her own back and tell Kate every sordid detail. Deciding to call it a day, he cleared his desk and left the office. As he climbed into the car, the phone rang and he almost didn't pick it up, really not in the mood for any more of her mewling. But then the thought that it could be Manuel, or someone else equally important, forced him to reply.

'Yes?' He held in a breath.

'Dermot?'

'Eddie, how are you?' He exhaled.

'Fine thanks.'

'I didn't know you were back?'

'We decided to take a break for a couple of weeks and, before we head off again, we're having a few people around on Saturday night and we'd love yourself and Kate to come over for a few jars. And this might interest you, I have a friend who's keen to buy some property in Torrevieja, so I told him that I knew just the man for him. No doubt you're interested in doing a deal?'

'Always Eddie, always.'

187

Chapter Twenty-Seven

Kate took her time getting ready and finally slipped into her new outfit which fitted her perfectly now. Dermot didn't get back until after eight and it took him a half an hour to shower, shave and change, so it was quite late when they drove over. But tonight she wasn't perturbed, content to slip in unnoticed and blend with the crowd, just another body. She was welcomed warmly by Eddie, hugged and handed a drink; but received a slightly cooler reception from Chris, who looked surprised to see her. Kate was puzzled at that, and wondered was there something at the back of it, or was it her imagination? But it seemed to be more the latter as she chatted for a short while, introduced Kate to some friends and excused herself, leaving her to make polite small talk. Although she made an effort to appear interested, she wondered if Jack might be here this evening, and occasionally she glanced across the room in search of his tall figure, but she couldn't see him and was forced to concentrate on the conversation.

'They know it all,' one woman complained.

'I can't get through to them, they simply won't listen,' another added.

'Have you children, Kate?'

'Two sons, but they're grown up now.'

'You're lucky, you don't have to be too concerned about them any longer.'

'Well, I don't know about that, we all worry no matter what age they are.'

'I'm the one that has the responsibility in our house, all my husband does is play games on the computer, I don't know who he's talking to.'

'It's the new addiction.'

'My kids are only allowed to watch television at weekends,' a petite blonde woman said.

'I wish you'd come over to my house and drag my lot away from the box.'

They laughed. Kate's mind wandered once more, the subject boring. She looked along the length of the large room again and her pulse began to race as she spotted Jack going into the dining-room.

'I see my chef has just served up, come on girls, let's get to it,' Chris called.

The group followed her, but Kate stayed where she was, suddenly feeling acutely shy. She searched for Dermot but he was in deep conversation with some man in a corner; she had just decided to join them when she heard Jack call her name. He walked towards her, smiling.

'How are you?'

'Fine, thanks.'

'I'm just off, I only came around for a short time to help Chris.'

Her stomach dived.

'But maybe I won't go yet, I might get myself a drink instead. Is Dermot here with you?'

'Yes, he's over there with a prospective client.' She waved in his direction, a whooping delight sweeping through her now that it appeared Jack was staying on because she was here.

'While I have you all to myself, I want to ask you something.' He moved closer.

She was puzzled.

'I need you to come over to the studio to look at some work I've done. Do you think you might be able to find the time?'

'Is it just me?' she stuttered, taking another gulp of her drink.

'Of course it's just you.'

189

'I thought maybe you meant the company, the others, a business thing?' She suddenly needed it to be that, afraid to even consider that he meant anything else.

'No, it's not business.'

'I suppose I could come over,' she said hesitantly.

'I'll phone you to arrange...' He looked around sharply as suddenly Eddie and Dermot appeared beside them, followed by another man, all in jovial mood after a few drinks.

'Kate, your glass is almost empty, you need a refill. Jack, can I get you something?' Eddie asked.

'No thanks.' This was the only drink Kate was going to allow herself this evening.

'Dermot, have you met Jack, Chris's brother?'

'No, I don't think so.' Dermot gripped Jack's hand.

'It's good to meet you.'

'Yea, likewise, likewise.' Dermot turned to Kate. 'This is Richard, he's interested in buying in Torrevieja. I've invited them over to dinner next Saturday.' He drew her attention to the man who had a hand outstretched towards her. She took his limp grasp. 'Now come and meet Barbara, Richard's wife.'

Kate found herself being propelled across the room, as usual not given a chance to say no, I don't want to meet this Barbara, whoever she is. She was annoyed with him, but she looked back at Jack, and the smiling glance exchanged between them made her feel so ridiculously happy, suddenly she didn't give a damn about Dermot.

Chapter Twenty-Eight

Dermot arrived at Manuel's offices in Alicante. He had not been here since all that fuss with Carmen and he wondered what her response would be when she saw him, assuming herself and Manuel had no doubt made it up by now. But to his surprise there was another girl sitting at her desk.

'Is Carmen out today?' he asked Manuel.

'She has gone.' His abrupt response was accompanied by a dismissive wave of the hand.

'She's working somewhere else?' Dermot decided to continue along this line to make it look as if he knew nothing at all.

Manuel shrugged as he drew Dermot's attention to the documents in front of him. It was the biggest project in which Dermot had ever been involved and made his business at home seem like a little roadside stall. He was excited. The original investment would double at least, and all those millions would be in his bank in the Caymans any day now. His plan was to transfer some of it into his account at home to pay off the mortgages that he had taken out, in particular he was anxious to clear the one raised on Mount Asher Road. Although those monies would have to be declared, the bulk would reside tax-free in the Caribbean.

Later that night when he had left Manuel's club and, with more than a few drinks on board, he tried Carmen's number, remembering only the good times they had together. As it rang out, he murmured slurred words of apology for what happened in Dublin, certain that she would forgive him. But he was frustrated when there was no reply, the line dead.

'Another whiskey.' He slid his glass across the counter towards the barman.

'Si, senor.'

Disgruntled, he sipped the drink, looking around the bar to find someone else with whom he might pass a few hours.

*

Carmen sat in the back of the car which was parked across the street from Manuel's office. There was one policeman in the driver's seat and another sat behind with her.

'It is on the first floor?' The bald-headed one turned to her.

'Yes.' Carmen was a little afraid now, but it was too late, she had made up her mind to expose Manuel. She knew about the fraud which was being perpetrated on the foreigners who had purchased property in Spain and had access to the information about the crooked notaries. This was her chance to establish herself again, the police would pay her for the information and she could make a fresh start somewhere else.

'You have the key, and know the alarm code?' the fat low-sized man spoke in a gruff voice.

'Yes.' She nodded. Her pulse raced; she was breathing fast, excited that she still had power over Manuel, and glad that she always had the good sense to keep an extra set of keys.

When the night security man went into the bar next-door for a break, as was his usual habit at one o'clock, she quickly took them inside to Manuel's office. There she nervously opened the safe and chose the particular files which she needed. Time was against them, there was a window of fifteen minutes only. The seconds were counted down as they photographed page after page, until finally she locked the safe again. They left the building with only a moment to spare.

Chapter Twenty-Nine

The bell echoed inside the house on Harrington Park with a peremptory sound. Kate glanced down at herself and brushed a tiny fleck of dust from her navy jacket. She had been in such a state getting ready that now she wondered if she had put on two odd shoes, or had smudged her lipstick, but before she had a chance to check any of those possibilities, the door opened and he was there in front of her.

'Kate, it's good to see you, come on in.' He stood back and ushered her inside, the almost-brush of his white shirt was so close the little nerve at the nape of her neck began to quiver.

They made desultory talk about the weather as they went through to the lounge which was softly lit, shadows thrown by the warm glow of the lamps and the leaping flames of the fire. She sat down on the couch and he poured two glasses of red wine from the bottle already opened on the low glass-topped table.

'You're looking well.' He sat opposite.

'Thanks.' She felt self-conscious and stiff.

There was an awkward silence. They sipped their wine.

'I asked you over because I'd like to know what you think about some work...'

'I'm flattered,' she quipped, slightly more like her normal self.

'I don't know if you will be, I'm almost afraid to show them to you.'

'I can take it.' She sipped a little more wine.

'Suppose we'd better go up, I won't be able to concentrate on anything else until we do.' He stood and put out his hand to take hers. She reached automatically, his touch sending messages from her brain through sinew, muscle, every nerve-tingling part of her. She looked somewhere over his shoulder, reluctant to meet his eyes, but she was drawn there in spite of herself, aware that his hand still held hers, and the inches between them were fast diminishing until their bodies melted together into one. Then her head was on his shoulder; his arms were around her, a silent giving in, without any decision made or even a considered will we or won't we?

Almost in slow motion he moved; his lips softly touched hers in a gentle searching exploration, and she knew that this wasn't some light-hearted kiss, but more than that. She opened her mouth just a little with a slight exhalation of breath; his tongue entwined with hers, warm, moist, and she could feel his body tense. Suddenly, she wanted to give him all of herself. She was fully sober now, not like before. Well, one glass of wine didn't count. The rest of her life faded into a dream place. Dermot, Conor and Shane belonging to another person.

He slipped off her jacket. Then his hands were under the fine silk top she wore, moving along the curvature of her back, and slowly around to the front, his fingers caressing gently. They undressed each other quickly, clothes ending up in a pile on the floor. Then moved down on to the couch, slowly making love until finally he slipped inside her, seeming to know his way so well like they had been together hundreds of times. They strained into each other and demanded the very enth until they were exhausted. But suddenly there were tears in her eyes and she hid her face in his shoulder.

'Hey, what's this?' He put his finger under her chin and forced her to look at him.

'I'm sorry.' She bent her head again. 'It was just...I can't explain.'

'You don't regret it, do you?' He wiped away the tears.

'No, of course not.' She clung to him.

'You won't run out on me?'

She smiled.

'Promise?'

'Promise.'

They lay together on the couch, quite relaxed. She ran her hands over his body, his lean limbs taut and muscular, his skin still dark with last summer's sun-tan.

'This is like a dream come true for me, you know.' He moved closer to her. 'I never expected this to happen, I thought you were someone unattainable, like royalty, or a big movie star.'

'Yea, with minders watching my every move.'

'I'm sorry about that first time,' he murmured, 'I felt I had forced you into something which you didn't want.'

'I was shocked at myself.' She stared into the leaping flames. The embers glowed. She saw things as in the imagination of a child. There were fairytale castles among twisted trees, weird distorted faces of people, animals, anything else which could be conjured up. She loved a real fire, at home it was gas, those insipid spurts of flame pale by comparison.

'But even though I felt it was just a one-off for you, I couldn't get you out of my head, particularly when we met again.' He reached for her and they made love again, this time a more leisurely exploration of each other, her response to him so strong it made anything between Dermot and herself shrink into obscurity.

'I wish we were back in Spain, continuing where we left off.'

'Let's go to the Alhambra tomorrow.'

'We'll have lunch in that little bar, remember? Although I think I'd prefer to have you for lunch, anything else would be stale and dry.' He kissed her again, and she breathed in the aroma of his body, that particular scent of the soap he used, the trace of oils, knowing him so intimately now as if they had been lovers for ever. But, inevitably, time seemed to pass with unusual speed. She had to force herself to surface.

'Do you have to leave?'

'Suppose I must go back to the real world, Dermot is away at the moment.'

'Stay the night.' He clasped her to him again. 'Don't leave me.'

'I wish.'

'I wish.'

'What were you going to show me?' She suddenly remembered the reason why he had asked her over.

'It doesn't seem so important now.' There was no more talk for a while, until eventually, he took her by the hand and they went upstairs to the studio.

'Close your eyes.'

She giggled.

'No peeking.' He led her across the room, tightened his hold on her hand and after a few seconds told her she could open her eyes again.

She stared at the paintings which hung in front of her; unable to believe what she was seeing. They were so exquisite she couldn't speak, floored by the extraordinary beauty of this celebration of a woman. He stood behind and put his arms around her, and it was only then that she was sure that it was herself. Jack had created something wonderful for her, and mirrored what they had expressed for each other tonight.

Kate didn't sleep very well, so glad that Dermot was away. Every part of her still pulsed, and her mind played over the events of the night again. She remembered Jack's brown eyes, and the delicate touch of his hands as he made love, so gentle, letting her dictate the timing. Their final coming together was something out of her experience; Dermot's always rushed congress never considered her needs. She tried to remember whether it ever had, but if it did, those memories eluded her. She must have slept eventually, but when she awoke in the morning, the romantic hue had faded somewhat. She struggled to deal with the guilt, Jack's question echoing in her head.

'What are we going to do now?' he had asked as they walked together to her car.

'I don't know.'

'I want to see you again.' He took both of her hands in his.

She nodded but couldn't find any answer for him. 'I must go, it's late.'

In the car she pushed the key into the ignition and then opened the window, which brought him closer to her again.

'Thank you for the paintings, they're beautiful.' She gripped the steering wheel. The car began to move. He raised his hand in a wave. She looked straight ahead and drove out through the gates, just letting the car take her home without any thought, stopping at lights, turning corners, still back in Harrington Park with him.

Dermot's wife, mother of Shane and Conor, showered and chose her clothes carefully. The grey suit, the crisp pin-striped silk blouse, her usual dark choice for work. There was nothing external to indicate any change within this person, but a bowl of muesli was left unfinished; a cup of hot water with lemon barely sipped. Her stomach was in knots as she took a casserole from the freezer for dinner, checked the fridge and the kitchen presses for shortages.

'You're looking good,' Carol said as they took the lift together. 'Sparkle in the eye, blush on the cheeks, Dermot must be behaving himself.'

'Yea,' Kate smiled.

'I've a heavy schedule today. That client in Delgany is going to take a lot of time.'

'Carol?'

She looked at her.

'There's a couple of things I need to discuss...' They arrived at her office. She was longing to talk and ask her advice about Jack, but a sudden fear swirled inside her at the thought of sharing last night with anyone, and she decided against it, sure that she would be quite unable to cope with any disapproval. 'I'll catch you later.' She went inside.

The phone rang, the first call of the day. She picked it up, her heart thumping, half-expecting it to be him.

'I've got Textile Images on the line for you, and Ryans are holding,' The girl at reception said.

She took the calls. The morning was busy. Each time the phone rang there was breath-held expectancy in those first seconds and then disappointment when she realised it wasn't him. She found it difficult to concentrate on what she was doing, almost irritated when Mags walked in looking for information on orders in the pipeline.

'Will you discuss timing for the blinds with the suppliers and I'll talk to the fitters?'

'Yes, I'll push them to deliver as quickly as possible.' Kate made a note.

'They're having a bash at the end of the month and we have to guarantee completion.'

Her phone rang again. Automatically, she put out her hand and picked it up.

'Kate?'

She hesitated for a few seconds, a pounding inside her as she recognised his voice. She shuffled the papers on her desk, immediately conscious of Mags beside her.

'Can you talk?'

'Just give me a minute.' She could feel her cheeks warm, and struggled to keep her expression normal and hide the happiness which had soared through her.

'I'll let you take that call, talk to me later.' Mags left the office.

Kate leaned back in her chair, glad he had phoned at last, and needing to say so much. But the conversation was general, about her well-being, and what he was doing, just a friendly chat with no mention of last night, until there was a pause as they seemed to have exhausted all those topics. With conscious haste she said something about work and he agreed...they said goodbye and see you soon...

Chapter Thirty

As the date of the opening of the play drew nearer, Jack spent most of his time at the theatre putting the finishing touches to the set which was already constructed on stage now. His own particular style was very much in evidence in the strong primary colours used. The free-hanging flats would move in coordination with the imaginative lighting design to create the shades of bright and dark in the lives of the young people in this contemporary piece.

On his way home, he always drove past Kate's office, in the hope of seeing her as she left. He had even toyed with the idea of sending her a ticket for the opening night, but dismissed that, still unsure of himself and waiting for her to make the first move. Then one evening as he approached Lee O'Donnell he saw Mags standing at the edge of the pavement waving energetically and he immediately pulled up and opened the door.

'I've been trying to get a taxi but not having much luck, and then my knight in shining armour appears.' She climbed into the jeep and settled herself in the passenger seat.

'Can I drop you somewhere?'

'I've to pick up the car at the garage before six, it's only a couple of minutes away, but too far for me to walk in these heels.' She clicked the seat-belt closed. 'I suppose you're painting like mad. I haven't seen you in yonks.'

'I'm doing the design for a play at the new theatre in the dockland.' He pulled into the traffic again.

'When is it opening?'

'Next Tuesday.'

'Could you get me a ticket?'

'It's mostly an invited audience, but I managed to get some for a few friends, so there might be a chance.' Suddenly the idea of inviting all three of them seemed like the ideal way to meet Kate again.

'I'd love to be there, I haven't had a chance to rub shoulders with the glitterati in ages; take a left here,' she directed him and he pulled up outside the garage. 'Please try to get a ticket for me?'

*

'Delivery for someone special!' Carol put her head around the door.

'What do you mean?' Kate looked up from the design on which she was working as Carol came nearer, one arm behind her back holding something.

'It's a bit late for Valentines - and it's not your birthday - or your anniversary, now I wonder what else it could be?'

'What have you got there?' Kate put down her pen.

'Voila!' With the aplomb of a magician, Carol produced a beautiful bouquet of long stemmed red roses wrapped in crinkly cellophane paper and tied with red ribbons. She handed them to Kate, who felt her face grow pink with embarrassment.

'For me?'

'Well, the card is addressed to Ms. Kate Mason. Dermot has gone all out this time. Let's see what he says, go on, open it, I'm dying to hear his attempt at romance.'

Kate instantly recognised the handwriting. Her mind darted around trying to think of what she was going to say, but just at that moment her phone rang and she put down the envelope unopened as the girl at reception told her there was someone waiting to see Carol. To Kate's great relief she hurried away. With her heart thumping at a ridiculous rate, she opened the card. A ticket fall out on to her desk and she knew instantly that it had to be for the opening night of the play but was disappointed at the casual tone of his invitation, particularly

200

unimpressed by the fact that it seemed he had sent one to Mags and Carol also. And just by way of an afterthought he suggested that she come around to the bar afterwards for a drink. She threw down the card, as a sudden irrational annoyance surged inside. It was so offhand, not at all the sort of card that went with red roses. Maybe she wouldn't go at all? But then she picked up the bouquet, touched one of the soft petals and her emotions dissolved into mushiness again. He had bought them for her, and arranged for them to be delivered, something which hadn't happened to her for a very long time.

Dermot was one of those men who always felt foolish buying flowers, or so he said, and hadn't even bothered to bring her a simple bunch out of the garden when she had been in hospital having the hysterectomy a couple of years ago. She drew the flowers closer, breathed deeply, and felt such a longing it hurt.

*

Just before eight, backstage was charged with tension. The actors waited for their first entrance in various states of concentration, but Jack held behind, anxious to stay out of the way; he might have been playing the lead he was so tense. Knowing that Kate was in the audience excited him as he stood in a room leading on to the stage, listening to the dim murmur of voices from the audience out front. He walked across the room and back again, unable to settle. He glanced at his watch, two minutes to eight, reached for the can of Coke on the window sill. Two of the girls in the cast rushed by him and disappeared into the darkness of the stage area. Then he heard the first strains of the music which had been composed for the show. This was it.

'There are some well-known faces here,' Carol said as they settled themselves in their seats.

'I recognise a few television people and politicians, there's that Minister...I can't think of his name.' Mags stared around her.

'You can chat them up afterwards.'

'I'm not interested in any of them. You know who I want to chat up.'

'Well, you have your chance tonight.'

'I can't wait, I was so excited when he asked me to come.'

'Hey, he invited all of us,' Carol retorted.

'Me first.'

Kate stared up at the set. She could see Jack's strong strokes in the dramatic reds, yellow and blues of the backdrop and wondered where he was now.

'The set is fantastic, isn't it?' Mags said.

Kate nodded.

'You'd know it was Jack's work, stands out a mile.'

'Ssshhh,' Carol whispered, as the lights went down.

The play proved to be a great success and the audience gave them a standing ovation. For Jack it was a most fantastic feeling to hear the rounds of applause, but after that high point, most of all he was anxious to see Kate. He went into the bar as soon as he could, but was drawn into conversation with the director, who introduced him to various luminaries in the world of theatre.

'I really like your work, I hope we'll see much more of you around,' one man said as he pumped his hand.

'It's amazing how easily you've made that transition from art to theatre.'

'We need someone with a new approach, it spices everything up.'

The plaudits came fast and furious.

'Marvellous show, and your design was terrific. I wouldn't mind talking to you about a play we are putting together at the moment, can you give me a call to discuss?' the artistic director of another theatre asked.

'I'd be very interested.' He pocketed his card.

'Jack, a pint.' The lighting man handed it to him.

He sipped gratefully.

'Everybody loved it, thanks be to God, I can breathe at last.'

He agreed, but was unable to make a move as a journalist collared him, then a photographer, and it was some time before he could extricate himself. He pushed through the noisy crowd to find the girls chatting with some of his friends. But the only person he had eyes for was Kate and, as he moved in her direction, Mags threw her arms around him in a wild enthusiastic embrace.

'It was great, really fantastic, and the set was wonderful,' she gushed. The others crowded around, shaking his hand, kissing, hugging, and the brief tingling touch of Kate's lips on his cheek was frustrating in the extreme.

'This is the first step of your new career,' Mags said, hanging on to him possessively.

'I don't know if I'll get a chance to do a second play, although a director from another theatre has asked me to discuss a project with him, so it could be promising.' He tried to meet Kate's eyes, but every time he looked towards her, she was looking somewhere else.

'Well, here's to a new future.' They raised their glasses.

'You'll be so successful we won't be able to keep up with you.' Mags clinked her glass against his, and reached to kiss him on the cheek.

Kate watched and forced a tense smile on her face as she listened to one of the girls talking about the play, but she didn't really hear what was being said as her mind was focussed on Mags as she played up to Jack. She had no opportunity to talk as everyone wanted a slice of him. When her eyes strayed in his direction, all his attention was taken by one of the others, and she almost screamed with jealousy as she watched the scenario being played out before her.

It grew even worse when they all went over to the Trocadero for a meal, and she found herself sitting at the end of a table with Carol, while he sat towards the middle with Mags at his side. Conversation whipped up and down the tables, the chat interspersed with much laughter. While they did exchange a few remarks, she felt awkward, her emotions running so high she thought she would never get close to him. And didn't, not really, having to content herself with a brief impersonal kiss when they left later.

The following morning she bought all the newspapers, but only found one review which praised the cast, the director, the writer, and, last of all, "Jack Linley, new on the theatre scene, his set-design dramatic, powerful, and atmospheric." She cut it out of the paper and put it in a zip-pocket in her handbag, hidden away like that secret part of herself which held the thoughts of this man, reminded of last night again, and how close he was to her, yet so far away. How she wanted to put out her hand to clasp his, but their every move was observed, the strain almost unendurable as she watched him chat with Mags, Carol and the others there. She went through the day feeling like a piece of taut wire, and by five decided that she would have to see him this evening.

After work, she drove past his house, thrilled to see the jeep in the drive. She parked down a side street and walked slowly back, feeling like some sort of zombie. Worried that she shouldn't be here; wondering what she was going to say and how he would respond. He took a couple of minutes to answer the door, and there was a look of surprise on his face when he saw her.

He smiled, opened the door wider as she moved inside and closed it with a dull thump as he reached for her. The breath swept out of her in a long sigh as she held on to him, his face against hers, their bodies close together.

'I thought you'd never get here.' He kissed her very softly.

Afterwards, they lay together looking at each other, and he pushed back her hair from her forehead and cupped her face in his hand.

'I love you, Kate.'

She smiled.

'I love you,' he said it again.

'And I love you.'

It was the beginning of something wonderful. He was like a magnet which drew her to him, and she was helpless in the grip of such an attraction. From the very first moments of her awakening in the morning to the last seconds before she fell asleep at night he was in her conscious mind, in her subconscious too, dreams and nightmares. He lived inside her like a spiritual other half.

Her days were planned around Jack. Her work arranged to allow time to see him during lunch, or on the way to or coming back from somewhere. Occasionally she called in the morning and they had breakfast together, but more often after work, or later in the evening, using fictional meetings, or Yoga class, or any other excuse she could find as a cover. The only time they met away from Harrington Park was when she concocted a desire to go walking in the Pine Forest on a Saturday or a Sunday morning, so early there was no-one else about. She had given her whole self to this man.

Chapter Thirty-One

Kate rang Mags' bell for the second time, moving from one foot to another with impatience. She hadn't really wanted to come over this evening at all and found her friend's preoccupation with Jack more difficult to handle, particularly since her relationship with him had deepened to such an extent she felt that there was a sticker on her forehead announcing to the world that he was her lover.

The door clicked. She pushed it open and made her way down the corridor to the apartment.

Mags greeted her with a kiss.

'You're dressed up, why didn't you tell me we were going out and I would have worn something a bit better than this?' Kate glanced down at her jeans and pale blue sweater, then back at Mags who was dressed in a black off-the-shoulder number.

'You're fine, sure we're only having a drink, in you go.' Mags propelled her into the main living-area.

'Is your electricity gone?' she asked, but at that moment the lights came on and there was a huge shout.

Surprise!

Surprise!

Happy Birthday!

People appeared from behind chairs, curtains, tables, or wherever they had been hiding and crowded around her. It was like everyone she knew or had ever known was there.

Mags and Carol squeezed her tight. A cork popped out of a bottle of champagne and an overflowing glass was pushed into her hand.

'Congratulations! This is it, the big 4-0!'

She was surrounded by people, Dermot, Shane, Conor, all the office crowd, even some friends from school she hadn't seen in years. The apartment was decorated like a fun fair, with flashing lights, balloons, coloured streamers and banners wishing her a Happy Fortieth Birthday.

Mags pushed through with a tray of finger-food.

'Help yourself.'

'They look gorgeous, you shouldn't have gone to all this trouble, girls, it's too much.'

'You're only forty once, and we wanted to surprise you.'

'You have certainly done that,' Kate beamed. She hadn't been aware of her birthday looming at all, so caught up with Jack these days.

'She threw this party for herself, Kate, look who's over there at the window.' Carol turned her head, and Kate followed her direction, stunned to see Jack standing there in conversation with someone. She could feel her heart begin to race, and was so taken aback she couldn't even think of anything at all to say to Mags.

'I couldn't believe it when he agreed to come, now I've got another chance to make it with him tonight.'

Kate smiled, a wave of excitement bursting through her, but thankfully Mags didn't notice her distraction as she moved away through the crowd of people with her tray. Kate looked towards Jack again. His eyes met hers and with a wide grin he raised his glass. For a long moment they stared at each other; she felt like there was no-one else in the room and began to walk towards him.

'Well, surprise, surprise!' Dermot appeared suddenly in front of her. 'Now you've reached the horrible forties, join the rest of us.'

'Mum doesn't look anywhere near forty, I'd say thirty would be more like it.' Shane put his arm around her shoulders.

'Yea, sure, definitely. Now, have I a little something for the birthday girl?' Dermot put his hand in his pocket and pulled out a rather bulky envelope which he thrust towards her.

'Thanks, Dermot.' She reached and kissed his cheek, the expected response of a grateful wife when she is presented with a bundle of money by her husband.

'Buy yourself something nice.'

'I will.'

'Mum, this is the most popular perfume at the moment apparently, it will get any man going within a five-mile radius.' Shane gave her a small box.

'Not too many I hope, or I'll be in trouble.' She hugged him. 'This party is amazing, did you know about it?'

'It was a well-kept secret.'

'Just a voucher Mum, sorry I couldn't be more imaginative.' Conor handed her an envelope.

'Thanks a million, I'll enjoy spending it. Where's Nicola?' She looked around.

'She couldn't come. She asked me to give you her apologies and to wish you a Happy Birthday.' He looked sheepish, with his hands stuck into his pockets, while his eyes were somewhere beyond her.

'Oh...'

'Let me top you up there.' Carol poured more champagne into her glass, the frothing bubbles bursting over the edge. 'Come on, drink up.'

And Kate did exactly that as she circulated. She met friends she hadn't seen in ages who were all anxious to catch up with the news. She regaled stories of the past with great hilarity. But her mind wasn't really with them, she was so conscious of Jack's presence, always just somewhere over there, a few feet away at any time. She hadn't actually had an opportunity to talk to him yet and was getting frustrated, positive she could make it seem so casual that no-one would think it was anything other than an ordinary everyday conversation. But now she saw that he had been commandeered by Mags, who stood smiling up at him with a provocative stance, giggling at whatever he was saying. She was looking absolutely wonderful tonight, golden-brown from her Caribbean trip. A flash of jealousy made itself felt, and Kate looked away sharply, to see Carol walk towards her carrying a large candle-lit birthday cake.

This was the high point of the evening when everyone sang "Happy Birthday" and cheered as she opened her present from the girls which was a generous travel voucher for a trip, anywhere, at any time.

'It's an enormous amount of money, you shouldn't have.' She hugged them both.

'It will do you good. You can go anywhere you like. What about a break in New York, or Paris or Rome, or wherever? Maybe you might make it a second honeymoon with Dermot, or we could take an all-girl's trip, how about that?' Carol was excited. 'It's your choice.'

'Thank you so much.'

There were lots of other presents as well, and she felt like a little girl again. She even shed a few tears amid all the hugs and kisses.

Suddenly Jack was there in front of her, and reached forward to kiss her on the cheek. Then someone else was there instead and before she could say anything he was gone, but he had put something into her hand which she now pushed into her pocket. She went around everyone in the room after that and thanked them, but to her disappointment she found Mags talking with him again.

'Congratulations,' Jack smiled.

'I don't want to think about the number, with that big zero after it.'

'It's not that bad, I've been there, next week you'll have forgotten all about it.'

'Thanks be to God I've yet to reach it, I'm a young thing compared to you two. I've been trying to persuade this old guy to hang around for a while, but he's insisting on heading off home to do something or other. I suggested that he could stay over and I'd tuck him into bed, but still no joy.'

'I'm sorry, Mags, but I'm on the night shift. I have to go with the flow whenever it takes me.'

He seemed a little awkward, and Kate could sense it as she watched him swallow the last of the wine in his glass. Then suddenly she knew why, as Dermot put his arm around her shoulder in that possessive way he always affected in public.

'Great party, Mags, great party.' He raised his glass of whiskey, and gulped quickly. Kate noticed with a sense of dread that his voice was slightly slurred. 'And how's my birthday girl enjoying herself?'

Will you shut-up you fool, drunk as usual, she thought.

'She's having a ball, Dermot.'

'Great night, thanks for arranging it.'

'Another drink?' Mags asked.

'Wouldn't say no.'

'Kate? Jack?'

Both declined.

'Dermot, have you met Jack? If not, you do the honours, Kate.' Mags hurried away to get the drinks.

Dermot shook Jack's hand. 'Good to see you again, I've heard your name somewhere else recently, but I can't quite remember.'

'Jack is an artist. Maybe you saw one of his paintings?' Kate mentioned.

'That's it. Manuel has two or three of your creations in his office, great big things in bright garish colours. He said he might try and pick one up for me, but apparently they are very hard to get. You're quite collectable apparently, a good investment.'

'That's a nice thought.'

'Of course, you could sell to us direct. You do take commissions, I presume? I'll be in the market very shortly and it's something I might consider, these days shares are so unstable.'

Mags returned and handed Dermot another whiskey.

'Normally I do, but I'm very busy at the moment on something else.'

'Maybe I'll call around to your studio. Where are you?'

'Harrington Park, he's in the phone book.' Mags stood just a little closer to Jack.

'I'm working in the theatre now, so I've nothing to show you until my next exhibition at the end of the year.'

'I mightn't be able to wait that long. Money can't lie idle. Surely you have something that hasn't sold?'

'Well, of course, there are works that...' he hesitated.

'Then I can buy those from you, a job lot at a knock-down price. They will probably fetch as much as any of the others in a few years. It doesn't matter what they look like, I'll put them in storage in the meantime. Why don't I come around and have a look? You might be glad of the chance to get shut of them, but I'm warning you, I drive a hard bargain.'

'I'm sorry, Dermot, but those paintings are ones I have no intention of selling at this stage. They're not good enough.'

'I don't care about that. It's your name that counts if you're as collectable as Manuel says. You could scrawl something on a piece of toilet paper and it would sell. Why don't you do that and I'll buy it, just for the craic. It will probably go for millions at auction in Sothebys when you kick the bucket,' he laughed, his face flushed from too much whiskey.

Kate was horrified at the tone of his conversation. He was gross, and she wanted to slap his face and shut him up before he said any more. 'Jack is an artist, Dermot. He paints for the love of it,' she said sharply.

'No-one does anything for the love of it, money is all that counts. It's your livelihood, Jack, isn't it?'

'Well...yes.' There was a glimmer of anger in the dark brown eyes.

'You have to pay the mortgage, eat, buy clothes, and run your car, so you can't do those things on love alone. It's got to be a commercial entity, and that's where I come in. It doesn't matter who writes the cheque once it doesn't bounce.'

'That's true, but I try to be selective, and I'm never keen to flog anything for a few euro.'

'Bring the wolf to your door and you would sell your grandmother.' Dermot's laugh was loud. 'That's what I believe and it applies to everyone.' He finished the glass of whiskey.

'Where's that gorgeous Mags?'

'I think we should be going soon, Dermot,' Kate said firmly.

'What are you talking about? The night's young. Don't tell me the guest-of-honour is going to run home to her little bed to get her eight hours sleep? You do that if you want, I'm getting myself another drink.' He wandered off unsteadily in the direction of the kitchen.

'I'm so sorry, Jack, he was at his worst. If I could have shut him up I would.'

'Don't you worry, he's had a few too many. I'm just sorry that we had to waste all that time, forget about him and talk to me.'

'I'm furious.'

'Relax, he won't remember a thing in the morning.' He glanced towards the kitchen. 'And you should be enjoying yourself.'

'I am. It's such a great party, and you're here, so everything is perfect. Thank you for my present, I'll wait until I have a quiet moment before I open it.'

'To celebrate your birthday I want to take you away somewhere you'll really enjoy.' He lowered his voice. 'I want to spoil you...'

'Still here?' Mags returned. 'Thought you were leaving ages ago?'

'I was diverted,' he smiled at Kate.

'Maybe I'll divert you a bit more. Persuade him to stay, Kate, you seem to have more influence than I have.'

'I don't know about that.'

'Sorry, I've got to go. Thanks a lot, Mags, great night.' He kissed her lightly, and then turned to Kate and kissed her too, just a touch of his lips on her cheek, innocent of anything until he whispered 'I love you'.

'I'll see you out.' Mags grabbed his arm. 'We have to make arrangements for the sitting, and I must decide what to wear. Should it be something dramatic, or casual, or maybe nothing at all?' she giggled. Kate watched them with sudden dread.

In the quiet of the kitchen after Shane and Dermot had gone

up, she made herself a cup of coffee, and sat down at the kitchen table. Then she took the gold-wrapped box from her pocket, tore off the paper and flipped open the lid. The diamond earrings designed by Rudolf Heltzel of Kilkenny were definitely the real thing, exquisite in their simplicity, and the tiny card inserted into the box just said "I love you".

The following evening, just before five she finished off the letter she was writing, shut down the computer and put away her files. There was a tremor in her fingers, a nervousness, and she quickened her pace, anxious to get there as soon as she could, frustrated when she had to join a long line of traffic inching out of town. As she approached the house, she decided to phone, suddenly worried that there might be someone there with him, perhaps even Mags. She punched in his number.

'How are you?' His voice was soft.

'I'm fine, thanks.'

'What sort of day did you have?'

'Mad, but I've just left it all behind.' She pulled into a parking spot.

'What are you doing now?'

'Well, at the moment I'm going for a short walk.' She put on her new earrings.

'It's a lovely evening, I wish I could join you.'

'Could be risky.'

'Don't I know it,' he groaned.

'Open the front door, and I'll wave to you as I pass by.'

'What are trying to do to me?'

'Nothing. Just obey me!' She walked quickly down the road, praying she wouldn't be spotted by someone she knew in the line of cars which drove past, but she carried her briefcase, and marched purposefully. She was out on a job, what else? Just when she drew abreast of the house, she hurried up the drive, into the open door, and his arms.

His declaration of love, and her own acknowledgement that she felt as much for him now emphasised those uncertainties always there when you bare your deepest self.

'I'm going to have to fit Mags in one of these days, she is so keen to have a portrait done,' he said later.

She was taken aback, even though she had known it was going to happen.

'Although I really haven't got the time, there are a number of commissions to complete before I head off.'

'Head off?' She asked the question, but knew instantly to what he was referring.

'Any other year I would be in Spain by now, but this year you've kept me here, and now I don't want to go at all.'

'I'd rather you didn't go either.'

'Needs must. It's the place where I do my best work, on my own in the mountains with only the goats for company. Although I can think of someone else I'd prefer...'

Her impulse to beg him not to go was a childish I-can't-live-without-you plea which she wouldn't indulge.

'Tell Mags I'll try and make a start next week.'

'She'll be delighted.' She tried not to react as a vision of Mags dressed in some sort of sexy outfit, or nothing at all, came into her mind.

Chapter Thirty-Two

Kate could sense a definite change in Uncle Bill on that Friday evening. It wasn't anything she could pinpoint, just a vague weakness which developed into something much more as they sat having a cup of tea in the kitchen. Suddenly he stopped talking mid-sentence and stared at her. His eyes were blank, the irises had reduced in size, there was a white fuzzy around the outer edges. She called his name, but received no response. His hands felt cold, and she knew that there had to be something seriously wrong. Panicked, she ran out the front door. Dr. Walsh lived nearby and would come up straight away if he was there, she was sure of that. But half-way down the path she realised how crazy it had been to leave Uncle Bill alone, so she rushed back inside relieved to find him still sitting in his chair, his hand by the cup of cooling tea as if he was just about to pick it up. Shaking, she took her mobile from her handbag, and dialled 999 quickly, then she put her arms around him, and, in tears, she held him close until at last the doorbell rang.

'He's in a trance, I can't wake him up,' she explained to the two men who quickly assessed the situation and within minutes he was being carefully lifted onto a stretcher and taken into the ambulance. Outside some of the neighbours had gathered.

'What's wrong with him?' Mrs. Murphy from next door enquired.

'I don't know, he's taken a turn.'

'Poor thing. I'll say a few prayers for him. And don't you worry about the place, we'll look after it.'

Kate ran back inside, locked up, and followed the ambulance in the car. Although it was long gone out of sight, she could still hear that scary threatening sound that was the siren wailing in the distance.

She rang Jack from the hospital, needing to talk.

'It was a stroke. I'm so worried about him.' She was in tears again.

'I'm really sorry to hear that, do you want me to come over? I can be there in ten minutes.'

'I wish you could.'

'That's the worst of it, all this secrecy.'

'I'm sorry.'

'No, I'm sorry, this is not the time for going on about our situation, just remember that I'm here if you need me.'

Bill stared at her out of puzzled blue eyes, opened his mouth to say something, but there was no sound. He hadn't made any real progress over the past few days; the doctors couldn't give her a very positive prognosis. She smiled at him, and wondered why they had taken his teeth out, knowing that if he had been in the full of his health he would have hated that indignity, and there was a tube inserted in his nose which must have been extremely uncomfortable. What was going to happen to him if he couldn't go home again?

She had talked to Dermot about the possibility of bringing him to stay at Mount Asher Road, and arranging for a nurse to look after him, but he had been totally against it, so she had had to consider the nursing home option. These days, when she wasn't at the hospital she spent her time checking them out, not terribly happy with anything she saw. But she put his name down in the best, aware that there was no guarantee that a room would be available when he needed it.

'Hi Kate.'

She looked up, surprised to see Irene standing by her side.

'How are you?'

'How is he?'

'Not very well.'

'Hello Bill?' she said loudly as she walked up the length of the bed and peered down at him. But Bill's eyes were closed, and she repeated the words a second time as if he was deaf, but there was no response. She put an expensive basket of fruit down on the trolley.

'He won't be able to eat the fruit, they feed him through a tube, he has no swallow.'

'The thought of that is awful,' Irene grimaced.

'Hope it never comes to either of us.'

'I'd kill myself first, and if I can't, you're to do it for me.'

'Sure, I'll think of something.' Kate had a mental picture of strangling Irene, or giving her an overdose of some lethal drug. She shivered at the thought.

'I'll leave the fruit anyway.' Irene slid it into the centre of the trolley.

'Why don't you take it home, it seems a shame to waste it,' Kate suggested.

'No thanks, don't fancy eating anything out of a hospital, God only knows what I might catch. Maybe the old guys might eat some of it.' She looked around at the other occupants of the ward, most of whom were elderly men like Bill. 'They're all look so crocked they would be better off dead. Who wants to live like that?' She fiddled with her white silk blouse collar.

'He'll get better, I hope.' Kate patted his hand.

'It doesn't look like there's much possibility of that. Sure isn't he paralysed all down one side, has lost his speech and God knows what else?'

'Sshhh, he might hear,' Kate warned.

'That seems unlikely too.' She stood up. 'Now I must be off, if he wakes up make sure to tell him I was here, and show him the fruit, even if he can't eat it, will you?'

'Yes.' Kate compressed her lips with irritation.

'Oh, I almost forgot, would you drop me to the airport on Wednesday morning, I'm going to New York for a few days shopping?'

'What time is the flight?'

'Eight, I check-in at six, so if you call for me just after five, we should get there in time.'

'It's a bit early,' Kate couldn't resist pointing that out. 'What about a taxi?'

'You know I don't trust taxis, remember that time when it didn't turn up and I missed my flight, I can't take the chance.'

Kate agreed, resigned to it.

'Why not come with me?' Irene smiled enthusiastically. 'We could take in a couple of shows and blitz the shops. I'll try to book you on the same flight, what do you think?'

'No, Irene, I couldn't go away at the moment, particularly with Uncle Bill being so ill.'

'He's being well cared for by the look of it, probably wouldn't even notice if you disappeared for a few days, he's asleep most of the time, isn't he?'

'No, I have to be here,' Kate was almost tempted to tell Irene that going to New York on a shopping spree with her was the last thing she wanted to do, the very last.

'Well, your loss, I'll see you on Wednesday morning, byee.'

She turned and clip-clopped her way across the shining floor tiles in her high-heels. Kate didn't even look up to see her leave.

But for all that, she was the only visitor. Kate had asked Dermot and the lads to drop in, but they hadn't bothered.

Chapter Thirty-Three

Carmen was becoming very nervous about the whole thing. These days she couldn't eat or sleep properly. She thought the time would never come until Manuel and the rest of them were behind bars, and when she could openly walk the streets again. But she knew that if Manuel's lawyers got him off on some technicality, then her life wouldn't be worth much.

Still, the police seemed to be taking it seriously. She watched the group of men who were huddled around a desk and urged them to hurry up. She tapped her long polished fingernails on the imitation leather of her handbag, uncaring about the marks; if it wasn't real leather it was nothing. Her once elegant wardrobe had been cleared up by the janitors at the apartments by now - a black scummy pile of ashes - all that was left of her wonderful life.

But she had managed to keep going, so glad she had that money saved. Somewhere in the back of her mind there must have been a premonition, a lack of trust in Manuel. So while her wardrobe wasn't designer, at least she had been able to afford to buy some new clothes. And although her little room over a dry-cleaners wasn't penthouse style and didn't possess a Jacuzzi, it was somewhere safe to hide. When she went out she wore a wig and felt sure Manuel would never recognise her even if he passed her on the street. After a long wait, they came over to her and explained that they planned to carry out a raid, seize everything and arrest Manuel.

'Have you got the photograph?'

She searched in her wallet for the one she used to carry around with her but couldn't find it. Manual had always liked the idea that she kept his image close to her, it had appealed to the enormous ego of the man, but now she was worried that perhaps it had been thrown away in a mad fit of rage, or just lost. She emptied the bag of its contents until at last she found it tucked behind some business cards.

'That is him.' She slid it across the desk, reluctant to look at it herself. 'You can have it, I have no further interest.' She pushed everything back and zipped the bag closed.

'We will keep in touch with you.'

It was done.

Manuel waited in the shadows behind the small stage, his fingers flexing in preparation for his act. There was a good crowd of appreciative people in tonight and he was looking forward to being the high point of their evening.

The two women in scarlet frilled dresses tapped their black shoes in a loud rat-tat-tat and clicked their castanets as the last bars of music sounded. The crowd roared. Manuel sucked in his stomach, straightened up and leapt on to the stage, feet pounding, every muscle finely tuned. His dancing was the love of his life, more than anything else, even women, or money. Well perhaps not money, particularly when in a matter of hours he would have a greater amount in his bank account than he had ever imagined. The last of the funds were being transferred, so many millions he could hardly control his excitement at the thought of it. Until the other investors received their cut, he would be richer than he ever thought possible.

Chapter Thirty-Four

One evening about five, the doorbell rang and Jack hurried down to answer it, hoping it was Kate. Since her uncle had been taken ill she hadn't been around so often, spending every night and a large portion of her weekends at the hospital. He didn't blame her, but he found it very difficult to tolerate being forced into third or fourth place in the priority stakes in her life.

To his disappointment it wasn't Kate, but Chris who stood outside. 'I thought you were still in Spain?'

'Flew in yesterday for a few days.'

'Eddie with you?' He looked outside.

'No, it's Dermot. He told me that you asked him to come around to see your work so I said I'd give him the guided tour.'

'I asked him?'

'Yea, when you met at Kate's birthday party.'

'More like he invited himself,' he muttered, definitely not in the mood to entertain him.

Dermot hurried up the path and shook his hand energetically. 'So this is where it all happens?'

'This is it.' Jack took a deep breath, ushered them into the lounge, and offered a drink, or coffee. Dermot opted for a whiskey, Chris a glass of white wine. He had a coffee himself, disinclined to drink as he was busy painting a large representational work of a stud farm for a client. The style of painting didn't really appeal to him, but he had accepted the commission. Although if he thought deeply about it, work like this probably had financial motivation just as Dermot had insinuated. They sat chatting for a while, talking mostly about

221

Spain, until Dermot asked when he was going to see the workshop.

'The studio, Dermot,' Chris laughed.

'Whatever. I'm looking forward to seeing some pictures. We have a couple already, Kate bought them, but I'm anxious to choose my own, maybe hang them in the office.'

Reluctantly, Jack led the way upstairs.

'This room is a grand size, and you've plenty of light.' Dermot swung in. 'That painting is really something.' He looked at the half-completed work of the stud. 'How long does it take to finish one that size?' he asked.

'It varies.'

'Could take months, could take hours, isn't that right?' Chris sipped her wine.

'Well, what have you got to show me?' Dermot stood in the middle of the room, and swallowed the last of his whiskey.

'As I said, I haven't much at all at the moment.' Jack struggled to keep his voice light and even, although he felt like telling Dermot to get lost, hating his intrusive attitude.

'What about that there?' He pointed towards a painting which lay on the bench. It was one of Kate, the last to be framed.

'It's for a client.'

'Well, I'll have a gander at it anyway.' He moved across the room.

'I think you should wait until my next exhibition, then there will be plenty of choice.'

'Maybe that would be best, Dermot,' Chris agreed.

'I don't want to wait, I'll be really flush with money soon.'

'What about some of the other galleries in town?' Jack moved towards the door.

'I had my mind set on you, Jack. I told Manuel I was going to invest and he thought it was a great idea. In fact, he's going to come over himself and have a look at your work.'

'I'll be exhibiting in Madrid next year.'

'You could fly over to the opening, Dermot,' Chris suggested.

'When he heard I was coming direct, he was really keen to do the same, cut out the middle-man so to speak.' Dermot picked up the painting of Kate and stared at it. 'I like this, did you get the bird to sit for you, like one of those French painters? She's pretty well covered as well, the Venus type. Do one like that for me, will you? It's just the sort of thing I like, maybe I might even provide the model,' he laughed in a gross manner which made Jack want to take a swing at him.

'You painted it out of your head, didn't you Jack, it's not of anyone in particular.' Chris raised her eyebrows at him. He wondered was that a warning, a don't admit it's Kate whatever you do?

'It's a once-off, Dermot.' Jack crossed the room and took the painting from him. Chris had lost it altogether if she thought for one second that he would inform Dermot that Kate was the subject.

'But if I paid enough, surely that could change your mind?'

'No, I won't be painting anything like that again.' He turned the painting against the wall, and walked purposefully to the door. 'How about another drink?' He guessed that was the best way of getting Dermot out of the studio.

'Never say no.'

They chatted for another hour, until finally Chris rose and decided that she had better go, so he got rid of him as well.

'Thanks a lot for showing me around, Jack, I'll call again. Maybe you'll have some paintings for sale next time.'

'I'll send you an invite to the exhibition.'

'If I'm in the area I'll drop in.'

'I don't expect to have anything.'

'Have a look around, you seem to have loads of pictures here. When I'm flush you could make a real killing. As I said before, I'm not fussy, it just has to have your name on it.'

Chapter Thirty-Five

Irene came over for dinner, Kate forced to ask her when she collected her from the airport this morning. I'd love to have you any time, Kate thought. It was just what she needed after hanging around for the delayed flight, then going in to see Uncle Bill, and after that having to cook a full dinner just to suit her. She had promised Jack that she would see him some time in the late afternoon, and now had to phone with her excuses. A silence at the other end of the line when she explained the exigencies of her day.

'I feel like I'm in a chatroom on the Internet, someone without depth or reality who spouts words on a screen,' he said, irritated.

'I'm sorry,' was all she could say, unable to give him a decent reason as to why she couldn't see him, the demands of her domestic life so petty.

'Well, I've got work to do, see you...whenever you can fit me in.' He cut himself off, leaving her feeling worse than ever. He was erratic by nature and could be short-tempered too, hating or loving a person instantly. It was the way he responded to her, his feelings so intense there was never any hesitancy, or doubt, he just loved with every breath.

Dermot arrived back in amazingly good form and sooner than she expected.

'Have you eaten?' she asked.

'Yea, grabbed a bite at the golf club.' He looked beyond her to Irene, and grinned. 'How was the Big Apple, Irene, all the shops out of stock now?'

'Fantastic, Dermot, I had a ball.' She waved her glass. 'Come and join me, I brought you a bottle of whiskey, and a nice silk scarf for you, Kate, which you haven't even opened yet, I might add.'

She undid the pretty parcel and admired the floral patterned scarf which was in shades of pink, not to her taste at all. Then she poured a whiskey for Dermot, another for Irene, and left them together while she pottered in the kitchen wondering how she could organise to meet Jack tomorrow. The morning was out as there was a breakfast-meeting arranged with a client. Lunchtime simply couldn't be predicted at this point. The evening was given over to Uncle Bill and whatever else needed to be done. Now she cooked a chicken dish for the next day, baked a lasagne, did some cleaning downstairs, keeping busy until she was asked to make coffee and felt obliged to join them.

'I was just telling Irene about the Spanish property deal. I thought we might move house, we can afford it now, what do you think? I've been talking to an estate agent about properties, perhaps we might run a business from there.'

'Are you serious?' She was puzzled and disbelieving.

'You can find somewhere in the country with a decent piece of land around it, mingle with the county set,' Irene added, puffing on her cigarette.

'I thought we might operate a stud farm, there's great money to be made in that racket. We could pick up somewhere like that place I saw in the picture yer man was painting. Chris took me around to his house yesterday, and I'm hoping to invest a bit of money there too if he has anything to sell.'

Kate stiffened.

'Who are you referring to?' Irene asked through a haze of smoke.

'Jack Linley, one of those artists who does that sort of impressionistic stuff, he's a brother of Chris.'

'I've heard his name, he's becoming quite well-known apparently,' Irene said with a knowledgeable air. 'One of his paintings was sold for a fair whack at a charity auction recently, it was a huge thing.'

'Bit of a wimp, you know the type.'

'We never found him like that.' Kate couldn't resist.

'Probably appeals to you women, nancy boy.'

'What do you mean?' Kate snapped, hating his denigration of Jack.

'He's not a man's man,' he scoffed.

'What sort of a man is that? One who drinks twenty pints in an evening, uses foul language, and spends all his time looking at sport on the television? There is certainly more to him than that!'

'Rushing to his defence? Listen to that Irene, all these culture-vultures stick together.'

'I'm not into the type Kate has described either, Dermot.' Irene sniffed.

'I'm just keen to invest some money when I get my share of the profits. Now let me show you a few brochures.' He went into his study, and returned with lists of properties which he spread out on the coffee-table.

'Kildare, near the Curragh, what do you think?' He passed a photograph to Kate.

'I can't move to Kildare,' she said.

'Why not?' He shuffled through the brochures.

'What about my job?'

'It's nothing compared to what I'm planning. Mags and Carol can get someone else, you're not indispensable.'

'I don't want to.' She could feel herself becoming angry.

'Don't be such a stick-in-the-mud, Kate. I'm giving you a chance to change your life completely, you won't know yourself. Have a look at this place in Tipperary, what do you think of that?'

But his words meant something entirely different to Kate. The idea of changing her life brought Jack into her mind, imagining what it would be like if she said no to Dermot, and woke up every morning and went to sleep at night beside him. To escape into a heavenly place where love was the only thing that mattered.

'We'll be an amazing team together. You'll be so good at the PR side of things, dealing with all the sheiks from Saudi Arabia with their fabulous bloodstock, and I'll handle the financial side. We won't know ourselves this time next year.'

'Yes, an amazing team,' she murmured.

'Maybe I could get involved as well, Dermot? I've plenty of contacts.' Irene was excited.

'It's a fantastic idea. Imagine living in the peace and quiet of the country, not a person for miles. Shane and Conor can live here, let them make as much noise as they like.'

Dermot laughed. Irene laughed. But Kate couldn't even manage a smile.

As it seemed the evening would go on for ever, an idea formed in her mind, something she couldn't resist.

'Dermot, I'm going over to Carol...I promised to...' She stood in the doorway.

'Bit late, isn't it?'

'I won't be that long,' she said nervously.

'I'll look after him,' Irene smiled.

He sat down, and flicked the television on with the remote. Kate quickly took her opportunity and left before he said any more.

In the car, she phoned Carol. 'Could you do me a favour?'

'Yea, sure, what is it?' She was her usual bright breezy self.

'If Dermot rings looking for me, would you say I've been with you, and phone me? I'll only answer if it's you.'

'When?'

'In the next hour...or so...'

'Sure.'

'I'll tell you about it when I see you, just back me up on this, please?' Kate drove through Rathgar.

'You're in the car?' Carol asked.

'I've somewhere to go.'

'Don't worry, I'll cover for you.'

'Thanks, I appreciate it.'

'You owe me one!'

Her next call was to Jack, to let him know that she was five minutes away.

'I spent most of the evening at home with Mam and Dad, I'm not back that long.' He put his arms around her. 'And please forgive me for snapping at you earlier. My patience just ran out at that moment, and you know what I'm like if anything upsets my plans.' He kissed her.

'You're like every man I know, you always want your own way,' she teased.

'I'll just keep all the impatience bottled up.'

'Then you'll explode some day and that will be worse than all the little gripes put together. You're a temperamental artist, never know what you might do or say.'

'I'm all those things, and worse probably, that's why I've lived on my own for so long. I wouldn't dare ask any woman to put up with me, that is, until now. So if I want you, I have to curb my irascible tendencies and behave like a normal human being.' He smiled down at her. 'I promise I will really try.' They sat close together on the couch, drinking coffee and talking. This evening there was no wild lovemaking, it was an unusually quiet time between them.

'We were married for five years, and it was good, I have to admit, we enjoyed life, that is until...' he hesitated, staring at some point across the room.

Kate was silent.

'Paula became pregnant...but it was unplanned, and didn't suit her, so she went to London...' His body was suddenly taut and he reached forward to put the empty coffee mug on the table. Kate could see the pain in his dark eyes knowing by the tight grip of his fingers that he was still hurting. He continued in a tirade about how he had struggled to deal with what was the worst thing that ever happened to him. On and on, until slowly the anger eased out, and he talked directly to her again. 'I'm sorry to have burdened you with this.'

'I don't think I've been much help to you.'

'It's the first time I've talked about it in years,' he admitted, 'it was good to get it out, important that you understand the things that matter to me. To have shared it makes me feel closer to you, if that is possible.' The shadow faded from his eyes.

She nodded.

'I have come to terms with it. That might be hard for you to believe, but it's been put away in the past and has no relevance to us. I wish I'd met you twenty years ago, it would have changed everything, but even though we're starting late, I know I want to spend the rest of my life with you, to marry you, take care of you.' He looked at her, questioning.

'It's a bit too soon for me, there is so much going on in my life now. Can you be patient and wait to see how things pan out?' she had to say it, had to disappoint him.

'I'll try. The new Jack Linley will try very hard.' He hugged her. 'All that matters is that you love me as much as I love you.'

She left shortly after that, her mind racing as she remembered the things he had talked about, and thought how much she would have loved to be able to have a child with him, to give him such a gift, even at this stage in their lives. But that wasn't possible now.

Chapter Thirty-Six

Dermot took out the files on the Spanish project and stared at the figures, thinking about the profits which should be deposited in his account in the Caymans today. As the bank wasn't open yet, he tried to concentrate on some other work, but it was impossible. He ran his finger around the inside of his shirt collar, loosened the knot in his tie, and poured himself a whiskey, fantasising about what he was going to do with the money, his plans ballooning out of all proportion.

He surfed the Internet looking for investment opportunities in the Caribbean, even checked the flights, hoping to take a trip out there soon to have a look around. There was a huge tourist industry and he was sure that he would find something waiting for him which would double or even treble his millions. Billionaire status loomed on the horizon. He wondered about buying one of the smaller islands with white beaches and palm trees, imagined retiring somewhere like that. He dreamed on until he reckoned the bank was open and checked the balance in his account using all the security codes, but to his disappointment nothing had been lodged. He rang Manuel's number, but was told he wasn't in the office. He tried his mobile, but couldn't make contact. A sudden worry began to eat away at the base of his stomach, but he tried to convince himself that he was being ridiculous. It was a huge undertaking, and timing could easily change.

*

The red Ferrari accelerated along the motorway and overtook the other traffic with a loud roar. Manuel loved his latest acquisition, the beauty of the sleek body, the softness of the leather upholstery, and above all the power of the engine which gave him that terrifying death-defying thrill when he pushed it to its maximum.

He slipped in a CD and relaxed back into the low racing bucket seat, as his favourite flamenco music filled the small space, tapping his fingers on the steering wheel in time with the rhythm. He was happy today, so many things whirling around in his head, most of all his business plans, and the new woman in his life.

The phone rang and he turned off the CD.

'Si?'

'Manuel...'

'Javier?' He glanced at himself in the mirror admiring his dark Moorish features. Ran a finger along one eyebrow settling a stray hair, and suddenly worried that there might be the slightest growth of beard, he took the electric-shaver from the pocket in the door and used it to smooth the already smooth.

'I have some information for you.'

He switched off the shaver and listened more intently.

'You are alone?' his informant asked.

'Si, si, get on with it.'

'There will be a raid on your office by the police today.'

'What?' Suddenly, his good mood of a moment ago drained away.

'It may be just a rumour but I think my source is reliable.'

'Why? What time?' Manuel asked, wondering frantically what this was all about.

'I have to go...' The man put the phone down.

Manuel continued driving, but his pace slowed as he began to compute the information which had just been imparted. His mind swept from one possibility to another. His stomach was twisted into a tight knot, and perspiration soaked the fresh white shirt. Suddenly, he pulled across the motorway into the side lane and took the exit back to Alicante, where he went straight to his bank.

He was nervous, worried that perhaps someone would become suspicious of him. While the bank manager checked the account, his heart thudded inside his chest, his hands clenched. He smiled at the man who was keying-in codes into the computer. The seconds counted down in his head far too slowly. He prayed that all the money would have been deposited, if there was any delay he was finished. Finally, after what seemed an age, the manager confirmed the amount lodged over the last few days, and he sighed with relief. Quickly then, he instructed him to transfer it to his account in the Caymans, making some rather lame joke about not lasting very long. They shook hands and he left, hardly able to believe that everything had gone so well. Now his fortune was made, all those millions sitting there waiting for him. To hell with the rest of the investors, he thought, only concerned with his own future now.

Once he had left the bank, he headed to the airport and took the first flight out. Within a short time he was in Madrid, a few hours later in London, finally catching a flight for the Caribbean.

Chapter Thirty-Seven

Kate spotted Carol getting out of her car, and caught up with her just as the lift door opened. They stepped inside together.

'I've something to tell you,' Kate said slowly, knowing that she would have to come clean.

'There's no need, Kate.' Carol put a hand on her arm in a staying gesture.

'But last night I...'

'You asked me to do something for you, and I did it gladly.'

'Thanks a million, but I feel I should explain.'

'I don't want to hear another word about it,' Carol said as the lift arrived at their floor and they walked into reception.

'About what?' Mags spoke from behind.

Kate turned sharply, with no explanation at the ready.

'I told her I was glad to see her finishing up at five o'clock these days, she has been working far too hard.'

'Yea, I agree. There's more to life than the hard slog,' Mags said, 'and for God's sake, will you take some holidays, how many weeks have you built up?'

'Only a few days.'

'You'd better take them or you'll lose them, that's company policy, isn't it Carol?' They walked down the corridor.

'When are you going to use that voucher?'

'I haven't decided yet.'

'Hurry up or it'll have expired.'

Kate was grateful to Carol for her generosity, but she would have felt better telling her about Jack, and confessing that she had used her as an excuse more than once; last night being the first time she had phoned to ask.

'She was so nice, it made me feel really guilty for putting her in such a position.' Kate felt downcast.

'Cheer up, my love, she's a good friend to have,' Jack reassured.

Her worries receded. It was always like that. He could take her with him into another world so fast real life just evaporated like spilled water in sunshine, as if it never existed.

'Love you.'

'I love you so much. When I'm with you, I'm someone else entirely.'

'That's because you are mine now, and I'm never going to let you go.' He threaded his fingers through hers. 'Some day I'm going to put a ring on the third finger of this hand.'

'I can't imagine that.'

'I am consumed with you. It's like we are marooned on a desert island, no-one else for thousands of miles.'

'I'll be Woman Friday, you can be Robinson Crusoe.'

'What an idyllic prospect.'

'It would be like a dream come true.'

'I'm not a dream, I'm flesh and blood, the real thing, and don't you forget it.' He pulled her closer and convinced her of that.

Afterwards, they showered together, but as usual time ran out far too quickly.

'I'm going to have to go, my love, tempus fugit,' she murmured.

'Don't. Stay here with me and send Dermot an email.'

'Wonder what he would say?' she mused.

'He'd be furious, of course, to lose the best thing in his life.'

He went to the wardrobe and opened it. 'Put this robe on you, I don't want you to catch cold.' He slid the white satin over her shoulders.

'What's this, very feminine, very sexy for a man?' She pulled it around her.

'It's yours, to wear when you're here with me.'

'A kimono, how lovely, thank you so much.'

'It suits you.' He helped her slip into it, and tied the belt to one side as she stood in front of the mirror admiring herself. He reached into the wardrobe and took out a matching pair of pyjamas. 'These go with it, not that I want you to wear them too often, but I'd like you to leave them here, then I'll have a part of you with me all the time, as well as that little scrap of lace I have tucked away in a drawer,' he grinned.

'I was mortified over that, although the girls thought it was hilarious.'

'You told them?'

'No, I just mentioned I'd met someone, you're called David by the way.'

'I wouldn't mind being called David if we could come out in the open and behave like normal human beings.'

She didn't answer him, and began to examine the intricate embroidery on the cuffs. 'You spoil me.'

'That's what I enjoy doing. I'm never happy unless you're with me, always imagining how it could be if we were together, sharing our home, sharing our whole lives. Tell me that it's going to be like that, tell me.' His eyes demanded an answer.

'I want it to be that way too, but with Uncle Bill...'

'If we were together, you could still look after your uncle, and I can help as well then. As it is, I feel I'm invisible.'

'I'm sorry, but I just couldn't walk out now.'

'Saying you're sorry is no use' He was suddenly annoyed with her. 'I sometimes wonder whether you feel as strongly as I do? Maybe it's a little less important for you, no need to make decisions yet or change the status quo.'

'It is important to me, how can you even suggest that?'

'It's the frustration of not knowing where I stand, that's the worst part of it.'

'Jack, I love you.'

'Being the "other man" in a triangle is...awful.' His expression was suddenly grim. 'And I hate the secrecy. Tell Dermot about us, make a clean break.'

'I'll think about it, I promise.'

'You mean that?'

'I mean it.'

The doctor announced that they could do nothing more for Uncle Bill and he would be discharged shortly. Kate immediately began to ring the nursing homes on her list, but they had nothing to offer, and she was forced to go further afield, in the end lucky to find one in Dun Laoghaire with an availability. She went to inspect the place. It was spotlessly clean, and the twin-bedded room on the first floor had been attractively decorated in shades of peach.

'The dining-rooms, sitting-rooms, conservatory and the garden will all add value to his life,' assured the Head Staff Nurse.

I don't think so, Kate thought savagely, seeing it as a kind of prison, with high walls around it, and that slight, ever so slight, whiff she had noticed once or twice. Tears threatened to overwhelm her, but she forced a bright expression on her face as she followed the nurse around. In the day room a man played keyboard and a few creaky female voices sang along with "Somewhere over the Rainbow". Other residents watched the television, or sat there unresponsive. These were the more agile who could get around by themselves; the stroke victims, like Bill, were confined to bed most of the time, although Staff Nurse assured her that he would be brought down in the wheelchair as much as possible.

So she accepted the room for Uncle Bill, sharing with a man who was well able to get around. But it was expensive and she prayed there would be enough money in the bank and that his house would never have to be sold. She was reluctant to calculate how long it would last, desperately hoping he would make a full recovery and be able to return home soon. She managed to get in every day to see him for an hour or more after work. It became part of her routine, going into the office earlier to balance that extra time, and preparing as much food as she could for the freezer at the weekends, or late at night. And in the middle of all that, Jack had to be kept happy as well.

Today Uncle Bill was asleep when she arrived, so she kissed his forehead, and at the touch of her lips his eyes opened and he smiled, reaching his one good hand out to her

'How are you?' she asked, putting down the bag she had brought with her and sitting beside him. 'Were you downstairs today? Was there any music? Did anyone else come in to talk to you?' The stream of questions and remarks probably made no sense to him, but she did it all the same, determined to be normal although there was no response from him other than when he squeezed her hand.

'Dermot says hi.' And that's about all, he won't cross the threshold, he hates hospitals, she thought. 'Shane and Conor send their love.' Which isn't worth anything really since they don't bother to come in and see you either. 'And I've got a Mass Card for you. Isn't it nice? Look at the picture.' She held it up so that he could see it, and he smiled again. 'We'll put it on your locker. And here are some lovely yellow chrysanths, like the ones that grow in your garden.' She still brought flowers, but found that the following day they had been removed, and usually disappeared forever. It bugged her, but she said nothing, anxious to stay on the good side of the staff, most of whom were really nice. However, there were some who had very short fuses and she didn't want Bill to be at the receiving end of their ill-humour.

She began her usual ritual. She took away any clothes to be washed, and put clean ones into his locker. She combed his hair, buffed his fingernails, rubbed moisturising cream into his hands and face, applied the special preparation for his feet which were affected with a dry skin rash. Then she read to him from a Western she had found in a second-hand shop. Although she didn't know how much of it he understood, she continued with a page or two of the story for him.

This evening the doctor called her into his office before she left and told her that Uncle Bill was weakening. He went on to mutter vaguely about the affects of the stroke and his age, and that he wanted her to be prepared. But how could you be prepared for something like that? she asked herself. He was only here a short time, and there hadn't been any great change in him, how could they see what she couldn't? They didn't love him.

'I've got the details of that trade-show in Bermingham next month. Who's going?' Mags asked.

'Sorry, I can't, not at the moment.' Kate wasn't in the mood for a junket, particularly with Uncle Bill being ill. She didn't know how long more he had and certainly wouldn't want to be out of the country if anything happened.

Carol shook her head. 'I don't think I can spare the time.'

'I'm having my portrait painted, so I'm all tied up,' Mags giggled.

'I suppose I could fly over for the day,' Carol sighed, 'how is the masterpiece coming along?'

'I haven't seen it yet. He won't let me look, but he says it's almost finished so I don't know how many more sittings there will be.'

'Let's decide on the advertising, I have to get back to the agency by this afternoon.' Kate spread the photographs out on the desk.

'Are you wearing any clothes, or is it a nude study?' Carol asked.

'I'm covered with a sort of gauzy thing, and I can tell you it's frustrating.'

'Wow! May I ask who made that decision?' She raised her eyebrows. Kate tightened her lips.

'I did, of course. I want to look my very best, and make sure everyone raves about my painting.'

'It will be interesting when you finish the painting bit, and get down to the real nitty-gritty. Tell us, has he succumbed to your charms yet?'

'Not quite. So far he's been very business-like about the whole thing, but I'm praying that it will all happen naturally one evening.'

'What does he charge? Maybe I'll have mine done as well, interesting to have myself hanging on the wall in the nude,' Carol asked.

'We haven't discussed price yet, but I'm hoping he won't charge at all, once things start to happen.'

'You're probably driving the poor man mad, teasing him until he can't see straight.'

'I hope so.'

To Kate's relief, they finally changed the subject and the morning passed as they argued about the options of the campaign proposed by their advertising agency. Although they didn't need to market the company as such, it was always good to have a corporate presence in the various glossy interior and architectural magazines. Planning to call over to Jack today, she was nervous as it began to seem as if she wasn't going to make it.

'Let's do lunch, we haven't been out in ages,' Mags suggested.

'Yea, good idea,' Carol agreed.

'I can't, sorry.' Kate felt embarrassed as she tried to think of an excuse.

'Why not?' Carol asked.

'Eh...'

'You've brought your egg-sandwiches and a flask, is that it?' Mags hooted with laughter.

'Come on, for God's sake, see you in five, we'll take a taxi.' Carol stood up.

'I have to go to see our solicitor with Dermot, some property deal,' she stuttered. It wasn't a little white lie, but a big black mortler, and she felt guilty as she drove over to Harrington Park, her insides churning.

'I've missed you,' Jack whispered.

'I saw you on Sunday.' She managed to smile, remembering the time they had spent walking in the forest, the morning mild and sunny, and so early there was no-one else to be seen. But underneath her normal exterior, her emotions were jangled, particularly since hearing that he was painting Mags in the nude. She really wanted to quiz him. Was she beautiful? And had she exaggerated the fact that she was partially covered? And did he fancy her?

'I've got some lunch ready, you must be starving.' He took her hand.

'For you.'

'You're something else, I can't keep up with you.'

She leaned and touched his lips with hers, moving softly, until they went upstairs to bed, forgetting all about the lunch. But today, her lovemaking was different. There was a sense of desperation in her, as if she wanted to imprint herself on his consciousness and blot out any influence that Mags might have exercised on him.

And then, just at a crucial moment, a delicate balance on the edge of love, there was a ring on the doorbell. She froze, and stared horrified at Jack.

'Ignore it.' He reached for her again.

'See who it is.'

'Could be anyone, forget it.'

'No, look out.'

He went over to the window, raised a wooden slat and peered down at the front door. 'It's Dermot.'

'My God, I hope he doesn't see my car, where is he parked?' She joined him, and for a few seconds she was unable to breathe with shock. She began to pull on her clothes.

'Don't worry.' He turned back to her. 'There's no need to dress, he'll go away.'

The doorbell rang again.

'I must. If he comes in I can say I'm here looking at paintings, or something!'

'He can't come in unless I open the door.'

'I know that, but the very thought of him being outside freaks me, it's horrible, almost like he was peering in the window at us.' She struggled with the zip on her trousers, tugging until it finally came up, and pulled on her jacket.

'Don't be silly, come back into bed.' He kissed her. 'I shouldn't have told you who it was.'

'I can't stay, I feel so weird.'

'He's forcing you to leave.'

'No, he isn't, it's just I...'

She ran a comb through her hair.

'Kate, don't let's waste our time worrying about Dermot.' He looked out again. 'He's heading back down the path to the car, you can relax.'

'Relax?' she exclaimed.

'He's gone, driven off.'

But she couldn't stay a moment longer. She rushed back to the office in a guilt-ridden heap, trying to behave as if nothing unusual had happened.

'It's finished!' Conor sat down heavily into a chair, his whole demeanour one of defeat.

'I'm sorry, love, what happened?' Kate asked.

'She threw me out, the bitch, would you believe?'

'But something must have caused it, she didn't seem like the sort of person who would suddenly do that.'

'You don't know what she's really like, all very nice when you met her, but at home it was something else.' He stood up and opened the fridge. 'Anything to eat?'

'I could make you a sandwich.'

'Thanks, make it a double-decker with plenty in it, I'm going in here to look at what I want on the television.' He disappeared.

Kate busied herself at the counter, thinking that the old adage was true. Come to live with me and you'll get to know me. If she decided to give everything up for Jack, would it turn out the same as Conor and Nicola eventually, or herself and Dermot? Were relationships doomed to failure regardless, and did most couples stay together unhappily for the sake of the marriage, or the children, or what the family might think, hurtling from one crisis to the next? Was she doomed to continue in this rut for the next forty years, if she lived that long? Now that Jack had told her

241

how he felt, she was split in two. Deep inside, her heart and emotions were centred on him, while outside she continued to play the part of the wife of Dermot Mason, who seemed to feel nothing at all for her, needing only those practical things that she provided. It was as if he were her child. She looked after him; always there when he wanted her to entertain his clients, or by his side at family gatherings.

Give me a script. Learn the words off by heart and spew them out when required. That's me, she thought, a boring nothing person. Part of the furniture, like a housekeeper employed to ensure that the environment of the Mason family was always in pristine condition.

Chapter Thirty-Eight

Dermot tried Manuel's phone for the hundredth time that day but still couldn't get through. No-one answered the phones in the office, or replied to faxes or emails. There had to be a rational explanation. The computers were down, or maybe the electricity had failed. It probably takes as long in Spain to have something repaired as it does here. Give it time, don't be impatient, he told himself severely. But as the days passed, all he could think of was his money. Nothing had been lodged yet, and it was the fate of his original investment that worried him most – the millions in profit he had hoped to make suddenly seemed less important. He pulled open the drawer of the desk, took out the whiskey bottle and poured a glass. It was the only thing that kept him sane now, his excuse that it was for medicinal purposes.

But towards the end of the week he grew more uptight, and eventually decided to go over to Spain himself. He flew into Alicante and took a taxi to Manuel's office immediately, determined to march in and demand to know what was going on. If there was even a suggestion of anything suspect, he would force Manuel to give him his money back.

The taxi-driver drove quickly through the sunlit streets, jamming on the brakes to avoid pedestrians as they stepped out without any warning, causing Dermot's already-jangled nerves to spin in crazy circles. He tried to calm himself. There was no point in arriving angry and aggressive to find that there was nothing wrong at all, only some breakdown in communication, a simply-explained glitch. He could imagine Manuel's smiling unconcerned face as he waved his hands about, reassuring him that he was worrying needlessly. By the time the taxi drew up outside the office, he began to feel a little foolish, and wondered if he had over-reacted. The building looked normal, so it hadn't been burnt down or blown up. He gave the taxi-man a big tip. Gracias. Thanks for the ride.

He walked into the foyer, but then his recently-elevated heart took a dive into the depths again as he saw that instead of the pretty receptionist, there was a policeman standing there, his cold eyes looking straight at him. Dermot froze. A nervous hammering reverberated through him, and he wondered what he was going to say to this man, as all the Spanish he knew had gone out of his head.

'Senor?' The policeman stepped towards him.

'I'm just looking for an office, oficina, donde es?' He had to think of a name, any name. 'Perez, Oficina Perez,' he stuttered, 'no hablo Espagnol.'

There was a puzzled look on the stern features, and one hand moved slowly towards the gun in the holster. Dermot began to shake.

'Donde, Perez, Perez and Sons, computers,' he said it slower this time, 'acqui?'

The man shook his head.

'Thanks, gracias.' He forced a smile on to his face and backed away, afraid even to take his eyes off the figure in front of him. He nodded and gave the man a vague sort of salute as he exited through the door. Then he forced himself to walk slowly along the street staring up at the buildings, keeping up the lost act although he was perspiring profusely with terror by then. He reached the corner, quickly hailed a taxi and directed the driver to the airport, hoping this time that the journey would be covered as fast as the previous guy had managed.

There was something going on there, and he was involved in whatever it was. He thought of the fraudulent property deals, and felt sick. It had never crossed his mind that anything could happen. Manuel was so sure of himself, and Dermot knew that he wasn't the only person who had invested money. There were people from all over Europe buying properties through Manuel, but who owned them now? And what about his interest? Did it even amount to a euro?

At the airport he tried not to appear too nervous. If the police had followed him, they could nab him here, or even on the plane. And they had guns. Perspiration dribbled down the sides of his temples. 'I need to get to Dublin, urgently.' He dabbed his brow with a handkerchief. 'Someone is dying, it is very important.' It's me, he thought, I'm going to die if I don't get away from here fast.

The girl tapped at the computer keys.

'There is no flight until 19.30.'

'It has to be earlier, what about London?'

'There is a flight at 18.00 hours.'

'Nothing sooner?' I'll have to hang around here, they'll be bound to spot me, he panicked.

'You could take a flight to Madrid and connect onwards?'

'No...no...that wouldn't suit, I could be further delayed there.' He needed to get out of the country fast. 'I must get closer to home, it is very urgent.' He leaned over the counter towards her, a tragic expression on his face.

She smiled in an understanding way, and tapped some more.

'There is a flight leaving in thirty minutes for Amsterdam, and with seats available, but you would need to hurry, they will be boarding shortly.'

'Yes, yes, I'll take that, no problem to get out of there,' he smiled with relief, and glanced over his shoulder. The airport was busy, people walking in and out, carrying bags and pushing trolleys. He couldn't see any police, but there were a couple of security men standing near the doors and he wondered were they watching out for him? He turned back to the girl, his stomach in a sudden cramp as he lifted up his holdall and made ready to go towards the departure gates. Taking his passport from the inside pocket of his jacket and putting it down in front of the girl with his credit card, he prayed that she wouldn't have any instructions to prevent a Dermot Mason leaving the country.

'Go straight to Gate 6, I will tell them you are on your way.'

'Thanks a million, I can't thank you enough, gracias.' He turned and walked quickly towards the departure area. Not too fast. Don't draw attention. You're just a person who's a bit late for his flight, it happens all the time in airports, doesn't mean you're a criminal on the run. The very idea panicked him again and he glanced over his shoulder, expecting someone to grab him from behind at any moment, stick a gun barrel in his back and shout stop.

The next hurdle was the security, and he stood in line, his heart doing a drum solo inside his chest. Nervously he moved back a little and stepped on the shoe of a man behind. He turned around to meet the eyes of a rather austere man who was obviously not very pleased to have his big toe crunched under Dermot's heels. The man looked down at his foot, moved the shiny patent-leather shoe this way and that, and Dermot followed his gaze wondering if he expected him to bend down, spit on it and rub it with his handkerchief? He smiled at him, shrugged in that typical Spanish fashion, then turned to find that he was next. He put his bag on the scanner, walked through the doorway, but the bleeper went off. His heart sank, his stomach cramped up again, as the security guard motioned him back, and indicated that he should empty his pockets. His keys, money, wallet, and lighter were put in a container, and he went through again and to his relief arrived on the other side without a squeak. At the boarding-area he was ushered down the stairs to the bus, the last person to depart.

Chapter Thirty-Nine

'Kate, I have a delivery here for you.' The girl at reception called out and she turned back, more than surprised to see her hold up a large bouquet. 'Anniversary?' She grinned.

'Eh...yea.' Kate was embarrassed, knowing instantly who had sent it. She hurried towards her office, hoping to get back without being noticed, but that didn't happen. Her heart sank when she spotted Mags coming towards her.

'More flowers?' She raised her eyebrows in surprise. 'Dermot is surpassing himself. Spill the beans.'

'Eh, we had a row, it's a peace-offering.'

'Let's see.' Mags took the bouquet out of her hand and pushed her face into the cluster, breathing deeply. 'Wish Jack would send me flowers...not much chance of that now.'

Shocked, Kate stared at her for a few seconds.

'You're so lucky.'

When they met together later, the main topic of conversation between Carol and Mags was the portrait.

'I'm dying to see it, you'll have to invite us to the unveiling party,' Carol said.

'No, I won't be doing that, I'm not that keen on it.' Mags didn't look happy.

'What?'

'I thought it would be more naturalistic, and that I would recognise myself at least, but it's very abstract.'

'Things didn't go according to plan then?'

'No.' Mags was sullen.

'I'm sorry.'

'And he probably knows how I feel after this.'

'You didn't tell him?' Carol seemed horrified.

Kate listened but made no comment, feeling treacherous as she hugged her secret to herself.

'Not in so many words, but when he brought it around, I took out a bottle of champagne, and suggested we make a night of it, but he was too busy apparently and had to rush off. He couldn't be bothered to take a few hours off for me.'

'That doesn't mean he knows how you feel.'

'He can't be that thick.'

'It was nice to have the painting done anyway and maybe just as well you know where you stand now,' Carol said gently.

'Thanks a bunch.'

'How much did he charge?'

'He didn't charge at all. He said he enjoyed doing it, and when I heard that I really felt over the moon, full sure that he...'

'So I can't ask him now.' Carol looked at Kate. 'And neither can you. It's such a pity, all my hopes of seeing myself reproduced on canvas for posterity are gone down the tubes.'

After that they concentrated on work, and it was only when she had returned to her office that Kate was able to open the card. A glow infused her as she read it, and she lifted the phone immediately. Jack denied that it was any more than a tiny gesture, and that he loved her so much more, and how about a room full of flowers, or a house, or the world?

'Dermot got the credit again, I'm sorry to say.'

'Once you know who sent them, that's all I care about. But when am I going to see you? It's been over a week and I miss you so much.'

She was silent then, not knowing what to say. She was still in fright since that day when Dermot had called, and had refused to go near Harrington Park since.

She brought in the flowers to Uncle Bill, but he took no notice, so she put them in the little oratory. There was a blank nothingness in his eyes during the last few days, and no matter what she said or did it made no difference to him. She couldn't help but see how feeble he had become and that the doctor had been right. His one good hand didn't reach out to her in greeting any longer. The little smile on his lips was something which she missed, and his blue eyes were sunken back in their sockets. Some of the time he didn't even recognise her. Very down, she walked out to the car. She had to search in her bag for the keys and didn't notice the black jeep parked beside hers, until a voice called her name and she looked up to see Jack standing in front of her.

'What are you doing here?' she asked, delighted to see him.

'I decided to surprise you, my patience ran out,' he smiled and moved towards her.

'It's so good to see you.'

He clasped her in his arms. 'How is your Uncle?'

'Not so good.' A cloud came over her again.

'I'm sorry to hear that, my love.'

'It's just...no-one in the family seems to care. They don't even bother coming in to see him, except Irene occasionally, and Carol, although now it probably isn't important, he doesn't even recognise me.' She couldn't help the tears which filled her eyes, and he pulled her close to him again. But just then a car appeared, and as Kate became aware of it she immediately broke away, and looked around, rigid with shock when she saw that it was Carol and Mags who were now climbing out of the car a few yards away from them.

Mags stood looking at them for a moment and then stalked towards the door of the nursing home without a word. Carol walked over. 'We're going in to see Uncle Bill.'

'You're very good, thanks.'

'Hi Carol?' Jack smiled at her.

'How're you doing, Jack?'

'Fine thanks, and you?'

'Great, busy as usual.'

Will you shut up, the pair of you, making stupid inane talk, Kate thought. Suddenly irritated with the back and forth of pleasantries which continued between the two of them while she stood there all embarrassed just longing to get away.

'We have to go now,' Kate said, as soon as she could interrupt. They said goodbye, and Carol followed Mags into the nursing home.

She glared at Jack, started up, and quickly drove out on to the main road, quite unaware of her speed. For a few minutes she didn't notice that he had caught up with her, and had flashed his lights a couple of times, indicating left.

'What do you want now, another chance to be seen by someone we know?' she muttered angrily, but she turned anyway at the next opportunity, and pulled up.

'I'm sorry about that,' he said when he sat into her car.

'I thought Carol and yourself would never shut-up, I was mortified,' she burst out, full of ire.

'Sorry, but I couldn't very well ignore her. Anyway, it's better to behave normally.'

'I thought I'd never get away.'

'Well, they know about us now, but they're hardly going to tell the whole world surely?'

'I suppose not,' she sighed, somewhat calmer. 'I'm sorry for losing the head there, but you must have noticed that Mags was furious?'

'I was only looking at you.'

'She'll be really angry.' Kate was upset and didn't know how she was going to deal with it, staring out through the windscreen at a group of boys kicking football, but not really seeing them.

He looked puzzled.

'She likes you, fancies you, I can't believe you've never noticed.'

'She's such a live wire, I thought she was like that with everyone, I didn't think it was me particularly.'

'Don't give me that!' Anger surged inside her again. 'And you painting her in the nude for the last few weeks.'

250

'Don't be ridiculous, Kate, I'm far too old for her.'

'She thinks you're perfect,' she snapped.

'For God's sake, Kate, you're letting your imagination run away with you altogether.' He put his arm around her.

'What about that night you brought her home from a party and tucked her into bed?'

'She was drunk, couldn't put one foot in front of the other.'

'Didn't strike you that it might have been exaggerated just to get you into her bedroom?'

'Will you stop, that's crazy thinking.'

'Might seem funny to you, but maybe she wasn't telling us the whole truth.' She had got herself in a state now, as jealousy mixed with suspicion to produce an irrational anger.

'Are you suggesting that something happened?'

'Well, how would I know?'

'Kate, I haven't been with another woman since that time with you in Spain, and I suppose I could have made the most of the opportunity, but Mags doesn't...'

'There, you're attracted to her.'

He sighed.

'Admit it,' she goaded him.

'Kate, that particular night was before we got together again, it had no bearing on us.'

'So you did make love with Mags?' She was horrified.

'Kate, I told you enough times that nothing happened, and if you don't want to believe me, that's your prerogative!' His anger matched hers now. He opened the door, stepped out and banged it behind him. Furiously, she drove up the road, to find herself in a cul-de-sac which necessitated a series of jerky turns at the top before she could go down again to the main road. She looked straight ahead, and ignored Jack, who still sat in his jeep. Her imagination went into overdrive to a place where she was being used by him, probably among a number of other women with gorgeous slim figures like Mags. Tears filled her eyes and she dashed them away with her hand wishing she had never met him.

Of course, Irene chose this evening to call after dinner. She always seemed to be around these days getting in Kate's way. Now she sat there sipping a glass of whiskey, watching Kate as she took out the ironing-board ready to tackle the pile of clothes which never seemed to diminish. Irene chattered on, her conversation always, but always, about herself. But Kate wasn't really listening, preoccupied with Jack, furious with him, and herself too. The first time in her life to have ever been with another man and now it seemed that it meant nothing at all. Jack only wanted her sexually, the delighted-to-oblige woman whose flagging ego was sparked into something which resembled confidence by the attentions of a practised operator. She hated him.

'I'm thinking of having some more surgery done,' Irene announced.

'What is it this time?' Kate asked.

'A few more lines have appeared, and I want to get them erased. I thought while I'm doing that I'll have a breast enhancement job, and tummy tuck, the lot.'

'I don't know how you can even think about it.' Kate shuddered. No matter how she looked she couldn't have undergone surgery. 'What if something goes wrong, or there are side affects?'

'I've an excellent man, and so far he's done great work, don't you think?' She took a small pocket-mirror out of her handbag and closely inspected her face. 'Now that you've lost weight, you should get all the flab tightened up.'

'Should I?'

'You're too big, I'm too small.' Irene stood up, and pushed out her chest to its fullest proportion.

'I don't know what you're talking about, they're perfect.'

'When I come out of hospital, can I stay here like I did before, you looked after me so well?' Irene asked.

Kate hesitated, not really keen on the idea, remembering that the last time she had stayed with them for over two months, and required first-class service in every department.

'I promise I'll be no trouble, you won't know I'm here.' She re-applied her lipstick carefully, and sprayed a cloud of some heady scent around the kitchen as Dermot walked in.

'How are you, Irene?' he asked.

'I'm fine, Dermot,' she smiled at him.

'Kate, make us a cup of coffee, will you?'

She immediately flicked on the kettle.

'You'll be having the pleasure of my company in a few weeks time. I'm going to have surgery done, so I'll be needing tender loving care from all of you.'

He looked at her for a few seconds. 'Nothing serious I hope?'

'No, just some cosmetic work.'

'Good, good.'

'Does that mean that you're looking forward to it?'

'Yea, yea, bring that coffee in when it's ready, Kate, and something to eat, I'm peckish.' He disappeared through the door which banged behind him.

The atmosphere in the kitchen became suddenly tense as Irene stared after Dermot, her cheeks flaming. Kate slapped together a sandwich - wishing she could tell him to make it himself, and that she was tired of being ordered about. But she had to hold her tongue in front of Irene, furious with the whole world.

Chapter Forty

Dermot stared at his computer screen, an expression of doom on his face. Since he had come back from Alicante he had been simply traumatised, unable to make any decisions at all, forced to the conclusion that something had gone very wrong with the Spanish property company. He couldn't make contact with anyone as he was afraid to ring the office, and there was still no reply from Manuel's mobile phone. He didn't know what to do. He was faced with huge repayments to the bank, which couldn't be covered by the rental income that he received on his properties in Dublin. The loan he had raised was short-term and the bank had been more than accommodating considering he had a number of mortgages already on the properties he owned, but as they had the deeds of everything, they would very shortly begin to repossess. He would be ruined.

Although it was only lunchtime, he poured a glass of whiskey and knocked it back, determined to work his way out of this. All of the banks had refused him, so he made a list of family and friends, and the only possibility out of that lot was Irene. She had plenty of money which had been inherited from Kate's father. Her investments were in sensible funds which would provide for her future, and she owned some property as well as paintings and jewellery.

He wore his good business-suit, with a crisp white shirt, a dark tie, and felt he looked the part. The man who was down on his luck but never let it get to him, and just needed a helping hand over a rough patch. He hadn't been very attentive lately, he realised that, regretting his short-tempered surly attitude. But all that pressure to leave Kate had got to him. Was she mad or what, to expect that he would trade Kate for her? But now he was determined to get back to where they were before, when she wanted him so badly she would have done anything for him.

As he rang the bell at the apartment, he felt anxious; his mouth was dry, there was a lump in his throat.

'Yes?' Her voice was husky over the intercom.

'It's me!' He was certain she would know instantly who it was.

'Who?' She sounded distant, as if he was the postman or someone.

'Dermot,' he laughed.

He took the lift up to her floor, so glad to see her waiting for him in the doorway, looking as if she just stepped out of the beauty salon.

'Sorry, are you going out, maybe I should have phoned?' Dermot suddenly realised that he could be barging into a situation here, and his knees wobbled as fear played a tune on his ego. Maybe she had another man in her life already?

She held the door for him.

'A present, Irene.' He handed her the perfume he had just picked up at the chemist.

'Thanks.' She was cool, and his earlier discomfort became even more acute.

'Look Rene, I'm very sorry about everything, but things have settled again, and I want to get back to where we were. Can you forgive me?' He had a hang-dog expression on his face.

'You may as well sit down.' She waved to an armchair. 'Drink?'

'Thanks.'

She poured a glass of whiskey, handed it to him, then she reclined on the couch.

'You're looking well.'

'Thank you, Dermot,' she smiled for the first time.

'I've wanted to say that to you more than once, but when you were over at the house I couldn't take the chance.'

She nodded slowly.

255

'I don't know why we're sitting so far apart, it never used to be like that.'

'You can come over here if you want.'

'Thanks.' He moved beside her. 'I've missed you so much, Rene.'

'I didn't get that impression when we met at your office.'

He drew back a little, disappointed, but then went at it again, determined to convince her. 'I was confused then. I didn't know what I was doing. I'm very sorry.'

She looked at him. Her expression guarded.

'Rene, can't we begin again? Love never dies, you know, at least it doesn't with me. Once I love someone it's for ever.'

'Really, what about Kate?'

'We got married so young we didn't know what real love meant. You're the only woman I've ever loved and I want you back.'

He reached forward again and managed to press his lips on hers. Once he got this close there would no turning back, and so it seemed as she responded in a half-hearted way.

'You are the most beautiful woman I know, Rene,' he murmured.

'Has the big deal come through yet?' She drew away from him, and lit a cigarette.

'No, things are pretty bad to tell you the truth.' He was relieved that she had brought up the subject first.

'What?'

'Manuel has dropped me in it, and done a bunk with all the money. Not a cent has been lodged to my account in the Caymans, and the police may even be involved. I don't think I'll ever be able to go back to Spain.'

'My God!' Her blue eyes widened with surprise.

'I'm facing bankruptcy, even the house could go.' He nodded sadly.

'You'll have to think of some way to get out of this, you can't let it happen.'

'That's all I'm doing these days, going from bank to bank to try to persuade someone to lend me some money so that I can get back on my feet again.'

'That's terrible.' She was sympathetic.

'It's such a relief to talk to you about it, Rene, I haven't told anyone else yet.'

'You can always talk to me, Dermot.'

'When can I see you again?' he asked. Irene had kept herself distant, and he hadn't made the progress he had hoped.

'I'll phone you.'

'Make it soon, I need you, Rene.'

'I'm busy this week, but I'll try to fit you in.' She walked with him into the hall.

'Oh, by the way, any chance you might be able to lend me something to keep me going, I hate to ask, but you're always so generous.'

'Is that the reason you are here?' she asked sharply.

'Not at all, Rene, no way. It just suddenly occurred to me, now we're together again, that you might consider helping me out. Sure who else would I ask only the person I love most in the world?'

'How much are you talking about?' She stood back a little from him, a suspicious look on her face.

'I need a lot of money to get started again, but I'd be grateful for a temporary loan.'

'You know most of mine is tied up.' She opened the door.

'Surely you can spare something, please Rene, don't let me down.'

'Well, I'll see, leave it with me.'

'Thanks Rene, thanks.' He just about managed to brush her cheek with his lips as she stepped away. 'I'll give you a buzz tomorrow.'

'Yes, do that.'

Chapter Forty-One

For Kate, the following day dragged interminably. There was no contact from Jack, and she was determined she wasn't going to phone him. Carol persuaded her to call around to see Mags after work, both of them a little worried about her as she didn't appear into the office and hadn't been in touch to explain why.

'Mags, it's me, open up,' Carol said into the intercom and the door clicked open. 'Right, told you she'd be here. I knew she had hit the bottle last night.'

Mags was curled up on the couch, her eyes red-rimmed, mascara-streaked from crying, and sure enough a half-empty bottle of gin on the coffee-table.

'I didn't ask that bitch to come in, I thought it was only you, Carol.' She sipped the liquid in her glass.

'Mags, I'm really sorry about this whole thing.' Kate sat down opposite, hardly able to drag her eyes away from the large painting which stood against the wall.

'I'm heating the lasagne in the micro wave. Are we invited to share this bottle?' Carol asked.

'Have what you like.'

'Hope you don't expect us to drink it neat, any mixer?'

Mags waved in the direction of the kitchen. Carol made up the drinks and brought in the meal for Mags on a tray.

'Eat up, you must be starving.'

'I couldn't touch it.' Mags shook her head.

'Come on, just a little bit,' Carol coaxed.

'No,' she snapped.

'Well, don't then, you can have it later if you want, but now we have to talk about this situation, which I would imagine is probably no one's fault, least of all Kate, who wouldn't harm a fly under normal circumstances,' Carol said, as if she was chairing a meeting.

'What was she doing there, draped around him, right in front of us?'

Kate felt very uncomfortable.

'He was the guy she met in Spain,' Carol explained.

'But you said his name was David.' Mags glared furiously at Kate.

'I couldn't tell you.'

'And you let me get involved with him, assuming he was free?'

'I didn't expect it to go any further.'

'We're supposed to be your best mates, and you knew from the very beginning how I felt.'

'Nothing happened for a long time, I only met him again last February. It's over between us now, so you can have him if you want.' Kate took a gulp of the G & T. 'Although I don't think you should bother, he's just a womaniser.'

'I feel such a twit, always hanging around looking for him, spending all that time with his boring friends.'

'Kate, I'm amazed that you even looked at another guy. You and Dermot are so close,' Carol said.

'It was just a crazy falling in love thing, and it will never happen again.'

'Twenty-odd year itch?' Carol laughed.

'Suppose it was something like that.'

'And Dermot?'

'Things haven't been good for a long time.'

'People have their ups and downs, it doesn't mean they're all washed up.'

'You've ruined my life.' Mags lay back on the couch, eyes closed.

'Kate couldn't help it if they fell for each other. He never gave you the come-on, even that night he took you home and you tried

259

to persuade him into bed,' Carol pointed out.

'Is that the truth?' Kate asked.

'Yea,' Mags mumbled. She reached for the bottle and poured herself another drink.

'Mags, you're drinking too much, you'll have an awful head in the morning, put some mixer into it.' Carol began to pour in the tonic, but Mags lifted the glass to her lips and it spilled.

'I need it to blank all this out, I feel a right fool. When I think of posing for that picture I could scream. I'm going to burn it,' she sulked.

As Kate listened, she realised that under the influence Mags usually told the truth, her exaggerations confined to her more sober moments. She was suddenly horrified at herself for accusing Jack of lying, when really she had nothing to base it on at all, just wild jealousy which had twisted the facts and sent her off on a crazy tangent.

Carol made coffee and persuaded Mags to have a cup. Then she brought her into the bedroom, and tucked her into bed. After clearing up the place, they left. Mags was already asleep by then.

'It will all work out, don't worry,' she assured Kate as they hugged goodnight outside.

Unconvinced, Kate drove towards home, but half-way there, she slowed and took a turn back into town, suddenly anxious to apologise to Jack. She drew up outside the house, but there was a red sports car in the driveway. Disappointed, she pulled away, her plan to beg forgiveness had gone down the tubes. Again, her suspicions ballooned out of control, imagining another woman with him. Drinking out of the same crystal glass she used, the coffee-cup, sitting where she sat on the couch, and worst of all, sharing his bed with him. The whole thing flashed before her mind in minute detail, the crisp white cotton bed-linen, the soft light from the bedside-lamps on the natural wood lockers, and the figures on the bed, intertwined. Her phone rang, but she was too upset to talk to anyone now, and let it go on to the voice-mail.

Hardly able to think straight, she reached Mount Asher Road noticing that Shane was the only one absent, and hoping that Dermot or Conor wouldn't want her to start making meals or do anything else at this hour. But as she was about to put her key into the lock the front door opened, and Conor almost knocked her down as he rushed out, followed closely by a bellowing Dermot, his face flushed crimson.

'Don't you walk out on me.' He grabbed Conor by the arm.

'What's going on?' Kate asked.

'He refuses to go back to work. He's just going to loll about here doing nothing, lazy sod.'

'Let's go inside and talk about this.' She ushered the two of them ahead of her into the kitchen.

'I thought he was just using up his holidays, but no, he's given up the job altogether, would you believe?' Dermot growled.

'I don't feel like working.' Conor lit a cigarette, and slumped in a chair. The unconcern of youth was there in his face, unlined, almost beautiful.

'Would you mind telling me how you're going to support yourself?' Dermot asked.

'I'll get a few bob from somewhere.' He pulled deeply and tapped the length of ash on to a small black ashtray, his own personal one which he carried around with him from room to room.

'I've provided for you and your brother ever since you were born, but I don't intend to do it until I'm getting the pension.'

'I'm not in the mood for work, Dad.'

Kate placed mugs of coffee, and a plate of biscuits on the table.

'Listen here to me. This isn't on, expecting everything to be handed to you. I won't have it.'

'Dad, you can't make me work, it's my choice.' Conor took a gulp of coffee, lifted his ashtray, and made towards the door.

'Let him go, we'll talk again.' Kate held Dermot's arm. But he shook off her touch and followed him, still shouting.

She sat down again, and sipped her coffee, remembering then the message on her phone. Retrieving it, she was thrilled to hear

Jack's voice. 'Did I see you outside just now? I thought for a second you were coming in, then presumed you noticed Vincent's car here, and decided not to. Please phone me. Maybe you could come back? He was just about to leave.'

But there was no chance for her to return Jack's call, as she heard Dermot coming down the hall again.

'He'll pick up something soon. With his experience in computers, it should be no problem,' she said softly, understanding what may have brought him to this. It had to be because of Nicola. He couldn't face her every day in the office, and backed away from it the only way he knew how. She understood exactly how her eldest son must feel, how deeply he was hurting. But, of course, he hadn't told her any of this; he wouldn't admit it for the world, big brash tough guy, no way.

'Might have known you'd side with him, the pair of you out to thwart me.' As ever, Dermot turned on her, and she took the blame, the full force of it's all your fault. 'You have them the way they are, wasters, lazy lumps, without a smidgen of responsibility.'

'He'll get a job soon, he's just a bit upset after losing Nicola.'

'Broken-hearted? Going to need his Mammy's arms around him to protect him from the rough-and-tumble of life. Is that how you see your role? Well, what I want to know is Mammy going to provide the money for whatever he wants?'

'I can certainly help.'

'If you support him in this, you can pay for everything he needs, I'm not putting my hand in my pocket, and the same for the other dosser, you can have them both. I'm going to bed.' Dermot stomped out of the kitchen.

Kate sat there, both hands around the mug of coffee, its warmth comforting; she felt worn out, and longed to feel Jack's arms around her, a little plan suddenly beginning to take shape in her mind. She tidied up the kitchen, taking her time for once, and then did the television-room as well. Her duster flicked over surfaces, she picked up newspapers, an empty beer-can, a half-eaten sandwich and binned them. Then she plumped the cushions, threw out some white carnations which had begun to wilt and looked around for anything else to do.

Later she went upstairs, opened the bedroom door, and listened to Dermot's snores. To her delight Conor lay prone under the duvet as well.

'Thanks for coming down. I'm so sorry about last night, I shouldn't have left you like that,' Jack apologised.

'It was my fault, accusing you of being with Mags.' They argued, each trying to take the blame.

'My fault, your fault, what does it matter, once you believe that I never laid a finger on Mags.'

'I should never have doubted you,' she smiled at him. The relief inside her was enormous, as all the aggravation and worry of the last twenty-four hours drained away.

'Is this our first real row? Should I mark it on the calendar?'

'You've seen the worst side of me,' she said.

'And another side to me as well. I was so angry, wondering how you could believe that I would lie to you, the most important person in my life? I didn't pick up a brush all day, just mooned about the place unable to concentrate on anything. I was itching to lift the phone, but knew that it would all explode again and make things even worse. Although I was planning to phone you tomorrow morning, I couldn't have waited any longer.'

'I was jealous,' she admitted.

'How little faith you have in me.'

'At times I'm unsure of myself, and of you.'

'Of me?'

'Of our situation.'

'Well, to be honest, I've been doing some serious thinking. I couldn't even sleep last night,' he said slowly.

She waited, wondering.

'This is difficult...' He drew her over to the couch and they sat down together. 'But I've come to the conclusion that I can't tolerate this secret life any longer, I can see more and more rows which will destroy us in the end.' He took her hand in his.

263

She nodded, fear whipping through her.

'Now that Mags and Carol know, I want to tell everyone. Then I can take you out to dinner, here, there, wherever we want to go.' There was sadness in his eyes.

'I don't want to lose you.'

'I'm here if you want me, but it has to be above-board.'

'I've been thinking about telling Dermot, but the time never seems to be right.'

'I don't want to push you into a decision. You have to make that for yourself, and if what you feel for me is not enough, then it's better to call it a day.'

Loyalty to her family, and her love for Jack fought a battle inside her, and as of now, she had no answer for him. She glanced at her watch. 'I'd better go.'

He walked to the car with her, and they held each other silently.

'Goodnight, my love, I'll talk to you tomorrow.'

He kissed her and she breathed in that aroma that was Jack, and tried to keep it in her memory so she could bring him back to her whenever she wanted.

As Kate lay in bed that night beside Dermot, tears flooded her eyes and soaked the pillow. How could she go on living without Jack? Had she the strength to consign herself to a barren loveless existence for the sake of the vows she had made, because she was a married woman?

She dragged herself into work, anxious to talk to Mags. But she didn't get a chance. When they met in the corridor, Mags averted her eyes, or disappeared into someone's office. Coffee breaks together no longer happened, and life in Lee O'Donnell Design took on an almost macabre quality. Worst of all, their daily meetings proved tortuous, and she wouldn't listen to anything Kate had to say about her department.

'I don't agree that we should take on someone to replace Bridget. We have enough staff, they can just work a bit harder,' Mags said flatly at a meeting a couple of days later.

'But this girl is excellent, and exactly the type of person we need. We have a lot of curtain orders in the pipeline,' Carol pointed out, 'and Kate and I feel...'

'What's next on the agenda?' Mags asked.

Carol gave in and drew a line through that item on the list with a despondent air. 'Now, do you want to go to the opening of the hotel? It's on Thursday night and should be an interesting bash.' She dealt with the next subject for discussion.

'No.'

'But I thought you would enjoy it.'

'No, it doesn't suit me.' She sniffed in disdain.

'Neither Kate or I can go, and someone should, it's good PR.'

'So I'm the fall-guy?'

'Don't be ridiculous. We both thought you'd enjoy it.'

'We both, I like the sound of that, it seems she's taken over my job. Don't forget she's only the girl, we run this company.'

'I'll go, don't worry,' Carol said, obviously annoyed.

Kate sat silent, her position in the company very clear to her now. She had to hold herself back from giving notice immediately. But to storm out would be foolish and hot-headed, and she knew Mags didn't really mean it.

'I don't need anyone to organise my life for me,' Mags said heatedly.

'Please yourself. Now let's get on, what progress has there been on our tenders, any joy?'

'Nothing yet,' Mags muttered.

'The order-book is reasonably full, but we need to be looking ahead to the autumn.'

'I'll chase them,' Kate offered.

They finished up, but she was worried; would this row with Mags ever be sorted? And she was still unable to make a decision about Jack. All week she had stayed away from him, but when they talked on the phone she could hear the despair in his voice as it seemed she had nothing to say to him.

She spent a lot of time with Uncle Bill now, very much aware of the deterioration in him, the thought of death so close she felt it was sitting on the other side of the bed, waiting. It made her think about herself too, and the inevitability of it, and wonder.

It was just after six when the phone rang. Kate woke up with a start. She hated to receive a call so early in the morning or late at night, always thinking it was bad news, and it was, the worst. The Staff Nurse told her that Uncle Bill had passed away. The polite unsympathetic voice explained what had happened, and she burst into tears. She lay back on the pillow so overcome with sadness she couldn't get her head around what she had to do next. It was some time later before she managed to force herself to wake Dermot, Conor and Shane and they drove in a convoy of cars to the nursing home.

On the way, she made a hurried call to Jack.

'Uncle Bill...' She couldn't say the words, just sobbed.

'I'm so sorry, my love, when did it happen?'

'Early this morning. I'm going there now. Why didn't I guess there was something wrong last night? I should never have left.'

'Can I do anything? Tell me there's something I can do?'

'No thanks, I can manage.' She struggled to get control of herself. I think I can manage, I have to, she thought.

'Could we meet later, maybe for a coffee or something? I really want to see you, particularly now. I know what I said about not seeing each other secretly, but this is different...'

'It's going to be very busy. People to phone. Decisions to make about the funeral, the Mass, and...'

'I wish I could be with you. Phone me later and let me know how things are, or text me if you can't do that, will you, please?'

'You know I can't text, anybody could pick up my phone...' she snapped.

'Try and make contact?'

'I will.' Of course I will, if I say I will, I will, she thought as a sudden irritation with him spurted.

'Soon, I'll be worried.'

She dabbed at her eyes, which simply refused to dry, filling up and spilling over like someone had left a tap running inside her.

'I love you,' he said.

'I love you.' She cut herself off, unable to listen to his voice any longer. She had to deal with this alone.

Uncle Bill was in a private room, a look of peace on his face as if he had just fallen asleep. She put her arms around him and kissed him. Then she knelt by the bed, covered his cold clasped hands with her own and whispered a prayer. Dermot, Conor and Shane stood behind. They did nothing, said nothing. She stayed there for a while, her head bowed, until finally she rose to her feet, kissed him again, and left the nursing home. From the office, she contacted the undertakers. Dermot had said he would tell the family, so she didn't have that burden. She was on automatic pilot, sometimes unable to remember exactly what it was she had done a moment before; constantly questioning herself, did I phone him, or her, send that fax, or email? why did I come upstairs, or go downstairs? She was in a daze, unable to believe it had happened at all; reminded of the deaths of her parents, an accumulation of grief weighed heavily upon her. She talked to Jack later, but although he wanted to see her, she put him off, decisions impossible to make now.

The small group of mourners crowded around the graveside, the priest spoke the prayers and the men lowered the dark wood coffin into the ground. Kate threw a single rose on top of it. It drifted softly, landing soundlessly on the brass plate with Bill's name inscribed on it. This was followed by a loud rattle as someone else threw a handful of earth. It spattered across the shining wood, signifying dust-to-dust, the end of a life.

After the funeral, Kate went through the motions in a vague numb way. The shock of Bill's death had hit hard, and her life seemed to have stopped at the time she received the phone call from the nursing home on that morning. She didn't seem able to start it up again. But there were things she had to do, the most important of which was to arrange a meeting with Bill's solicitor. The Executor was a distant cousin, but she still had the key to the house, his bank account details, and wanted to hand them over. The solicitor greeted her in friendly fashion and they chatted about Uncle Bill for a few minutes, and then got down to business.

'I'm sure you are anxious to hear the contents of the will?'

'Not really, I don't have any expectations,' she smiled. Her uncle might have left his estate to any number of people, God knows he had made enough wills.

'I'll just read the basic few items - "I, William Crawford, of 18 Berwick Road, Rathmines, Dublin 6, being of sound mind etc. etc., hereby bequeath the house and lands at 18 Berwick Road, to Catherine Crawford Mason, and various monies..." - that consists of his full estate with the exception of some bequests,' the solicitor said.

Kate stared at him, astonished.

'He left you everything. I know he was very fond of you.'

'I can't believe it.' Tears moistened her eyes.

'It's a substantial property, and if you decide to sell, it should fetch quite an amount of money.'

'No, I'm not going to sell, he wouldn't have wanted that,' she said immediately.

'I have to inform you that there will be inheritance tax on the estate.'

Suddenly the excitement burst like a balloon.

'But you could take out a mortgage to cover it, your husband and yourself...'

'No, I'll handle it.'

'Right. I have a few contacts and when probate is through we can look into it for you.'

Kate turned the key in the heavy door, and pushed it open. Bright coloured sunbeams shone down into the hall of Berwick Road through the stained-glass window on the landing, and she felt she was caught in a magic rainbow.

'Thank you, Uncle Bill. Thank you for giving me your home, I love it,' she said aloud to his invisible presence and walked down the steps into the kitchen. She longed to find him sitting in his chair in front of the fire, but the place was empty, silent. She hadn't been here since he died, unable to walk in the shadow of his footsteps knowing he was never coming back. As she slowly wandered through the rooms, she could hear his voice and smell his cigarettes, as if he was following her around making some crabby remark or other, something she would have given anything to hear.

Although she didn't like the thought of it, she had to start going through his things, to clear out the presses, wardrobes, dressing-tables, of the accumulation of many years. But the most difficult was his old wooden box which held his private papers. It was his seaman's chest where he had kept his personal things when on board ship. She took it home, but didn't want to open it at first, it seemed intrusive. So she put the mahogany box in her room where it sat like Uncle Bill himself daring her to push the little key into the lock, until suddenly one evening she plucked up the courage, and began to go through its contents. She found his birth certificate, also that of his parents, and other papers relating to his naval career. There were letters from friends, and to her surprise, a bundle tied in faded blue ribbon from a woman called Grace who wrote lovingly to a young naval officer in the years before the Second World War. Kate had never heard him mention her name, and wondered what had come between them. It saddened her to think of it, and she stopped half-way through unable to read any longer. After she had finished in the house, she turned her attention to the garden which he had loved. It was hidden from prying eyes by high trees, chestnut, beech, an abundance of luxuriant shrubbery. In summer the borders burst with those old-fashioned flowers which come up every year and need very little attention. Huge clumps of white dog-daisies, blue cornflowers, yellow peonies, honeysuckle, wallflowers, his precious pink roses. And her favourite, the pale blue clematis which trailed over the old mews and stable building at the back.

She spent as much time as she could at Berwick Road. It gave her an excuse to escape from the tension at home, which was building, with Conor still without a job and Dermot in foul mood. There she had a chance to think. She yearned to walk away confidently to a new life with Jack, but she was held back by that scared uncertain person who existed deep inside, drawn to him by the strength of her new love, drawn to Dermot by old loyalties. But there was another small voice in her heart now, reminding her that Uncle Bill and his Grace were kept apart for some reason, and that he had paid the penalty – a sentence of a lonely isolated existence.

Chapter Forty-Two

'Did you have a chance to look at your finances, Irene?' Dermot asked when he phoned.

'I can't just pull money out of the air, Dermo, it will take time.' She kept him hanging on, loving it.

'Oh but I thought...'

'I will check with the bank.' She was glad it was a phone-call, because she couldn't have kept her face straight. She had him now.

'As quick as you can. It's just for a few weeks...you've heard the good news?'

'What good news?'

'Kate has inherited Uncle Bill's place, and when probate is through, we'll sell it, and I'll be back in business.'

'Oh, that's really great.' She was taken aback as her plan to have him grovel for as long as she wanted suddenly vanished.

'If you can manage to let me have some money, there will be no problem paying it back with interest.'

'I suppose I could let you have a couple of hundred.'

'Oh.' There was disappointment in his voice. 'Thanks, that's good of you, I'll call over to see you, maybe later on this evening, how about that?'

'Yes...see you then.'

After she had put down the phone on Dermot, she sat and stared into space, depressed, wondering whether Dermot's need for money was the only reason he was taking any notice of her. To cheer herself up, she phoned the beautician booking in for a session the following day. Facial, massage, eyebrows, eyelashes, manicure, pedicure. She had him now, and she was going to hang on to him. Looking so beautiful after her surgery, he would never be able to resist her again.

*

Dermot sat at his desk, which was a mess of papers covered with figures, tots, lists and scribbles. The phone rang and his heart raced; every time he lifted it he hoped to hear Manuel's voice.

'I'm afraid we have a problem with your account,' his bank manager said.

'I know I'm at the edge, probably shaving the overdraft level?' Dermot gripped the empty glass on his desk, his fingers tight around its serrated edge.

'You're way over the limit and I need to see you urgently.'

'But it should sort itself out soon, I've funds coming in from a number of projects.'

'Could you get in to me today?'

'I don't know, let me check my diary.' He feigned busy-ness and flicked the pages. 'Yes, I think I can manage a few minutes before you close.'

John was unfriendly, his attitude very different to the usual fawning, so-anxious-to-please approach.

'Sit down, Dermot, sorry to bring you in at such short notice, but something has to be done.' He swivelled his chair around to where his PC was positioned, flicked a few keys, and Dermot held his breath as he saw his bank statement flash on to the screen. 'We've written to you a couple of times but received no response.'

'Did you? Give me the dates, I'll get my secretary to check.' He took a notepad and pen from his inside pocket.

'But now we must ask that a large lodgement be made. Until that happens then I'm afraid we have to insist that you write no more cheques.'

Dermot stared at him, aghast. This was the worst possible scenario, ruination faced him. 'John, you can't mean that! I

272

won't accept it, my business will fold overnight, I'll be bankrupt.'

'Lodge a substantial sum as quickly as you can, then we will take another look at it.' He flicked a key and the screen-saver replaced Dermot's statement.

'That's a bit difficult at the moment. Give me more time, I promise I'll put the account in funds the first opportunity I get, but don't pull the rug out from under my feet, please?'

'As soon as you come to me with a proposal I'll consider the position, that's all I can say.' His face was expressionless.

'But in the meantime, I can't pay a bill, or the staff wages, or even fill the car with petrol...'

'I'm sure it's not quite that bad.'

'It is, that's what I'm trying to say to you, it's as bad as that and worse.'

John stood up, moved around his desk, and Dermot felt himself being shepherded out of the office.

'Look, John, I've always dealt with you...' He was very worried.

'And we want to continue doing business with you, Dermot, but there are limits.' He opened the door.

'I don't know what to do, John, you've really thrown me in at the deep-end.'

The manager took his hand with a limp uncompromising grip, the firm man-to-man handshake was gone.

'Please, can't you reconsider? Just give me a few days, monies are coming through shortly. I'll be able to clear the overdraft as soon as my investments in Spain come to maturity.' He almost choked.

'Keep in touch, Dermot, I'm looking forward to hearing your proposals as soon as you have something concrete.' They were out in the general area of the bank now. Dermot felt self-conscious, his collar tightening around his neck as he caught the eye of one of the staff who had obviously overheard.

'Right, yes, I will, can't run a business without a bank account.' He managed to grin, and left the place muttering to himself. I won't be banking here again, mate. When I get back on my feet, you can say goodbye to my millions.

Chapter Forty Three

'When will probate be through, Kate?' Dermot asked.

'Could take up to a year.'

'That long?'

'So the solicitor said.'

'Uncle Bill turned out to be a generous old sod in the end, he must have appreciated all we did for him. I hope the market keeps on the up by the time we sell the house, but in the meantime, we can use it as collateral for a loan. I'm a bit strapped for cash at the moment, so it's a godsend.'

'I told you I'm not going to sell. I've no intention of using it as collateral either. There's a large tax bill, and I'll have to take out a mortgage to cover it,' Kate pointed out.

'Come on, Kate, the Spanish development is taking longer than I expected and my cash-flow is under pressure, so I really need money.' He was still hoping he could work through the situation with the bank. The thought of telling Kate and everyone else how bad things were stuck in his throat.

'And if you raise a loan, that means the house could be lost if your business gets into trouble, no way, I'm not agreeing to that.'

'Not at all, Kate, it's purely paperwork, it means nothing.'

'Uncle Bill wouldn't have taken a risk with his home. I feel the same, and that's the end of it.' She went into the utility-room, changing out of her shoes into wellies.

'I'm asking you to do me a favour.' He followed her, glaring balefully.

'Sorry, I can't do it.' She went into the garden to prepare the earth for bedding-plants.

'You'll have to change your mind, Kate,' he snapped.

'Will I?'

'Yes, you will.' He marched back inside.

Later, she looked around the beautiful garden, realising that most of the flowers and shrubs could be taken up, re-planted in different positions, and next year they would all come up as healthy as any of this year's crop. Could she as easily uproot herself, and live in another place?

Chapter Forty-Four

'We're going out to Spain again next week, when are you planning to head?' Chris asked.

'I'm not sure.' Jack was aware that he had been so consumed with Kate he had lost track of time and should certainly have been in Mojacar by now.

'Kate keeping you here?'

'You could say that.'

'I hate coming the elder-lemon, but what's in it for you in the long run?'

'I don't know.'

'I think you're wasting your time. You need to get on with life, meet someone who is anxious to start having babies and all that sort of thing.'

'I'm a bit past the baby stage, Chris.' He tried not to over-react at the mention of that sensitive subject.

'It's irresponsible of Kate. She is nicely settled, has had her family, and is quite content to string you along. Worst of all, you seem to have accepted the whole set-up.' She was becoming irate.

'It's not like that, Chris, you don't understand.'

'I understand well enough.'

'Look, I'm old enough to do my own thing, Chris. God sakes, I'm forty-three.' He tried to keep from losing his temper. Too many times in the past they had clashed, their volatile temperaments so similar.

'It's not funny to waste your life away. What about having someone to share everything? You have to admit that you've missed out on that. All you have is paint and brushes, inanimate objects, cold and unresponsive, it couldn't be enough for you.'

'I have been there, Chris, I know what it's all about. Although of course we had no children, but you come to terms with that, like yourself, I presume.' He was unable to meet her eyes.

'I couldn't have children, but you have a chance. Take it before you get too long in the tooth. You'd never keep up with your kids the way they are these days.'

'I don't see that happening, Chris, and I'm not going to choose a partner so I can have a family. I love Kate, and I'm hoping that some day we can be together, that's enough for me.'

'There's no way she's going to give up her life with Dermot. Sure they're the happiest couple I know. I feel really guilty that my brother is trying to break up their marriage.'

'You feel guilty?'

'Yes.'

'That's crazy. You'd think Kate was a child, unable to decide what she wants.'

'If you hadn't pursued her, nothing would have happened. You knew she was married and that they were friends of ours. I don't know how you can do this to me.'

'Chris, I told you before, I didn't plan it.'

'I saw you that night at the party in Spain, you were all over her.'

He was silent for a moment, and tried to gather his thoughts. 'I think we should leave the subject, Chris, I don't want to say anything I might regret. Can I get you a drink? I'm going to have a whiskey.' He took a bottle from the drinks cabinet, and poured some into a glass. He gulped it quickly, needing something to calm the anger which had evolved in the last few minutes.

'No, thanks, I'd better go.' She picked up her bag and he walked her to the front door.

'You haven't mentioned our situation to anyone else, have you?' he asked, wondering did half the family know about it.

'You must be mad, the less people who know about this the better. Poor Dermot. I feel sorry for him.'

'Goodbye, Chris,' he said, his mouth a grim tight line.

'Mother insisted on coming over to see you, and we had to get two buses, she wanted to make sure you're still in the land of the living.' Jack's father had a very disgruntled expression on his face as he shook a spattering of raindrops on to the floor from the black umbrella.

'Are you all right, Jack?' His mother stared up into his face, searching, her faded blue eyes anxious.

'I'm fine. Didn't I talk to you on the phone the other day?' He kissed her and brought them into the lounge. 'How are you?'

'We'd be grand, if we didn't have all this worry,' his father grunted.

'Sit down, I'm delighted to see you.' He helped his mother off with her coat and took her over to a chair.

'I'll keep mine on, we won't be staying long.' Thomas Linley stood awkwardly in his heavy grey overcoat.

'Please sit down.' Jack indicated the other armchair.

'No, no, I'll stand, I wouldn't want to be dirtying your chairs, I don't know what you were thinking when you bought such a light colour, sure they'll last no length.'

He offered them tea, regretting the only thing he had to give them to eat was a few biscuits. 'Why don't you stay for lunch? I could organise something.'

'You know we always have dinner at two o'clock, and we'll be home by then.'

'Well, I'm glad to see you both, it's a long time since you were over here. How is everyone?' Jack sipped coffee, knowing exactly what was going on. But as he looked at his mother, he noticed that she seemed tired, a slight paleness about the face against the pink-toned blouse she wore. A wave of guilt overcame the annoyance that always made itself felt when they fussed over him as if he was still a child.

'We thought you weren't well, or something, you haven't been over in weeks,' his mother said.

'I told you it was all in your imagination, he's just not bothered, that's what it is, I told you.' His father's cranky mutter was barely audible.

'I've been really busy.'

'Doing what, I'd like to know.' There was a loud clink as he put the mug down on the coffee-table, but he lifted it again quickly and kept it in his hand.

'Come up to the studio and I'll show you.' He helped her up.

'Take it slowly, she's no teenager, you know.' The remark followed him as they walked upstairs.

They both admired the painting on the easel, but he could see that it wasn't to their taste. They simply didn't understand his work.

'I don't know why this place is in such a mess, paint, brushes, pictures everywhere. God almighty, it's hard to know where to put your feet. What's that?' There was a look of disdain on his face as he kicked something with his brightly-polished black shoe.

'That's just a rag.' Jack picked it up. 'The woman who cleans for me is never allowed in here. She looks after everything else, washes, and irons, but this place is taboo. Anyway, I never was very tidy when I lived at home, was I?' he laughed.

His mother smiled.

'And why can't you paint ordinary pictures? With mountains and rivers...a few sheep in a field...something normal...instead of all this weird stuff?' Thomas looked around, and examined some of the other paintings which were on the work bench, peering closely at the finished work of the stud farm. 'This is more like it.'

'That's a commission.'

'Well, it's good, what do you think, Mam?'

'It's lovely,' she agreed.

'But what sort of thing is that?' He pointed to one of Kate.

'A portrait of sorts.'

'Not my cup of tea. Right, we'd better be off.' He steered his wife towards the door.

'Stay a little longer,' Jack persuaded, but there was no stopping his father. He was the one in charge today and his mother bowed to her husband's will.

'I'll be doing a nice leg of lamb this Sunday, will we see you?' she asked.

'And there are a few things I need you to do for me, make sure you have enough time.'

'I'll be there,' he agreed, fastening the top button of her coat, and settling the collar.

'We'll be looking forward to seeing you.' His mother put her arms round him, and he held her close.

'Now we must be off, it's stopped raining.' Thomas glanced out the narrow window beside the front door, and picked up the umbrella.

'I'll drop you home.' Jack picked up his keys from the hall table.

'There's no need, we'll get the bus.' He shook his head.

'You're too busy,' his mother said.

'I'll bring you home, and that's that.'

'We don't want to take you away from whatever you were doing.'

'You're not, so stop arguing about it.' He was quite determined. The look on his mother's face when she arrived had been enough to convince him that long bus journeys were far too tiring for people in their late seventies. He regretted now that his absence had been enough to cause them to come all this way. He opened the front door and stepped out, more than surprised to see Kate hurrying up the driveway.

'I was just passing...I thought I'd call in to see how you are,' she smiled.

'Kate?' He stretched out his hand to her.

'I'm on my way to an appointment, so I only have a few minutes. Let's go inside and I'll show you how much I love you.' She moved towards him, but her smile faded as the door opened wider and she caught sight of the two elderly people standing behind him.

'We'll make our own way home, Jack, don't worry about us,' his mother said.

'Mam, Dad, this is Kate, a friend of mine.'

'It's good to meet you both.' She shook hands.

'We're going out to Inchicore, it shouldn't take very long, why don't you wait for me?' he asked, a secret smile in his eyes.

'Thanks, but I have to meet with some clients,' she said a rushed embarrassed goodbye, walked quickly back to her car and drove off with a brief wave.

'I didn't know you had a girlfriend, you never told us about Kate before,' his mother remarked when he had settled her into the passenger seat. 'Why don't you bring her to lunch on Sunday, I'm sure all the family would like to meet her.'

'No thanks Mam, maybe some other time, and don't you be getting ideas into your head.'

'But I thought I heard her say...' she murmured.

'I told you this wasn't a good idea,' his father said, but neither Jack or his mother made any response as he drove out through the gates. He was aware of her hand patting his arm in a sympathetic manner, knowing that she had put two-and-two together and came up with the right answer pretty fast. While she may have looked a bit tired earlier, there was obviously nothing wrong with her mind, she was as sharp as ever.

As soon as he had left them home and was back in the jeep, he phoned Kate, but was disappointed when he heard her voicemail. He left a quick message, his mind full of her as he tried to discern the nuances in her words, and whether her unexpected arrival had any particular significance.

Chapter Forty-Five

Kate was heading along the corridor towards her office when she met Mags face-to-face, and because of the short distance between them there was nowhere for her to go. She smiled but was given a blank stare by Mags. She appealed to her. 'Can't we talk about this? Let's clear the air between us and get back to the way it used to be, I miss you.'

'I have no interest in talking to you ever again.' Mags pushed around her.

'I can't cope,' she said later to Carol.

'It's getting difficult for me as well, I'm between the two of you like a referee.'

'I tried to talk to her earlier, but she's just furious with me and so unforgiving, it's not like her at all.' Kate gathered her papers for the meeting. 'I don't know what I'm going to do, Carol, whether I should stay on or resign. I will be taking some time off anyway, all those holidays due to me are going to be called up now,' she smiled.

'I'm glad to hear that, maybe a break would be a good thing for both of you.' Carol ran a comb through her dark hair, applied lipstick, and slipped on her jacket.

At the meeting, all went well for a while, and at one point Kate was enthusiastically talking about what they might consider for the overall theme, and she looked around at the others for endorsement when Mags spoke for the first time.

'I don't agree, I think it's weak, lacks any versatile thinking.'

'I've done quite a bit of work...' Kate's face was pink with embarrassment.

'What work you might have done, after you've finished playing around with your lover-boy, isn't worth a toss!' Mags seemed quite oblivious to the fact that there were a number of other people present.

Kate stared intently at her lap-top screen, mortified. There was a shocked tension in the room, and for a moment no-one said anything, they just avoided each other's eyes and shuffled their papers.

'It could be considered, and will certainly be one of a number of different treatments which we will offer you,' Carol smiled at the clients, anxious to dispel the sudden coolness.

'Well, you needn't bother, I'm not going to support that one.'

'I think we should go on to the next theme.' Carol cut in quickly.

The meeting continued, but it had lost any momentum, and by the end of it, Kate was beginning to think resignation might be the only option for her.

'Twice in one day, to what do I owe this honour?' Jack asked.

'It's been too long, I've missed you so much.'

'Tell me about it.'

'Fancy meeting me in Galway on Friday night?'

'Sounds interesting,' he smiled.

'I have some business to do in that direction. It could necessitate an overnight.'

'And you might like some company, I presume.'

'Yea, I hate to sleep alone.'

'Just give me the details and I'll be there,' he held her close.

That night it was uncomfortable in the bed, Dermot hugging most of her side, and the duvet. She tried to ignore his whiskey snores, and thought about the dullness of twenty-three years of marriage, grown stale like last week's bread. And a more recent phenomenon, the speckles of mould which told her that it should be thrown out. She slipped out of the bed, pulled on her dressing-gown and went downstairs, feeling the soft carpeted edge of the stairs with her bare feet in the dark, her hand sliding along the banister which was polished to a high gloss.

She turned off the house alarm, put on a pair of old trainers, and went outside. The garden glimmered in the moonlight, its shapes weaving in and out to draw the eye to a feature, the pergola or the fountain. She sat in the swing-seat moving gently back and forward, the only sound in the quiet the creak of the wood and ropes, her heart aching for all she would leave behind.

It was like a honeymoon. Jack already waiting in the foyer of the hotel when Kate arrived, trying to be so cool and unaware of him as she booked in. But they took a chance and went upstairs together in the lift, making a quick dive into her room, giggling like teenagers.

'It's wonderful to see you.' He flung his arms around her. 'All the work done?'

She nodded.

'I can't believe this has actually worked out. Let's go around to my room, I'm on the next floor.'

'I'll just shower and change first.' She took off her beige linen jacket. 'It's so warm.'

'Let me help you.' He began to unbutton her blouse.

They moved together, two people who wanted so much from each other. Time meant nothing, their lovemaking slow and wonderful, no need to watch the clock, or think about rushing home to make the dinner, or anything else, until much later when Jack realised that he had forgotten the booking he had made at the restaurant.

'I'll have to phone and apologise, we won't make it now.' He picked up the phone. 'Is it really three hours since we came up here?'

'I never noticed the time.' Half-covered with the white sheet, Kate lay in the large bed, and stretched like a lazy cat lying in the sun.

'You must be hungry, I know I am.'

'Not particularly.' She reached for him again.

284

'We'll ask Room Service to send something up,' he murmured through a kiss.

Another hour passed before they surfaced again.

'Better phone before they close for the night, or we'll be dying of hunger,' he said, 'I've just remembered, I ordered a bottle of champagne and it's in the fridge in my room, I forgot about that as well, my mind is so full of you everything else is just blanked out, no wonder I can't survive without you.'

'Go and get it, and put on some clothes or you'll be arrested.' She giggled.

In his absence, she stared around the room, the décor quite attractive even to her own practised eye. It had a Scandinavian look, the woods natural, a rich red theme in the drapes and bed-linen. But she couldn't have cared less, so she closed her eyes on it, as the married woman inside suddenly pushed an unwelcome presence into her head, reminding that even now she could still get up and go home. That there was enough time to gather her shattered morality without the ultimate stain on her character of spending the night with another man. She wondered about the degrees of harm between that, or snatching an hour here and there, and decided that there wasn't a whit of difference.

Jack returned after a few minutes, uncorked the champagne, and poured it into two glasses.

'To us.' He clinked his glass against hers.

'To us,' she repeated his words.

'And the future. Now close your eyes.'

'Why?' she laughed.

'Do as I say.'

She could feel his fingers placing something light around her neck.

'Come over here.' He drew her off the bed and across the room. 'Countdown...three-two-one...'

She opened her eyes immediately, and was taken aback when she saw the simple beauty of the fine gold necklet with a glittering diamond set in the centre, and gave a gasp of surprise.

'Jack, it's beautiful!' She touched it. 'You shouldn't have, it's far too much, but thank you.'

'I was hoping you'd like it.'

'I love it, and my earrings match.' She stared at herself in the mirror.

'I wanted to take you out tonight all dolled up but you sent my plans askew.' His arms curled around her. 'But I have to admit that it looks even more beautiful on you without anything on.'

'I'm a perfect foil.' She posed.

'Perfect.'

'I've something for you, but it's nothing compared to this.' She felt suddenly shy as she went to the wardrobe, took the parcel from her suitcase, and handed it to him. 'It's just something small to remember tonight,' she accused herself of having no imagination at all.

'Thank you.' He smiled, and ripped off the wrapping-paper, letting it fall to the floor as he examined the book on Impressionism which he had mentioned while reading the reviews in one of the Sunday newspapers. 'It's sweet of you to remember I wanted this.' He flicked through the pages, examining some of the reproduced paintings, and only then noticing the few words she had written on the fly-leaf. 'And I'll always remember tonight as well.' He reached for her again, but just then the bell rang and they parted reluctantly.

They had a banquet, one of those simple meals so tasty because they were together. They laughed like children on a secret adventure as she fed him chips dipped in salt and he popped tiny bite-sized salad sandwiches into her mouth, the whole lot washed down with champagne. They hardly slept at all that night, both reluctant to close their eyes and lose a second of such valuable time together. But somewhere in the small hours, when the intensity of their passion for each other had been satisfied, he wanted to talk.

'I'm sorry that I forced you to choose. More than once I was quite prepared to take anything at all you could give me.'

'No, you were right, it made me look at things properly,' she admitted.

'And?'

'If you still want...' She paused, even at this stage a part of her was a little unsure.

'If I?' he smiled broadly. 'How could you even think it would be necessary to ask such a question? My darling Kate, I can't believe you're willing to give up all you have for me.'

'I love you,' she said, knowing at last that this was right for her. The thought of all day, every day, and every night too, was so intoxicating she was swept into a happy excited mood where anything was possible. 'Dermot only wants me as a housekeeper. Conor will probably move out as soon as he gets another job, and Shane has said that there might be a tour of Germany in the offing for the group.'

'Thank you, my love, for having the courage to take a chance with me, you have made me so happy.'

In the morning, as they ate breakfast in the room, they talked practicalities.

'Will you divorce Dermot? Although that doesn't really matter, I just want you to live with me, to be mine. And if you do get a divorce down the line then we'll make it official.' He tackled the full Irish breakfast, with obvious enjoyment.

'I haven't thought that through yet, but it would probably be better to make a clean break.' She spooned grapefruit, more careful than ever about her diet. While she had continued to lose weight she still wasn't as close to her target as she would have liked.

'How soon will we be together, my love? I'm impatient now, I can't wait.' He covered her hand with his. 'I want to wake you up in the morning, every morning, bring you breakfast in bed, get back into it with you, and...' He reached across and kissed her.

'Breakfast in bed...what luxury.'

'Just let it be soon, Kate.'

'I'll have to tell Dermot and the lads...and that's going to be difficult. But I've mentioned to Carol that I intend taking all the holidays due to me soon, so that means...'

'You can come out to Spain with me for a few weeks. If you want to stay on in your job we can live in Dublin, and I'll commute. I've been asked to design the sets for another play later on in the year so I'll have to be back for that.'

'I've been thinking about resigning anyway, the situation with Mags is too difficult, so maybe we might live in Spain permanently.'

'You can set up a business.'

'But if I'm around all the time, what about your work? You need to do your own thing, and be able to paint whenever you feel like it. I wouldn't want to tie you down.'

'We can compromise on that, I'm certainly prepared.' He stood up.

'But have you really thought carefully about the disadvantage of having to consider someone else in everything you do?' she asked, suddenly determined to point out all the negatives to him. Not that it counted for much, there was no guarantee in any relationship.

'I can't say that I have, to be honest I hadn't dared hope. I want to be with you and my work will have to fit in. It's not the most important thing in my life now, you are.' He drew her back with him to the bed, and pulled her down beside him.

Chapter Forty-Six

'Have you done any more thinking about Bill's house?' Dermot demanded the moment she arrived home.

'I told you I'm not selling,' she replied, putting down her overnight case in the hall and walking into the kitchen.

'I thought you might have changed your mind so I didn't tell you. I wanted to avoid worrying you, but you've pushed me into it.'

'Tell me what?'

'The business is gone, washed up.' He stared bleakly at her. 'Look at the figures.' He waved a bundle of papers. 'This is serious stuff, I'm at my wits' end.'

'What are you talking about?' Kate asked as she took the scribbled pages from him and examined them, a sense of dread sweeping through her.

'Manuel's done a bunk, we've lost millions.' His face was ashen.

'When did that happen?'

'A few weeks ago.'

'Why didn't you tell me about it before now?'

'I was hoping to work through it, but then the bank stopped honouring my cheques and the whole thing went belly-up.'

'You should have explained exactly, all you did was mutter about cash-flow. Anyway, why can't we sell off some of the property?'

'The bank owns it all now.'

'There has to be something you can do.' She tried to get her mind around this, but was too numb to make any sense of it.

'We'll have to use Berwick Road as collateral to raise a loan to cover some of the moneys owed, we've no choice.' He looked at her with a sad crooked smile. 'We'll tart the place up in the meantime, and get as much as we can for it as soon as probate is through.'

'But I told you I don't want to do that, Uncle Bill didn't want his house sold.' She sank down into a chair, her legs suddenly weak, as all the happiness of the past twenty-four hours drained away.

'Sure he's dead and buried, what does he know?' he barked, his face darkening with sudden anger.

'That's an awful thing to say.'

'You're a sentimental twit.'

'That may well be, but it's the way I am,' she said, her heart thumping.

'You know we could lose our home if we don't become solvent again, there's a hefty mortgage on this house as well.'

'But I thought you paid that off a few years ago?'

'Re-mortgaged.'

She was horrified, as slowly the meaning of what he was saying began to clarify in her mind.

'So Berwick Road is the only thing that will save us.' He put his hand on hers, but she pulled away quickly.

'No.'

'For God's sake, this is for us, for the family. How are we going to manage if we can't find an injection of cash? None of the banks I've been dealing with will give us any money. It's a drastic situation; it needs drastic measures, and all this emotional hogwash about Uncle Bill is just nonsense.'

'I've made up my mind.'

'But can't you understand that we have no other choice, otherwise we go to the wall and lose everything?'

'I'll approach our bank.'

'I've been everywhere, Kate, including your bank, and they're just not prepared to support us.'

'I can't believe that, it was a solid business.' Her voice trailed away, unable to make any real contribution. She should be trying to make sense of Dermot's scribbles, asking some relevant questions, but all she could think of was Jack, and their plans.

'The market is so good at the moment we'll be made, Kate.' He put his arm around her, but she shrugged him off. 'It will save us, and we won't have to worry about the Sheriff.'

'Let me look at those accounts again,' she said slowly, trying to force herself to think logically instead of bursting into tears.

'Anything to eat, Mum?' Conor sloped through the door, and interrupted the conversation.

'I can get you something in a while.' She stared at Dermot's figures.

'I'm starving.'

'Didn't you hear what your mother said?' Dermot barked.

'I just want a snack, a quick sandwich.'

'When you can pay your way, you can have extra snacks around here.'

'What about Shane, he doesn't have a job?' Conor asked, lighting a cigarette.

'He'll have to cough up as well. As I was just saying to your mother, I'm in bad financial straits so I can't afford to support either of you any longer.' He poured himself a glass of whiskey.

'What do you mean?'

'It means I've lost all my money, so you'd better get yourself organised and find another job.'

'I have to be in a good frame of mind, and it takes time.' He squinted at Dermot through the smoke he had just exhaled.

'Well, you can start buying your own cigarettes for starters, cover your drinking, petrol, anything else you want.'

'Dad, you can't do that to me.'

'As of now.'

'Mum?'

She didn't answer, still trying to make some sense out of the figures, but knowing she hadn't a hope.

'Your mother couldn't support you. When I say you have to stand on your own two feet that's that, and Shane is going to be informed right now.' He rang Shane's mobile. 'Come in here to the kitchen, I want to talk to you.'

Kate could imagine all the excuses produced by Shane who was, no doubt, in the middle of something or other which was vitally important to him, but she said nothing. When Dermot was in a mood like this to remain silent was quite the safest option. Anyway, she didn't have anything to say, as with sinking heart she realised that this sudden situation was going to change everything.

Shane appeared.

'Sit down,' Dermot roared, building up to a crescendo again.

He pulled a chair towards him with a loud scrape on the tiles.

'Watch the way you treat this house, wait until you have your own place, then you can do what you like.'

'Stay cool, man.'

'I am cool.' He stood out in the middle of the kitchen, his shirt sleeves rolled up. He looked as if he was ready to take on both of them. 'Now, it's time the two of you looked out for yourselves, I've run out of money.'

Shane looked shocked; Conor pulled hard on another cigarette with a grimace.

'You'll have to find a job immediately if you're going to continue living here, we can't support you any longer. Conor has already been informed of that fact.'

Kate stared at the drama being played out in front of her. Her husband and sons acting out the farfetched plot in which she was reluctantly caught as well.

'But we only play an occasional gig, it's not enough to live on, no way,' Shane protested.

'That's your own business, get something in a factory or somewhere. Conor, if you weren't so stupid giving up your good job then you'd have no problem. But oh no, you throw the lot up and assume that Dad is going to keep forking out for ever. Well, you can think again.'

'What will I do for a few jars?' Shane raised his arms helplessly. 'The tax and insurance on my jeep are due.'

'Start looking for a job, you'll find something.' Dermot laid down the law.

That mention of the insurance, a more normal everyday matter, brought Kate back to the conversation. She could pay that for Shane, but it was the bigger picture, the repayment of the mortgage and all the other household bills that worried her. A high mounting pile of expenses which normally had been settled without a thought of whether there would be enough in the bank account or not. A wave of loss washed through her as the cold hard facts hit home.

'Mum, is Dad really serious, are things that bad?' Shane asked.

'Don't worry, I can support us for a while. But you'll have to get a job, even a part-time one, and Conor, I'm sure you would prefer to be working.'

'Oh yea, always contradict what I've said. Make it easy, smooth over troubled waters, protect them from reality, instead of forcing them out into the real world.'

'You can't throw your sons out the door without a thought for them,' Kate said softly.

'We can't live on your few bob, some life we'd have then. The only answer is to borrow against Uncle Bill's place until we can sell it, and for me to get back into business.'

'Yea, surely that would be the best thing to do,' Conor said, 'it would sort everything out.'

'Yea,' Shane agreed.

'It's worth a lot of money, even the site alone. You could build another house beside it, and the mews has huge potential. If I could only get hold of the money I'd do it myself, but someone else will be only too delighted with the chance. The lads even agree. They're adults now, they have a say in what happens around here. It's a unanimous decision.' Suddenly, Conor and Shane were worthy of an opinion. 'And I thought you had a good brain, a good business brain, but now I'm beginning to wonder,' Dermot sneered.

She hated herself for not doing what they wanted. But there was something intractable inside, the I'm-not-going-to-give-in streak of stubbornness which had been born that day she had travelled alone to Spain.

Kate went down to the workroom to check on the job for the Minister's Office, still going through the daily routine with a dogged determination, trying to hide her depression. She hadn't said anything to Jack yet, hoping that through some miracle Dermot's financial problems might be solved, and she would wake up to discover the whole thing was a nightmare. When she arrived, the girls all nodded or smiled or said something to acknowledge that she had come in, except Mags, who happened to be there before her.

'We should have the Mulvey job finished by the end of the week,' Mary began to bring her up-to-date. 'And DWS were on about that delivery we're waiting on, it should be out to us tomorrow.'

'Have those chrome poles from Powers arrived yet?'

'Yes, they're in stock, the burnished brass from Coopers as well.'

'That's good, I'll be able to arrange the fitting this week then.'

'Mary, I was asking you about this fabric, do you think it's suitable for curtains?' Mags interrupted.

'It seems a bit on the heavy side, what do you think, Kate?' Mary handed the sample to her.

'Give that back to me,' snapped Mags.

'Kate might have an opinion,' Mary said.

'I don't want her opinion.' Mags grabbed the fabric out of Kate's hand.

'She is the expert.' Mary seemed quite oblivious to the fact that there was something going on.

'Oh yes, she is the expert on everything.' Mags glared at Kate. 'She knows it all. This place would collapse without the wonderful indispensable Kate, I don't think.'

No one said anything, the only noise in the room was the steady groan of the machine which stopped and started again as one of the girls joined two widths of a curtain. The others continued with their hand-sewing.

'I'm not too sure about the fabric, but I'll leave it up to yourselves to decide.' Mary went over to the workbench. Kate and Mags stood looking at each other for a few seconds of highly-charged emotion, protagonists sizing each other up. Then Mags swept out of the room, banging the door behind her. Kate was embarrassed, knowing that every word was heard by the girls, sure to be discussed at coffee break, and lunch. It was bound to be the main topic of conversation for the day. Did you hear what Mags said, can you believe it? She hated to be the subject of gossip, knowing that the words would be exaggerated like the script of a soap, their lives outside the office wondered about too. 'Did they do this, or that? What about the shindig at a meeting with a client?' someone would ask, 'I heard it was Mags took the floor from under Kate.' The heads would bob close together, the eyes widen with horror, as they tried to imagine them at each other's throats - and all over a man?

'Mum?' Conor stood in the doorway, a dissatisfied look on his face.

'Yea?' She looked up from her bank statement.

'Can I talk to you?'

'Sure.'

'Dad's really putting pressure on me to get a job, but I can't get myself motivated, I need more time out.'

'I know.'

'Shane and I were talking...he's putting together a demo at the moment...what will we do if Dad has no money?'

'Why don't you ask him?'

'He doesn't want to know. We can't even mention the word money. And my jeep needs a service.'

'I'll talk to him.'

'Thanks Mum, and would you have a few bob for the

weekend? There's a crowd of us going to a barbecue in Wicklow on Saturday; we have to bring our own beer and stuff.'

'Sure, I can manage that.'

'We'll be bunking down there so I'll need my sleeping-bag. Do you know where it is?'

'I think so, I'll get it out for you.'

'Thanks.' He left the kitchen and met Dermot in the hall. He was still in his dressing-gown, looking definitely under the weather.

'You got yourself a job yet?' he barked.

'No, still looking.' Conor went up the stairs.

'Get the paper out and start making a few applications. I want you out of here next week, I'm sick of looking at you loafing around doing nothing, lazy lump,' Dermot yelled after him. Then he flopped down opposite Kate at the table. 'What are you doing?'

'Working out our budget.'

'It wouldn't be necessary if you did what I asked you,' he said, his voice rough after a night's drinking.

'I'm doing my best. We should be able to manage on what I have.'

'That doesn't help me. What am I expected to do? How will I get back into business again without an injection of cash?'

'I don't know, Dermot.'

'Your best is like my worst. If things were reversed and the girls' company was on the line, I'd stand on my head for you, don't you know that?'

She looked at him with surprise. Would the better side of Dermot come to the fore if she appealed to him for help?

'Kate, you're my wife. We're in this together, for better, for worse, remember? You don't realise how bad I feel. Sometimes I want to hang myself or take an overdose, anything to get away from it all.' He snuffled into his handkerchief.

'You'll get back on your feet. There's bound to be something left when the accountants have finished their work.' She was suddenly worried that he would crack under all the pressure.

'God knows when that will be. Anyway, there's never enough to pay everyone after the Revenue and the banks have got their share, it's usually zilch. I'm relying on you to help me out of this. There is only one solution, sell or mortgage,' his blue eyes begged, 'won't you do it for me?'

'I can't, you know that.'

'You don't care about me, or Shane or Conor, don't care about any of us,' he mumbled.

'You know that's not true, I care very much.'

'You don't love me.'

'Of course...I do.'

'We're your family, Kate. You can't turn your back on us.'

'Why don't you go over to Spain and try to find out what happened? I can cover the flights. There must be other people who are in the same boat. Get a solicitor, put a private detective on the case, if you all work together maybe Manuel will be found.'

'That's all in hand, do you think I'm an idiot? I was over there a few weeks ago; I had a meeting with the other investors and a plan of action was decided.' He glared at her.

'But what about the development, the buildings, the place itself? If that's still owned by the investors, maybe it could be sold onwards?'

'That's being considered, yes, it might happen down the line. But who owns what now, that's the problem. Maybe it's the bank or the government, or the kids on the street, who knows? Spanish law is convoluted, nothing gets done quickly. In the meantime I'm bankrupt, that's all I know, bankrupt.'

Dermot was never very interested in what she had to say about business, or to take advice about anything, except maybe which tie to wear with which shirt or suit. He had never told her what was going on. She just knew that he was doing well in his property company, all the signs were there so it was never a concern to her. But she was very worried now and the few euro she had saved in a building society assumed enormous importance. It would have to see them through this really difficult patch. If the boys didn't manage to get jobs, they were expensive to run. For God's sake, stop calling them boys. They're men now. Have I spoiled them so much I've kept them boys? The heavy weight of responsibility crushed down on top of her.

It became more difficult for Kate to meet Jack now. Dermot was around the house all of the time, demanding to know where she was going and when she'd be back.

'You said you would be home by six, it's a quarter-past now, I'm starving.'

'Why didn't you start the dinner? The casserole just needs to be heated in the oven.'

'I didn't know that.'

'You could have phoned me.' She was getting tired of this.

'You'd have probably been too busy to take the call,' he grumbled.

'Don't be ridiculous, Dermot.' She began to empty the bag of shopping.

'When will it be ready?' he demanded.

'In about an hour.'

'An hour?'

'Have a snack in the meantime.'

'What sort of snack?'

'Maybe some cheese or ham on a cracker?'

'Where is it?'

'In the fridge.'

He opened the door and stared gloomily inside.

'I can't see any cheese.'

'It's in a small container.' She reached past him and took it out. 'There you are.'

'What about the crackers?'

'Look, wait a few minutes, I'll do it for you.' She put the casserole in the oven, buttered crackers, sliced cheese, made tea, just to keep Dermot happy, she couldn't bear another row. She had to go down to see Jack later, and dreaded that. It was time she told him the truth about her situation, it wasn't fair to keep him hanging on any longer.

298

Chapter Forty-Seven

'It's great to see you.' Jack welcomed her in.

She just about managed a smile.

'Glass of wine?' He poured without waiting for an answer. 'I've been checking flights for you, ferry-sailings for myself. It's going to take me a few days to get there, and I want to do a bit of work around the place before you arrive. Some of the family have been out recently, and I don't know what condition the house is in.'

She sipped the wine.

'Any idea when you might be able to get away?'

'I'm not sure....'

'Have you spoken to Dermot?'

She shook her head.

His fingers tightened around the glass, white-boned.

'Things have changed,' she said slowly, her eyes downcast, aware that the bubble had burst. All day she had thought about it, even tried to think of the words she might use so as not to hurt him. But in the end there was no easy way, and she simply told him the details of the collapse of Dermot's company.

'Does that mean...?'

'I can't leave them now, they need me,' she whispered.

'And I don't? Is that the way it seems to you?' He was angry.

'You're a stronger person.'

'How do you know that?'

'I feel it.' She tried to keep from crying.

'You only know what I've told you, no-one knows what's inside here.' He thumped his chest. 'So the bottom line is that

Dermot's flavour of the month again, and I'm to be ditched?'

'It's not like that, you just don't want to see it the way it is.' She pulled a tissue from her bag, and dried the tears which had begun to drift down her cheeks. 'You wouldn't want me to let them down, would you?'

'You expect me to be magnanimous and unselfish where you are concerned, and I just can't be...I only know what I feel...to hell with the rest of the world.'

'For you it's easy. You're an unattached man, and can swan off to Spain whenever you feel like it.'

'Not the way you have me at the moment...'

'For a mother it's different. It goes against our nature. However free we think we are, a woman can't sever ties when her family is in trouble and needs her.'

Jack leaned forward, his head down.

'I'm sorry.' She put her hand on his head and ruffled his hair. 'I can't leave now. Dermot's drinking too much; he's making no effort to get back to work and there's no sign of the lads doing anything either.'

'And they just let you do everything for them, selfish...' He looked at her, his eyes bleak. 'I could give Dermot some money, would that help?'

'No thank you, I couldn't accept...it's not your problem...'

'So we've been sacrificed?'

That got to her. She longed to tell him what he wanted to hear, but she had to force herself to go against the grain, to let the man she loved go away without her and, no doubt, end their relationship for good.

'I don't want to give you false hope because I don't know what's going to happen. I love you, never doubt that, but I once loved him, and for what that meant, I can't let him down.' She painted it like she would have painted a picture, as it was, not like Jack's work which was vague and impressionistic.

'So it's not all about money?'

'It's...complicated. Although if I could sell Berwick Road that would sort everything, but I don't want to. You know how I feel about the place.'

'Perhaps it would be the best thing to do. You'll get a very good price for it, certainly enough for Dermot to build up his business again.' He suddenly seemed brighter, more hopeful.

A small unwelcome realisation curled its insidious way into her mind. He wants me to sell Berwick Road as well, she thought. No-one cares about me, they're only interested in themselves. It was a strange conclusion, relegating Jack to the level of Dermot, Conor and Shane. She felt guilty even thinking that way.

'I can't sell the house and go against Uncle Bill's wishes, you don't understand.'

'I understand very well, you're putting a pile of bricks before us.'

'Don't get annoyed at me, I couldn't take that now,' she sighed.

'Don't get annoyed! Are you mad? My life is suddenly devastated, the best part of my life, and I mustn't get annoyed?'

'I'm sorry,' she mumbled, twisting the torn tissue between her fingers.

'While you make the decisions, I have to pick up the pieces of the life I had before?'

Suddenly there was a silence between them. He stood up and moved across the room to stand before a large painting on the wall. She followed him, put her arm around him, but his back was unyielding, so she let her hand fall. It seemed to be his final retort, his leave me alone, I don't need you any longer either. But after a moment he turned back to her and they held each other. There were no angry words now, just a terrible sense of loss.

'Come up to the studio.' He led her upstairs to look again at the paintings which now hung in his bedroom.

'I still can't believe that's me,' she said.

'It's the way I see you, the way I'll always see you.' He stood close behind her.

'Sounds like I've died.'

'For me, it's as if you have.'

*

301

Jack was angry. Whatever happened at the house on Mount Asher Road influenced his life as well, leaving no room for manoeuvre on his part. Like a carnival horse on a merry-go-round, he moved up and down in response to the man who pressed the button, unable to take the reins and run free with Kate. He remembered Chris warning him off, but it was too late even then, his feelings for her had already taken root. He looked at the paintings and remembered that when he had held her earlier he was aware of his heart beating, an echo of her own which wasn't quite synchronised, but like their lives, slightly out of kilter.

He began to pack that night, a desperate need to get away. He couldn't have endured seeing her again - listening to the same explanations for what she was doing; it seemed she had her mind made up. Luckily he had finished all of his commissions and had been playing around with some new ideas to pass the time. He had enough canvas, paint and stretchers; extra quantities of his own particular brands could be sent out by courier as soon as they came into stock at his suppliers. After that, it just meant a few clothes had to be thrown into a bag. The following day he had the jeep serviced and booked the car-ferry across to Holyhead, not the best route but the only one available to him at such short notice. Lastly, he phoned a few friends, tidied up a bit of business, and went out to Inchicore to see the parents, always a tough task.

'You never told us you were going?' His father was quite put out. 'And I was hoping you'd help me with some new paving I want to put down on the back patio.'

'Stop going on at Jack,' his mother chided.

'But he's going to disappear for months on end.'

'Maybe it's not going to be that long.' She was already putting something into the grill.

'I'm not hungry, Mam.'

'This is just a toasted-sandwich for you to have with your tea, Dad, will you have one?'

'Never say no.'

'Thanks, Mam.' Jack put his arm around her shoulder.

He had his tea, then did as much as he could for his father in the garden, and said goodbye reluctantly in the end.

'Try and get in touch more often?' his mother asked wistfully.

'I will.'

'Your Dad likes to know where you are.'

'It could be two or three months, or longer,' he hated saying it, but was unable to put himself into a situation where he wouldn't have the freedom to go with the emotion which often took him over when he was working.

Back home, he loaded the box on to the roof-rack. Then he went next-door to Paddy who looked after the house while he was away. Lastly, he phoned Vincent. 'That series of paintings I showed you a while ago, are you still interested in them?'

'Yes, yes I am.'

'Right, I'll wrap them and leave them in the hall. My neighbour on the left will let you in, just give him a call first.' He gave him the number.

'What about price?'

'It's not important. I'll leave it up to you,' he said abruptly.

All the time he waited for Kate to make contact, hoping to hear that she loved him above anything else in her life, and would follow him over to Spain as planned in a week or two. But while there were a few other calls, it was never her, and finally, he set the house alarm, locked the front door, and drove to the ferry.

Chapter Forty-Eight

Kate felt sluggish and weighed down. Her normal sleep pattern was disturbed; as if she spent her nights on a train existing somewhere between the consciousness of the rumbling clickitty-clack and the velvet darkness of total blackout. She tried to persuade herself that she had done the right thing in breaking with the man she loved, stepping back into the shoes of Kate Mason, wife and mother. The bad times, the worst times were when she lay beside Dermot who slumbered most nights in an alcohol-induced coma. As she tried to sleep all those physical things about Jack pushed their way into her consciousness. She remembered again the moist taste of his mouth, the warmth of his breath, the aroma from his skin. She wondered was it humid in Spain, and did he lie in bed thinking about her? The vibrancy of the life he wanted to share with her was like his palette, all the colours of the spectrum there, from the bright glimmering heights of their passion, to the bleak depths of their loss.

To keep going from day to day, she planned things to fill the empty hours when she wasn't working. She purchased paint from her limited resources, hired a high ladder, and gave Berwick Road a new look. She threw out the old carpets and with the promise of some money, persuaded Shane to help her sand and varnish the wooden floorboards. The curtains were dry-cleaned, repaired, re-hung, and she made up some throws for the couch and armchairs to cover up some of the wear. The kitchen wasn't the most modern in the world, but it was adequate and hopefully the tenants, whoever they were, wouldn't be too fussy. Then she approached an estate agent she knew, delighted when a group of French students were prepared to take a lease for three months.

'What did you go and do that for?' Dermot shouted when she told him. 'If probate comes through quickly, then we can't sell it.'

She didn't answer, just continued to clean the windows.

'Look, let's talk about this properly, discuss it in depth,' he said, his tone suddenly quite gentle. 'Come down from there. All we've been doing is shouting at each other.'

You've been doing the shouting, she almost snapped. I'm perfectly calm about the whole thing. But then she felt a tremor in her hands, and had to admit she was anything but calm. There was a thin veneer, but it was like the delicate shell of a newly-laid egg, liable to crack at the slightest touch.

'Kate, I'll make us a cup of coffee, we haven't had a decent chat in ages.'

Not for years, Dermot, she said in her own head. But she did as he asked and decided to give him a few minutes, unable to take another row. She watched him make the coffee in a sloppy fashion, throw a few chocolate biscuits on a plate, quite aware that he was trying to force her to do what he wanted.

'Kate, please help me? You're the only one I can turn to.' His blue eyes had a tragic look.

'It's not just about money, Dermot, it's about family. Berwick Road is where my father grew up, and Uncle Bill, I can't sell it.'

'Just let me borrow a little money against it?'

'No, it's too risky.'

'I'm a good businessman. The house is safe. This whole shambles wouldn't have happened if it hadn't been for Manuel.' He slurped his coffee, ate another chocolate biscuit.

'I can't do it, Dermot. You'll have to find another way.'

'Kate, you don't know what you're doing to me.'

'Why can't you find yourself a job? How long are you going to laze around here? You're as bad as the lads. Surely one of your builder friends would have something for you to do?'

'You mean...labouring?' He looked at her in horror.

305

'No, not necessarily, but you're an experienced businessman, and if you don't get something, it's going to be tough with Conor and Shane.'

'I told them to get the hell out of here,' he muttered, his earlier good mood disappearing.

'You can't do that.'

'Watch me, I could take the two of them on, just a few body-blows and they'll collapse. Why does nobody do what I want? There I was being nice, and you still don't want to help me. I thought you loved me, Kate? I thought marriage was all about being rich or poor, healthy or sick, 'till death us do part.' He massaged his temple.

At that moment the phone rang. She rose to answer it, glad to have a reason to end the conversation, but not glad to hear Irene at the other end informing her that she was being discharged from the clinic the following day, and would Kate please pick her up?

So Irene settled into Mount Asher Road. Not as beautiful as usual, it had to be admitted. She was a bit bruised around the face, but she didn't seem to care about that and was looking forward to the results which she hoped would take another few years off her age.

Kate was kept busy. While she couldn't get Jack out of her mind for very long, there were the inevitable spells when he drifted away, and she was forced to concentrate on her work, and look after them all at home. Irene required the most attention. In the morning, coffee, orange-juice, toast, marmalade, had to be brought up to the guest bedroom. After that there was the shopping-list to be written. Special creams, magazines, her favourite biscuits, chocolates, flowers; she couldn't bear a room without flowers. That seemed to be the last parting shot this morning as Kate went downstairs. But as soon as she reached the last step she heard the little bell ring and had to double-up again, to be reminded to pick up a copy of The Irish Times. She almost screamed, wondering how long she could put up with her.

In the evening she had to cook meals that Irene liked - that succulent little bit of fillet steak, or fish or chicken - and open a bottle of red wine; their stock of which was fast being depleted. But neither Dermot or Irene considered the fact that there was no money to replace it. The only good thing about her stay was that Dermot made more of an effort with himself. He showered, shaved and dressed in something other than a tracksuit, and didn't nag her about selling Berwick Road so often. But there were a lot of bad things. The worst being that they drank for most of the afternoon and on into the evening - the pair of them usually quite intoxicated by the time Kate arrived home.

Shane's friends in the band, who practically lived in the garage, were another burden on her tight budget. Shane lacked any understanding that she bought enough food for themselves and couldn't manage to stretch it to include Kev and the others. And when her offer of a cheese sandwich wasn't acceptable, the rows would erupt, Dermot always in the middle of it, ranting and raving, until one evening Irene intervened.

'Can I bail you out with an advance until things get sorted?'

She looked pretty good now, and most of the bruising on her face had faded.

'There's no need, Irene, thanks,' Kate said.

'I was only going to lend Shane enough to get a take-away for the lads,' she explained, her voice slightly slurred.

'Look who's talking, the one who's got us living like paupers says there's no need.' Dermot laughed.

Irene reached for her handbag. 'Here's fifty.'

'Thanks, Irene.' Shane pocketed the note.

'Much appreciated, Rene. At least someone we know has a spark of generosity. Come on, let's have another drink.' Dermot went into the dining-room.

'There's none here, Kate, where's the whiskey?' he yelled from inside.

'We must be out of it,' she said, with deliberate disinterest.

Irene rushed after Shane and asked him to pick up a couple of bottles at the off-licence, pulling another fifty from her purse.

'In the meantime, we'll have a glass of wine.' Dermot peered into the depths of the sideboard again. 'But there seems to be no wine either.' His voice echoed hollowly.

'There's some in here.' Kate took a bottle of Merlot from the top press where she had been hiding it, the last one.

Dermot came in, grabbed it from her, botched his attempt to open it, breaking the cork in the process.

Kate served up as quickly as she could, anxious to get food into the two of them. They were in fits of raucous laughter for the duration of the meal and it turned into a party in the end. Shane was despatched to the off-licence again. The band brought their instruments into the conservatory, and Irene danced to the sort of music she would absolutely hate if she was sober.

To get away from it, Kate went into the front lounge for some peace and quiet, but when she stepped inside she knew there was something wrong in here, but couldn't put her finger on it exactly. Her brain computed the signs, but so shocked it didn't come up with the explanation immediately, until finally a few seconds later she realised what it was and rushed into the conservatory where the party was in full swing.

'Dermot, we've been burgled!' she screamed above the noise, but he was completely oblivious as he swayed in a corner, a glass in his hand. She grabbed his arm. 'Did you hear me, we've been burgled, our two paintings have gone, I'll have to call the police,' she shouted.

At that he seemed to come back to the present.

'I was the burglar,' he grinned foolishly.

'What?'

'Get the police, put on the handcuffs, I'm ready to be taken away.'

'What do you mean?'

'I sold them,' he slurred with a self-satisfied smirk.

She stared at him, speechless.

'Yea, got a good price.'

'When did this happen?'

308

'A couple of days ago.'

'You stupid idiot, I loved those two paintings. I had to pay for them on-the-drip. It took me long enough, as you well know.'

'What yours is mine, what's mine is my own,' he laughed, but then turned suddenly vicious and grabbed her arm. 'And don't you call me stupid, do you hear me?'

'Let go.' She tried to free herself, self-conscious when the music stopped temporarily.

'Say you're sorry.' His fingers tightened.

'Dermot, let go of me.' She pulled away from him, but his grip was strong.

'Say sorry.' He leered into her face.

'Sorry,' she muttered reluctantly, and he released her. Embarrassed, she hurried out of the room and went straight upstairs to the bedroom to check whether he had included Jack's painting, but was very relieved to find that it was still there. She took it down, realising that the other paintings were unimportant, this was the only one that meant anything to her.

Chapter Forty-Nine

Carmen lit a cigarette, sipped her glass of champagne, and rearranged the turquoise silk beach wrap allowing just the right amount of tanned leg to be viewed. She enjoyed being here in the luxury of the Hotel El Castillo, looking out over the sparkling blue sea from where she sat at the terrace bar. It was such a change from her dull life in Alicante. She had lived like a fugitive in that grimy little room without a penny to her name, or one decent item of clothing on her back, until the police had coughed up the first of the money they had promised her, and she had enough to escape here to Acapulco.

'Carmen?'

She turned around with more than a hint of irritation.

'Ross, where have you been...?' her voice trailed off as she stared at the man who stood looking at her, and she could feel the blood drain through her body.

'How are you?' Manuel asked smoothly.

'I'm fine...Manuel.' Terrified, she shrank into her chair. He sat beside her, uncorked the champagne bottle with a pop and poured some of the sparkling liquid into the glass which was meant for Ross.

'I need to ask you a few questions, Carmen, but it's too public here, let's go up to your room.' He took one sip of the champagne, then put down the glass on the white marble surface of the table.

'I'm waiting for Ross,' she said nervously.

'I don't have any time for waiting around, and I'm not particularly interested in meeting this Ross, whoever he is.' He stood up and held out his hand to her.

'I told you, I have to wait for Ross.' She looked over the heads of the other patrons towards the entrance, praying that her tall tennis-player would appear soon.

'Carmen.' There was a sudden hard edge in his voice.

Slowly she picked up her leather bag, walked back into the hotel, followed by Manuel who was dressed casually in a grey linen suit. At the lift, she tried to dawdle, frantically wondering should she go to reception and tell someone that Manuel was harassing her, or just scream for help. But he had a tight grip of her arm and forced her into the lift so quickly she had no chance to do anything.

When they arrived in her luxurious suite, he pushed her inside.

'Can I get you something, coffee, drink?' she offered hesitantly.

'No, I just want you to sit down and answer my questions.' It was an order. Without another word, she obeyed him.

'You informed on me, didn't you?'

'What do you mean?' She stared at him with innocent eyes.

'Someone told the police about my business, and showed them where to find the files they needed to commence an investigation. The person who did all of this had access to everything, possessed a key, was aware of the combination of the safe, and also knew when the security man would go for his cup of coffee.' He leaned towards her, his smooth dark-skinned face only a few inches from hers, so close she could actually see the tiny beads of moisture which shone on his forehead and around his nose.

She stared at him, immobile. How could he know all of this?

'No, that's not true.' She shook her head, and her long gold earrings flashed. 'Someone told you that to blacken me, to take the heat off themselves. How could you think that I'd ever dream of doing something so terrible?' She put a hand on her chest and tried to give the impression of total innocence.

'So you still love me?' A half-smile hovered on his lips for the first time, and it gave her hope.

'Of course I do, Manuel, I was devastated when we parted.'

'But you had time for another man. You were seen that night. I was very sorry I didn't get there in time.'

311

'How do you know we were doing anything? Perhaps he was a friend?'

'You don't have any men friends.'

'Yes I do,' she stuttered, realising that she was digging a hole for herself which was getting deeper and deeper.

'His name?'

'I can't remember.'

'His name?'

She shivered.

'His name?' he demanded, and suddenly a narrow silver blade appeared in his hand.

She stared at him, and the knife, hypnotised. 'Dermot Mason.'

'The Irish? That lump of an Irish? How could you waste your time with him? He's ignorant. How could he be more attractive than me?' He was furious now, his face contorted. 'Tell me what he had?' The blade glinted in his hand.

'Nothing, he was never like you, but I...' She burst into tears.

'It is the worst insult of my life to be replaced by him.' He dragged her head up by the long black hair, and forced her to make eye-contact with him. 'And he won't ever want you again, Carmen.'

'Please don't kill me, please Manuel, don't...'

'No, I won't kill you, Carmen, but every time you look in the mirror I want you to remember me.' He slashed at her face. She screamed. A thin red line appeared across the smooth tanned skin, and widened as blood spurted. He threw her back on the couch. 'And I'll take my revenge on that Irish pig as well.'

Chapter Fifty

There was a sense of unreality about the following weeks. Kate's subconscious mind kept account of the length of time since Jack had left, and constantly reminded her of his absence. But she had to force him out of her head, so that anger which had spurted when she realised that he too wanted her to sell Berwick Road, was stirred up and clung to. He didn't understand her. He couldn't love her. She had made a mistake.

It was important to think only of those things that had to be done from the moment she snapped out of sleep in the morning to when she tried to shut down at night. She made lists on little yellow notepads and stuck them everywhere. They were like a paper-trail, the only way to clamber from hour to hour.

'Are you feeling OK?' Carol stared worriedly at her one morning. 'You're losing the weight very quickly, your clothes are beginning to hang off you.'

'I'm OK.' She didn't respond to Carol's comment about her figure, but it was true, she had lost weight. She was thinner than she had ever been, and should have been thrilled, but her looks were the last thing on her agenda these days. She didn't even bother to weigh herself. She only vaguely noticed that the waistbands of her skirts and trousers were loose and thought that she must make some adjustments one of these days, but it always slipped her mind. It was ironic really, her dream of achieving that magical nine-stone target had come true without effort. She wished she was back in those days of hating the flab, but being able to laugh at it, knowing that her life was good, her family safe, and Dermot loved her regardless of how she looked.

'Why don't you come back to Yoga?'

'Sorry, we're going out, it's business...' she lied.

'Are you doing a few postures at least?'

'Oh yes,' she lied again. It had got easier, and she did it more frequently, deliberately keeping up the sham that everything was normal.

But Carol wasn't fooled so easily. 'Is all this business with Mags getting too much for you?' she persisted until finally Kate nodded. 'And you're really missing Jack, am I right?'

'No! I was glad to see the back of him,' she snapped. Tears moistened her eyes as Carol hit the point exactly, and she pressed a tissue to dry up the signs of telltale emotion. 'But I blame myself for the way things are with Mags,' Kate admitted, aware that their friendship was strained almost beyond repair at this stage.

It was so childish, the I'm-not-speaking-to-you-ever-again thing. And if there were times it needed all three heads, Carol and Kate struggled to ensure that the rift was not too obvious, but assumed everyone knew something was going on. Site meetings began to consist mostly of Carol and Mags or Carol and Kate, very seldom did they discuss projects as they had done in the past. If Kate had a query, she went through Carol. If Mags had a query she went through Carol, who said she felt like an arbitrator for two opposing sides in a union dispute.

'There's no such thing as all one person's fault. It's like a marriage, your fault today, my fault tomorrow. It's bound to settle eventually,' Carol advised, but Kate wasn't persuaded.

At home, Dermot and Irene continued to party. He was still lying low, keeping up the sham of being in Spain. Kate wondered when he was going to surface. He seemed to have no intention of going back to work for anyone else, and began to nag her about selling Uncle Bill's house again. It was all he talked about. Of course he had Irene, who was obviously financing the party, but Kate was still expected to produce rabbits out of hats. She had a couple of thousand left in her savings account, and although she managed the everyday expenses out of her salary, as time passed

314

and various calls were made on it, her nest-egg began to diminish.

'Don't forget to pick up some wine when you do the shopping,' Dermot reminded.

'And cigarettes for me,' Conor added.

'And a few cans.' This from Shane, who was really the most harmless of the three of them, working away at his music.

'Mum, can I have some money for the weekend, about two or three hundred will do?' Conor had asked the other evening when they were alone.

'I don't know if I can give you that much, two or three hundred?'

'It's Donal's stag and everyone's going.'

'I can't afford it.'

'But you knew he was having a stag.'

'I gave you the money for the wedding-present, new gear, and that's as much as I can manage.' She was determined not to give in. 'What about down at the local, the way we used to do it?'

'Mum, those days are gone, you should be glad we're not heading off to Greece, Tom is planning that for next year.'

'Then you had better start saving.'

'I will, but I can't manage it for this weekend. What are they going to think if I back out?'

'They all have jobs, Conor, they work. Can you even spell the word?' Kate demanded.

'Look, you're my mother, you have to support me.' He grew heated, and she could see Dermot in his angry features.

'I don't, you're over eighteen.'

'You have plenty of money, I know it.' He moved closer to where she stood at the counter and leaned over her, his outstretched arm against the wall.

'I don't have plenty of money, I can just about manage to pay the mortgage and support all of us.'

'I'll pay you back as soon as I'm in funds, with interest.'

'You've never paid anyone back, Conor, never, not a bean,' she snapped - loathe to let him bully her.

315

'I've always paid my debts, don't you insinuate...'

He glowered down into her face.

Suddenly she felt slightly afraid of him.

'Take that back,' he demanded roughly. She stared at him, shocked. She couldn't believe that this irate man was her son.

'Take it back.'

'Conor, how dare you speak to me like that.' She found her voice at last.

'You can't insult me,' he retorted.

'I'm your mother, I can say what I like. If that doesn't suit, you can move out.'

But of course she gave him the money, almost glad to see him gone for the weekend, knowing full well that there was no way he could afford to move out.

Then Shane asked for his portion of dosh.

'A friend of Kev has offered us the use of his studio at a really low cost, just a pittance really, so we've decided to give him five hundred between us, plus the CD expenses, so do you think you could manage to let me have my share?'

He had an innocent expectancy about him, a doesn't money grow on trees and can I have some look.

'Shane, I can't keep giving you money, you will have to find a job of some sort to pay your way.'

'But I don't have time, Mum. I need every minute to concentrate on this demo, it's really important.'

'I'm sorry Shane, it's becoming a real problem.'

'Can't we borrow some money?' Shane suggested, but neither of her sons understood anything about repayment.

But she gave him what he wanted as well, and vowed that she was really going to try to resist the pressure, and the constant arguments between the four of them. The "I want" syndrome was something to be expected from four-year-olds, not supposedly mature adults.

With their financial situation deteriorating, Kate had to force herself to talk to Dermot, and prayed this time he would see things from her point of view. She tackled him one Saturday morning. Waiting until he finally surfaced, she made him a tasty brunch, determined to be pleasant and non-judgmental.

'I'm worried about our situation, Dermot, when do you think you'll get back to work again?'

'When you decide to sell Berwick Road.'

'We can't manage on my money.' She ignored his remark about the house.

'I supported all of you for long enough, it's your turn now.'

'But my salary is not like a piece of elastic, although I'm sure Conor and Shane think it is.'

'Ask for a raise, can't you?'

'Don't be silly.'

'I told you what to do,' he growled, 'but of course you won't do it. You would prefer to grind us into the ground rather than do something to help us get out of this mess we're in.'

His phone rang. He listened to whoever was on the other end, and Kate could see his face pale. 'I'm in Spain at the moment. As soon as I get back, I'll be in touch and give you an update. It's just a bit of a delay, the workers in Spain aren't exactly Speedy Gonzalez, but it shouldn't take much longer...no problem...OK...right, talk to you soon.' He clicked off the phone. 'You see, that's another thing. My clients who have given me deposits on apartments and houses in Spain are all wondering when they're going to be able to take possession. What am I going to do about them?'

'Give them back their deposits if you can't complete the contracts, you should have some money from the sale of the paintings.' She tried to eliminate the sarcasm which coated her words.

'That only kept me going for a few days.' He forked up the last butter-filled mushroom on the plate. 'The next thing to be sold is Berwick Road.'

'You can't go over my head on that.'

'But I can get into your head, Kate. Never forget, I know you since you were twelve.'

'You don't know me at all, Dermot.'

Chapter Fifty-One

Jack travelled to the north of Spain this time, an area unfamiliar to him. He was reluctant to go back to the south yet, all of his dreams for a life with Kate rooted in that place. He wondered would he ever get her out of his head again, or would he be forced to travel around Spain like a nomad unable to settle anywhere for long? Now he was a tourist, exploring the ancient castles and monasteries along the route to Santiago de Compostela. This part of Spain reminded him more of Ireland in its green-ness and the amount of rainfall. Andalucia, where the sun burned day after day out of a cloudless blue sky, was a very different place.

He spent a couple of days in Santiago itself, an ancient medieval city built of warm golden granite. In an aimless fashion he wandered through the quiet back streets and squares. He didn't bother to look at a guide-book, or visit the cathedral where the bones of St. James were supposedly buried in the crypt, the focus of most pilgrims' visit. He just soaked in the atmosphere, and tried to talk to local people he met, the old man feeding bread to the birds, the woman sitting by the fountain watching her grandchildren play at her feet, the dark-faced kids who gathered at every corner, the girl in the grocery shop with the flashing smile. But to his frustration his efforts to communicate were limited as the language spoken by many was Gallego, a mixture of Castilian and Portuguese.

Among those people, he searched for inspiration which would encourage him to begin to paint in his usually obsessive way, but no one caught his imagination or his heart, not even the smiling girl. He travelled on to the west coast. To the old town of Muros, which ascended in tiers of narrow streets from the curve of the seafront, the place once known as the end of the world. He booked into a small hotel and waited for something to occur to him, until bored and depressed, the germ of an idea finally struggled to the surface of his mind. While at first he dismissed its presence, reminded too much of the way he had painted Kate, it came back again as he wandered around the town, until he persuaded himself to make a few sketches at least. So what if it never went any further, it would be something to do.

He began with the people he met, taking their features one by one, a head, a hand, and the feet, particularly the feet, remembering the pilgrims who had travelled the dusty road to Santiago from ancient times to the present day. He isolated the essential detail. With a bunch of children staring wide-eyed, he sketched the fishermen as they mended their nets, a sense of history about them as they worked in much the same way as their fathers before them, and the black-clothed old women who sat in doorways, their gnarled brown fingers moving rapidly as they created wisps of white lace from a single strand. There was a surfeit of subjects, but the final results were darkly shadowed, reflecting his innermost thoughts and his grim solitary mood. He felt it was the end of his world. The weather changed suddenly, black threatening storm-clouds marched in from the horizon. From the balcony Jack watched the small town nestle in shadow as all the bright sunshiny colours, the whites of walls and blues of sea, were dulled. The people hurried past, hidden under umbrellas angled against the torrential rain which slanted down like sharp rods pounding on the cobblestones, pools of water suddenly created.

He had tried to escape from Kate, but she was always there in front of him. Once he saw a woman who had a look of her, with the same blonde hair and figure. He stopped what he was doing, heart banging inside his rib cage, until she had disappeared around a corner. He almost followed to see whether by some huge coincidence it was her, but he resisted the urge, reminding

319

himself that things like that didn't happen in real life. But he went on daydreaming, remembering so many things about her, and how much she had seemed to love him. But that uncertain little word "seemed" threw him off balance. He came to the reluctant conclusion that for her it was just being in love, a short-span interlude, and not real love, not the way he felt. He should have been back in Mojacar by now, but the thought of returning was something which he did not relish. He felt the same about Dublin. Lately he had even begun to consider going further afield altogether, to one of the South American countries perhaps. It might be just what he needed. For now he decided to move on down south, and take a slow meander through places he had never been before which might spark something new in him, inject a fix of adrenalin to shoot him back to where he had been a couple of years ago, before Kate, a contented man with a narrow solitary life, who had no expectation of anything other than his art.

Chapter Fifty-Two

It was a very humid day. By lunchtime, Kate felt so uncomfortable she decided to go home to shower and change. There was a meeting with some new clients arranged in the afternoon but she really couldn't have faced them the way she felt. Walking quietly down the hall, she guessed that both Irene and Dermot were probably still in their beds - the usual thing these days after a late night. On the stairs, she heard a sound above, and stopped to listen. Was that someone running? But there was no further noise and she continued on up presuming that she had imagined it. In the bedroom, Dermot lay in a crumpled heap of sheets; the duvet trailed on the floor. Luckily he made no move as she took out her burgundy suit, a pale-pink blouse, fresh underwear and went into the bathroom. As she dressed she glanced at herself in the mirror and only then thought about putting on her gold chain. She returned to the bedroom to get her jewellery-box, but when she opened it she gasped. There was only a cheap bracelet and a pair of earrings inside. She searched through the drawers of the dressing-table, the tallboy, the bedside-lockers, but couldn't find a trace of all the other pieces, particularly worried about the necklet and earrings Jack had given her.

'Dermot.' She shook his shoulder.

'Wha?' he groaned, but didn't open his eyes.

'I can't find my jewellery...' She dragged at the sheet which was wrapped around him. 'Dermot, wake up, wake up!' She shook him again.

'For God's sake, stop thumping me. What's got into you?' He sat up angrily.

'Haven't you heard a word I've been saying?' she demanded.

'I couldn't help it, shouting in my ear like that. Anyway, what jewellery have you got, only a couple of things worth anything at all?' he scoffed, and climbed out of the bed.

'It's not the value, it's the...I'm ringing the police.' She lifted the phone.

'Don't bother, I took it. I thought you wouldn't notice, you don't wear jewellery that often, and I was going to replace it as soon as I've got money.'

'You took it?'

'Yea, I had to raise a few bob. Although I don't know why you couldn't mention that you'd invested in stuff like that as well as pictures. I felt a right fool when my jeweller friend pointed out how valuable the neck thing was, and the earrings. I can't even remember how many carats he mentioned. He thought I'd bought them for you, but of course, I had to try to cover up the fact that I'd never even seen them before.'

She stared at him in horror.

'Anyway, I'll buy you some more as soon as we get on our feet again, just as good.' He grinned and went towards the bathroom.

'You bastard!' she ran after him, catching up as he went in the door. 'They're irreplaceable.' She grabbed his sleeve.

'Nothing's irreplaceable.' He threw off his pyjamas and stepped into the shower.

'Where did you sell them?' she screamed in panic. But he didn't hear her above the noise of the water, so she pulled open the door and grabbed his arm. 'Get out here. I want to know what you've done with them.'

'Kate, I'm trying to have a shower.' He slid the door closed again, and forced her to wait outside trying to contain her anger until finally he stepped out. 'Where's the towel?' He held out his hand.

'Do you think that's what I'm standing here for?' She grabbed one from the rail and flung it at him.

'You might as well make yourself useful,' he grinned.

'Give me the name of that person. Was he one of those pawnbrokers?'

'No, no, much more high-class than that, although I doubt if he still has the necklace and earrings. He said he had a client who would be delighted to find such an item, they're by some designer apparently. I have to say you always had a keen eye for a good investment.'

'But they're mine, mine, not yours!'

'Needs must.' He dried himself off with a towel. Wandering back into the bedroom he dressed in a pair of trousers, and white shirt.

'I want to kill you, Dermot.'

'Relax Kate, for God's sake, you're doing my head in.' He swung out through the door and she followed him downstairs.

'Why didn't you sell something else, your car or the lads' jeeps?'

'How would we survive without cars? And what would people think if your banger was the only one in the driveway?'

'You're obnoxious...'

He reached for the whiskey bottle which stood on the counter.

'Give me the name of the man who bought my jewellery,' she demanded, moving closer to him.

'No, I told you I can't do that.' He poured a glass.

'Tell me!'

'No.' He swallowed the whiskey quickly.

'I'll never forgive you...'

'What's so vital about them anyway? You didn't go on like that over the pictures, what gives?' He poured another generous measure.

'They're just more...' She grabbed the glass in his hand.

'Hey, what are you doing? Let go.' They struggled with it.

'If you'd only stop drinking you might make some attempt to get going again, as it is you're out of it most of the time.'

'It's the only consolation I have, can't you see that?' He succeeded in pulling the glass away from her, spilling most of the contents.

'You're pathetic, self-centred...uncaring...' she shouted furiously.

'Thanks a lot. Kick a man when he's down, you're good at that,' he sneered, and turned on the television.

'What's going on?' Irene appeared in the doorway, wrapped in a sheer black negligee.

'Nothing!' Kate said, and pushed past her. Desperately upset, she drove away from the house towards the mountains, almost unaware of where she was going. At the Pine Forest, she pulled into the car park, and stopped there among the tall trees, no-one else around. After a while she got out, followed the path upwards to one of the topmost points, a place where she had spent many a morning with Jack. In the solitude, she sat on a rock and looked out across the landscape. Devastated over the loss of the jewellery, she wondered how she could ever replace it. Even apart from that, the thought of trying to explain to Jack what had happened was a pretty awful prospect, if she ever saw him again. She phoned Carol to say that her car had broken down, apologised for missing the meeting, and thought about what she was going to do.

It was almost five when she returned. The meeting was still in progress, but she didn't join them. She was far too tired, with her head throbbing, her suit and hair damp from a heavy shower which had fallen as she walked back to the car. She didn't do any work as such, just tidied away the papers on her desk, and made herself a coffee. She swung slowly from side to side on the swivel-chair staring out the window at the buildings opposite, the sky a hazy blue over the city, the day still warm. As she sat there her mind began to clear, and she realised one obvious glaring truth. She couldn't continue to live with Dermot. Turning back to him, Conor and Shane, sacrificing herself because they needed her was nonsense. She had been fooling herself into thinking she was indispensable. All they wanted from her was money, and saw her as one-dimensional, a cardboard cut-out. They didn't love her, and might not even realise that they had once loved her until she left them. She made the decision reluctantly, as her emotions dragged her back into the memories of their lives, and left her wondering how she could live a solitary existence for the first time ever.

Carol came in when the meeting was over.

'Did you get your car fixed?'

'I got it going, it was something to do with...I'm not sure exactly...how did the meeting go?' Kate tried to act normally.

'Very well, I'd say we have it in the bag, but I'm sure you don't want to go through the details now, it's a bit late.'

'No, I'm afraid my brain wouldn't be able to absorb it.' Kate stared vaguely out of the window, and then after a few seconds, turned back again to look at Carol.

'You definitely seem out of sorts. Come on, let's go home.'

'I'm leaving Dermot,' Kate said abruptly. Saying the words suddenly gave reality to her decision.

'What?' Carol gasped. Then she put her arms around Kate, the two holding each other in silence for a moment, until she moved back and stared down at her. 'Tell me about it.'

'It doesn't sound like much, but...' Tears glistened in her eyes as she recounted what had happened earlier.

'Maybe you should give yourself some time to think it over. It seems a bit drastic to leave because he sold the jewellery and paintings. After all, he's probably in a desperate state over money, that sort of thing has sent many a man over the edge.'

'Are you on his side?' Kate snapped.

'No, I'm just trying to introduce a bit of logic.'

'It was the last straw. There's so much going on I just have to get away, I'm worn out.'

'Come and stay with us for a few days, give yourself some space. Then you can go and talk to him.'

'Thanks very much, I appreciate that.'

'What about Conor and Shane?'

'I'll keep them going with money until they get jobs.'

'It might give them a bit of a jolt if you didn't.'

'To leave them the way they are at the moment is difficult enough; anyway money doesn't matter - there's more to this than...money.'

'Right, I'll sort out the spare bedroom for you, come over whenever it suits you.'

'Thanks a million. Love you.' Kate hugged her.

She felt strange going into her home, aware that this might be the last time she would open the front door, walk down the hall and into the kitchen. The last time...the last time...repeated in her head like a premonition of some awful catastrophe as she went through into the conservatory where Dermot sat watching television. As soon as he saw her, he switched it off and stood up. There was a sudden quiet, only vague noises impinging on them. The sound of birds twittering through the open patio door, the distant plink-plonk of Shane's electric guitar, other things she couldn't identify.

'I'm very sorry about your jewellery, Kate, but I was desperate, I thought I'd replace it when I was flush.' He moved towards her.

'I'm leaving you, Dermot.' In the end it wasn't that difficult. It came out easily, as if she was saying she was going to work, or getting her hair done.

'What did you say?' His eyes widened.

'You heard me.'

'Getting your own back for selling your stuff?' he laughed.

'It's not only that...'

The smile on his face faded.

'You're not the person I married, Dermot, I don't know you any more, and I don't want to live with you.'

'But you can't leave me! And what about Conor and Shane?' he shouted.

'You can sort them out, they won't do what I tell them. Anyway, they only see me as an unending source of money. I'm tired of that too.'

'But where are you going to live?'

'With Carol.'

'For God's sake, you can't just walk out on us because of a misunderstanding. Things like that happen in marriages, it doesn't mean that the whole thing collapses. Please Kate, don't go,' he begged.

'I'm not discussing it. I'm leaving...'

*

It was more difficult to tell Conor and Shane. Luckily, Irene was out for the evening, and when Dermot disappeared into his study with a bottle of whiskey, she took her opportunity. She made them a snack, busying herself buttering bread, placing thick pieces of baked ham between three slices, the way they liked it, Conor's seasoned with French mustard, Shane's with mayonnaise. She took extra care and tried to stretch out the time before she had to start explaining.

'I want to talk to you,' she said lightly, as if it was nothing out of the ordinary.

'When is the dinner going to be ready?' Conor asked.

'I've made you a sandwich to keep you going.' She put the plates and mugs on the table.

'I'll have mine inside,' Shane said.

'Hold on, I need to have a chat with you.'

'Will it take long? I'm in the middle of something.'

'It's important, Shane.'

He sat down at the table as she searched in her mind for the right words, but none came. Instead, she found herself wondering about small inconsequential things that suddenly seemed terribly important. How will Conor sort his socks? Who will boil up lemons when Shane goes down with one of those bad throats? What will happen to them if they eat nothing but junk food? The questions ambushed her. She poured herself a coffee from the percolator, just to do something, to be her usual self. A mother. Mam. Mum. That all-consuming role of women, all freedom relinquished when they marry and take on the mantle of motherhood, bound with invisible strings to their babies for ever. She had a sudden vision of the boys in their prams, one dark, one fair. Her heart twisted.

'Your Dad and I...' she tried to drag resistant don't-want-to-be-spoken words into life. She couldn't look directly at them, her eyes somewhere above their heads. 'We have decided to separate...for a while.'

'What?' Conor looked shocked.

'Things haven't been going very well, and I, we, think it's best.'

Shane didn't say anything.

'Is Dad moving out?' Conor asked.

'No, I am.'

'But where are you going to live?' he asked, always the practical one.

'I'll stay with Carol for a while.'

'You can't go,' Shane burst out.

She struggled hard not to cry, knowing that they wouldn't be able to take that. Emotion had to be kept under wraps. It was too volatile and could run them all ragged in a moment. Accusations flung wildly, things said which would always be regretted.

'What about Dad, what does he think?' Shane demanded, beginning to lose his cool. Knowing the boy man so well, she knew her younger son never liked things to change and hated having to adjust the routine of his life. He wanted the family to revolve around him, all his needs served.

'He'll tell you himself.' She could imagine Dermot's awkwardness, stuttery and embarrassed in front of his sons.

'What will we do about our food?' Shane asked.

'You're old enough now to look after yourselves, between the two of you it shouldn't be that difficult.'

'But we're not used to it, we can't do all those things you do for us.' He was sullen.

She wanted to put her arms around him and hold on tight for as long as it took to chase away the look on his face, and tell him that she would always be there for him, but she was afraid to do that.

'I can't believe it. I didn't think it was all roses with you and

Dad, but I never thought it would come to this.' Conor folded his arms across his chest with a bullish you-should-have-managed-it-better attitude.

She searched for a response.

'Are you selling the house, splitting things up between you?' he asked, 'that seems to be the usual thing with most of my friends.'

'We're not doing that. I'm going.' She turned to clean up the remains of the sandwich-making, her back to them now.

'But I don't want you to go.' Shane moved closer to her.

'Maybe it won't be for long,' she had to say it, to make him feel more secure. Her second son was tall and broad-shouldered like her first born, but softer, much softer.

'The mother never leaves, it's always the father. You can't go off, Mum, it's your place to be here,' Conor growled.

'It's going to be awful without you.' Shane's face was pale, he looked as if he would burst into tears at any moment.

'How will we live? Dad has no money,' Conor demanded angrily.

'I'll give you as much as I can.'

'Mum, I'll try to find a job, please change your mind.' Shane came over and put his arms around her. They held each other tight for a moment, then unable to say any more, she went upstairs to pack. Lastly, she took Jack's painting from the wardrobe, wrapped it in a sweater, then put it carefully in the suitcase.

It was strange living with Carol and Amanda, a displaced person without any ties. She missed Shane, Conor and Mount Asher Road so much there was a physical pain inside her. The silliest things nagged at her. Would they remember to water the flowers, mow the lawn, put out the feed for the birds? Who would wash Conor's football gear? Who would cook their favourite dishes? Who would...?

She phoned them every day and met Shane as often as he could spare the time away from his music. To her surprise, he seemed to be getting used to her absence, whereas Conor was curt in his response to her enquiries, and so unforgiving.

But the habits of years die hard, and she still found herself driving in the direction of home regularly. Mostly it happened when the day's work was finished and she was heading for Carol's house. But she was never able to take that turn, some deep-seated need inside forcing her to continue on to Mount Asher Road, longing so much to open the door of her home, close it behind her, sink into its warm comforting embrace.

Home. A place of loving and holding close, of tears dried, of hurts mended. A place which had always been there for her, safe, secure, where she could shut out the world.

Why had it all gone sour?

Chapter Fifty-Three

'Your dinner's ready,' announced Irene. She was wearing a frilly polka-dot apron over a simple black dress, totally unsuitable for the kitchen. But she was determined to make herself indispensable to Dermot, and had no intention of ever looking like someone who had slaved over a hot stove all day. She forked a rather well-done sirloin on to a plate, added oven chips, a few peas, and put it down in front of Dermot. The same for Conor and Shane.

'I'm fed up with steak every night, can't we have something else to eat?' Conor moaned.

'I thought you liked steak,' Irene said, as she delicately ate a small piece of salmon.

'I do, but not every night. Why can't you make some of the dinners Mum used to make?'

'Shut-up Conor, you're lucky to be eating steak, particularly when Irene's paying for it,' Dermot grunted.

'Mum makes great lasagne, and spaghetti bolognese, and super sangers.' Shane swallowed his beer.

'Enough about...we're so fortunate that Irene's prepared to look after us, just be glad she's here,' Dermot cut through his steak.

There was a silence then, the noise of cutlery scraping plates, and the chewing of food the only sound.

'I could do salmon for you?' Irene offered.

'We hate fish,' Conor said.

'What would you like?' She smiled helpfully at them, but received nothing in return.

'That chicken thing Mum cooks in the oven is really tasty. You could do that,' Shane suggested.

'It sounds far too fattening. Maybe I'll do burgers?'

'Yea, OK.'

'Right, burgers it is. I'll get the supermarket to include them tomorrow when they deliver.' Irene finished her meal, and dabbed at her mouth with a napkin.

'Mum makes them herself, she doesn't buy them in the supermarket.'

'I'm not sure how to make them.'

'If you don't like it, you can lump it, or cook for yourselves, you should be well able,' Dermot rasped.

He wasn't in good form. He hated having to put up with Irene, but she was paying for everything, and there was plenty of food and drink in the house now, even if the lads didn't like it much. Best of all, she had agreed to put up a property she owned on South Circular Road as collateral so that he could borrow money to start up in business again. But while she provided everything he needed, and sneaked into his bed at night, he hated being beholden to her and wanted her out of the house.

He phoned Kate at least once a day, and tried to persuade her to come home. But he had no success, suddenly not knowing the woman who spoke so coldly to him at the other end of the line.

Chapter Fifty-Four

Kate was slowly fitting into her new routine, and detoured when she found herself near the house these days. Shane was the only one she saw regularly, and she treasured any opportunity to meet him.

'Irene is a real pain, Mum. She can't cook, and is always complaining about having to do the housework, so it's not the greatest. Why don't you come home? I'm sure Dad would be delighted. And we'll try to make things easier for you. He's going back into business with Irene, so that means there shouldn't be any money problems, please come home?'

She would have given anything to go with him, but forced herself to say goodbye again, each time harder than before. Carol made her very welcome, and although money was tight Kate still felt that she had to pay her way.

'I don't want that much, it's ridiculous. I don't want anything at all, I'm not running a B & B.' Carol slid the cheque across the table towards her.

'Look, you're really kind to me, but I can't just take without giving something in return, so please?' Kate pushed it back.

'OK, I'm going to buy you something with it, and you can't do a thing about that.'

'Don't you dare, that's towards the bills, food, drink, and Amanda.'

'Listen, you're my best friend, and there's no charge for friendship in my book.'

Nowadays she really needed Carol, and felt the loss of Mags in her life, the final showdown occurring unexpectedly one evening as she left the underground car park. She had planned to meet Shane, and was driving slowly along the line of parked cars towards the exit when her phone rang, forced to slow down to a stop as she listened to his rushed apologies because he wouldn't be able to make it. Suddenly, there was a dull thud at the side of her car. Shaken, she looked around, unable at first to grasp what had happened exactly, then climbed out to see the back of Mags' green Morgan embedded in her Corolla.

'What were you doing, you stupid idiot?' Mags demanded furiously.

Kate stared at the two cars, suddenly feeling weak, the bang had really unnerved her.

'I waited until you had passed, began to reverse, and then you were still there.' Mags pointed to her dented bumper.

'How did I know you were reversing? I didn't know you were even in the car. My phone rang and I had to stop.'

'You should have seen my lights. You were only thinking of yourself as usual. Look at my car, it'll cost an arm and a leg to repair that.'

'The insurance will cover it,' Kate said, glad to be talking to Mags at last. Even if the circumstances weren't exactly ideal, at least they were actually communicating for the first time in months.

'It will never be the same again in my eyes, first time I've ever had a prang.' Mags' pretty features were ugly with anger. 'You're a right bitch. Everything's gone wrong in my life, and it's all your fault.'

At that moment Carol drove up in her car and jerked to a halt.

'Oh my God, Mags, what have you done?'

'It was her fault.'

'You should have been looking where you were going.' Kate's patience ran out. 'I've had it with you, Mags, and your attitude. It's become impossible to work with you, and all because Jack chose me. I know it seems crazy to you that he preferred me, but he did and you can't change it.'

Mags stared at her silently.

'Right, girls, let's get the cars separated, we'll be causing a major hold-up in a minute.' Carol took control and as both cars had sustained relatively minor damage and were still driveable, they all left without another word between them.

That evening Kate decided to resign from Lee O'Donnell, aware that her relationship with Mags would probably never improve. She had always imagined working until her old-age, simply passing away at her desk, but now the prospect of that wasn't so attractive. She broached the subject later, and as expected, Carol was horrified.

'But I don't think I could manage without you.' There were tears in her eyes.

'Look, all this stuff with Mags has affected our work, you know that. It's dull and uninspired. Maybe some new blood would be the answer?'

'I'll get Mags over here, we have to thrash this out.' She picked up her phone.

'Don't bother, Carol, it's too late for that now. I've used up all my enthusiasm, so I'm probably no good to the company any more.'

'How long have you been thinking about this? You never said a word,' Carol accused.

'It only occurred to me this evening after the accident.'

'But how can you make a decision like that in a matter of hours?'

'I just did. Dermot's going back into business again, so hopefully I won't have to support them all for much longer. So I'm going to look for another job or I might set up something myself.' She suddenly knew she was doing the right thing.

'Look, why don't you take a break, a long break? You said you were planning that. Maybe when you come back Mags might have got herself sorted. Go on, get on to the travel crowd and check the flights, you've never used that voucher we gave you,' Carol tried to persuade.

'No. Now that I've made the decision I want to finalise it immediately.'

'It's forty, the menopause, the mid-life crisis, isn't it?'

'Well, it could be all of those things.'

'What if you really regret it?'

'I can always come back and apply for a job with you, can't I?' she laughed.

*

Dermot rang just before five. It was the second time that day.

'Kate, I wonder, could you, would you meet me after work for a bite to eat and a few drinks? I've really missed you, please?'

'I've already told you that I'm busy, Dermot, don't you remember?' She flicked the keys, making some changes in a letter.

'Please Kate, don't shut me out like this. I'm sorry about everything, I shouldn't have done it, I realise that now.'

She didn't reply.

'Please Kate?'

She could hear the appeal in his voice and wanted to laugh. 'Sorry, Dermot, bye.' She put down the phone with a sense of triumph, and couldn't help smiling as she continued with her letter, but she stopped again after a moment unable to concentrate on the content. Even if Jack hadn't come into her life, she would eventually have been ground down by Dermot's lack of interest in her and his obvious boredom with their marriage.

As she left the office a couple of hours later, she saw him standing by the car waiting for her.

'Kate.' He moved closer, handing her a bunch of flowers. 'For you, it's a long time since I gave you any.'

He was dressed in his best dark suit, looking as if he had really made an effort with his appearance. She was caught off-guard and with stuttered thanks, accepted the bouquet although she would have preferred if he hadn't bothered. It just wasn't Dermot and trying to recreate himself was laughable.

'Let's go somewhere for a chat, please Kate. It's important. We have to make decisions about what we're going to do,' he begged in that old way. While she wanted to refuse, she knew they would have to talk eventually and decided it might as well be now.

'I haven't got much time,' she said quickly, wanting him to know that she wasn't going to sit listening to him for the night. It was so different to a couple of years ago when she would have given anything for the opportunity.

They went to Murphy's. She sipped a glass of water, and he downed a first glass of whiskey quickly, a second at a more leisurely pace.

'Have to say you're looking very well. Where are you living?'

'I'm still with Carol.'

'That must be difficult.'

'No, it isn't actually, it's very pleasant.' She watched him, and noted the slight shake in his hands as he fiddled with his cuff links, which were inexpensive; his gold ones had obviously gone the same way as her jewellery.

'Would you consider coming home, Kate, giving me a second chance?'

'Isn't Irene still with you, fulfiling the housekeeper role?'

'I'll be getting rid of her soon, she gets on my nerves,' he pouted, a sad crumpled look on his face.

'What about your business? Shane said you were setting up again.'

'We've formed a new company, Irene's the front-runner because of the situation, so I'm stuck with her. But now I can offer you something, Kate. We'll be back to where we were.' He put his hand on hers, but the rather hard grip was demanding and held no love or softness. She shook him off, and reached for her glass. 'Believe me Kate, the only thing I want is for us to be together again. Shane and Conor miss you terribly, they've told me.'

'Perhaps they do, but they show it differently. Conor refuses to meet me, although I see Shane frequently.'

'You can't blame Conor, he's very sensitive.'

'It must be very difficult when your mother isn't around to

pick up after you, or fork out money whenever you want it. What I give them now doesn't come near what they expect.' She could hear the edge in her voice but she made no effort to soften it.

'There'll be no need for you to pay anything towards their expenses, or the household bills now.'

'Does that include the mortgage?'

'Yes, I should be able to manage it all.'

'That's great, I'll cancel my payments with the bank.' She was delighted.

'And will you come home?'

'You know things haven't been good between us for a long time. Can you even remember when we last made love?'

'It wasn't so long ago, just before you left, I remember...' he mumbled.

'We haven't made love for years, Dermot. We might have had sex, but there was no love in it.'

'Of course there was. I love you, Kate, believe me, I do love you.'

'Dermot, you don't even understand what love means,' she said bluntly, longing to tell him about Jack.

'Maybe I didn't show my love to you in the past. I've been so busy with the Spanish project, all that worry and stress, please give me another chance?'

'No Dermot, I've made my decision, it's finished between us.' She reached for her handbag.

'Kate, you can't do this to me, you're breaking my heart.' Dermot caught her hand again and held it tight.

'Don't be so melodramatic, Dermot, it doesn't suit you.' She pulled away from him, and walked out the door to where her car was parked.

He followed. 'Kate, please come back to me, please?'

'See you, Dermot.' She turned the key in the ignition, shifted into first gear, and pulled out into the traffic. And he would pay all the bills in future! That was a surprise. She wondered when he would have informed her of that. She laughed, really pleased that his ploy did a nice little reverse-cartwheel and hit him right between the two eyes.

*

Dermot pushed past Irene into the dining-room where he picked up the whiskey-bottle, and poured quickly.

'What's wrong?' She watched him from the doorway.

'Nothing.' he swallowed a mouthful.

'I'll have a drink as well.' She took a glass from the sideboard. 'Come on, pour one for me.'

'Get your own,' he muttered.

'Dermot?'

He slumped into a chair.

'Maybe I will! And maybe I'll let you do everything for yourself in future too. I'm not going to hang around here and be treated like Kate, I'm not surprised she left.'

'I'm sorry, Irene, sorry, I shouldn't have spoken to you like that, forgive me.' He reached out to pour the whiskey into her glass.

'Don't bother, Dermot, I've had it. All you expect me to do is to pick up after you. I'm tired of that, I wasn't cut out to be a servant.'

'Dad?' Conor appeared in the doorway. 'Can I borrow your car tonight? There's something wrong with my jeep.'

'No,' he muttered. Kate knew what she was doing, took her chance to get away from all of this, and left him holding the baby instead.

'I must have transport.'

'Get the bus.'

'Dad, don't be ridiculous. By the way Irene, have you seen my black T-shirt? I left it in the bathroom yesterday.'

'It's probably in the launderette. I put a bag in there yesterday. If it smells, or even looks like it smells, I assume it's for the wash.'

'Would it be ready by now?'

'Probably gone over to the woman who does the ironing. You'll have to pick it up yourself, I'm off-duty,' she laughed.

He wandered off, disgruntled.

Just then there was a weird jangling sound as Shane walked into the room, plucking his electric guitar, trailing a long lead behind him.

'Shut up that racket,' Dermot shouted.

'Keep your hair on.'

'You can serve your own dinner, Dermot, it's in the grill. I'm going to pack.' Irene removed her apron, threw it over the back of a chair, and left the room.

'Irene, for God's sake, wait, you can't go off now. We're in business.' He ran after her.

'Make an appointment.' She hurried upstairs.

Dermot's phone rang and he searched for it in his jacket pocket.

'Yea?' His reply was curt.

'Dermot?'

'Manuel?' He whispered the name, hardly daring to believe that it was him.

'Si, it is I.'

'You bastard, where have you been? And where's my money?'

'I am so sorry, but it was not my fault. There were other people involved, and the police. I have lost everything also. It is only now I have got away from Spain with a little cash that I thought of you, always so sharp, and said to myself, Dermot is the man, he will be interested in doing some business, I am right, si?'

'Does the cash you're talking about belong to me by any chance?' Dermot asked.

'No, sadly. It is a small inheritance from my grandfather who died some months ago. Not that I am happy about his death, I would rather he was still here enjoying himself than for me to have his money, but such is life.'

Dermot could visualise the shrugged shoulders, the hands waving about. He wondered could he ever trust the man again?

'I'm sorry about that.'

'It will take some time before I forget. But now I am here in Dublin for a few days and I would like to meet you. Perhaps we might have dinner this evening, you and your lovely wife?'

'My wife is away.'

'That is a pity.'

'I'll have to check my diary.' This could be an opportunity, Manuel always thought big, and it might be to his advantage. Businesses folded all the time. People were left with nothing and established themselves again. 'I'm very busy at the moment, but I think I can fit you in with a bit of juggling. Let me see...shall we say eight o'clock?'

Chapter Fifty-Five

Jack wandered in and out of towns and villages, followed rivers through valleys, climbed in the mountains, only too aware that the summer was passing into autumn, and there was no work done. But he didn't really care. In Andalucia, he bypassed Granada deliberately, unable to walk those streets again without Kate. Her loss tainted his view of everything, and took the edge from its beauty. One morning, he suddenly found the isolation just too much to bear, and an unexpected need for contact with those he loved sent him towards Torrevieja.

Chris hung onto him with tears in her eyes, Eddie shook his hand, and Jack felt good, but regretted he hadn't met or talked to Chris since that day at home when they had clashed over Kate.

'I'll bring my stuff in and we can open some very nice wine I've got.' As he carried in his bag, he walked towards the house next-door and wondered whether they were there, knowing that she was the real reason why he had come. But as he moved closer, he saw the burnt grass, the dry leaves, the debris blown by the wind and felt as if someone had punched him.

Chris joined him. 'Our man would maintain the garden, but we can't get in. It does nothing for the area to have a house looking so run-down.'

'They haven't been out for a while?'

'Just as well, I really couldn't look her straight in the face.'

A wave of anger spun through Jack, but he pushed it away, reluctant to begin another row with Chris. There was an awkward silence between them.

'Have you done much work this summer?' she asked after a moment.

'No. I intend to try and get down to it now.'

'Surely you did something?'

'Some sketching, but that's about it.'

'I'm surprised, you're normally so prolific.'

'One can't always predict how work evolves. Maybe I've worn myself out, perhaps there's nothing left in me.' He didn't look at her, just stared at some point in the middle-distance as he contemplated the prospect of taking up accountancy again.

'You can't suddenly come to a stop, there has to be something wrong. You seem a bit down anyway, what's the matter?'

'Nothing really, it's probably like writer's block or something... artist's block,' he just about managed a wry smile.

'What about the theatre, did they ask you to do more work?'

'They did actually, but I'd have to be in a certain frame of mind to tackle that successfully.'

'It's all about Kate, am I right?'

'I suppose it will take some time to put it behind me.'

'I told you she'd dump you, she was just playing around. I'm furious with her, she's a...'

'Don't say that to me again, Chris.'

'I'm sorry.' She lowered her eyes and had the grace to look ashamed. 'It's just that I hate her for what she's done, that's all. I'm only thinking of you.'

'Let's join Eddie, I feel like getting drunk tonight.'

Chapter Fifty-Six

The tenants in Berwick Road moved out and Kate took possession again. It was the real start to her new life. Such a relief to be able to open her own door, close it behind her, do what she wanted when she wanted, and not have to step gingerly around other people.

Shane called in regularly, sometimes sleeping over if he was in town with the lads, and to her delight, Conor wasn't so distant any longer. That last night had been a turning point when she had gone home to collect her computer. She had knocked on the door out of politeness, with a strange sense of not belonging here any more, and waited until Conor answered, his expression more of a scowl than anything else.

'I'm so glad to see you, how are you?' She moved towards him, but he stepped back.

'Not bad, are you coming home?' His tone was slightly sarcastic.

'No, I'm sorry, I'm moving into Berwick Road. I told Dermot I'd come over.' She walked through quickly.

'He's gone out.'

'Why don't you call over to see me?' She put out the invitation not knowing what to expect. 'I'm leaving the company shortly, so I'll be working from there.'

'I might,' he grunted, surly.

'Come down tomorrow night with Shane for dinner, and we'll celebrate.'

'What?'

'The formation of my new company, "Crawford Design".'

'I 'dunno.'

'Please?'

'I'll see.'

There was a silence. A waiting. Then suddenly he moved, long legs eating up the space between them, and threw his arms around her. 'Why did you have to go, Mum, why?' he whispered.

Once she had given her formal resignation to Carol, her interest in the day-to-day work had waned, and although she put in as many hours as ever, maybe more, her mind was always on her new venture. She had inserted an advertisement in the back of The Irish Times, describing a specialised curtain design company and hoped it would bring her some work. Her financial position had stabilized radically when Dermot began to pay the expenses on Mount Asher Road, and she managed to save a good proportion of her salary.

Her leaving was celebrated with dinner at the Vadore Bistro on the evening of that last day she worked in Lee O'Donnell Design. All the staff were invited and the atmosphere was one of festivity, no-one else aware of the sadness she felt as they raised their glasses to toast her new venture. This year had seen the end of so much, probably the worst in her whole life, the break-up of her marriage, leaving home, and Jack too. It wasn't a year she wanted to revisit. She had become quite good at hiding her emotions, and smiled, and laughed, only allowing a few tears to escape when they presented her with a most exquisite bronze sculpture of a woman which would have pride of place in her new home.

The only downside was that Mags was absent. Kate would have loved for them to bury the hatchet. But supposedly it was impossible for her to be there, something about the family, a lame excuse which she didn't believe.

Kate barely picked at her dinner. The grilled lamb-chop, potatoes, mixed steamed vegetables, looked unappetising, and she pushed the plate away. Eating alone was difficult.

Accustomed to a noisy table at home with much talk and loud arguments, to sit in a room with only the radio or television for company was so strange it reinforced her single-ness, her newly chosen status. It allowed unwelcome questions about the wisdom of leaving Dermot to intrude. But she pushed them aside telling herself that it was natural to feel that way. She would get over it, eventually. It probably wouldn't have been so bad if she had been busy, but she found time heavy on her hands with nothing to do, the phone silent, and no business opportunities banging down the door. Her new workroom remained tidy and unused.

To fill the hours, she continued to redecorate, turning her attention to the kitchen and bedrooms. But as the weeks passed without a single enquiry she grew worried, watching her bank balance dwindle, and wondering if the advertising was going to bring in any return. Her biggest expense would soon kick-in, as probate on Uncle Bill's estate was nearing completion and she would have to begin making the repayments on the mortgage which she had arranged. She could have asked Carol if she needed her assistance, even on a part-time basis, but her pride wouldn't let her do that.

So she changed her marketing strategy, dropped the newspaper ad, and produced a flyer on the computer which she delivered to homes in the area in the evenings. She also placed them on the supermarket notice boards; there had to be business out there. To fill the empty hours, she developed her own ideas, creating specious light-filled rooms in a distinctive style, there was no need to take the opinions of other people into account.

'I love your stuff,' Carol admired the plans which were spread over the table. 'If I'd known you could produce this quality of work, I'd never have let you go.'

'I suppose I needed to do my own thing, develop myself,' Kate said shyly.

'Whatever it is, you've changed out of all recognition. Is that a size twelve you're wearing? And your hair is much softer now that you've let it grow a little. You look a million dollars.'

'I lost the weight through stress probably, although I wouldn't recommend such a method,' Kate laughed, certainly not going to inform Carol that her diet was suffering as a result of her tight budget. The little luxuries which she loved, biscuits, chocolate, and all those savoury high-calorie foods were no longer included in her weekly supermarket basket. 'Come on, I'm buying lunch.' She wouldn't have admitted for the world that there wasn't a client in sight even to Carol, who would bend over backwards to help if she had any idea of the true situation.

'You seem to be doing really well, I'm so glad for you,' Carol said as they sat in an alcove seat at the pub.

'It's not all sweetness and light. I've never lived alone before and there were times I almost had myself convinced I could put up with Dermot, but something made me stay here and dig my heels in.'

'If we'd gone to a fortune teller a couple of years ago and she foretold this, you'd never have believed her.'

'Maybe it was meant to be - fate.'

'I don't believe in that rubbish. You make your own way, carve out your niche, that's if you have the strength to do it.' Carol munched a fresh salad-filled roll.

'Is Mags well?' Kate asked, enjoying her vegetable soup.

'Great. She's fallen for some computer-wizard fellow she met, and Jack's history. It was obvious it was going to fizzle. When she's keen on someone, and the guy doesn't respond, she tries twice as hard.'

'How are things at work?'

'Now that you're free, have you thought about getting in touch with him again?' Carol's question shot in just at the same time as Kate's effort to change the topic.

'No, it's finished.' Kate shook her head adamantly.

'We were trying to make contact, but there was no answer from his phone.'

Kate put the spoon down. She didn't want Carol to notice that her hand had begun to shake.

'We needed some more paintings for Bob Benson, but we had to buy them from The Nestor instead.'

'I really don't want to talk about him. He's no better than the rest of the men I know. He's completely self-centred, and doesn't have a clue about me, no understanding at all.' Anger built up.

'But surely he was the reason you left Dermot in the end, a deep down in the subconscious sort of thing. He gave you the gumption to leave. You have to thank the guy, that's if you think you've made the right decision for you.'

'He wasn't...the reason.'

'But I thought when Dermot sold the jewellery Jack gave you it was the last straw?'

'I left Dermot because I didn't want to live with him any more. I was so tired of trying to please them all, including Jack.'

'But you can't ignore the fact that you love him. Here you are living all on your own, and he could still be out there for you. I think you're mad.'

'He's probably got someone else by now. Anyway, you didn't run after the first man you met and shack up with him just because you were on your own.'

'I never met anyone worth shacking up with,' Carol grimaced.

'Why do we need men at this time of our lives?'

'Well, there is the obvious!'

'I can live without that for now, and you've obviously managed, unless you're having a bit on the side you're telling no-one about,' Kate grinned.

'No, unfortunately, I don't even remember what that experience is like any more.'

'And I'm quite happy on my own.'

'Load of bull, if Jack walked in here you would change your tune so fast, we wouldn't see you for dust.' Carol burst out laughing.

'No, I don't think about him all that much, I'm content with my business, and the house, and...'

'Yea, but every time you get into bed that's all you think about.'

Kate had to laugh in spite of herself. 'I do not!'

'You're trying to fool me and fool yourself as well. It isn't working.'

'Well, I must get back, I don't know about you but I've a lot to do.' Kate stood up, and the two walked towards Berwick Road still laughing as they went along.

'I had to have the outfit altered, and I'm really under pressure for time, can you please pick it up for me?' Irene asked.

'I'm busy, Irene.' Kate continued sanding one of the kitchen chairs, only half-listening to her stepmother, whose voice crackled through the microphone.

'Please, Kate, I'm getting my colour done first. I'm booked in at the beauticians after that, and I wanted to wear the dress this evening, won't you oblige me?'

'I'm sorry but I'm busy.' She refolded her piece of sand-paper.

'How can you do this to me, Kate, I don't believe it's you I'm talking to.'

'Well, it is, Irene, it's definitely me.'

'I'm furious with you. You're not yourself at all.'

'I must go. Sorry Irene, bye, see you.' Kate continued sanding.

The phone rang again. It was Dermot. 'Can I see you, Kate? I need to talk to you.'

'What is the point?'

'How can you ask that, you know how I feel?' He sounded surprised.

'I've nothing to say to you, bye.' She put down the phone.

Determined to succeed, she continued with her nightly sales pitch. Armed with her flyers she spent hours running up and down driveways. Ringing the doorbell, handing the leaflet to whoever answered with a very quick explanation, already half-way down the path before the person realised what she was on about. Or if there was no reply, she slipped it through the letter-box, and hoped that her fingers wouldn't be bitten off by the snarling dogs which seemed to lie in wait for victims like herself. While it was tiring, it took care of her exercise programme, as well as any gym. She became very fit, timing herself when she was finished, delighted to cut a few minutes off her record for the previous night.

It was one of those evenings she found her first client. A woman who informed her that the painter was arriving on Monday and she didn't know what to do about new curtains and blinds, her old ones already thrown out in the skip. 'I went into town recently but I was so confused I came home and decided to put it off until another day, so you're just the sort of person I need.' She showed her around the old Victorian house.

Kate followed, her mind immediately full of ideas. She promised the lady she would come back the following day, and bring samples to show her. At home she opened up the computer, only finally giving up about two in the morning, praying that the woman would like her suggestions. The next day she went to some of the companies which stocked the type of fabrics she had in mind for this particular job. Unable to afford to build up her own collection just yet, they were very obliging and lent her the books she wanted to show her client. It took hours of consideration, cups of tea, and numerous wholegrain biscuits, until finally, as Kate was wondering if she had given it enough time, the woman pulled a chequebook out of her bag and offered to pay a deposit against the order. Kate smiled broadly, finding it difficult to control the delight which swept through her.

It was a great start, and that first client recommended her to neighbours, friends and relations. She was on her way at last. As more orders came in, her bank balance began to look more healthy, and she was kept busy right up to Christmas. She felt more optimistic and sure of herself than she had in years.

One evening, the doorbell rang.

'Happy Christmas!' Dermot handed her a box wrapped in shiny red paper, and a bottle of wine. 'We had to come around with your present, didn't we, Conor?'

'Yea...' Conor shuffled in after his father, looking no different to usual in his faded jeans, crumpled T-shirt, and black leather jacket.

'Must say this place is looking good.' Dermot stood in the hall and gazed up at the ceiling. 'The plaster work is terrific and I like the way you've picked out the design in gold, very swish altogether.'

She brought them into the sitting-room and they sat down. 'Can I get you something to drink,' she offered, thinking how strange it was to be entertaining her husband and son in her own home.

'I wouldn't mind a beer.' Conor sat on the edge of the chair.

'The usual for me,' Dermot grinned.

'I don't know if I have any of the usual, beer is about as far as I can stretch, or I could open the wine.'

'No, no, you keep that, beer is fine, thanks.' He nodded.

She gave each of them a can and a glass. Then she sat down opposite. 'Well, how have you been, Dermot, is the business going well?' she asked politely.

'Not bad.' He poured the beer slowly into the glass.

'What of your own clients, have you been able to sort them out, or do they get swallowed up?' she asked, although she had very little interest.

'I don't know yet. I've been so pestered with calls I had to change my phone number, I must give it to you.' He pulled a card from his top-pocket and reached over to hand it to her.

'And Manuel? Have you had any news from him?' She was suddenly curious.

'Oh yea, he got his fingers burned as well, and had to leave Spain apparently. Anyway he flew in a while back and we met, so I've decided to set up a joint operation with him.'

'Are you mad? I thought he had dropped you in it, and run off with all the money?'

'Apparently it wasn't quite like that.'

'But why would you do business with him again?'

'I can't turn down the opportunity, and it's the only way I can find out exactly what happened.' He shrugged. 'Now, enough about business. We came over to see you because we wanted to tell you that we miss you, didn't we Conor?'

'Yea,' he grunted.

'I miss you too.' She looked at Conor.

'Mum, any chance I can watch the TV, there's a match on?' he asked.'

'Sure, go ahead.'

He went downstairs and they were left alone.

'I'm glad he's gone, I want to talk to you.'

Kate waited.

'I must say you're looking very well, your hair is different, more like it was in the old days. Remember? And you are so thin I hardly recognise you,' he murmured softly, 'Kate, I miss you, please come back to me. Life is unbearable without you. I only brought Conor over for moral support because I felt so nervous.' He twisted his hands. 'I want us to be together again for Christmas. The house hasn't even got a decoration up, no tree, or crib, it's nothing without you.'

She almost felt sorry for him.

'I promise I'll do everything I can for you. The thought of waking up on Christmas morning on my own is awful. Remember how we used to open the presents, and go to Mass together, and the great dinner you always cooked, this year there's no pudding or cake or anything.'

'I can't go back now.' Kate stood up and turned to stare out the window. 'Too much has happened.'

'You mean the paintings and the jewellery, is that it?' There was a nervous jitter in his voice. 'I can buy you more, whatever you want. How could they count for anything when you love someone?'

'We don't love each other, not the way we used to.' She chose her words carefully.

'That's not true.' He came over, slid his arm around her and tried to kiss her.

She stepped back from him.

'Kate...' His grip tightened.

'No, Dermot.'

'I love you, I can't live without you.' He pressed his lips on hers, and tried to force her mouth open. She struggled to escape his grip, feeling claustrophobic as he pressed her against the wall. She tried to speak, but her words were garbled. He wasn't listening anyway, as he burst open the top buttons of her blue striped shirt, and his hands moved underneath, his body pushing hard into her.

'Dermot, stop, please stop.' She thrust him away, but he was heavy, and her efforts ineffective.

'Come on Kate, let's do it like the old days, come on.'

'No, Dermot, I don't want to, no!'

He pulled her down on the floor, opened the zip of her jeans, and tried to drag them off, crushing her with his weight. Suddenly, she was afraid, and realised that she didn't know this forceful man, he was a stranger to her. But as he pressed down, fear gave strength, and she brought up one knee with as much speed as she could manage into his groin, and he rolled off with a tortured shout.

'Oh...fuck...' He curled up in obvious pain.

'You bastard, you bastard!' She pushed herself up from the floor, dragged her jeans up, re-zipped them, and held the edges of her shirt together.

'What did you do that for?' He held himself with both hands. 'For God's sake, are you trying to ruin me for ever?' He crawled up on to the couch, and sat there, moaning.

'Don't you ever touch me again, do you hear me?' she yelled, but then remembered Conor downstairs, and lowered her tone. 'How dare you force yourself on me, how dare you...' She moved closer to the door, still wary of him.

'I'm your husband. I have my rights, and anyway I thought you might feel like a bit of the other. You haven't had it since you left.' He rocked back and forward.

'You have no rights over me!' she flashed, angrier than she had ever been before.

'You're like a nun bouncing around this big old place on your own. What a way to live. You should be back with us where you're needed, doing your duty as a wife and mother. I don't know how you could have walked out, turned your back on a beautiful home and left us to fend for ourselves.'

'Dermot...I just have one thing to say to you...just one.' She was shaking and had a mad urge to rush at him and beat the living daylights out of him, wishing she knew Karate, or Judo or something.

'What's that? You'll be entering a convent next week?'

'Listen, you sarcastic shit, get out of here. This is my home and I never want to see you again, or hear your stupid voice on the phone. So make no contact at all with me, if you do I'll call the police.'

'Taking a vow of silence as well?' He stood up slowly, and adjusted his clothes.

'Where you're concerned, yes.' She opened the door. 'And by the way, far from entering a convent, I've met someone else, and I'll be filing for divorce shortly.'

He stared at her.

'Pull the other one, Kate, who'd be bothered with you? You're boring, and you never were much good in bed anyway, no wonder I had to look elsewhere over the years,' he sneered.

'What?'

'Do you want me to spell it out?'

She stared at him, silenced, and rushed out. In the cloakroom, she pulled on a sweater, and stood there in the gloom, shaking, and trying not to cry. After a few minutes, she returned to see him standing in the hall, head down, shoulders slumped, a twist in the collar of his navy wool coat. When he heard her footsteps he looked up.

'Is it true about someone else? Will he be moving in here?' he asked.

She opened the front door. 'None of your business,' she snapped.

He nodded, a disgruntled twist to his mouth, and went out on to the step. But then he turned back. 'I'd better get Conor.'

'I'll drop him wherever he wants to go.'

'Oh, I almost forgot. I was going to give you some money for Christmas, you must need it.' He put his hand into his pocket.

'Stuff your money, Dermot.'

There was an unexpected look of loss on his face, but she only caught a glimpse as she banged the door, double-locked it with the key, and slid across the bolts top and bottom. Then she leaned against it and touched the cool painted surface with her hot forehead. Her mind racing around as she tried to get to grips with his sudden admission. After a moment she went down to the kitchen again and told Conor she was taking a bath.

He nodded, still engrossed in the match.

She ran the water until the bath was almost filled. Then she stripped off and soaked herself, anxious to wash away the touch of Dermot, so offensive to her now. She felt like she had been through a mangle, terribly hurt that her husband and the father of her children, whom she had once loved so much, had actually attempted to rape her. The thought that he had been playing around all these years was awful, but she had to admit, in all honesty, that she wasn't much better.

After changing into fresh clothes she took Conor around to his friend Dave. Returning home, she gathered up the underwear, the jeans and shirt. Then she threw the lot in a black bag, together with the unopened present, tied a knot in the top and dumped it in the bin. Lastly, she uncorked the bottle of wine and emptied its contents down the loo.

Chapter Fifty-Seven

Jack flew back to Dublin on Christmas Eve, a return flight to Spain booked for St. Stephen's Day. The airport was crowded as he walked into Arrivals, everyone hugging and kissing all around him with much laughter and tears of joy, the atmosphere electric. He walked through, a solitary man coming home with no-one to meet him. Of course, he hadn't told anyone what time he was arriving, crazily imagining that Kate might be there, waiting for someone else perhaps, they would meet accidentally and...the automatic doors opened...he went outside to join the queue of people at the taxi rank.

It was festive this year, two of his brothers home from London with their families, everyone glad to see him.

'And you're looking far too thin as usual, and why are you staying only one day? I can't believe it, we won't even have time to talk to you,' his mother complained.

'I'm going to Brazil for a while.'

'Where's that?'

'South America.'

'Oh my God.' She blessed herself.

'What's this?' Tricia asked.

'I've decided to go further afield to work.'

'How long are you going to be away?' Rose handed around a platter of brown bread topped with smoked salmon.

'I don't know, and unfortunately I won't be able to come back as often as I did from Spain.' He helped himself to a slice.

'Why do you have to go so far away, surely you can paint

here?' his father asked, in good humour with his family around him.

'With the sort of pictures you paint, what difference does it make where you are? They all look the same,' Brian said, and there was a loud guffaw of laughter.

'That's not fair.' Tricia patted Jack's back sympathetically.

'I'm hoping for new inspiration.'

'What do you need that for? You just have to throw a few tins of paint at the canvas, and there you are, a completed picture in minutes. Wish I could do it, beats IT.'

'You're all Philistines, and you don't know how good this guy is. People queue up to buy his paintings.' Chris put her arm around him.

'I bought a lovely one recently from a guy who called to the door. It's about two by two, and a nice scene of a harbour at sunset,' Terry said.

'Why don't you go back to accountancy? It would be a steady job, nine-to-five,' his mother asked.

'A permanent pensionable job,' they chorused, laughing again.

'Don't mind them. We're all going to miss you.' Chris hugged him.

'Yea, of course we are,' Rose added.

No-one took things very seriously in the Linley family, and within minutes they had gone on to a new subject. What he did for a living or where he was going was no longer of any interest.

Christmas Day was as mad as ever, the whole crowd of them enjoying Mam's cooking, no deviation allowed in the menu which had been the same for as long as he could remember. He enjoyed the chat and the laughter, glad to be home, but in the back of his mind, Kate hovered, and he wished she was here with him - that he would only have to put out his hand to touch her and know his life was complete. He wondered should he call to find out how she was, but he didn't. He left early the following morning, a man running away from his feelings, hoping to make a new life for himself on the other side of the world.

*

Kate had indulged herself at Christmas, determined to look good this first year on her own. All her long hours of hard work had paid off, and she was thrilled to be able to try on a size twelve in a full-length black suit. It was the first time she had spent any money on clothes in the last few months, and she felt she was entitled to splash out just this once. There was nobody else going to do it. Although Carol insisted on buying her the shoes and bag to compliment the outfit.

Her sons received clothes, always needed and appreciated by both of them. She was presented with the usual voucher from Conor, and body lotion from Shane, who never forgot her even though he hadn't much money. They came down to share dinner with her. Dermot had gone to his sister, Mary. Irene was in the Caribbean. Everyone in the family quite aware of the situation now.

She tried to create a festive atmosphere with a real tree in the front bay window. Christmas garlands graced the old marble mantles, and white candles glimmered. She produced a meal as good as any she had put on the table at Mount Asher Road, with its top-of-the-range kitchen. She was really happy that the lads wanted to share her Christmas, and that Conor and herself were on good terms again. They enjoyed dinner in front of a roaring fire in the sitting-room and raised a glass in a toast to her new life, both of them apparently quite accustomed to her absence from home by now.

'How are you getting on at the new job?' she asked Conor.

'Great, I'm earning a good salary now so I'm looking for an apartment, you never know when Irene might turn up again. It was embarrassing trying not to notice her creeping in and out of your bedroom...' he stopped talking abruptly and lowered his eyes.

Kate stared at him. 'What did you say?' she whispered, suddenly reminded her of that day she had come home unexpectedly at lunchtime and heard the noise upstairs. She couldn't believe it, Dermot and Irene?

'Nothing, Mum, nothing,' Conor muttered.

'We've been booked to do a tour in Germany, so we might stay on and pick up a few gigs, there's plenty of work over there apparently.' Shane opened another can of beer.

The television was moved up to the sitting-room, and they watched a video, but the images and sound track were meaningless as all she could think about was this unexpected scenario which had entered into the scheme of things. So Irene was the one who occupied Dermot's mind, the person who lay between them in the bed and drove them apart. She was horrified at the thought of her stepmother being with her husband, and wondered how long it had been going on. Still, she couldn't really blame him, she carried her own guilt. But somehow, it was just too close to the bone, incestuous...almost. She shuddered, feeling sick, as suddenly, she was forced to look at the past from a new perspective, and realised what a fool she had been to let Dermot treat her like a doormat, and Irene to cleverly manipulate her. To have turned away from Jack was the worst thing she had ever done.

As the light darkened and the candles flickered, she looked at her watch. It was five o'clock. She imagined him in the middle of that big family, replete after his mother's turkey and ham dinner, or perhaps he wasn't in Dublin at all, and was spending a romantic Christmas with the new woman in his life?

'Mum, do you think you could let me have some cash? I'll need extra money for the deposit and some stuff for the apartment?' Conor asked.

'I'm sorry, Conor but you'll have to finance it yourself,' she said firmly, trying to ignore that sudden disappointment in his eyes.

'It's going to be difficult to get it together,' he said dourly.

'You're going to have to economise. We all have to make sacrifices to get what we want. And Shane, if you go to Germany you can't ring up looking for money to be sent over, you'll have to support yourself as well.'

'I thought you might be able to help with the flight, and until we get paid...'

'Had you two got this nicely planned?' she asked, slightly irritated with them, pretty sure that she was being set up here.

They shook their heads in vigorous denial.

'OK, I believe you.' Though she didn't. 'I know it seems that I'm being very mean, but regardless of money, I still love you both,' she smiled.

'Yea, Mum,' Conor muttered.

'We know, Mum.' Shane looked sheepish.

When the lads left a short time later to meet their friends, she sat in the light of the flickering candles unable to drum up enough enthusiasm to call to Carol which had been a loose arrangement if she should feel like it. She opened another bottle of wine, poured herself a glass, and watched some stupid film on the television until it was time to go to bed, glad this day was over.

On St. Stephen's Day she immediately threw herself back into work, even refusing Carol's invitation to dinner. She had had enough of the Christmas celebrations for this year. But the days were sluggish as they dragged up to New Year's Eve, and she accepted Carol's invitation this time, but she dreaded it really, and as she made her way over about nine had already decided to leave as soon as possible. But in the end it turned out to be surprisingly enjoyable, some of Carol's family there and Amanda's friends.

She busied herself helping in the kitchen, baking trays of finger food.

'Guess who's arrived?' Carol came in carrying some empty dishes.

'Who?' Kate asked as she took a tray of samosas from the oven and tossed them into a serving bowl.

'Mags.'

Kate's eyes widened with surprise.

'I told her we'd have a few people around and to come along, although I didn't expect her to accept. I'm sure she realised that you would be here as well.'

'Is the new boyfriend with her?'

'He had to go home apparently. She was asked but decided against meeting the family just yet. Being a bit cautious I think, for a change.'

'I'd better take these around, they're getting cold.'

'I'll do it.'

'Let me, I'll offer some to Mags, maybe she'll accept and we might break the ice.'

'Yell if you need any help, I don't want to have to send for the police to separate the two of you.' Carol took some more food from the fridge.

Kate worked her way around to where Mags sat chatting with some of Amanda's friends, to her surprise she helped herself, and murmured thanks, but there was no eye contact. She continued on her way, and then went back into the kitchen.

'Well, how did it go?' Carol asked.

'She took one.'

'First step. She'll throw her arms around you next.'

'Yea, some hope.'

Twelve o'clock was counted down on an old drum by Carol, then everyone cheered madly, hugged and kissed. Suddenly Mags was in front of Kate, and they did the same, all of the antagonism swept away.

'I'm so sorry. I've really been horrible to you, I don't know what I was doing. Forgive me?' Mags whispered.

Kate glanced at her watch and crossed Grafton Street. She had plenty of time to get to her appointment and thought she might wander around Brown Thomas for a few minutes. As she walked through the doors of the shop, she almost bumped into a woman hurrying out, laden down with bags.

'Chris?'

She looked as glamourous as ever in a cream outfit, a brown fur wrap thrown around her shoulders. Kate's heart skipped a

361

beat, as she was immediately reminded of Jack. They chatted for a moment and then she took her chance.

'How is Jack?' She had to know that, at least.

'He came home for Christmas, but went back to Spain on St. Stephen's Day to get things organised, he's off to Brazil soon.'

Kate said nothing. What was taking him all the way to Brazil?

'He's not satisfied with his work. He didn't mount an exhibition this year, he's just not himself.'

'What do you mean exactly, is he ill?' Kate asked, suddenly worried.

'No, not exactly, but if you saw what he produced this summer, compared to a couple of years ago, you wouldn't believe it.' A bitter expression flashed across her face. She stared at Kate with a hard accusing look.

'I didn't know,' Kate murmured, taken aback.

'It's finished between the two of you, I believe?'

'Yes.' Kate felt crushed by her tone.

'I was very surprised. I would never have expected you to do such a thing. To use a man and dump him, and not care what affect it had. Jack isn't the type you can treat like that, he's sensitive. Creative people always are, but you obviously didn't know him well enough to understand that.'

Kate was silent.

'So he's heading off to South America, and it's all your fault. None of us are pleased to see him going, particularly in his present frame of mind. And where is poor Dermot in all of this I'd like to know? Does he even know what you've been up to, or is he the innocent husband, always the last to find out?' It all spewed out.

When Kate didn't reply, her pulse racing with shock, Chris suddenly turned back into the shop, and disappeared into the crowd.

Chapter Fifty-Eight

Although she wasn't really in the mood, Kate was persuaded to go to Bob Benson's house-warming party with Carol and Mags, all the anger between them a thing of the past.

'This is like the old days, girls.' Carol drove into the car park, and Kate smiled at Mags, so glad they were back to their own friendly selves again.

'How do I look?' Mags stood for inspection before they went to the main door and produced their invitations to the security staff.

'You look perfect, as usual,' Kate admired.

'Not as good as the new Kate, Mags, you'll have to watch yourself, she's passing us out in the glamour stakes.'

'Yea, yea, yea!' Kate led the way through into the main hall. The place was packed, and she felt particularly good tonight. Accepting a glass of champagne they mingled with the crowd until they met Bob himself, holding court among a crowd of people in the entertainment business.

'Ah, my designers!' he called, and introduced them to the group, who were in awe of the job the girls had done. They talked for a while, reassuring everyone that it would be no problem to travel to the U.K. or the States or anywhere else in the world, should their services be required.

Later, they had a good look around.

'Its great, isn't it? A super job, wonder who did it?' Carol grinned.

'Some design company run by talented beautiful women, the only people worth talking about in the world of interiors.' Mags swaggered.

'We're sure to get lots of jobs out of this, there's such a mix of people here. Keep your business cards to hand.'

'I have mine stuck on my forehead,' Kate smiled.

'You can rub off us if you want.'

'What do you mean? I was involved with this whole project, plenty of me went into it, so I don't need to rub off you two,' Kate retorted.

'Oh, feisty.'

'I'm the up-and-coming new talent in my field, a specialist, who can do things with fabrics no-one could even imagine.' She sipped her champagne, and they wandered down into the underground block.

'We want to show you how the studios finally shaped up.' Mags led the way into the huge foyer. 'We hung Jack's paintings in here. These are the ones we bought from The Nestor direct.'

Even as she stepped in through the door, Kate's heart began to hammer inside her. She had no choice but to follow the girls and stand before the series of paintings, the only work hung on a vast wall.

'What do you think of these, aren't they amazing?' Carol asked.

'We couldn't judge them until they were properly hung, but once we saw them we knew they were a perfect choice for an area as large as this.'

Kate nodded, but she was unable to see the paintings through the tears, as the memory of the last time she had looked at them hurtled back. She could feel Jack standing behind, his arms around her.

'I love the way all the smaller ones come together in the main portrait, wonder who it is?' Carol mused.

'They're fantastic.' There was a reverence in Mags' voice. 'I wish it was me.'

Kate couldn't say anything.

Carol turned to stare at her. 'You're looking a bit...are you all right?'

Kate nodded, although she wanted to run she couldn't move, her feet were rooted to the spot.

'My God...it's you, isn't it?' Carol stared at the paintings again and back at Kate. 'Mags, it's Kate, I don't know how I didn't spot it before.'

'The one he did of me wasn't anything like those,' Mags murmured slowly.

'You're immortalized on canvas, Kate. When you're old and grey you can look at these and know that you were really beautiful. You'll be like the Mona Lisa. People will throng to see you for centuries to come.' Carol put an arm around her shoulders.

'He seems to have captured something special in you.'

'But Jack said...he was never going to sell.' Kate struggled to control herself.

'May have needed the money.'

'He wanted to get rid of them,' she retorted angrily.

'What about being unable to look at them? When a relationship is finished, you don't want to be reminded every time you look at a picture on the wall. I got rid of all the photographs of Tim, remember?' Carol reminded.

'He must feel something special for you,' Mags admitted.

'I've tried to persuade her to talk to him again, at least fill him in on what's happened, but she's too stubborn. She won't forgive the guy for not understanding what makes her tick, as if anyone could do that. I ask you, can we even understand her?'

Kate turned away.

'Come on Mags, back to the party, we're going to get a few more glasses of champagne into this one here, never know what we might persuade her to do!' Carol said firmly.

Chapter Fifty-Nine

But it didn't need the champagne, or the girls' efforts to persuade Kate to try and contact Jack. Seeing the paintings again had unlocked something in her heart, and by the time she arrived home, she had forgiven him his lack of understanding.

Luckily, she had completed all her orders, and was able to leave for Spain a couple of days later. In Alicante she booked into a small hotel which was just about adequate, with a clean bed and bathroom. But Kate didn't care about the luxury or otherwise of the place, all she wanted was a good night's sleep, to look her best for him. The following morning, she awoke at seven, surprised at the warmth of the day even at this hour. Breakfast was a quick bread-roll and a cup of coffee in a bar on her way to the bus-station where she bought a ticket to Mojacar. She had considered hiring a car but decided against that plan when she thought about the bother of having to return it if Jack happened to be still there.

It was midday when she finally walked in through the doors of The Alameda where she had stayed before. There were very few tourists around, just some clusters of people on the beach, tall leggy girls in skimpy G-strings, partnered by deeply-bronzed muscular men, further along a few older couples, wearing a little more clothes, and groups of young boys playing football. She quickly showered, changed and took a taxi up to the town.

She went straight to the house, but sudden terror gripped as she lifted her hand to press the bell. For a few seconds she left it in mid-air, until finally she reminded herself that there was no point in coming all this way without at least knocking on his door. And if there was another woman in his life...she pressed the little black circle, took a deep breath and prepared to meet him. The bell echoed inside. As the seconds passed there was no sound of footsteps, or the rattle of a door handle; she tried Paqui's bell also but there was no reply there either. Confused, she slowly walked away, her feet dragging. A lonely woman out of place among the busy throng of local people on the streets, trying to convince herself that Jack hadn't already left. To phone would have seemed the obvious, but he never carried a mobile when he was here.

After a long walk on the beach, she returned to the hotel where she changed again, and this time took more trouble with her appearance, finally deciding to wear the pretty red linen top and the shortest skirt she ever had the courage to buy during a mad rush around the shops before leaving Dublin. Then she passed some time in a little restaurant on the square forcing herself to eat some mixed fried fish, a green salad, and drink a glass of wine, feeling more relaxed by the time she decided to go over to the house again. Hope that he had returned bursting its confident way through her. But he wasn't there and her heart-thudding excitement died down after a few seconds. She tried Paqui's bell, delighted when the door was opened after a moment and the woman stood there smiling at her.

'I'm looking for Jack, but there's no answer, do you know if...' Paqui stared at her for a moment with a rather puzzled look on her pleasant features.

'I'm a friend of his from Dublin.'

'Ah, si,' she smiled.

'Kate.'

'Of course, I remember, come in, come in.' She ushered her through to her apartment. Kate passed the little fountain, glanced upwards, but all the doors on the upper level were firmly shut.

'Please sit down, can I get you something to drink, a glass of wine, or coffee? Yes that might be better, it is so cold.' She disappeared into the adjoining kitchen.

No, I don't want any wine, or coffee, I just want to know if he's still here, and he probably isn't, judging by all this palaver, Kate thought impatiently.

Paqui reappeared with two cups of coffee on a tray and handed one to her. Kate had to go through the motions of polite etiquette, drink her coffee with delicate sips, make irrelevant small talk, about the weather, the holidays, what she was doing, what Paqui was doing, like someone who had been invited for afternoon tea and cucumber sandwiches.

'Is Jack here these days, or is he away?'

'Ah, he is going to Brazil, I will miss him very much.' She waved her hands in a sad gesture.

'When is he actually leaving?' Kate asked urgently.

'He is visiting now with his sister in Torrevieja, I am not sure when he is flying exactly.'

A wave of anticipation swept through Kate as she listened; suddenly possibilities evolved into probabilities. She smiled with relief, finished the last of the coffee, anxious to get out of there now, her mind computing ways of reaching Torrevieja as quickly as she could. There was no transport that night and first thing in the morning she went to the car-hire office, but it was closed, so the only option was the bus. A taxi would have been far too expensive.

The journey seemed to take much longer today, stopping in every little village, passengers getting on and off. Being Sunday, there was an even slower more relaxed mood about the people, and she almost screamed with impatience. Finally, she arrived in Torrevieja, stiff, crumpled, hot, and knew that she couldn't possibly approach the house in this state. After that last session with Chris, it could be embarrassing to say the least, and she might be thrown out on her ear, accused of being some sort of a wagon, or worse.

In a bar, she drank a glass of Sprite, and afterwards slipped into the Ladies, locked the outer-door, quickly freshened up, and changed. But then there was the nuisance of her case. She was delighted when the girl behind the bar put it in the back room, closed the door and assured her in broken English that it would be quite safe there.

The journey to the house overlooking the sea only took a few minutes by taxi. Outside she noticed a lot of cars parked up on the pavement, it was obvious that there was a crowd of people in to lunch. She walked up to what used to be their own gate, shocked at the condition of the garden. The grass was brown, the flowering shrubs withered, and it had a look of such abandon about it she turned away, hating her vulnerability, and that a house could cause such a sense of loss.

Summoning up her courage, Kate negotiated the cars parked on the driveway. The level of voices from the patio grew louder. She wondered was Jack here? Would he want to see her? Then, right at the top, in front of Eddie's car was the black jeep. Her heart thumped. She pressed the bell, but there was no reply. She pressed it again, beginning to think it would be necessary to go around into the middle of that partying-crowd, when suddenly it opened, and Chris stood there, a vision in lilac.

'I thought I heard the doorbell as I came into the kitchen...' she smiled, but then her eyes grew cold, and there was that same bullish expression on her face as the day they had met after Christmas.

'I wonder is Jack here?' Kate asked, very much aware of the antagonism which emanated from Chris.

'No, what would he be doing here? He's gone to Brazil, I told you that.'

'Well, I saw his jeep, and I...'

'He left it here while he's away.' She began to close over the door.

'Do you have an address for him, or a phone number?'

'No-one knows where Jack goes, and he never takes a phone with him either. Anyway if I had a number I wouldn't give it to you.' Her lips curled contemptuously.

'Would you mind if I come in for a while? Our house is closed up,' Kate asked softly, ignoring the attitude of the other woman, and still hoping to get inside.

'I certainly would, this is a private party, invited guests only.'
The door was banged in her face.

Shocked, Kate stepped back, and then stumbled down the driveway again. She half-walked, half-ran along the narrow road, just anxious to get away from there. After a while she found herself at the top of the steps leading to the beach, slipped off her sandals and wandered across the sand to the edge of the surf.

*

'More people arriving?' Jack asked when Chris came out from the house again.

'Just some neighbours.'

'Can I top you up?'

'Yea, please.'

'Sit down, you've been rushing around organising everything, I'll answer the door next time.' He poured some white wine into her glass and they sat at a table at the far side of the pool.

'Wish you weren't going.' She was morose.

'Me too, in one way. But in another, I'm looking forward to the challenge, which is something I need badly.'

'Brazil is so far away,' she sighed, 'how long do you think you'll stay?'

'Haven't a clue really, I might never come back.' He stood up and moved close to the balustrade which bordered the cliff overlooking the beach.

'Don't say that,' she wailed.

'No point in saying otherwise, I simply don't know, Chris.' He sipped his wine, staring along the line of the surf which stretched away into the blueness, and noticed a woman walking slowly along its edge, the only person for quite a distance. Her long black skirt floated in the breeze, and she had a rather lost look about her, like a girl wandering home in the morning from an all-night Debs, he thought.

Eddie appeared and announced that the food was ready on the barbecue.

'Come on, let's eat,' Chris said.

But Jack didn't hear, his eyes still focussed on the woman who had just stopped, turned back and begun to walk across the beach. 'It's Kate!' he gasped. Even in the distance he knew her.

'Is it?' Chris followed his gaze.

'I'm sure.' He moved nearer the balustrade, and shaded his eyes against the sun with his hand. All those feelings he had held in check these last months were suddenly released.

'That woman doesn't look like her at all.'

'Hey, you two, anyone giving me a hand here?' Eddie called.

'It's definitely Kate.'

'Come on, she's past tense.' She put her arm through his and they walked around the pool.

'After all this time...' A sudden longing to rush down to the beach swept through him.

'Where are the catering staff?' Eddie waved a fork in his direction.

He joined him and began to serve tandoori chicken, brown black steaks, and a mixture of other food to the guests who had already formed a queue. As he filled the proffered plates, he wondered if Dermot was with her, and if he did go down, what would happen? 'Steak or chicken?' he asked automatically, like someone in a factory-canteen serving hundreds of people, repeating the same words with a bored take-it-or-leave-it attitude. But why not? he argued through the logic with himself. I could bump into either of them at any time.

'There are salads over there, help yourself,' he smiled at the guests, but their identities didn't register. The thought of being close to Kate even for a moment was tantalising and suddenly, just as he was about to serve the woman in front of him, he stopped and put down his fork. 'I'm sorry,' he said, and walked back towards the house.

'Where are you going?' Chris asked when she saw him move away.

'I'm going down to the beach.'

'But we'll be opening the champagne any minute now.' She seemed annoyed.

'Leave it 'til later, Chris.'

'You can't walk out on your own party.' She followed him into the kitchen.

'I'll be back, Chris, and will probably bring Kate with me, and maybe Dermot too.'

'But she wasn't invited,' she hissed.

'If she isn't welcome, then I'm not.'

'That's ridiculous, Jack, I thought you'd put that bitch out of your head.'

He stared in silence at her for a few seconds, then went through the house, and hurried down the drive.

Chapter Sixty

The room was strewn with old newspapers, empty whiskey bottles, cans, mugs, overflowing ashtrays. Dermot sat in the middle of it looking at the television, a glass of whiskey in his hand. There was a ring at the doorbell, but he took no notice. It rang again. He pushed himself up out of the couch, wandered down the hall and pressed the intercom, wondering who was in the dark car which was pulled up outside the gates.

'This is the Gardai, sir, we'd like to talk to you,' a voice said. Dermot felt nauseous as he pressed in the code and watched it swing in. He opened the door as two men walked towards him.

'Dermot Mason?' one of them asked.

He nodded.

'Detective Inspector Gallagher...could we have a word with you?' He waved some ID at him.

Dermot brought them into the lounge. 'What's this about?' he stuttered.

'We'd like to talk to you about your business interests in Spain...but we can discuss it in more detail down at the station,' the man spoke politely, and Dermot knew he was being given no opportunity to refuse. Desperately afraid, he put on his coat, and they left together, their footsteps loud on the wooden floor. A thumping sound which echoed through Dermot's heart, a sudden reminder of those days when he came home from school into the empty house to hear that same reverberation.

Suddenly, he wanted to scream out loud for his mother. And Kate. The only women he had ever truly loved. But he knew it was too late now, too late.

Chapter Sixty-One

Kate wandered across the beach and sat down on the sand, idly picking up handfuls of the fine white powdery grains and letting them sift through her fingers. She stared out to sea with a blank lost look on her face and noticed a large heart with two names inside drawn in the sand nearby, reminded of that last day when Jack had written her name in the sand, and she his. Unexpectedly, a gust of wind whirled up a mini-dust storm on the surface and all but obliterated the words. Cynically, she thought how transient love could be.

But after a moment, she began to run back to the steps, furious that she had allowed Chris to treat her in such a fashion. Not even bothering to put on her sandals, she turned up the road which led to the house, unaware of the sharp gravel which pierced the soles of her feet, determined to find out for herself whether Jack had left or not. As she ran along, she made crazy plans, and decided that if he wasn't here, then she would camp out at Harrington Park until he came home. She would wait as long as it took to tell him how much she loved him. Her breathing was short as she climbed uphill, the beginning of a stitch in her side as she turned a sharp corner, and suddenly, he was there...

THE END